A Riley the Exterminator Mystery

Lethal Fetish

Jeffrey Alan Lockwood

𝓟

Pen-L Publishing
Fayetteville, Arkansas
Pen-L.com

Lethal Fetish

ISBN: 978-1-68313-190-8
Library of Congress Control Number: 2019931486

First Edition
Printed and bound in the USA

Pen-L Publishing
Fayetteville, Arkansas
Pen-L.com

Cover design by Conor Mullen
Interior design by Kelsey Rice

CHAPTER ONE

I wasn't in a good mood. January was shaping up to be as bone-chilling as San Francisco gets and that's saying a lot. My romantic plans for Nina to join forces with me in a warm, sweaty battle against the city's cold dampness had vaporized. Instead, I had a celibate weekend looking after Tommy so my mother could drive down to LA, where there was presumably sunshine and definitely an opera. Mom and Gladys had treated themselves to a performance of Puccini's *Gianna Schicchi*. For the two church ladies, the opera's tale of moral judgment offset the decadent journey into California's city of fallen angels, where movie stars snorted their coke and Bo Derek wannabes jiggled their boobs.

Meanwhile, Tommy and I had gone on a "Saturday safari"—my kid brother's term for insect collecting. We'd spent a few hours in the hills above Berkeley, breaking open fallen logs in search of six-legged treasure. We nabbed a couple of nice ground beetles, and when Tommy found a spectacular millipede along with some skittering centipedes he decided to expand his collection beyond insects. We'd gotten drenched, muddy, and worn out.

On my way to work this morning, I hoped that the day's biggest decision would be which pastry to pick for breakfast. Most hopes are destined to be crushed, but at least Gustaw was sympathetic to my current indecision.

"There is only one blueberry pierogi left, Riley," he said, gesturing with a beefy arm at the display case."

"But the farmer's cheese flavored with vanilla is a delicious filling," said Ludwika, coming from the back room and wiping her flour-dusted hands on an apron that was unable to conceal the ample bosom that lured Gustaw forty years ago in Gdansk.

"People think it is sweetened cream cheese. One of America's few, great mistakes," said Gustaw.

"You should explain these things to our customers," Ludwika said, giving her husband a smack on the side of his massive head.

As I pondered my options and Ludwika wiped down one of the four tables in the shop, Gustaw leaned over the counter and whispered. "Riley, you have—how you say?—sweet tooth. But there is other possibility."

I generally favored something sugary to counter his 'strong like dockworker' coffee. "And that would be?" I asked, unsure of why we were using a conspiratorial tone unless his alternative pierogi involved a shot of vodka which Ludwika strictly prohibited before noon.

"I make for you a special treat. Ludwika does not approve. She says it makes me fat, but you are not so, so *gruby*," he said giving up on the English word and patting his generous belly.

I grabbed a table by the window and Gustaw disappeared into the kitchen. After a few minutes he returned with a heaping plate and a steaming mug. The pierogi was topped with caramelized onion and browned kielbasa.

"This is real meat. Is not what Hillshire Farms calls Polish sausage," he said with a disgust suggesting he'd someday find and pillage Hillshire Farms, as if the place actually existed. It's good for a man to want justice, even if it involves sausage.

All I wanted was a quiet half hour to savor a Monday trifecta: a custom-made pierogi, a cup of coffee thick enough to pass for San Francisco's answer to the La Brea tar pits, and the sports section of the *Chronicle*. But in my experience, the universe cares precious little about what I want.

I had settled into a story featuring Joe Montana's reaction to the 49ers winning their first Super Bowl. Tommy and I had watched the game with Father Griesmaier in the rectory of St. Teresa's. It was the high point of the weekend, what with my kid brother shouting himself hoarse and the priest serving up a running biography of Montana—the cleft-chinned, All-American who played for Notre Dame and provided living proof that the

Almighty favored Catholics. The Trumer Pils from the priest's Austrian homeland didn't hurt. Tommy could let loose and be himself around the gentle cleric. Having reached his forties, Tommy was increasingly aware that having a child's mind locked in a damaged adult's body made him an object of stares and derision. I knew people could be cruel, but I was about to discover how twisted they can be.

Larry came through the door, the brass bells tinkling his arrival. He knew that Gustaw's was my sanctuary on Monday mornings, and I was not to be disturbed before eight unless there was an emergency at the shop.

There was.

Carol had taken a call from a homicide detective who told her that Goat Hill Extermination was connected to a couple of dead bodies. My old pal from the force strongly suggested that I should drop whatever I was doing and pay him a visit at the scene. Neither the cosmos nor the SFPD gave a shit about my plans.

I got up and slid a fiver across the glass counter to Ludwika who gave me a worried look and a grandmotherly pat on the hand.

As Larry and I hustled down the hill, he filled in some of the sordid details that Carol had charmed out of the detective. For a lesbian, she sure knew how to beguile men. Larry had his calloused side which was pretty much his only side, other than a penchant for dark humor. But even this seen-it-all Vietnam vet figured the old Polish couple didn't need to hear that the victims were elderly, dog-collared and nude.

When we got to the shop, Carol was at her desk, looking worried and adorable with her new bobbed haircut—a style I found far more appealing than the popular bouffant style that makes a woman look like an electrocuted lion. Her radio was playing some moron who kept the beat by snapping his fingers while singing that he loves a rainy night. The guy had never spent a winter in San Francisco.

"Riley, what's going on?" she asked as if whatever was going on was my fault.

3

"Slow down, babe," I said, knowing that she hated this 'sexist label' which is why I stuck with it. "All I know is what you told Larry. A cop I knew while I was on the force is investigating a scene with two old stiffs in an embarrassing situation."

"Not that dead folks can blush," Larry noted.

"Good point," I said. "But I don't suppose their friends and family would approve of gramps and gramma playing doggy sex games when they went to the great kennel in the sky," I said.

"You two are sick," Carol said.

"Sick puppies," Larry said.

"Stop it," she said suppressing a grin. "What does this have to do with Goat Hill Extermination?" I was technically the owner, but Carol was the bookkeeper, receptionist, scheduler, and payroll clerk. In short, she ran the place and took great pride in our reputation.

"Beats me," I said. "I guess something at the scene links us to the deaths."

"Maybe Dennis knows." Larry poured a cup of coffee from Carol's bottomless Mr. Coffee carafe.

"I doubt it," I said.

"Besides, he's not here yet." Carol glanced at the salvaged kitchen clock hanging above the filing cabinets, its sunny, smiling cartoon face mocking the citizens of San Francisco. She knew the guys were dependable, but it was eight-o-five after all.

"Probably still in la-la land after that Smokey Robinson concert this weekend," Larry said. "Nice to know that a geezer can still be boss." He glanced at me with a sly grin. I didn't take the bait.

"If nobody has a clue what the hell is going on, let's get to work," I said. "I'll head into the weirdness and you two make some money so you can post bail if this whole thing goes sideways. Assuming I'm not detained by the city's finest, let's meet back here for lunch so I can share what I've learned with everyone at the same time."

Larry headed down the hall to the warehouse and called over his shoulder, "Carol, when Dennis gets in, I'll tell him that you said he'd better work his black ass double-time to make up for being late."

Carol suppressed another smile and handed me the address that the detective had given her. "Riley, I'm serious. Watch yourself on this one. We can't afford bad publicity with Orkin and Terminix trying harder than ever to steal our customers."

I gave her shoulder a reassuring squeeze and leaned over to give her a peck on the cheek. She grabbed a handful of my graying hair, looked me in the eye, and explained that she'd straighten my boxing-bent nose with a left hook if I messed up. Some women just refuse to accept that men have the world under control.

I took the old rust-bucket from behind the shop and clicked on the radio. KDFC was playing Chopin's Nocturne in E-flat Major, Opus 9, No. 2, in the hope of lifting the spirits of commuters on a dreary Monday. Not many people know that Chopin was Polish, although Gustaw is keenly aware of this fact and also insists that his countryman Henryk Górecki will be the next big thing in classical music—once the world hears his work. The old Pole might be right. He knows his sweets and symphonies.

On the drive across town, I turned off Van Ness onto California so I could pass by Grace Cathedral—the gothic behemoth built by the Episcopalians to show up the Catholics. It never ceases to impress me with its Old World feel and I imagine myself in the heart of London. But if I was God, I'd hang out in St. Ignatius Church, not because the Catholics are any holier but the Jesuit Baroque architecture is classier and looks better in San Francisco.

After a few more Chopin pieces, I ended up in one of the city's most exclusive neighborhoods—Snob Hill. Arriving at the appointed address, I came to a pair of wrought iron gates decorated with gilded, hand-sized, five-petalled flowers of St. John's wort—the herbalist's remedy for anxiety, depression, sleeplessness, menopause, heart palpitations, cancer, hepatitis, herpes and most likely hangnails and rabies. I knew this because I remembered having visited this estate a few months ago along with Dennis and treating the carpets for a flea infestation while the owners regaled us with the wonders of herbal medicine—my wonder being that anyone shells out big money for dried leaves. But Mr. and Mrs. Linford were the tycoons of weeds, demonstrating that P.T. Barnum was right about the birthrate of suckers.

The gates were open and the circular driveway swept past a four-car garage with a black Ferrari 308 featuring vanity plates that read "1 Lane" parked alongside. The drive curved up to a brick Tudor mansion adorned with bay windows featuring little glass panes, dormers, gables and the requisite half-timbering on the second floor. Reagan's trickle-down economics were apparently forming quite a puddle on Nob Hill.

In front of the house, a slew of black-and-whites was haphazardly scattered. Cops park that way to remind citizens that the boys in blue can do whatever they want. I left my truck blocking a cruiser as a petty rejoinder on behalf of the public. When I identified myself to the uniformed officer at the door, he flicked his head toward the sweeping marble staircase indicating that I should head up.

At the top, I was greeted by Dimitris Papadopoulos decked out in a pinstripe suit like some *GQ* model. He was ahead of my class in the academy by a year and we were both assigned to the Mission station in the early Sixties. Our careers diverged: I got kicked off the force, he made lieutenant. We exchanged pleasantries and I shook his manicured hand. He looked like Greece's answer to Jack LaLanne, one of San Francisco's strangest gifts to the world, along with Jerry Brown and Dianne Feinstein.

We headed down a hallway illuminated by miniature crystal chandeliers and turned into a master bedroom featuring Queen Anne furniture— probably the real deal from a couple centuries ago. The contorted, nude bodies of a man and a woman in their seventies were nestled in the ankle-deep carpet.

"So, what linked my business to your loving couple?" I asked wondering how the cops had figured out they were customers of mine.

"This," the lieutenant said, handing me a business card from Goat Hill Extermination. "We found it on Mr. Linford's bureau, along with a sticky note that said 'Call.' That, and the fact that they're wearing flea collars, made me think you might have something to share with me."

"Maybe they overtightened their collars during some sort of kinky game," I said.

"Nah, we checked," he said, slipping a finger between the collar and the wrinkled neck of the old man. "No sign of strangulation. But enough with the distractions, Riley. Did you know these people?"

"Maybe. We might've treated this house awhile back, but I'd have to check our records. In any case, spraying for pests is a long way from convincing folks to wear flea collars."

"So, you have nothing that would help with the investigation?" he asked.

"Not right off. Mind if I look around?"

"Go ahead. The medical examiner and my boys have been over the scene and found everything worth finding. I'm going to talk with the victims' grandson. He found the bodies this morning and might've composed himself enough by now to be of use." Papadopoulos turned to the door. "Don't leave the house until you've checked back with me."

I started with a careful look at the bodies. There wasn't much to see that would explain the bizarre circumstances of their deaths. The couple appeared relatively fit but underweight. They'd both taken a healthy crap upon exiting from this world, which made getting close to them disagreeable. But looking more closely, I saw they had rashes across their shoulders and backs, along with patches of abraded skin on their torsos as if they'd furiously scratched to relieve itching or perhaps scrubbed themselves with a scouring pad.

I checked out the contents of their walk-in closet that was slightly larger than my bedroom. There were monogrammed shirts, silk ties, custom tailored suits, rows of designer dresses (Armani and Dior according to the labels; I understand that a single name means an expensive fashion), and enough Gucci handbags to hold my net worth in Italian lire. On the opposite wall of the bedroom was a locked door, presumably leading to an adjacent room. Next, I went into the bathroom, knowing that's where people tend to keep things they consider private—and a good investigator considers important.

The first dozen drawers under the granite countertop with a double vanity and high-end fixtures revealed normal, if over-priced, toiletries. There was nothing unusual until I came across a drawer filled with lice combs for removing nits, fine-tipped forceps, and magnifying glasses. And in the cabinet under the far sink was an assortment of gallon jugs of Lysol and rubbing alcohol, along with quart bottles hand-labeled as 'chrysanthemum tea' and 'citrus/eucalyptus drench'. I took a whiff from a couple of mystery containers including one with a pinkish liquid that smelled like vinegar mixed with kerosene and another that might've been a distiller's nightmare of lavender and geranium schnapps. The vapors were dizzying. On the floor of the bathroom was a set of rumpled, silk pajamas with a fleur-de-lis pattern and a demure, lavender nightgown with delicate lace. I picked over the clothing but didn't find anything interesting.

I checked out the other rooms along the upstairs hallway—an opulent lounge draped in maroon velvet curtains exuding an intoxicating blend of Castro's cigars and Napoleon's cognac, a couple of guest bedrooms that would put to shame anything at the Fairmont (or so I imagine, not having stayed there myself), and a library of leather-bound books on shelves reaching from the oriental rug to the twelve-foot ceiling. The house was immaculate, except that in the corner of each room hung a No-Pest strip, looking like a miniature apartment building with yellow windows. And in the library under an oak table with a green-shaded reading light was a spent bug bomb—one of those canisters that releases a fog of insecticide making homeowners feel much better and the pests feel worse. It seemed that the Linfords had lost their faith in botanical miracles, along with their dignity.

CHAPTER TWO

I went downstairs to find Papadopoulos and play the game of pretending that neither of us knew anything while hoping the other guy slipped up. He'd never been very good at this game when he worked vice because he couldn't bring himself to even feign knowing less than the scumbags he interrogated. Instead, he was really good at giving the impression that he knew everything about the perp and was just using the interrogation as a chance for the poor, dumb bastard to come clean and get a little leniency. Because Papadopoulos was probably a descendent of some Greek god—or at least he had the ramrod posture, swarthy machismo, and humorless presence to convey a sense of divine authority—lots of lowlifes broke down and admitted to the perversion du jour.

The same door-watching cop caught my eye again and flicked his head toward a wide opening off the entryway, managing to both dismiss my importance and indicate the lieutenant's whereabouts. I smiled in mock appreciation and hoped that I'd parked behind his cruiser. I went into a living room large enough for a half-court basketball game, furnished with a grand piano polished to a mirror finish and clusters of tastefully upholstered sofas and wingback chairs. The ceiling boasted enormous wooden beams, the fireplace was big enough to roast a whole pig, and the dark-paneled walls were decorated with antique prints of various plants. There were no oil paintings of family patriarchs since the Linfords were New Money. On the far side, a pair of French doors opened onto a brick terrace where the lieutenant was standing.

Papadopoulos had donned a tailored trench coat which was a bit classier than the 49ers sideline jacket I wore, having bought the souvenir after "The Catch" by Dwight Clark a couple weeks ago. The lieutenant was leaning against the stone balustrade separating the patio from a formal garden complete with fountain and goldfish pond. I assumed most of the shrubby plants were medicinal herbs, given the Linfords' entrepreneurial affinities.

"Find anything?" he asked as I crossed the expanse of brick, punctuated with black wrought-iron furniture and a grill that probably put out more heat than the furnace in my house.

"Nope," I said, wondering what it would be like to sear a steak on that gas grill instead of my charcoal hibachi.

"Liar," he said. I shrugged. "But I don't think you came across anything of importance that the crime scene boys missed." He looked out across the garden and the immaculate lawn, which sloped down toward a manicured hedge. On a clear day, there was probably a great view of the bay. Today, low, steely-gray clouds with leaden streaks threatened something between drizzle and downpour.

"How're you enjoying homicide?" I asked, hoping some chitchat might get him to loosen up and share information.

"Better than vice," he said.

"A higher class of criminals, eh?" Papadopoulos gave what passed as a smile for him, which would count as a wince on any other face.

"This case was tailor-made for me, according to the captain."

"You hit the jackpot—naked corpses and dog collars. This could be a high point in your career." He shook his head, rejecting my analysis.

"The cap needed someone with time in the trenches." Papadopoulos was probably a couple years my senior, maybe mid-forties. But his hair didn't have a strand of gray, his face didn't have the slightest wrinkle, and his gut lacked even a hint of paunch. Cosmetics, genetics, whatever. Asshole.

"The brass figured this was likely to be complicated, eh?" I asked, hoping to feed his ego.

"There's that," he said with evident pride. "And the word from the top is to keep a lid on this case. We have some gung-ho detectives who just moved to homicide and they'd be happy to get some ink." I understood: the politicos wanted the case buried along with the Linfords, discretion being one of the perks of wealth. To serve and protect—and conceal, as necessary.

"Sure, but with your experience in vice, nobody in homicide would be better prepared to unravel the weirdness upstairs. How do you figure it?" A bit more ego stroking was a small price to pay for whatever he knew. He loved being the guy with inside information.

"While you were poking around and finding 'nothing,' the M.E. gave me his initial findings." I waited. Papadopoulos couldn't stand not sharing what the medical examiner had revealed. I'd learned that during an interrogation, silence is an effective technique—even when the guy being questioned knows all of the tactics. He shifted his gaze toward the shrouded bay. "Poisoned. Both of them."

I gave a low whistle, to convey a sense of conspiratorial discovery and sustain his self-aggrandizement. "How'd it go down?"

"Can't say, yet. Could be murder-suicide or double suicide," he said, still staring into the distance with an air of authority. I continued to play along.

"So, your instincts don't point to a double murder?" Most of Papadopoulos' instincts pointed to himself, which made sense given that the Greeks came up with Narcissus—one of the few things I remembered from Sister Mary Leon's eighth grade course. I actually read a fair chunk of *Bullfinch's Mythology* because adolescent rumor had it that the stories involved lots of sex. I was mostly disappointed, although the possibility of gods humping nymphs was more intriguing to a hormone-fueled kid than the idea of virgin birth.

"No. The only suspect would be the grandson who lives in the house, but he doesn't have a motive."

"How about money?"

"Look around, Riley," he said, sweeping his arm toward the mansion. "How many guys in their twenties are living in the lap of luxury? From my interview with Lane Linford, it was evident he received a very generous allowance." That explained the vanity plate on the Ferrari.

"Greed's a funny thing," I said. San Francisco was up to its Golden Gated armpits in millionaires these days—and up to its Tenderloin in homeless folks.

"Maybe there's some convoluted way he could get richer, but the twisted aspects of this case point to the grandparents, not the kid."

"I guess an ex-vice detective would focus on the fact that the victims were naked. But I also suppose that stripping your grandparents before poisoning them might be a little too weird even in your experience."

"I've seen plenty of cases more perverse than that," he said.

"So did the grandson offer any explanation?" I had Papadopoulos on a roll and he was enjoying playing teacher to a wayward student who'd fallen from the graces of the SFPD.

"The kid says it must have been an accident. He claims that for weeks they'd thought something was crawling under their skin. They couldn't make it stop."

"Hence, the flea collars."

"Sort of like old Howard Hughes. Money and madness."

"Except with the Linfords, the germs were moving," I said.

"Precisely. So in their desperation, they doused themselves with chemicals."

"Better dying through chemistry. Seems like a tidy explanation."

"Maybe too tidy," Papadopoulos said, adjusting the knot of his tie to let me know that a godlike judgment was forthcoming.

"Meaning?"

"Meaning I might buy some germophobic craziness, but the bug story is lame. I worked the City's alleys and dives. There were plenty of crazies, but I never heard about imaginary insects except with some cokeheads and alcoholics, and the Linfords don't appear to be either."

"Don't seem the type," I said. "So, what's the kid trying to hide?"

"These upper crust types value their reputations. You know, social connections and all that."

I suppressed a snicker, given the suave lieutenant's effort to cultivate his image.

"I figure that the kid's trying to cover up suicide. Just because you're rich doesn't mean you're happy."

"Could be that there was a fat life insurance policy that wouldn't pay off with suicide," I said, still trying to find a financial incentive for murder. Greed is a helluva motive, almost as good as sex which is where Papadopoulos was headed.

"Or, more likely, he knows that his grandparents were into some sort of sick, sexual game."

"And if the word gets out, San Francisco's elites won't welcome perverts—or their grandperverts—into the best restaurants, clubs and parties," I said.

"That's right. Playing doggy with each other is one thing, but S&M is really sick—and dangerous. I'm no M.E., but I could see their skin was rubbed raw."

"Okay, but that's a long step from suicide," I said.

"So perhaps the kid's half truthful. Maybe it was an accident of sorts. Some people get off on strangulation, so why not intoxication? Maybe adding poison to their repertoire was exciting. Could be something like Ecstasy. You know, that hot, new psychedelic that's supposed to be an aphrodisiac?"

"I gotta start getting out more." I had no idea what he was talking about other than I enjoyed the hell out of sex without suffocation or hallucination. "Damn, you spent too much time in vice," I said.

Papadopoulos fell quiet and then started walking down the steps from the patio into the garden. I followed behind, waiting for what might come next in the strangest conversation I'd had in months. Discussing which poison is most effective in killing rats or roaches is lightweight banter compared to where this was heading.

The lieutenant's pace slowed to a pensive amble. "The assistant district attorney, Grant Roberts, is putting pressure on the vice squad to hunt down perverts. And I'm not sure where this case is going to fit into his grand plan to clean up the City," he said with a deep sigh. "The guy is a Moral Majority hardliner, a second cousin or some relation of Jerry Falwell. Roberts was hired to placate the Christians and their political allies who figure San Francisco is the poster child of sin." He stopped to pluck a camellia blossom. It might be winter, but these defiant flowers didn't care.

"Seems about right. Summer of love, the Castro District, nude beaches. And your bottom line—so to speak—is to both publicly root out deviants and privately cover up this case. Sounds like you have a problem." He nodded and started to absentmindedly pull petals from the flower.

"There's major political pressure, what with Reagan in the White House and Falwell condemning fags to hell. Don't get me wrong, I think the Gipper is what America needs, and guys screwing guys is disgusting." From what I knew of the ancient Greeks and young boys, Papadopoulos was on thin ethnic ice when it came to condemning homosexuality. But I thought better of sharing my cultural critique.

"Whatever two guys, or a guy and a gal, or two gals, or a whole roomful of genitals wants to do is okay with me," I said. Carol and Anna came to mind. They were happy and whatever they were doing in the bedroom didn't do me any harm, so I couldn't figure why it should matter. "Hell, we got nuclear missiles ready to vaporize whole cities, American fighters shooting down Libyan jets, ozone holes, and acid rain. The world's got bigger problems than where guys are putting their cocks or girls are putting their tongues." Papadopoulos smiled, if you looked closely and used your imagination.

"When I worked vice," he said, dropping petals along the soggy compost of the garden path, "I was just trying to make the city a decent place for normal folks."

"I'm with you. But did you ever wonder what 'normal' meant? These days, girls have pink, spiked hair and tattoos on their tits, and guys put safety pins in their noses and rings through their lips. God knows what they're doing in the bedroom, although you have to imagine that the hardware doesn't make things any easier," I said.

"Lips and noses are mundane, Riley. Think lower." I tried not to. "So what's normal? Normal is a mom sending her kid to the park without some deviant flashing his junk. It's a dad going in the public restroom and not hearing a couple of guys butt-fucking in the next stall." Having plucked the last of the petals, he tossed the sad remains into a patch of lavender and took a deep breath. "My job was to keep the perverts, pimps, and prostitutes off the streets."

"Something like trying to keep the Irish from drinking?" I asked, attempting to lighten the mood with ethnic self-deprecation as the sky darkened. The lieutenant didn't take the bait. We got to the end of the garden and looked back at the mansion.

"I really don't care what the Linfords were doing behind closed doors," he said. "Decency is a public matter, sex should be private. But that's not how Grant Roberts figures it, and if I cover-up the details of their death and Roberts finds out, then I can kiss my pension goodbye."

"And if this thing blows up, then Goat Hill Extermination might get dragged into the muck along with the Linfords, eh?"

"Seems like a good bet. If they were poisoned by insecticides and your company is linked to them, the press will have a field day." I could also imagine that a nosy reporter trying to sell papers or an eager detective trying to please Roberts might have a heyday with my business manager being a lesbian. This could get ugly, fast. "Your reputation could be trashed along with the Linfords," he added.

"Onward Christian soldier, eh? With a connection to Jerry Falwell, Roberts has some big-time allies," I said.

"And political clout. The Chamber of Commerce is pushing hard to clean up the city's reputation. Fisherman's Wharf merchants are leading the charge and the Board of Supervisors knows that tourism is critical to the economy," he said, as we started to head back to the house and the foggy mist began to turn into actual rain.

"AIDS has everyone spooked and with San Francisco as ground zero, I can imagine that uptight tourists might decide to take the family to Disneyland where the kids can fondle a duck who doesn't wear pants and hug a terminally youthful boy in green tights."

"I've heard Roberts told his staff that the Almighty sent fire and brimstone to Sodom and Gomorrah and He sent AIDS to San Francisco," Papadopoulos said.

"That son of bitch," I said.

"Roberts or God?"

"Both, if Roberts said that or God did that. Roberts is an ignorant ass. But if God provided the parts and they fit together in ways the Big Guy didn't figure, then so much for his being all-knowing. Speaking of which, I'm still trying to figure what the Linfords were doing when they died."

"That makes two of us," Papadopoulos said, as he pulled up the collar of his trench coat and stepped onto the patio. A cop who looked to be about sixteen opened the French doors in anticipation of our arrival. Make that the lieutenant's arrival. Rookies are committed to pleasing their superiors, not raggedy-ass exterminators.

"I wouldn't have figured old folks for kinky sex," I said. Papadopoulos paused and the rain pattered on the bricks. He turned to me while we were still out of earshot of the young cop.

"After putting in fifteen years on vice, I learned the young are supple. You wouldn't believe the positions that twenty-year-olds can manage in alleys, cars, and bathroom stalls." He wiped the wetness from his trimmed eyebrows. "The young may be limber, but the old are twisted." Papadopoulos finally flashed an unmistakable smile which disappeared when he turned toward the open doors and headed into the Linfords' living room.

CHAPTER THREE

Papadopoulos gave me the green light to interview the Linfords' grandson, saying that I probably couldn't do any harm. In reality, he'd not been in homicide for long and his vice-cop approach to punks and perverts wasn't likely to have shaken loose much from a rich kid. He knew that I sometimes worked cases on the QT since a felony conviction kept me from acquiring a private investigator license—and my business kept me too busy to moonlight anyway. Most of the guys on the force looked the other way when I got involved, knowing I wouldn't get underfoot and my off-the-books legwork could pay dividends for their overworked caseloads. So, I promised the lieutenant I'd give him anything important. We both knew I was lying unless sharing was to my advantage, and he was gambling on that chance. Betting on the truthfulness of an unlicensed PI is a bad wager.

Lane Linford didn't have his own room. He had his own wing. A gleaming, hardwood hallway on the first floor was paneled to the ceiling, and even the damned ceiling was wood paneled. On one side of the hall was an office with all the standard furnishings in dark-stained maple with brass hardware. One of the filing cabinets probably cost more than all the furniture in Goat Hill Extermination. On the opposite side was a game room with the de rigueur pool table (red felt was a nice touch) and an obnoxious video arcade along one wall, with images of jumping frogs, frenzied gorillas, and a yellow ball wandering through a maze. Pinball might've been just as senseless but at least the machines were beautiful.

Further down the hall was an exercise room with various metal-framed devices featuring tension springs, elastic bands, and rubber wheels. I wasn't sure what they did, although I did recognize a stationary bike and a treadmill—inventions that people buy to stay indoors so they can work hard and get nowhere. Much like the cubicles in an office building. There was also a bathroom with enough marble to rival the Taj Mahal and what looked to be a drinking fountain for midgets next to the toilet, but I'm pretty sure it was meant to satisfy the other end of the digestive tract.

At the end of the hall was a half-open door leading to a massive bedroom with plush, forest-green carpeting. The bed would've slept a family of four, and across the room was an elegant writing desk, where Lane Linford was seated, wearing an outdated argyle sweater vest over a shirt with a too-big collar. It didn't help that he was a notably unattractive young man. His head was too big for his scrawny body, which hadn't spent much time in the home gym. His face was pale and horsey; his limp hair was parted down the middle and didn't reach his ears but yet seemed too long. He'd been writing in a notebook and turned toward the door as I knocked softly.

"Yes?"

"Mr. Linford, I know this is a difficult time but I wonder if I might have a word with you."

"Who are you? The police have already questioned me, and I've told them everything I know." He was understandably annoyed. Now was the moment for tact, otherwise known as deception.

"I'm C.V. Riley, the owner of Goat Hill Extermination. Lieutenant Papadopoulos asked me to come to the house because of a possible link between my business and your grandparents." That much was mostly true. "He suggested my expertise could help wrap up this awful situation with minimum intrusion. Doing so would seem advantageous to both your interests and my own. After all, nobody has anything to gain from publicity regarding this tragedy—other than those who market smut and relish innuendo." I was hoping to put us on the same side, against the scandalmongers.

"What do you need from me?" he asked, turning fully toward the door. The young Mr. Linford was nibbling at the bait.

"May I come in for a few minutes?"

"Yes, if you must," he said, gesturing to a tufted leather chair. The shelves over his desk caught my eye. There was a pair of ant farms, like the ones you find in toy stores, except these were a couple feet long and the glass was framed by oak. There were also several terrariums covered with black cloth—a very odd approach to growing plants. As I sat down, I caught a vaguely familiar whiff I couldn't quite place. Sort of a combination of fryer grease and moldy leaves.

"Thank you, Mr. Linford."

"Please, call me 'Lane.'" I told him that I went by "Riley." The poor fellow looked wrung out. I didn't figure he was a paragon of posture in the best of circumstances, but his shoulders sagged and his head looked too heavy for his neck to hold upright. The tight-fitting sweater vest wasn't helping.

"Those are impressive ant farms," I said in an effort to ease into the conversation. He glanced briefly over his shoulder and looked as if I'd caught him with a *Playboy* centerfold.

"Just a hobby continued from my childhood. Now, what do you need from me?"

"I'm trying to provide some information to the authorities regarding the chemicals that might have contributed to your grandparents' deaths. But it might help if I knew just a bit of background about the family." I set the hook with my best fatherly expression, given that he was about twenty years my junior and clearly in need of emotional support. The patter was mostly manipulative on my part, but I honestly felt sorry for the guy—homely, and now alone.

My non-threatening, non-question gave Lane the chance to tell me how his parents had died a couple years ago in a foggy, fiery crash on Shoreline Highway. He moved in with his grandparents while finishing his degree in business management at Stanford. As the only grandchild, Lane was being groomed to take over HerbalVitae, the family business which had grown from a 1960s storefront operation in Haight Ashbury to a multimillion dollar enterprise. I couldn't see any motive for him to knock off his elders—especially in a way that would generate negative headlines (Herbal Tycoons Use Pesticides to Kill Selves: Is Your Tincture Tainted?). Maybe Papadopoulos was right. Eventually, Lane's story wound its way up to the present.

19

"My grandparents were very suspicious of synthetic chemicals, so the flea infestation upstairs must have been pretty bad for them to call an exterminator."

"Can you remember the details of the situation?" I asked.

"Not much to recall. Barney, he was their Golden Retriever, had the run of the yard. He apparently brought back a load of fleas which took up residence in their bedroom, where the dog slept. My grandfather tried lavender and cedar oils which made Barney smell good but didn't kill the fleas."

"Lots of people try home remedies and then end up calling us."

"Herbs can provide miraculous results, but sometimes a problem is too intense for a gentle and natural solution." He made it sound like HerbalVitae was the social worker, and Goat Hill Extermination was the SWAT team. Probably about right.

"Were they happy with our work?"

"Absolutely. Surprisingly so, to be honest. They were impressed with the professionalism of your technician. A Negro. I can't remember his name, but he was very polite—as it should be." I didn't know whether politeness was incumbent upon service workers or black men. Probably both for the Linfords.

"That would've been Dennis. He's a good man." I let that hang for moment. "So, what went wrong?"

"Wrong?"

"Lane, your grandparents ended up wearing flea collars."

"I'm not sure what happened. I took a trip to London to set up an import deal. And when I got back after a couple of weeks, my grandparents were convinced that something had infested their bodies."

"Fleas?"

"No, they said these bugs were tinier, black insects crawling under their skin. I couldn't see anything, but they were convinced there was a new pest in the house. They blamed Barney and gave him away. Poor dog, he was so loyal and trusting." Lane shook his head and ran his fingers through his oily hair.

"So what did you do?"

"I sent them to our family physician. He's very good and very discrete. Doctor Comly couldn't find anything but gave them calamine lotion for the itching. I don't think they used it, preferring to formulate their own treatments. Nothing seemed to help. Grandfather started mailing his skin scrapings to the insect experts at UC Berkeley on a regular basis. And grandmother had your technician come back and conduct an inspection. But nobody could find anything."

"Not to be rude, but it sounds like your grandparents needed a shrink more than an exterminator."

"Exactly!" Lane said, showing a spark of life. "The problem was that Linfords would never be seen going to a psychiatrist. Imagine the embarrassment if others found out. That's why my grandparents dismissed the house staff when their condition intensified."

"I've never been able to find a trustworthy butler," I said. He snorted softly and continued.

"There are plenty of affluent families with members tucked away in facilities recovering from stress and 'nervous conditions,'" he made air quotes with his fingers. "They're mostly drying out, but drinking isn't a stigma. Betty Ford is opening a posh center down in Rancho Mirage later this year. That should be a magnet for San Francisco's wealthiest alcoholics in need of a tan next winter."

"But your grandparents wouldn't qualify for a sunny junket to southern California, I gather."

"Right," Lane said, "they were psychotic, not addicted." I raised a curious eyebrow at his diagnosis. "I did a lot of reading and it became clear that they suffered from a shared psychosis."

"Meaning?"

"Meaning they convinced each other that they were infested. From my research on the condition, it crops up in couples where one person develops a delusion, say of being persecuted, and then the other individual 'catches' the insanity. From there, they feed off one another in a downward spiral. Pretty soon, both people are sure that the world is out to get them."

"Or that itty bitty creatures are out to get them," I said.

"Exactly. There are medications that sometimes work, but the prognosis is poor." He then digressed into a lecture on psychoactive drugs, an analysis of how aging affects one's critical faculties, and finished with a critique of the mental health system in the United States. If nothing else, Stanford had taught the kid to do his homework.

After twenty minutes, Lane leaned back and rocked his head to each side, generating an audible crack in his skinny neck. I took this to be an expression of satisfaction with his lecture, which he punctuated by cracking his knuckles. I was impressed with his knowledge—and suspicious. The young man knew a very great deal about a very unusual condition. Perhaps he was just worried about his grandparents, but his interest seemed deeper than that of a concerned grandson.

"If they were delusional, as you suggest, why did you allow them to continue their mad belief of being infested with invisible insects?"

"Riley, the bugs weren't invisible to them. They could see the things. And I couldn't get them to see what they really needed—a psychiatrist."

"And so you let them concoct various treatments, wear dog collars, hang No-Pest strips, and set off bug bombs?" He looked hurt. "I apologize if that sounded judgmental." I wasn't sorry, but I wanted him to keep talking.

"That's okay, I know how it looks. But they were so insistent, so utterly convinced. And those crazy interventions calmed them. Grandfather could conduct business by phone and fax, and grandmother could visit her friends—at first. It didn't take long before they became reclusive and obsessed with developing new formulations of herbs and God knows what else." I knew, at least in part from my bathroom inspection: Lysol, alcohol, vinegar, and kerosene to extract magical cures from every imaginable herb in their personal storehouse. But these concoctions shouldn't have been deadly. Irritating, smelly, and revolting—but not lethal.

"Did you share all of this with Lieutenant Papadopoulos?" I asked.

"Most certainly not," he said. "That man was insulting and accusatory. I would never have harmed my grandparents, but the detective was looking for someone to blame. He wanted a simple solution—murder or suicide—rather than tragic madness leading to a horrible accident."

"Well, I want to understand. It's a matter of professionalism and, quite frankly, self-defense. Exterminators are one step below personal injury lawyers these days, as you are surely aware given the surge of interest in all things 'natural.' So if my business or products contributed to their deaths, then I need to know and get ahead of any story that might develop. And, of course, I want to protect your good family name."

"Of course," Lane said, with a slight smirk. "Go ahead and tell the detective anything I told you that is crucial to his investigation."

"Of course," I said, with a conspiratorial smile. We both knew how the game was being played. "Is there anything else that might shed light on this tragedy?"

"There might be, and because I believe we understand each other," he said, opening a drawer in the writing desk, "I'm going to loan you the key to my grandfather's study." He handed me a lever lock key—one of those old-fashioned gizmos consisting of a long brass rod with uneven teeth protruding from one side. I was glad to have the key because lever locks are harder to pick than modern pin tumbler locks. "This will open a door from their bedroom, opposite the walk-in closet. When you're done, lock the door and leave the key in the top drawer of their nightstand. I'd rather that my grandfather's materials not become part of the police investigation and public record. So please be discrete with whatever you find, taking into consideration our . . ." he paused, "mutual interests."

I thanked him and headed back upstairs, trying to avoid drawing attention to my movements. I needn't have worried. The uniformed officers had moved inside to avoid the rain and were far more interested in ogling the house than watching me.

Chapter Four

Mr. Linford's study was like a museum display of an old-time, gentleman naturalist. The room was about thirty feet deep by fifteen wide. One of the long walls featured floor-to-ceiling bookcases. The volumes were arranged by topic and age, from what I could tell by opening a few. There were modern texts about medicinal plants from around the world, along with some intriguing books from the last century such as *King's American Dispensatory* which consisted of a monumental list of plants and what they were good for. I checked out the entry on coffee to be sure that the herbalists knew what they were doing. I was informed that, "An infusion of roasted coffee is an agreeable stimulant," its effects include, "increasing peristalsis, thus favoring a free action from the bowels," and it can be used to, "overcome the soporific or intoxicating effects of opium, morphine, or alcohol." Okay, brewed coffee facilitates a good morning crap and helps a bad morning hangover. Fair enough.

The oldest book was too high to reach, so I used one of those fancy rolling ladders connected to a rail along the upper shelves to reach Nicholas Culpeper's *Complete Herbal*. The publication date was 1653, which was pretty damned impressive. I climbed down and understood why there was a dehumidifier humming contentedly in the corner, along with some sort of special thermostat on the wall. The winter wetness would turn Linford's antiquarian literary collection into a mildew farm without some modern climate control. And the books weren't the only things that would have been a haven for mold.

Along the other long wall was a series of elegant, wooden cabinets. The drawers were about two feet wide and three inches high, just perfect for holding plant specimens mounted on thick sheets of blotter paper. Everything was labeled with a scientific name which meant nothing to me, along with what I assumed was the name of whoever yanked up the plant (only a few credited Linford), the date of the deadly deed (going back to the late eighteen hundreds), and the location (my brief nosing around yielded nearly twenty countries). I was impressed, again. There was an antique apothecary cabinet at the far end, next to a walnut worktable that filled the width of the room.

The table had just enough dings, scratches, and stains to prove that Linford used it, rather than kept it as an objet d'art—a term I had learned a couple weeks ago walking through the De Young Museum with Nina to check out the carvings of an Inuit sculptor (I had also learned that we don't call them 'Eskimos' anymore for some confusing reason that made sense to Nina and other Native Americans). In the center of the table was a Wild Heerburg stereo microscope that would set you back nearly the price of a new car—maybe a Datsun 210, but still. I know because I shopped around for my second-hand scope and still couldn't touch one of the German models. The krauts know how to grind a lens and make a buck. The table also held what looked to be a desktop model of a torture device, but it turned out to be an old-fashioned plant press with a cast iron plate that could be screwed downward against the base to gently crush an unsuspecting specimen between sheets of blotter paper and force it to confess its magical powers. At least that's how it worked for witches in Salem. Impressive, but the really interesting items were at the other end of the table.

There were stacks of books about insects. One pile was mostly general texts: *The Science of Entomology*, *Fundamentals of Entomology*, and other volumes promising to cover a field, "too vast for any single human intelligence to grasp" according to a character in an Oliver Wendell Holmes novel which I never read. I found the quote on a poster of California insects that I bought for Tommy at the Essig Entomology Museum. There was another stack of medical entomology books including: *Insects and other*

Arthropods of Medical Importance, Entomology in Human and Animal Health, Insects and Hygiene, and the always popular, *Scabies*—a title sure to generate raised eyebrows and arm's length handling from the librarian at the checkout desk.

Another pile consisted of back issues of the *Journal of Medical Entomology*. Linford had bookmarked various articles. There was one about the control of chiggers (dimethoate works well; score one for the organophosphate insecticides) and another about what environmental conditions allow fleas to survive (they like it warm and humid; go figure). I was grimly fascinated by the summary of a study reporting "myiasis"—a four-dollar word for when fly larvae set up house in the tissues of live animals, including the vagina of some poor woman in Texas. I quit reading at that point. Even seasoned exterminators can live without mental images messing up their libidos.

Linford had quite an assortment of stains and dyes, along with other laboratory paraphernalia, all neatly organized. He kept a daily log in a leather-bound book with recent entries such as: "Ask Lane to replace pest strips," "Remind Lane to mail samples to Cal Academy," and "Have Lane acquire ointment ingredients" with a bizarre list including sulfur powder, carbolic acid, mercuric iodide, and Crisco. It seems the old coot was shifting from herbalism to chemistry in a desperate effort to treat whatever he thought was afflicting him and the Mrs.—unless Papadopoulos could come up with some erotic interpretation of this nasty lubricant. So it appeared that Lane was lending a hand and not just passively allowing his grandparents to pursue their strange hobby.

I rifled through a couple of two-drawer filing cabinets tucked under the worktable. Mostly there were neatly organized photocopies of scientific reports and magazine articles. But one drawer was devoted to ziplock bags, each placed in a file folder and labeled with the date, the name of ma or pa Linford, and descriptions such as: "swabbing from neck and shoulder," "brushing from scalp" and "scraping from pubis." That last one was a point for the lieutenant's theory, but I seriously doubted that collecting this specimen was arousing. The baggies held clumps of hair, flakes of dried skin, and what looked to be blackened scabs and yellowish crusts.

Some file folders included a note card indicating that a subsample had been sent to a laboratory, most often "UC Berkeley/Essig Museum." A baggie from two weeks ago had "Proof!" written in bold, black letters along with a note card indicating that material had been sent to the Cal Academy. I took that one, along with a random selection of others. They were easily hidden in the pockets of my bulky jacket. I locked up, put the key in the nightstand, and thought I had about as much information as I could get in one bizarre morning. I was wrong.

I found the front door open and caught the unmistakable scent of Malcolm Machalek. Well, not exactly Malcolm but his cigar. There's nothing worse than the smell of a cheap cigar, but Malcolm smoked only the best—a blend of Dominican and Nicaraguan tobaccos which he claimed put the Cubans to shame. In the soggy morning air, the smoke was reminiscent of leather and coffee with a hint of vanilla. I knew it had to be Malcolm because nobody else would be contemplating a corpse and puffing on a fine cigar before lunch.

The morning's pondering was over since the bodies were already bagged and being carted down the stairs. So, I followed the odor plume along with a softly whistled rendition of the Toreador song from *Carmen*. Around the side of the house, I found the grizzled medical examiner contemplating a bloomless rose garden. The thorny branches complemented the winter mood. The rain had slowed to something between a heavy fog and a light mist.

"Riley, you spray-happy, nature-hating bastard," he said with a gleam in his eye, "what brings you here on this lovely day?" Ever since my forced exit from the ranks of San Francisco's finest, we expressed our mutual admiration through insults.

"Just thought I'd stop by and see if the body snatchers were willing to brave the weather, knowing how much you and your henchmen like fluorescent lighting and indoor recreation."

"Fuck you," he said with a crooked grin. "Really, what are you doing in this neighborhood?"

"Hey, even the rich folks need my services. And Goat Hill Extermination is known for being discrete."

"Right, so you just happened to come by to gas some roaches only to discover that your customers no longer required your discrete services. You're full of shit." He took a long drag on his cigar and exhaled with a sigh of almost pornographic pleasure.

"Okay, we treated the place for a flea infestation awhile back. Papadopoulos found our business card and connected us to the Linfords' peculiar death scene—flea collars not being considered a fashion accessory among the upper class. So, I'm trying to figure out if we're going to be dragged into this case."

"Could be," he said.

"Could be what?"

"Could be that they were poisoned."

"I thought you told Papadopoulos that was your finding," I said.

"My preliminary finding, yes."

"Did you find anything else that you could share with me?"

"Not with you, but I might be willing to chat with Mr. Jameson," he took a slow drag on the cigar.

"Suppose you tell me what you found while we're here, and I bring Mr. Jameson, wearing his Limited Reserve label of course, to your corner of the Medical Examiner's office later this week?"

He closed his eyes and slowly exhaled a cloud of smoke. "I suppose I can trust you to deliver," he said, knocking a lump of ash onto the ground. "I didn't give Papadopoulos the full story. The pretty boy has a stick up his ass, and he can wait for the official report."

Papadopoulos was about as smooth as Malcolm was coarse, although the body bagger was a season ticket holder to the San Francisco Opera. I've always said that classical music has a bad rap for being snooty—and Malcolm pretty much makes my point.

"And so Malcolm, to borrow from Paul Harvey, what might be 'the rest of the story'?"

"I believe that they probably died convulsively, given the fecal material smeared on the carpet as well as the anterior and posterior surfaces of the bodies."

"So, they rolled in their own shit?"

"How delicately put, my friend. In addition, the male decedent's arms were oddly tucked beneath his body, and the female's legs were positioned in a way that suggested a seizure rather than simply losing consciousness. Hence, I'm tempted to guess acute poisoning."

"But the flea collars shouldn't have delivered a lethal dose. And certainly not an acute poisoning," I said.

"True enough. But did you notice the white film on their torsos, like the deposit you'd expect from a deodorant?" I hadn't and Malcolm nodded sagely. "It was the remnant of two products we found on the bathroom counter and bagged as evidence."

"I'm guessing it wasn't roll-on antiperspirant."

"Try bottles of Major's Mange Cure and Centurion Flea Dip."

"Damn, so they drenched themselves in insecticides?"

"Ah, but it gets better, my boy," Malcolm said, taking a series of light puffs.

"Do tell."

"I don't suppose you detected anything unusual about their scalps?" he said, enjoying the professorial tone that came from forty years of examining corpses.

"They looked to have thinning hair and bad cases of dandruff."

"Very good. You noticed the obvious. But you missed the white powder and the pungent chlorine scent," I hadn't wanted to spend overly long with the reeking bodies, but Malcolm could focus on a whiff of chlorine and set aside the stench, like most of us could chat on a downtown sidewalk while blocking out the traffic noise.

"They used bleach on their hair?"

"It certainly was white, and bleach would account for the chlorine odor. But you're overlooking the powdery material."

"An organochlorine insecticide?" I offered.

"I'm guessing that they dusted their scalps with chlordane."

"That's quite a witch's brew of toxins that they used."

"Exactly. No single product was deadly. Most likely they were cumulatively intoxicated by the flea collars and chlordane dust. Swabbing themselves with mange and flea dip we—didn't find anything to suggest that they diluted the concentrates—pushed their nervous systems to the breaking point." He nipped the end of the cigar and spat the wet mush into the roses.

"So that's how it went down?"

"We'll have to run toxicology tests and perform autopsies, but I'm betting that the final report will be some version of what we just covered."

"It won't look good for exterminators in general or my business in particular when this goes public. I'll have to check to see if we provided any of the products to the Linfords."

"Might be a good idea, Riley. As it stands, the newspaper story written by some hack reporter will be that your company sprayed the mansion of a trusting, elderly couple and callously poisoned two of the city's venerable business leaders." He took a final drag on the cigar butt and tossed it into the roses.

If Goat Hill Extermination and my people were going to avoid being thrown into the thorn bush of public opinion, I needed to get back to the shop, figure out what we had done, and devise a plan to avoid stinking as much as the Linfords.

CHAPTER FIVE

I should've been listening to one of the radio stations reporting traffic conditions every few minutes, but I was intrigued by a program on KDFC. I caught the end of Suite No. 1 in G minor by Johann Berhard Bach (the obscure second cousin of the renowned J.S. Bach), then Frederic Chopin's *Minute Waltz* brilliantly played by Arthur Rubinstein, followed by the catchy *Radetsky March* by Johann Strauss I (the lesser known father of the famed composer). Although perplexed by the eclectic selections, I was enjoying the music far more than the drive. There was complete chaos heading up Van Ness toward Market.

The tangled mess of music and traffic made sense when the program host revealed the unifying theme. All of the composers died in a year ending in 49, which was the announcer's attempt to connect classical music listeners to the mindboggling celebration of the 49ers Super Bowl championship. Half a million people were starting to pack the parade route along Market. The insanity wouldn't peak for hours, but I had the sense to detour over to 3rd and make my way back to the shop.

Arriving late meant that Dennis and Larry had already picked their favorites from what Carol had bought for us. She'd refused to acquiesce to the gloomy weather and walked the nine blocks over to The Sandwich Shop in Dogpatch. It was one of the least cleverly named lunch spots located in the most intriguingly named neighborhood of Potrero Hill. Nobody really knows why it's called Dogpatch. Some people argue that in the Forties any obscure backwater was called "Dogpatch" after the middle-of-nowhere setting in Li'l Abner. Others contend that it was named for the weedy dogfennel that grew in the vacant lots—a plant that resembled chamomile from the Old Country and fooled our Hungarian neighbors into trying to make tea out of the stuff (but only once, as the story went). But my favorite explanation is that the neighborhood hosted packs of dogs that used to scavenge discarded meat from the slaughterhouses up the bay.

Whatever the origin, Dogpatch never gentrified. The area boomed with the shipyards during World War II and kept its gritty feel. The residents were screwed by the city in the Sixties when Interstate 280 cut through Potrero Hill and folks were paid a pittance for their homes. But the freeway gave the Dogpatch neighborhood a separate identity with a brawny blend of industrial operations, boxing gyms, working class neighborhoods, and unpretentious restaurants, which is a long way of saying that I ended up with a BLT after Dennis and Larry nabbed the pastrami and roast beef sandwiches. No complaints—The Sandwich Shop makes the best BLT in San Francisco, with generous bacon, crisp lettuce, ripe tomatoes and just the right amount of mayo on toasted sourdough. No frou-frou sprouts or fancy spreads.

We ate in the back, where the guys had arranged low bookcases of crumbling particle board to set aside a corner of the warehouse as their "living room" which Carol called "the dump." In their defense, there was something homey about the decaying couch, decrepit chairs and sagging coffee table holding down an unraveling, braided rug. To refute Carol's claim, the guys had gone out and bought an almost respectable, floral upholstered Louis XV-style chair—which they referred to as the "throne"—for her visits to their lair. She was not amused, mostly.

"S'up, boss?" asked Larry, while unwrapping the remaining half of his sandwich.

"Thanks for waiting," I said, as Dennis shoved the last of a roast beef on pumpernickel into his mouth. Carol was having something with cucumbers and a fringe of sprouts poking out.

"This is some choice grindage," said Dennis, dabbing at his lips.

"You're an absolute Pac-Man," Larry said, "I'm betting that if any mustard was on the napkin, you'd be scarfing it down too."

"Okay Riley, out with it," said Carol, "I assume you have something to tell us that will justify our falling behind before the week's barely started." I had a half dozen, pink, "While you were out" notes taped to my office door, so I could see why Carol wasn't too happy about my absence.

"There's a good reason, but not good news," I said. Then I explained the whole situation, or as much as I'd been able to understand—two rich senior citizens who died naked and collared; a wary grandson who played amateur shrink; an assistant district attorney on a crusade to save the city from perverts, a detective who doubted the grandson and suspected deviancy, and a medical examiner who suspected poisoning with the tools of our trade.

"And to make matters worse," I added, "the Linfords were richer than God, so if this goes public, we can be sure that the lawyers will make us the villains."

"According to Anna, the herbal market is booming. So maybe HerbalVitae isn't as profitable as it once was," Carol said. I figured that if anyone knew what was happening in the world of botanical scams it would be someone in the world of New Age nonsense. Carol's girlfriend, Anna, was a sweetheart, but selling tinctures, crystals, incense and past life guides at a store called Unblocked Chakra was equivalent to curing the plague with posies.

"Whether they's worth a million less than before, it sounds like we's in deep trouble," said Dennis.

"No shit, Sherlock," said Larry, crumpling his sandwich wrapper and aiming for a trash can in the corner. He missed, as had several Styrofoam cups, a few candy wrappers, and a half-eaten burrito in a microwave sleeve. The microwave had been my Christmas gift to the guys.

"Fuck you, Watson," said Dennis, who got up and went over to the repurposed aquarium that we used for the colony of Madagascar hissing cockroaches to impress potential clients. When he lifted the lid to drop a crust of his sandwich among the egg cartons where the insects hid, a musky scent reminded me of what I'd smelled in Lane Linford's bedroom. He evidently had a thing for rearing insects, which counted in his favor as far as I was concerned. Little did I know.

"Enough of the clever repartee," said Carol. "This could be bad news in lots of ways."

"It's bunk," declared Dennis, and Larry nodded agreement.

"Maybe, but we're involved," Carol said, reaching to grab a folder that she'd set on the bookcase. She winced in pain.

"Still working out at Marty's?" I said.

"Yeah, sparring is one thing but boxing hurts even when nobody's getting hit," she said, opening the file. "According to our records, the Linfords called us on September 7th of last year because they had red welts on their ankles and legs. Dennis did the inspection on the 9th and found flea activity in the carpet of the master bedroom. Then on the 10th, Riley and Dennis applied FleaGon to all of the carpeted areas where the dog spent time, including the grandson's bedroom. The family was instructed to sleep in the guest rooms for a few days. A note here says that the Linfords were also advised to have their dog treated for fleas, as he was the likely source of the infestation. They paid their bill with a check on the day of treatment."

"Nothing unusual so far," I said. "The mix of permethrin and methoprene usually does the trick."

"It gets weird, trust me. Mr. Linford called on October 21st and complained that 'bugs' were infesting their house again. Something was crawling on them and the itching was intolerable. Dennis went out the next morning. According to his report—and Dennis, your handwriting is atrocious—the Linfords were very upset. So, he did an exceptionally thorough inspection."

"That be me. Sloppy writing, awesome inspections," Dennis said, leaning into the mushy cushions of the couch.

"From what I can read," said Carol, clearing her throat and giving Dennis 'the look,' "he checked the dog, the dog's bed, and the bedroom carpet with a magnifying glass and found no fleas, no eggs, and no flea dirt." She paused. "Flea dirt?"

"That's the nice word for flea shit," Larry said.

"Looks like black pepper," said Dennis, "but smear it with a damp cloth and you get bloody streaks. Them's some badass insects."

"The report also says that Dennis put on white socks and walked through every upstairs room, which I presume is a good way to find fleas."

"The hungry little bastards hop out of the carpet and they're easy to see against white socks," Larry explained.

"Just like in the city. They's no way to hide yo' black ass when surrounded by whiteness." Dennis had grown up in the projects, so he knew the deal.

"We all have our burden to bear," said Carol. Being lesbian has its own challenges, even in the land of free love. And Larry's being a Vietnam vet was not without its difficulties, especially in the land of peaceniks. They were all damaged goods, like me. But we sometimes needed to remind each other to just play the cards we're dealt. No whining, no excuses.

"Mos' definitely," Dennis said. "But this boy didn't stop with the socks."

"That's right," said Carol. "It says here that you set up a 'bubble bath trap,' whatever the hell that means."

"Allow me," said Larry. "What my homey means is a shallow bowl filled with water and a few drops of liquid soap, set on the floor with a desk lamp to provide mood lighting and warmth. Fleas are all about body heat . . ."

"That was one fine movie," Dennis interjected.

"I'd hop into a bubble bath with Kathleen Turner," Larry said. "But in our case, the fleas jump toward the light and into the bowl."

"And the soap?" Carol asked. The guys shrugged. Larry moved over to the weight lifting bench and started one-arm curls with a forty-pound dumbbell.

"Riley says do it, and we always do what the boss man says." Larry grunted agreement.

"Since when?" I asked, and then added, "The soap assures that the fleas sink and drown. And as long as we're reviewing Dennis's report, that's one helluva service call. You weren't getting tipped, were you?" We had a no-tipping policy. Everyone earned a good salary and the best benefits I could afford.

"No way. They was nice folks and they liked me, which can't be said of all our customers." He was right. Even the liberal capital of the country had its share of bigots. "And, they shore seemed uptight about whatever was messin' with 'em. They blamed the dog, but he was clean. Prob'ly had him washed and fluffed at one of them fancy grooming places."

"The report says that you consulted with Riley and returned on the 22nd with flea dip and a package of flea collars that you picked up from Pat's Perfect Pets."

"I remember that," I said, "we were running full tilt around here, and I told Dennis to give them some off-the-shelf flea treatments. I didn't figure it'd do the dog any harm. But I also didn't figure that they'd start using the collars on themselves."

"Is that what killed 'em?" asked Dennis, leaning forward and looking very serious.

"Maybe, in part," I said.

"So, the thing is I gave the old folks the poison they used on themselves. Sheeit."

"That's heavy, man," said Larry, referring to the poisoning, not the dumbbell that he switched to his other hand. "But you . . . didn't do . . . anything wrong . . ." he said between curls. He set the weight between his feet and looked at Dennis, "You were trying to help."

"He's right, Dennis. If anyone's to blame it's me," I said. "I should've gone back over there and talked to them. And I shouldn't have sent you with flea dip or collars without confirming a new infestation. It just gave them ideas. They were loading up their bodies with organophosphates between dichlorvos in the pest strips and flea collars and chlorpyrifos in the flea dip and mange treatment."

"Probably a pyrethroid in the bug bomb, so that wouldn't be as bad," said Larry. He reached for the dumbbell.

"Maybe not, but their nervous systems must've been fried. I suspect they were diluting the flea and mange dip until that last dose, when they swabbed themselves with the concentrate," I said.

"The file indicates Dennis had one more visit in November. There's just a short note saying he found nothing," Carol said.

"That be right," Dennis said. "They was lookin' mighty bad by then, what with their skin being red and flaky. I could tell they both lost weight."

"Looked as scrawny as you?" Larry teased, trying to lighten the mood. Dennis went on.

"The mister, he showed me some baggies with hair and lint and other messed up stuff. He wanted me to tell him there was bitty insects crawling in there. I had my magnifying glass but I couldn't see nuthin' but what you'd get out of a vacuum bag."

"Was he upset?" I asked.

"Not so much angry as disappointed. Or maybe frustrated. He kept askin' me to look closer in better light. But I couldn't lie. I noticed the dog wasn't around, but I saw a bottle of flea dip on the dresser. I should've asked to take it back."

"Were they wearing flea collars?" Larry asked.

"Lemme think. He was wearing one of those nice blue coats with a gold patch on the pocket . . ."

"A blazer," Carol offered.

"Yeah, a blazer with a white turtleneck. Now that I picture that, I also remember she was wearin' a turtleneck sweater. I remember thinking to myself that they were both so old and wrinkled that they looked like turtles."

"Sounds like they were already wearing flea collars and hiding them from visitors," I said.

"Oh man, oh man," Dennis said. "They was doin' all that with what I gave 'em. It was like givin' drugs to kids in the projects. They trusted me and ended up dying."

"Dennis, stop," I said. "It is not your fault. I should've gone over there and checked out the situation."

"The Linfords called one last time on December 9th," Carol said, closing the file on her lap.

"And?" I asked.

"I left you a note to return their call because Dennis was out with the flu."

"And I never got back to them because they'd become one of those never satisfied, problem customers. Goddammit." We all sat in silence for a minute.

"What's next, boss?" asked Dennis.

"I've got two leads worth following. First, I need to talk to a shrink about what the hell was going on in the Linfords' heads."

"Other than chlordane dust, eh?" said Larry.

"Right, although it probably wasn't helping. And then, I want to meticulously examine what's in the bag that Linford labeled as 'Proof.'"

"In other words fellas, Riley is going to be trying to get in front of where this whole mess is headed and save our business," said Carol, getting to her feet. "Which means we're down a man, which means you two will need to cover."

"At least it'll feel like I'm helpin," said Dennis unfolding his lanky body from the couch.

"I'm down with that," said Larry, rubbing his biceps. "So the dynamic duo had better bounce if we're going to get in front of Carol's job schedule."

The guys headed out the back to the vans, Carol headed up to the office, and I called Nina for a psychiatric referral.

Chapter Six

"Hey sweetie, what's up?" Nina seemed cheery given our celibate weekend and my calling her at work. The church secretary had grumbled when I asked to speak to Nina, who was supervising the daycare for retarded adults. I sympathized since Nina's coming to the phone meant the secretary had to handle Tommy and the others, who were probably in the middle of a messy craft project.

"It's a long story, but I need the name of the psychiatrist you've been seeing."

"She's a psychologist." The distinction was lost on me. Whatever the title, the person was supposed to fix your head. "Is everything okay?" she asked.

"With me, yes. With the world, no. I need professional advice on a pretty twisted situation that has not-so-pretty implications for my business."

"Is Larry okay?"

"Larry? Yeah, he's fine." Nina knew about Larry's nightmares of his time in Nam. She worried about him. Actually, she worried about Carol and Dennis, too. And me. Her own messed up background connected her to the gang at Goat Hill Extermination. With that much to worry about, no wonder she was seeing a psychologist.

"What aren't you telling me?"

"I have—or had—a couple of customers who went bonkers and might've poisoned themselves with chemicals we provided."

"Riley! That's a big deal. People committing suicide with your pesticides will be disastrous for your reputation. Who will want to be associated with the purveyors of death?"

"Thanks babe, I hadn't quite put the situation in such stark terms. But we don't know whether their deaths were suicide or accident or something else."

"By which you mean murder? Somebody used your products to kill people? Oh God Riley, that would be even worse."

"It's unlikely, but I can't close any doors at this point. The police are suspicious but withholding judgment for now. I need to stay in front of this one, which means I need some professional help."

"I can imagine the stress and anxiety this must be causing you." Her tone shifted from alarm to sympathy.

"Not help for me. I need to get into the heads of the victims—and maybe their grandson, who's my only suspect if it wasn't an accident. The old folks had delusions about insects that might've caused them to misuse the chemicals. Or there might be some sort of sexual deviancy involved. Like I said, it's a long story."

"I'm not sure I follow you, but I am sure Dr. Chen can help. The woman is brilliant."

Nina gave me the shrink's number and reminded me of our dinner date at her family's restaurant tomorrow night before hanging up.

Nina had been seeing Dr. Chen for nearly a year. I doubted that an hour's therapy was worth ten hours of Nina's wages at the daycare center, but the counseling seemed important to her—and she was important to me. For that kind of cash, I'd almost be willing to sit in a plush office and feign sympathy. Almost. After a week of "uh, huh" and "say more" I'd need a shrink to keep me from killing myself.

I had been required to see the police psychologist after I killed a perp—a wannabe revolutionary who knew the whereabouts of a sick, kidnapped child. I explained that I didn't have any feelings other than mild regret that the punk decided loyalty trumped survival. Even that was admirable in its own way, as I told the shrink who eagerly jotted down this revelation in my file. He seemed incredulous that I wasn't traumatized. I couldn't convince him I had a sworn duty to protect vulnerable people from criminals—and if that meant beating a punk to obtain crucial information about an innocent kid and if that beating ended up being unintentionally lethal, then I would calmly accept whatever came next. What came next was losing my badge, but not my sanity.

I called Josephine Chen's office and asked to speak to the doctor. The receptionist said the doctor was unavailable. I asked when she'd be available. The receptionist explained the doctor was available only by appointment. I asked for an appointment this afternoon. She said the earliest time would be next Tuesday afternoon. I said the matter was urgent. She asked if next Tuesday at three o'clock would work or whether I'd prefer to be transferred to the mental health unit at San Francisco General. I hung up.

So, in the spirit of 'if you can't beat 'em, join 'em,' I went up front, gave Carol some brief instructions, and had her call Dr. Chen's office. Using her most authoritative voice, she introduced herself as Dr. Carroll and explained she was setting up a new counseling practice and she wanted to get to know those in the field, particularly such a highly respected colleague as Dr. Chen. Would her colleague be available to discuss professional matters over lunch, say at the Hang Ah Tea Room? Carol hung up and smiled. I would need to do some fast talking tomorrow at noon.

I went back to my office and pulled out the baggie labeled with "Proof!" With a hand lens, I could make out a few louse-like insects mixed in with hair and scabs. I needed better magnification to identify the little scoundrels. I decided to put off my taxonomic challenge until evening when I could use the microscope back at my house. So, as long as we were still in business, I spent the afternoon doing work to pay the bills.

San Francisco's ants, along with a fair number of residents, had been driven indoors by the winter weather. My first call was to a distraught woman in Richmond. An address on the other side of the city gave me the chance to hear the opening strains of Havergal Brian's symphony No. 1, *The Gothic*. The address was on Clement, which wasn't the ritziest neighborhood, but there were plenty of swank places. I'm not sure how the affluent Russians and Chinese ended up in the Inner Richmond, but I was intrigued how America's two communist enemies had mastered capitalism in San Francisco. Carol's note on the work order said, "Mrs. Wang asks you to park at the Dupont tennis courts, not at her house."

Like many well-to-do, Mrs. Wang didn't want the neighbors seeing an exterminator's truck parked in front of her home, which was an ostentatious collision of Edwardian and Spanish Colonial architectures. Like many in the area, this house was built with exterminators' job security in mind. The full basement—an unusual feature elsewhere in the city—put moist soil adjacent to poorly sealed walls and virtually assured the arrival of six-legged tenants.

I introduced myself and Mrs. Wang declared, "Mr. Riley must do something. Ants all over basement. They eating coconut. I crush them. They stink like rotten coconut. Where they get coconut? You kill them fast." I managed to get her calmed down, suggested she make some tea for us—my standard ploy to keep the homeowner from being underfoot—and headed to the basement. I already knew the culprit, as there's only one kind of ant that invades homes and reeks with the odor of decaying coconut, although not from eating the stuff. The solution was as simple as the identification—the infamous, odorous house ant.

The upstairs was decorated with silk hangings, jade sculptures, and elaborate cork carvings of temple scenes set behind glass in lacquered frames. Conversely, the basement provided a 'stink ant' haven. For starters, there were a couple of kids' bedrooms. Along one wall of the boy's bedroom (my Sherlockian deduction being based on posters of Wonder Woman in her armored bodice and Farrah Fawcett-Majors in her red one-piece swimsuit, along with the smell of gym clothes and Old Spice) was a pyramid of soda cans in an apparent effort to display one of every brand known to man. The sugary remnants of the collection provided a feast for the ants, and the wall backed to the utility room with a washer, dryer, and hot water heater providing tropical conditions for the sweet-toothed ants.

An hour's work bagging up the cans (the kid would need another hobby), putting down some bait stations, and caulking cracks was followed with a bout of landscaping outside the house. After I trimmed back the boxwood hedge to make it harder for the ants to access the foundation, I was cold and wet. Mrs. Wang's tea hit the spot. She told me it was lapsang souchong, the smoky tea equivalent of a peaty Scotch—that comparison being my own. I explained she'd done well to call me before the problem was severe, as many people in nice neighborhoods are ashamed of having pests and wait until infestations reach staggering levels. It's funny how people consider having ants to be a character flaw but a case of athlete's foot is not a moral failing.

I told Mrs. Wang how the ants had gotten in and what they were eating. She muttered something motherly in Chinese that probably meant, "I told that son of mine not to pile trash in his room. Wait until his father gets home." Mrs. Wang was both embarrassed by having hosted vermin and grateful for my assistance and discretion.

I walked back to my truck and caught the end of *The Gothic* which is, I think, even longer than Mahler's Symphony No. 3, neither of which is particularly good but both allow a lazy radio program host to take a nap. And I must say that Brian's symphony has a huge almost-ending, but he didn't know when to quit and dragged out the music into a sixth movement that concludes with a whimper from the choir rather than a bang from the orchestra. My work agenda involved heading across Golden Gate Park to a carpenter ant infestation in Sunset—the land of twenty-five-foot-wide lots and stucco facades. The customer's back porch was listing like a sinking ship. The good news was that carpenter ants are easier to control than termites. The bad news was that having carpenter ants doesn't prevent termites, as he'd heard from neighbors.

At the end of the day, I dropped off the truck, locked up the shop and headed over to Marty's Gym for a title fight with the heavy bag. The bag won in the eleventh round, but I got what I wanted out of the bout—serious sweat and pleasant pain. I chatted with Marty for a few minutes at the apron of the sparring ring while a white kid with heart was getting schooled by a black fighter with talent. Marty chewed his stogie and expressed his admiration for Carol, who had absorbed my tutorials and came every weekend to pummel the bags (heavy and speed), jump rope (including criss-crosses and double unders), and shadow box. He even put on the target mitts and called out combinations for her. In his estimation, she showed the young turks what hard work looked like, along with a desirable and unobtainable body.

She brought physical dedication and sexual frustration to his gym. The old codger loved it.

I took a steam which felt great but brought out a rash on my hands and wrists, which I attributed to brushing against poison ivy while collecting insects with Tommy last weekend. On the walk home, the cold drizzle soothed the itchiness while the residual warmth from the sauna lasted to my front door. Anxious to take a closer look at the contents of Linford's baggie, I rewarmed some leftover coddle which I'd made over the weekend to use up other leftovers. The combination of bangers, rashers, potatoes, onions and whatever else needs to be eaten (in my case, a few aging carrots, a sagging stalk of celery, and a bundle of wilted chives) can vary, but the secret is to never omit a pint of Guinness—half for the pot and half for the cook.

I wolfed down my dinner and went to the living room, furnished with a reclining chair, a declining television, a stereo system with new Realistic 'Mach One' speakers (my Christmas present from Nina which was far too expensive, but at least I had the good sense to get her a pearl necklace), a wall of twenty-five-drawer insect cabinets, and a massive, well-worn oak table where I worked on my collection. I poured myself a generous two fingers of Black Bush and put *Rigoletto* on the stereo with Placido Domingo as the Duke of Mantua and Ileana Cotrubaș as Rigoletto's daughter, Gilda.

I hadn't managed to draw Nina into symphonic music, but she had become enchanted with opera. Although attending the San Francisco Opera wasn't a cheap date, she was transfixed by the spectacle and the grand tales of skullduggery, loyalty, vengeance and, of course, romance. So an Indian and an Irishman found common ground in Italian theater. Sometimes, you gotta love this country.

Savoring the smooth sweetness of the whiskey, I got down to work, shaking the contents of the "Proof!" baggie onto a watch glass. Tangled in the detritus of skin and scalp, I found lice. I've seen my share of head, body and pubic lice over the years, from people variously humiliated and desperate to be free of the little bastards. But these lice were different. Under the scope I could see that instead of having comically small heads, their noggins were as wide as their bodies. It was as obvious as the difference between the head of a lion and that of a cheetah. I went through my various insect guides, and the best I could figure was that these were chewing, rather than sucking, lice. However, most of the chewing lice lived on birds, not mammals, such as the Linfords. Beyond this crude identification, I was stuck. But sometimes knowing where to get an answer is almost as good as knowing the answer—and tomorrow would provide the opportunity to find the person who'd know what vermin had excited the old man in the days before his death.

I spent a soothing hour pinning a few grasshoppers that Tommy and I had collected in the early fall. We'd driven down to the Zayante sandhills and spent a whole day in search of a particular band-winged grasshopper that was reportedly rare. If spending eight hours to net six insects constitutes being "rare," then we can confirm this status. But it was a great trip, leaving us sunburnt and exhausted. I'd stored the specimens in my freezer, and they thawed by the time Rigoletto was swearing vengeance against the Duke at the end of Act 2. The grasshoppers weren't impressive, with grey bodies and pale yellow hindwings, but spreading the left wings (never the right) of the small insects made for an enjoyable challenge.

The story of Rigoletto had me wondering about the Linfords—and the contrasts between appearance and character. Rigoletto's deformity was provided by nature, but his twisted personality came from his fellow man. In the end, the hunchback couldn't shield his daughter from the deadly corruption of the world. Nor could the Linfords, in the end, protect themselves with the marvels of modern chemistry—or from themselves. I headed up to bed after Gilda died in Rigoletto's arms.

CHAPTER SEVEN

Traffic on the Bay Bridge was moving slower than a chilled dollop of Baileys Irish Cream. Listening to the morning program on KDFC reminded me of last summer and how what seems to be a keen idea at the time doesn't always work out. Carol had spent an entire day with our seasonal help—a college kid whose work ethic grossly exceeded his common sense, to the extent that he had misread a job order and sprayed the front yards of an entire block in Parkside for aphids before a Greenpeacenik neighbor called the cops, who contacted Carol, who sorted out the mess. Under her subsequent, close supervision, he organized the chemicals in the warehouse into alphabetical order, which seemed like a fine plan. The pesticides were easier to find for purposes of inventorying the stock, but Larry and Dennis had situated the containers so that the most frequently used products were nearest to the loading dock. So the new arrangement made their daily loading much more strenuous and the organizational plan was abandoned.

I was also reminded of Nina's plan in the fall to spend a Saturday visiting the "ten best" stained glass windows in the city. She'd found a listing in the *Chronicle*, and decided it would be a good idea for us to saturate ourselves in chromatic beauty. It was great for the first two, alright for the next trio, increasingly tedious at the following four, and we gave up on the last one after circumnavigating the city and concluding that humans can take only so much kaleidoscopic artistry.

Likewise, the radio host figured that it would be great to organize a program around the theme of felines. He started off strong with some tracks from Andrew Lloyd Weber's *Cats* which had become a phenomenon in London last spring. The show was coming to Broadway later this year, but the host had managed to get his hands on a recording. I caught only the latter half or so, and I must say that "Mr. Mistofflelees" and "Macavity: The Mystery Cat" were quite entertaining. That said, things went downhill as the program dug into the litter box of classical music and played Scarlatti's *Cat Fugue* performed on the harpsichord (other than bagpipes, banjoes and accordions, no instrument is less musical). This was followed by *Duetto buffo di due gatti* which I'd once heard performed with two sopranos meowing the piece; it was no less annoying with a soprano and a tenor. It's cute for about thirty seconds and then it becomes clear why the composer used a pseudonym—after the guy heard the song performed, he understandably decided on anonymity.

I turned off the radio once I got into campus traffic around Berkeley. As a matted calico dashed across the street, I thought that cats were probably the most likely animals to enjoy classical music. Certainly the scruffy feline expending one of its nine lives sprinting across Oxford Street would have appreciated Andrew Lloyd Weber's arrangement of "Memory" sung by a scraggly old cat no longer touched by people. Moreover, feline intestines were never used for "catgut" strings, although barnyard animals might be justifiably appalled by violins and cellos.

Having failed to find any street parking between the downtown and the university, I pulled into a lot alongside University Hall—one of the uglier buildings on campus—and found a spot marked "Reserved: University Service Vehicles." I placed my "On Job" placard on the dashboard, a ploy that avoids a ticket about half the time when used in combination with the magnetic "Goat Hill Extermination" sign which I stuck to the door of my pickup.

I walked a couple blocks west of campus, found People's Pancakes which I assumed was a reference to politics not cannibalism, and enjoyed a short stack. They had no sausage or ham because in vegetarian breakfast joints pigs are evidently people, too. Then I headed onto campus, through the eucalyptus grove and towards the Essig Museum of Entomology to find my good pal, Scott Fortier. Along the way, I mentally tallied posters proclaiming the Berserkly students were variously anti-nuke, pro-choice, anti-PCB, pro-PLO, anti-apartheid and pro-whale. By my count, Palestinian whales planning to have abortions came out on top.

I'd called Scott before I headed across the Bay, but he greeted me like my arrival was a wondrous event. Curators of insect collections don't have many groupies, and my brother Tommy was the honorary president of Scott's fan club so I qualified for an enthusiastic welcome.

"Riley! How good to see you." Scott put down the latest volume of *Systematic Entomology*. I glanced at the title of the article he'd been reading and wondered how much arcane knowledge was stored under that blond Brillo pad of unruly hair. Like an insect pulling itself out of a cast skin one appendage at a time, Scott unfolded his gangly body from behind a gray, steel desk covered in a half-dozen teetering stacks of scientific journals and esoteric identification guides. As he came around to greet me, he knocked one of the piles with his elbow which caused the top volumes to slide onto the adjacent stack triggering a cascade onto the floor. He shrugged and gave me a handshake much firmer than one would expect from a human scarecrow.

"Always happy to visit," I said.

"And I'm delighted to have you, although even more so when you bring Tommy."

"He's looking forward to your 'Roly-poly Roundup' in a couple of weeks." As Scott became exuberant, I worried about further avalanches.

"We'll take folks up into the hills," he declared, swinging his arm in what was presumably the right direction. "They'll start with finding isopods and then hunt for any arthropod with more than six legs to show folks that entomologists are open-minded. There should be plenty of soil mites, millipedes, centipedes and whatnot to find even on a cold, rainy day." He gave a crooked-toothed grin and sighed like a kid looking forward to a birthday party—which is probably why Tommy, a middle-aged man with the brain of an eight-year-old, connected so deeply with the scientist.

"Now then," he said, taking a few rangy strides next door to a preparation room for the museum, "you said on the phone that you had some lice in need of names." I caught up to him, as he was settling himself in front of a high-end Olympus stereo microscope.

"They came from a fellow who thought he was infested with insects, and all I can say is that whatever's in this sample doesn't look like any lice I've seen." Scott dumped the baggie onto a sheet of white paper and used a camel's hair brush to lift the specimens onto a petri dish which he slipped under the microscope. He hummed to himself with evident pleasure.

"Well, these are most assuredly lice," he said, "but not likely a species that would afflict a human host. Look here." Scott leaned over so I could see through the eyepieces. "Human lice are in the suborder Anoplura. And as you noted in our conversation, they have little heads. What's more, they also have one big claw at the end of each leg to latch onto hair. The fellas you're looking at under the scope have big ol' heads and two tarsal claws." The triangular heads and body hair of the lice were reminiscent of a tackle on my high school football team, a thickset Swedish fellow with a blocky noggin, who might've made a passable louse if reduced in size by about a million times.

"And so?"

"So these are in the suborder Mallophaga. They're chewing lice, rather than sucking lice."

"And they wouldn't be chewing on people?"

"Well, not so fast. Most of the species in this group feed on birds, but there are a few notorious pests of dogs and cattle and such." He reached for a paperbound *Key to the Mallophaga*. "I'm pretty sure I recognize these beasties from my medical and veterinary entomology course, but that was more than a decade ago." He began flipping through the identification guide.

"I'm getting the sense I ought to settle myself into one of these comfy chairs," I joked, pulling up a wobbly plastic seat perched atop of a metal pole that was presumably adjustable at one time.

"Why don't you pour us some coffee," Scott said, gesturing toward a coffeemaker atop an insect cabinet. "I'll take two sugars and a large dose of creamer." I filled a couple of Styrofoam cups, took a sip from mine, and decided to follow Scott's lead in attempting to mask the burnt bitterness with granulated sugar and white powder.

"Here you go," I said, setting his coffee next to the microscope. But Scott was in a trancelike state, mumbling about maxillary palps, concealed antennae, and abdominal spiracles.

"Alright," he declared after a few moments, taking a sip of coffee and wincing at the flavor or the heat or both, "these are definitely in the family Menoponidae."

"Which means?"

"Not a whole lot. Most of the species in this family feed on birds, but a few feed on mammals. So, we need to figure out the genus," he said, rubbing his hands together with nerdish glee.

"Do you have the right taxonomic key?"

"In principle, yes. In practice, no. I'm not an expert on louse anatomy, and the diagnostic structures get pretty technical. So it's time to switch to the tried-and-true tactic of taxonomists."

"Picture books?" I asked, based on how often a good diagram had led me to an identification. A smile spread across Scott's horsey face.

"Spoken like an experienced collector. But I'm going to do one better," he said. Striding like a man on a mission, he disappeared around a stack of wooden cabinets and returned in a couple of minutes with a box of microscope slides. "There's nothing better than comparing an unknown critter to a set of identified specimens." He settled into his chair and systematically slipped prepared slides of lice under the microscope. I tried to drink the coffee. His task was more enjoyable.

"Kind of an entomological lineup, eh?" I observed. Scott nodded and hummed. Actually, this approach to identifying a suspect is pretty much a joke. Any detective worth his salt can provide a witness with the necessary cues to pick out the right guy without violating official protocol. If you can read body language and hear subtext well enough to pick up a one-night stand at closing time, you can figure out who the perp is in a lineup.

"Check this out," Scott said, leaning away from the microscope to give me a view. On the stage was a slide with a louse and next to it was one of Linford's specimens. The match was perfect. "As I suspected, you're looking at the common chicken body louse. They chew on feathers or technically they feed on blood by gnawing through the quills and skin."

"So, the lice in the baggie didn't come from a human?"

"Well, they might've been provided to you by a human who was working at a poultry operation. These lice are abundant in a mangy chicken flock. But they aren't infesting your client unless he lives on Sesame Street and wears a Big Bird costume with real feathers." I doubted that any of the Linfords had ever been to a poultry operation, but I suspected that Lane might have been less than forthcoming in our conversation.

"What would've happened if he'd sent specimens to the Cal Academy—or to the Essig?"

"Standard protocol. We'd return the samples and direct him to contact the County Extension folks who probably would've just told him that these were lice. The Academy would just toss the stuff into the trash. My former student manages the collection. You met him a couple of times. Really nice guy. On his own time, he helps out with field trips that the Essig organizes for the public. But his lab doesn't have the time or responsibility to identify insects that people find in their homes and gardens."

"Or their chicken coops?"

"Right. But for you—and Tommy—we make an exception." Scott gave me an aw-shucks smile and viselike handshake, reminded me to bring my brother next time, gave me some photocopies of articles he thought would interest me, and sent me on my way so he could get back to reading about a new genus of midge from Bhutan.

When I got back to my illegal parking spot, I was delighted that my sign had worked or the students employed by the university's parking office hadn't found my truck. Or more likely, one of them found the truck, saw the signs, thought about writing a ticket to punish a capitalist (whose taxes subsidized the university), but realized he'd met his quota so slipped into the eucalyptus grove to smoke a joint.

On the way back to the City I tried to piece together a story of how the Linfords ended up with chicken lice. I didn't come up with anything, although thinking about lice made my hands and wrists start itching again. Maybe it was an allergic reaction to the music program being played on the radio. I get that we're supposed to appreciate other cultures. I love most ethnic food (although I can't fathom the allure of the kimchi Mrs. Park brings to church potlucks that Nina and my mother expect me to attend), and I can even sit through the occasional Eastern European folk dance performance at St. Teresa's. However, there is no way that a classical station should expect listeners to tolerate an hour of sitar. I'm sure that Ravi Shankar plays a mean sitar, just like Mrs. Park can rot cabbage and ferment radishes with the best of them, but the result isn't palatable in either case.

At the office, I called Lane Linford to set up a visit for tomorrow morning. He asked about the subject of our meeting, and I told him that a sample collected by his grandfather had yielded a most interesting specimen—and some associated questions. I wanted to build anxiety in his mind. Uncertainty and inner turmoil are potent allies during an interrogation. Lane became wary and said he had a morning commitment of indeterminate length. I told him I'd swing by in the late morning and wait for his return to the house. There was a long pause on his end before he mumbled that I might be there awhile. I told him I was good at waiting. He hung up.

Carol had noticed my itching—not much gets past her—and found a tube of hydrocortisone cream in the first aid kit. I appreciated her caretaking if not her music which featured a bunch of guys expressing their plaintive and insistent desire for Elvira. I took Carol's advice and called my mother to see if Tommy had a rash on the assumption that we'd contacted poison ivy over the weekend. No dice; the kid was fine. The reddish bumps extended to the palms of my hands, as if I'd grabbed whatever was causing the reaction. I couldn't think of any suspicious plants we'd encountered, although I'd handled Tommy's trophy millipede—he'd been too excited and jittery to get it into the killing jar—and these creatures can release some nasty chemicals. But then, so can exterminators.

CHAPTER EIGHT

I caught 3rd to Market and then made my way into Chinatown. Dr. Chen's office was just a few blocks down Stockton from the Hang Ah Tea Room, which claimed to be the oldest Chinese restaurant in San Francisco. Who am I to argue? I'd taken Nina there for lunch a couple of times after her sessions with the good doctor, so I knew it was affordable—as confirmed by the customers being mostly shopkeepers and cops.

I grabbed a table and waited for a woman who looked like a Chinese psychologist, which turns out to be a challenge in Chinatown. After a couple of false leads resolved with minimal embarrassment and confusion, a very pretty, very intense woman wearing a sharply tailored gray suit, black silk blouse, and necklace of jade beads came in and glanced around, evidently seeking a lunch mate. I stood up and introduced myself as Dr. Carroll.

"Dr. Carroll, my secretary led me to believe you were a woman. My apologies for looking surprised," she said with enchanting grace and a firm but feminine handshake.

"And you were also probably expecting a fellow practitioner who wanted to talk shop," I said. Her face went from warmth to ice.

"I was, and if you've deceived me I shall be leaving." She stiffened and half-turned to the door.

"Please hear me out, Dr. Chen. I'm Nina Cabrera's boyfriend." The term invariably strikes me as odd given that I'm more than three decades from boyhood. She paused, turned back toward me and raised an eyebrow. "And what I need from you could be a matter of life and death," I continued.

"Is this about Nina?" Deep lines of concern furrowed her perfect skin. She looked to be well into her thirties but her complexion was that of a teenager.

"No, no. Nina is fine. In fact, she's better than ever, thanks to her time with you." She gave a slight nod.

"I suppose that your attempt at flattery is preferable to deceit, mister . . . ?"

"Riley. Just 'Riley.' My father was Mister Riley. And I would sincerely appreciate your staying. I would've made an appointment, but I'm afraid that time is not on my side in this matter."

"I suppose that I have to eat lunch sometime, Mr. Riley," she said without a hint of warming up to my charms. "What's more, Nina speaks very highly of you. Apparently, some unseen virtues offset your propensity for lying." Evidently my dashing good looks weren't among them. I gestured to the table and we sat down as a petite waitress in a pleasingly too-tight floral print dress brought us water and menus.

There weren't a ton of options at Hang Ah like at some Chinese restaurants, but a man can eat only so many things at one sitting, so having a hundred items untried doesn't add to the pleasure of a meal. Besides, I had a dinner date with Nina tonight, so I needed to keep lunch on the light side. Dr. Chen ordered a pot of green tea, glanced at the menu and set it aside.

"What is this life-and-death matter that justifies your having brought me here under false pretenses?" she asked. For a professional who spent hundreds of billable hours listening to people make up shit about their childhoods, spouses, and dreams, you'd think that my little deception wouldn't have been such a big deal.

I gave her a quick synopsis of the Linford case—the flea collars, chemical treatments, what Lane had said about their fixation on being infested, and his diagnosis along with Papadopoulos's speculations. I skipped over the chicken lice, figuring that detail might best be kept under wraps until I had an inkling of its relevance.

"That's all quite interesting," she said as the waitress came to take our order. The place was too small to wheel dim sum carts around, so they fixed everything to order in the kitchen. She had the bok choy in garlic sauce and the Chinese broccoli in oyster sauce. I went with the barbeque pork bun and pot stickers. I figured that she was probably vegetarian—the oyster sauce notwithstanding—and I also figured on my being famished by dinnertime.

Dr. Chen poured herself a cup of tea and continued, "But Mr. Riley, I don't quite see that there's a dire situation at the moment."

"Well," I said pouring myself a cup of tea to stall for time, "I don't suppose that anyone is about to die, but my business and employees have been dragged into the case through the insecticides used by the deceased, and that connection could be lethal for our reputation."

She nodded. "I understand the importance of honor. And being a businesswoman, I know the importance of one's professional credibility—at least in fields where practitioners have extensive training and certified expertise."

I was relieved—and offended. But I needed information more than pride at the moment. "Okay, we're on the same page, then." She gave the most subtle eye roll imaginable. I continued, "So, what do you make of the grandson's diagnosis?"

"Well, he's unusually well informed about such a disorder." I substituted 'suspiciously' for 'unusually' in my mind. "But I suspect he's on the right track."

"So, being crazy is contagious? Could one of his grandparents have caught it from the other?"

"Let's begin with what you mean by 'being crazy.'" Dr. Chen then schooled me on the proper lingo for mental illness—craziness not being among the accepted terms, and I assumed that nuts, bonkers and loony were likewise out.

While waiting for our food, I was tutored on the subtle differences among delusions, illusions, and hallucinations. I also learned how they were triggered and absorbed the details of some famous cases, including—if I have the particulars right—a wave of near-panic that swept Seattle in 1954 with thousands of people reporting their windshields were being pitted by sand fleas (always blame an insect), cosmic rays or supernatural beings. But what can you expect from a city that thinks that a flying saucer mounted on a tower is comparable to the Golden Gate Bridge?

The psychology lecture was concluded by the arrival of our lunch. The darling waitress refilled the tea pot and wriggled off to another table.

"Okay, I get the big picture," I said, dipping a pot sticker into a delicious sesame-scallion sauce. "But what about my customers who suffered from delusions? It would be a delusion, right? They had a false belief based on a misinterpretation their itchiness."

"At least you're an attentive student, Mr. Riley. Yes, they exhibited a classic case of delusory parasitosis combined with folie à deux."

"Slow down. I assume that delusory parasitosis is the mistaken belief that you're infested with fleas, or lice or some other vermin. I've seen mild versions of this, usually among women. They feel some tingling sensation and attribute it to tiny insects. The trade journals refer to an outbreak of delusions as 'mass hysteria.'" I thought back to having treated a swank office with a smelly placebo to break the cycle of itching among the staff. My guess is that a professional psychologist wouldn't approve of my amateur tactics. But they worked—and I didn't charge $50 an hour to murmur "uh, huh" while the secretaries scratched.

"That's right, although 'hysteria' is an anachronistic term that denigrates women and you and your colleagues should avoid using it. And, by all means, you should direct individuals in these cases to a professional."

"Of course," I lied. Nutty people don't generally want to pay big bucks to have a shrink tell them they're nuts. "But what about this other condition?"

"Folie à deux."

"Meaning an irrational passion for French companionship?"

"Meaning 'madness of two' or what the grandson called a shared psychosis. It's a relatively rare disorder in which one person transmits a delusion to the other through fervent repetition. And then the pair mutually reinforces the mistaken belief. The syndrome was identified by a pair of French psychiatrists in the 19th century. Hence, it's also called Lasègue-Falret Syndrome."

Her French sounded fluent to me, but I'd mispronounced 'lingerie' for years, as I learned when shopping for Nina at Victoria's Secret—one of San Francisco's gifts to the world. A temptress salesgirl corrected me. I can't remember exactly how she said it, although I recall spending nearly twenty bucks on a black satin camisole. Dr. Chen brought me back from my lecherous reverie.

"Let me ask you a few questions to test my interpretation of their condition."

"Sure," I said, washing down a bite of barbequed pork with the green tea, which made for an interesting combination of tangy and bitter flavors.

"Was there an infestation in the house before the delusions began?" she asked, gracefully lifting a bite of broccoli and oyster sauce with her chopsticks.

"The family dog had fleas awhile back, but we treated him and the carpets."

"I don't doubt the efficacy of your work, Mr. Riley. I assume that you're competent in the spraying of chemicals. I asked because in many cases an actual infestation sets the stage for delusory parasitosis. Now then, did the couple collect samples from their bodies in an effort to prove the presence of insects?"

"Two for two, doc. The man had quite an inventory of ziplock baggies filled with hair and skin scrapings."

"Psychologists used to refer to this symptom as the 'matchbox sign' but maybe we should update this to the 'baggie sign.' Next question. Did they see jumping black bugs?" she asked while polishing off the broccoli and moving on to the bok choy. The garlic smelled fabulous and I wondered if I should've ordered another dish.

"Their grandson said they referred to little black bugs, but nothing about jumping. The couple was convinced the insects were burrowing under their skin," I said, shoving the last corner of the pork bun into my mouth.

"Good enough. And finally, I gather that their belief was rather unshakable—that negative diagnoses and failure of others to see the insects did little to dissuade them."

"According to the grandson, they didn't believe their own physician, and they weren't fazed when others couldn't affirm their condition. They just used more and stronger treatments until . . ."

"Until they accidently poisoned themselves in an effort to relieve their suffering," she said. "There's no reason to infer anything sexual, as your police detective proposed, nor would I suspect murder or suicide. It sounds to me like a tragic ending to a case of severe mental illness. But I can't make a formal diagnosis based on secondhand information."

"Of course not," I said. "It would be like my listening to a person complain about itchy, red bumps on their ankles and identifying a flea infestation—which would be a good guess, but nothing to stake my reputation on."

"Perhaps something of that sort," she said, with the dismissive tone that professors, lawyers, and doctors reserve for students, cops, and nurses—or exterminators.

"What I don't get is how they seemed so normal before all of this. Even during their meltdown they managed a major business and had a social life, at least for a while."

"People are surprisingly skilled at hiding mental illness. They compensate for their condition in various ways. We celebrate uniqueness, but only as long as it doesn't make us uncomfortable. There is such shame in our society for being abnormal in any way." She slowly shook her head. "If I've learned one thing as a therapist, it's that you can't infer what's going on inside a person's mind from what you see on the outside." I chuckled as the waitress came to clear our dishes and leave the check.

"You find that observation amusing, Mr. Riley?"

"Not at all. I'm laughing in agreement. Actually, I'm thinking back to last night when I was listening to *Rigoletto*."

"You enjoy opera?" she said, unable to disguise her surprise.

"I do indeed. Remember, Dr. Chen, you said that one ought not to judge a book by its cover. Even an exterminator can enjoy some of the finer things."

"Touché, Mr. Riley. Now, you were saying?" I sipped my tea and savored her near apology, which I knew was petty. But sometimes petty feels good.

"Rigoletto is a hunchbacked jester who acts with clownish frivolity. But inside, he's tormented and wants nothing more than to protect his beautiful daughter."

"Intriguing. But my tastes don't extend to opera. Is there some music from this one that I might recognize?"

"You'd know the aria sung by the Duke, 'La donna è mobile,'" which a lingerie salesgirl would presumably pronounce correctly. I hummed the music while paying for lunch and leaving a generous tip for good service and a tight dress.

"Ah, that reminds me of the cancan song. The one that goes, ta-ra-ra boom-de-aye," she said.

"So your tastes reach to dancehall music." Dr. Chen acknowledged my insolence with a half-smile and dabbed the corners of her mouth with a napkin, a gesture which somehow reasserted her status. We rose, shook hands, and parted with a strange sort of mutual respect. She was smart and successful. Me, less so but holding my own.

I spent the afternoon working on a problem no shrink could've diagnosed. A taxi company in Mission Bay had found the seats and wiring in their cabs were being gnawed. A smattering of mouse turds identified the culprits, but finding the little beggars was more of a challenge. Turned out that the furry freeloaders were hauling upholstery stuffing from the cars to build comfy nests behind the stove and refrigerator in the break room next to the garage. The appliances provided a warm, dry home along with a daily allotment of crumbs from the cabbies. A few strategically located traps were sure to solve that problem.

And then down to a row of warehouses at Pier 80, to meet with Larry and Dennis so we could check on a major rat control project. They'd spent the day swapping out the nutritious and delicious bait we'd used to convince the suspicious rodents of our pure intentions, for a lethal chow laced with zinc phosphide and warfarin.

Successful exterminators and investigators know a great deal about bait and switch.

CHAPTER NINE

After a few hours of crawling around garages and warehouses, a shower and change of clothes was in order before dinner. A blast of scalding water on a cold day can be transformative. In light of my picking up Nina for dinner at her folks' restaurant and my hoping the evening might have an intimate ending, I opted for a dapper look.

Last fall, I'd bought a Donegal Tweed jacket in charcoal gray with understated flecks of color. It was my way of celebrating a lucrative pigeon control contract for Pier 39, the tourist mecca of Fisherman's Wharf where the merchants have plenty of money and the customers have no tolerance for bird shit. Harris Tweed is perennially popular, but County Donegal is just across the bay from County Sligo, the homeland of my parents—along with William Butler Yeats, as I was often reminded.

With a heather shirt and black slacks, a close shave and a splash of cologne, I was positively dashing—in my own estimation. However, the Riley spell was arguably broken by picking up Nina in my sea green, two-tone (three if you include the rust spots) 1970 Ford F-100. She runs like a top. And like Dr. Chen said, you can't know what's happening under the hood by just looking at the body.

I don't know what Nina was thinking about the evening when she came out of her apartment, but I hoped it matched her exterior. Her hair was silky black with a few strands of gray appropriate for a mature woman, and her lips had touch of gloss, enough to pass along a hint of fruit when we kissed.

She was wearing the outfit my mother had given her for Christmas. Nina looked sumptuous in an Aran jumper (my mother never having accepted the Americanism of 'sweater' as she thought it sounded like gym clothes) hand-knit in black wool with a cable pattern. It was pleasingly snug in all the right places and invitingly roomy in the others. I wondered if my gift of the satin camisole was hiding underneath. She had on a wool skirt in the Sligo tartan—a cobalt background with faint maroon and mustard striping— that stretched across her posterior to create the perfect balance of taste and temptation. No wonder County Sligo's motto is "land of heart's desire."

What didn't please me was the location of her apartment at the edge of the Tenderloin. But looking after mentally handicapped adults at St. Teresa's wasn't financially lucrative. The rent in her neighborhood was affordable, as evidenced by the recent swarm of Asian immigrants who crammed entire families into studio apartments. However, they worked damned hard and the Vietnamese made great coffee and croissants, so there was much to admire. But the long lines of homeless men at Saint Anthony's Dining Hall felt strange as young millionaires worked a half mile away in the Financial District.

We parked in a "Reserved" spot at Cabrera's—the best Spanish restaurant in San Francisco, a couple blocks from Telegraph Hill and the gleaming monolith of Coit Tower. The dignified hostess at the front podium abandoned all decorum and rushed to embrace Nina. I got a polite smile and an approving nod. As we made our way to the kitchen past the tables, I noticed the white linens had been replaced with burgundy tablecloths which gave the place warm ambiance on a damp night.

Nina's father welcomed me with a rock-hard handshake, and her mother gave me a long hug and an approving peck on the cheek. He'd put on a few pounds over the last year, but they only added to his aura of Old World pride. Her mother was as beautiful as ever, with long, braided hair and onyx eyes avowing her Indian heritage. Among the Cabreras there were kisses all around.

"Tonight," her father declared, "I have had my chef prepare pulpo á feira, a special dish in honor of familial roots. Or at least our Spanish and Irish ancestries." Nina's mother nodded and smiled at his recognition that her Native American heritage was acknowledged as missing. "It's been very popular among our customers, but I've reserved portions for my lovely daughter and her handsome *novio*."

He went on to explain with great enthusiasm that northwest Spain contains the region of Galicia, where people speak a Celtic dialect and play the bagpipes in a lush landscape reminiscent of Ireland. And yes, the Irish as well as the Scots have bagpipes. My countrymen's instrument includes the intelligent feature of a bellows under the arm to inflate the bag so we needn't destroy brain cells by huffing and puffing like our hard-drinking, good-hearted cousins.

Being on the coast, Galicia is famous for its seafood. The chef had slowly boiled an adult octopus—not one of those little things served as appetizers—until tender, then snipped the purple tentacles into medallions, which were garnished with olive oil and smoked paprika. Slices of the tentacles were prepared with boiled potatoes and a decadent sauce. The meal was complemented with a salad of orange and fennel, a loaf of crusty bread and a bottle of Albariño from Rías Baixas in Galicia for me and mineral water for Nina.

The food was nearly as pleasing as my dinner companion. She was keenly interested in what had led me to contact Dr. Chen, so I told her the story of the Linfords and what their strange demise might mean for the future of Goat Hill Extermination. I could tell she was worried, but I assured her everything was beginning to make sense, while omitting that I was perplexed by Lane Linford, the chicken mites, and delusory parasitosis which amounted to most everything.

"So, what about the start of your week?" I asked, mopping up some of the olive oil with a hunk of bread.

"It seems that nobody's Monday went well," she said while crunching a piece of fennel. "Petey, the street kid who had been coming by the daycare, hasn't shown up for a week." Nina had described him as being oddly silent around adults and way too naïve to make it for long on his own.

"Is Tommy worried?" My brother was terribly empathetic to other, vulnerable people.

"Both Tommy and Karsa were asking about Petey. They treated him like a big brother."

"The kid was something like nineteen, right? That would've made the two guys more like father figures," I said, sipping from my third glass of the Albariño and reminding myself that falling asleep on Nina's couch would be bad form.

"Their chronological ages are mixed up with their developmental ages. But the trio has fun whenever Petey shows up. They carry on with three-man touch football, trying to get Father Griesmaier to play quarterback."

"There's no sense contacting the police. The kid's out there somewhere, but the cops won't look for him if he's not wanted." I immediately regretted putting it that way.

"He is wanted, at least by Tommy, Karsa, me and the others at the daycare."

"Sorry, that's not what I meant. I presume there are no wants or warrants in the legal system. But it could be worth calling Social Services. You said that Petey had a heart-shaped birthmark on his cheek. They might recognize him and let you know if he's tapping into their programs."

"I know you didn't mean he was disposable," she said reaching across the table to give my hand a gentle squeeze. "It's just that people push aside anyone who's different. I get angry with the looks and comments Tommy gets about how he walks and talks."

The chef came by the table and rescued our conversation. He asked about our meal and Nina raved, deservedly. I teased him that while the food was exquisitely refined, I'd been craving blackened octopus. From a previous visit, I knew the chef was aggravated by the fad of Cajun cooking, but it was fun to inflame his Latin ire. My comment triggered an animated exposition on the culinary shortcomings of scorching seafood. He concluded by raising his face to heaven and pleading with the Almighty to explain to His lowly servant if burning food to a crisp made sinners happy by preparing them to enter the fires of hell. Then he shook a scolding finger at me and lifted Nina's hand from the tabletop, bent deeply and delivered an adoring kiss. She was beloved by the entire restaurant staff from hostess, to chef, to owners. For two glorious hours, everything seemed right with the world.

The rain picked up on the way to Nina's. Being a gallant sort of fellow, I dropped her off in front of the building and drove around the back to an alley that functioned as a parking lot, as long as you pulled in far enough for the garbage trucks to pass. She'd suggested coming up for a cup of mint tea which was our favorite nightcap and meant an invitation to stay until morning. We kept separate places because she liked her space and I needed mine. The appearance of propriety also pleased her father and my mother. Mrs. Cabrera seemed utterly at ease with sensuality and didn't need the illusion of her daughter being chaste.

As I came around the corner of the building, I saw Nina had been stopped at the ground floor. I'd noticed the guy before and he emanated a creepiness that Nina discounted by saying, "Tim struggles with boundaries." His close-cropped hair was flattened against his high forehead, and he looked haggard with a day's growth of beard and bloodshot eyes. The fatigue jacket was consistent with his claim of being a Vietnam vet, as if that excused his leering. Larry had been through horrible shit in Nam and didn't come back with a need to accost women. Nina's work primed her to interpret abnormality in charitable terms. My time in the city had taught me that there are a million ways of being messed up, but what matters is how a person plays the cards they're dealt. And Tim was playing his hand way too close to Nina.

With the patter of the rain, he didn't hear me coming from behind as he cornered Nina at the foot of the staircase. He was muttering something about having, "some 'ludes and Wild Turkey we could share." Nina and I had both been cops back in the day, although she'd been promoted into the big time and I'd been kicked off the force. I knew she could handle herself, but that wasn't the issue. This creep triggered my protective instincts. If that's sexist, then too bad.

I grabbed him by the collar with one hand and latched onto his wrist with the other, yanking his arm behind his back and upward to inflict a memorable lesson in avoidance. He yelped and struggled until I pulled his hand up to his shoulder blade and the pain froze him.

Nina stepped back and said, "Don't hurt him, Riley. He wasn't going to do anything."

"I won't dislocate his shoulder, this time," I said lifting his hand another inch which brought him up to his toes with an audible wince. "If you'll go up to the apartment Nina, then Tim and I will have a brief chat." She looked both upset and relieved.

"The lady said not to hurt me," Tim hissed through clenched teeth. I waited until Nina was out of earshot.

"I'm going to put this as simply as possible, sleaze ball. If I see you within twenty feet of her again, I will send you to the hospital for a very long time. Do you understand me?"

"Yeah," he grunted and I gave him a shove that sent him sprawling and cursing.

Unsure that the warning would be sufficient, I went up to Nina's apartment. The furniture was Mission style, the walls were painted an adobe brown and decorated with photos of redwood groves and paintings of seascapes; her houseplants were flourishing ferns and sinuous philodendrons. She'd lit a set of candles in an arch of driftwood and put on a recording of *La bohème*, which she loved for the heartrending romance of the story. The kettle was whistling as I came in, so I settled myself onto the sofa and enjoyed the music. Nina brought our tea from the kitchen, turned down the volume, and curled her legs under her in the way that women have to suggest flirtatious comfort.

"Now then, Riley. I appreciate your desire to protect me, but I don't want you assaulting my neighbors. Tim isn't dangerous, he just doesn't recognize social norms."

"I think he and I have an understanding of what's an acceptable distance from you. I know you feel sorry for the guy, but we both know how his sort needs to have lines drawn to keep things from becoming dangerous."

"Alright," she sighed, "let's not allow him to mess up a wonderful evening." Our conversation drifted into more pleasant topics until Nina stretched, took me by the hand and led us down the hall. She opened the bedroom window so we could hear the rain and feel a breeze. The cool air intensified the contrasting warmth of her body.

Nina liked combining sex and nature—the soft dampness of a forest floor or the sandy heat of a beach dune. This wasn't about exhibitionism, which would've struck me as deviant. She always sought private settings

65

for these encounters. Nature connected her to the land, our bodies and her Indian roots. She explained that when her people had lived in houses shared by extended families, the woods provided the only privacy to enjoy uninhibited sex.

Although we were indoors this evening, I enjoyed the drumming of the rain as a background to our love making. After slowly readying one another, we moved to a favored position embodying our passion as loving and tender creatures to be sure but, in the end, animals. The Church wouldn't have approved—unmarried, un-missionary, and unnatural. Unnatural, if sex is solely for procreation. But the whisper of the wind outside the window was natural, as were her gasps and final sigh.

CHAPTER TEN

I woke up buried under a downy comforter and pressed against a fleshy comforter. I considered a reprise of the evening's intimacy, but decided that a languorous back rub might be appreciated. Nina purred as I worked her lower back, and she hunched her shoulders in pleasure as I dug gently into the base of her neck.

Her skin glowed with a tawny radiance in the diffuse morning light. This sense of health contrasted with the inflammation of the Linfords skin—and with the similar blotches that returned to my forearms with the steamy heat of the shower. I'd been so focused on attributing the irritation to my weekend outing with Tommy that I'd not noticed how much it resembled the condition of the old couple. I added this connection to the questions I had for Lane.

I pulled together a breakfast of scrambled eggs, wheat toast, and strong coffee while Nina showered. As the toaster did its thing, I poured a cup of coffee and delivered the mug to the bathroom when I heard the shower door open. Timing is everything.

When Nina headed to St. Teresa's, I cleaned up the dishes and then called Carol for the day's schedule. She told me Dennis had solved a mysterious case at Wilson Prep, one of the city's exclusive private schools. Students had been coming home with inflamed skin across their shoulders and necks with complaints of pinprick sensations but no observable cause. Dennis had discovered that all of the afflicted students sat in the back corner of an upstairs classroom for a European History class, which turned out to be the vital clue. Carol suggested Dennis might appreciate my presence when he met with school officials first thing this morning.

When I got to the unpretentious, Spanish colonial building filled with pretentious adolescents, I was directed to the office of the headmaster. I knocked softly and was commanded to enter by a nattily dressed man in his sixties, who was clearly not enjoying a lecture by a black man in coveralls. Dennis was explaining that last week he'd found a small colony of Mexican free-tailed bats in the attic above the afflicted classroom. He'd hung some sticky traps from the ceiling and was now eagerly showing the headmaster his catch. I leaned over for a look as Dennis pointed out the incredibly tiny red creatures that speckled the surface of the trap.

"You see," he said, "what we got here's not your standard bat bugs, which be like bed bugs. And they's surely not bat ticks 'cause they's a quarter inch long and the students would've known if they'd been raining down. These be something rare that it took me awhile to figure. I went through some books that Riley keeps back at the shop and no question—you got bat mites. They don't normally bother people, but I guess the conditions in your school be just right." Dennis glanced up at me and I nodded my approval.

I'd never seen bat mites, but the miniscule vermin adhered to the trap were most certainly mites, there were bats in the attic above the problematic classroom, and the students had some skin disorder in addition to their acne. I was impressed and stepped back as Dennis explained the process of bat removal. All the headmaster wanted was my assurance of discretion. We were not to park a vehicle with our company logo on school grounds, we were not to whisper a hint of there being bats, and we were to do all of our work after the school day. For his part, he'd move the afflicted class to another room and he'd pay a premium for our efficacy and secrecy.

Dennis headed off to get a case of boric acid for cockroaches in a housing project and I headed off to get some answers from a rich kid at a mansion.

I had to wait a half hour in front of the Linfords' house, getting nasty looks from a woman walking her Pomeranian and a jogger who nearly fell off the curb while turning his head to memorize my license plate number. KDFC was playing Beethoven's 3rd Symphony, the *Eroica*. However, "heroic" wasn't a fitting description of myself on this grey morning that couldn't quite bring itself to drizzle. That said, the second movement was ending with the famous and ponderous funeral march just as the rumble of a black, Ferrari 308 broke into the music. The iron gates to the estate opened automatically and Lane pulled slowly into the driveway.

After a polite but curt greeting, he directed me inside to a room adjoining the entry hall. It was like going into a museum with a collection of antique apparatuses featuring elegant glass bulbs and sinuous tubing held in place by polished brass fittings. I presumed these were once used to make herbal extracts. In the middle of the room was an oriental rug with an exotically carved coffee table supported by legs looking like trees wrapped in vines. A sideboard and three leather upholstered chairs completed the furnishings. Lane perched himself on the edge of one chair and I settled into another, feeling like I'd landed in a 19th century men's club. I sat silently, letting the tension rise.

"What did you need to ask of me?" he began. "I have an appointment at noon, so we don't have much time. And I don't think I can add anything to what I've already told you."

"Since we last chatted, a few matters have arisen. And these lead me to believe that perhaps you were too shaken during our first visit to give a full account of your grandparents' affliction." I provided him with an excuse for having omitted information as a way of making my questioning less accusatory. Beginning with a confrontational approach tends to back a suspect into a corner. It's best to let them dig their own hole and then apply pressure.

"Meaning what?"

"Meaning your grandfather had samples of hair and skin scrapings that included lice. But perhaps you didn't know he'd found a cause for their symptoms."

"He never said anything about this to me."

"Really? I might've thought that his excitement with having finally established what was plaguing him and your grandmother would have prompted him to share the information with a grandson who'd been so helpful in concocting treatments."

"I said he didn't, Mr. Riley. Now is there anything more?" He shifted, as if readying himself to get up.

"What's most curious to me is that the lice were not a species that infests humans." Lane froze in place, his body language speaking volumes. "They were chicken lice that couldn't have come from your grandparents. I don't suppose you know how they might've acquired these insects, given that they hadn't left the house in weeks."

"I can't imagine," he said, cracking his knuckles and looking steadfastly at the carpet.

"What's more, I spoke with a psychologist, which seemed to be a sensible approach to understanding your grandparents' condition. But you never sought professional counsel. Or maybe you forgot to tell me about this in our last conversation."

"I learned all I needed to know from reading scientific journals and technical books. There was nothing to gain from speaking to a shrink."

"Nothing to gain other than affirmation of an amateur diagnosis of a serious condition. Nothing other than insights as to possible courses of treatment. Seems to me that a loving grandson might've wanted professional guidance on how to relieve the suffering of such an unusual mental condition." Lane said nothing in reply but rolled his head from side to side to elicit an audible crack. His leg began a subtle jackhammering.

"And then there's this," I said, showing him the inside of my forearms. The rash was fading but still visible. "A few hours after I was in your house, I developed a skin condition rather similar to what I saw on your grandparents. Now then, I don't have chicken lice but I have to wonder if you also have a rash."

"I do not, Mr. Riley. And what's more, I do not know what you're implying with these questions," he said, swallowing a few times and starting to rise from the chair.

"Sit down." He paused. "I said, *sit down*," and he complied. I didn't directly threaten physical violence but the right tone with a skinny kid, even in his own mansion, makes clear that force will be used if needed. "You know what I'm after, Lane. I want the whole story." He put his head in his hands and began rocking.

"I can't . . ." he mumbled. I ignored him and continued.

"When we parted company on Monday, we had a mutual interest in keeping your grandparents' condition from being made public. I now understand that your interests included providing me with just enough information to insulate you from the cops. So either you come clean or I pay a visit to Lieutenant Papadopolous, tell him what I've learned, and let him sort out what led to your grandparents' deaths. And believe me, he has some theories that will scandalize San Francisco's elites."

"What's to keep you from going to the police with what I tell you?" he sputtered, on the verge of tears.

"Maybe nothing. Or maybe our overlapping interest in keeping this out of the papers. You have nothing to lose, given that I'm your only potential ally in this mess."

Lane gave a deep sob. "My grandparents' delusions started after the flea infestation. They reinforced one another's belief that something was crawling in their skin. I read about their condition and realized they were on a downward spiral."

"Okay, but why not get them the help they needed?"

"They had been stubbornly old-school about the family business, refusing to modernize, to develop a marketing plan, or to explore new avenues. We were losing ground to competitors, and I figured that if their mental illness was bad enough, I could have them declared legally incompetent and save the company." He paused. I waited. "So I fostered their delusion."

"By planting lice on them?

"Not on them, but in my grandfather's clippings and scrapings.

"How'd you get the insects?

"I obtained a vial of lice from someone a friend told me about."

"A friend? How did this 'friend' know where to get lice?" Lane bent his fingers inward one at a time to crack each knuckle as he answered.

"The guy was into some weird stuff and knew a man named . . ." he paused as if trying to recall the name, " . . . Mitch, who owned a sex shop in, uh, the Tenderloin." Lane was an inept liar like most people, and like most people he crafted his deception from a core of truth. My challenge would be to find that core.

"Insects from a sex shop, eh? Go on."

"This guy supplied people with any creature they wanted for whatever kinky thing turned them on, including worms, spiders and insects. Anything."

"What was the name of this shop?"

"Pleasure something. Or maybe passion. The Passion Place, I think. Anyway, I ordered some lice, Mitch provided them, and I sprinkled a few in one the baggies my grandfather left next to his microscope."

"Why? Weren't your grandparents doing fine on their own sustaining their delusion?"

"He'd begun to express doubts about their being infested, so I thought that with the addition of some real evidence he'd keep going."

"Didn't you worry that a laboratory would identify the lice?"

"I thought the lice came from people. I figured Mitch had paid some sap to collect them from bums on the street. Besides, I knew which samples had the lice, and I was careful not to mail those out. I just threw them in the trash and sent his usual debris."

"I'm guessing you didn't know your grandfather kept his own reference material. That's how I came across the specimens in his study."

"I didn't think of that," he said, shaking his head and sniffling.

"And I bet you didn't think anyone would touch their pajamas and make contact with whatever you put on the material to irritate their skin," I said, scratching my arms. I was guessing wildly at this point, but my suspicion fit the emerging story. And if I was right, the existence of physical evidence would drive him to provide an account closer to the truth.

"Fuck, fuck, fuck," he blubbered, the emphasis fading with each repeat. "When I acquired the lice, I also wanted to amp up their symptoms. I used rubber gloves to collect poison oak from around Golden Gate Park. Then I rubbed the leaves on the inside of their nightclothes to make the whole thing more real to them." He gave a gurgling sob and said, "I didn't mean for them to die. I just wanted them out of the way so I could keep the business from going under. Once I had control, I would've made sure they got help. It all just blew up on me."

"Sounds to me like you worked your way into a psycho train wreck." Lane was looking for sympathy. I couldn't provide any.

"Are you going to report this to the police?" He looked at me for the first time, his eyes wet, red and pleading.

"Hell, I don't know if there's a crime in all of this wreckage. You're a manipulative shit who betrayed his grandparents. I suppose a prosecutor could find a way to charge you with reckless manslaughter. Beats me."

"And so?" he said with childlike hopefulness.

"And so, I'm done with you," I lied. I knew he was still hiding something—and that whatever he was hiding could be important if Lane ended up being interrogated and melted down under police questioning. My people and business could get drawn into a public relations disaster if I didn't figure out the whole sordid tale and prepare for a media onslaught. Whatever the real story, it sure as hell didn't involve a "friend" linking Lane to a guy named Mitch at The Passion Place in the Tenderloin, but somewhere in that fabrication was a lead worth following. And I knew one person who might shed some light into this darkness, if I handled the matter with delicacy, which wasn't generally my strong suit.

I walked out of the house and down the drive to my truck as the low, skittering clouds began spitting rain. I pondered the process of tracking down a sicko who provided animals to perverts, and I began to envy Dennis crawling around in school attics filled with bat shit and housing projects infested with cockroaches.

CHAPTER ELEVEN

On my drive back from the Linford's, I headed through Civic Center—not typically a clever route given the congestion around the government buildings. But I had a craving for lunch at a little joint squeezed between a soulless bank and a heartless insurance office. The rotund and balding guy behind the counter at Gyro's Welcome greeted me like Jason returning with the Golden Fleece.

Mr. Constantanides made his own pita bread from scratch, and a couple years ago he had a spectacular infestation of pita pests. The flour bins were crawling with confused flour beetles which deserve the name, given that they seem perplexed by what qualifies as food. They'll eat almost any dry good from snuff tobacco (as I'd discovered at a tobacconist's shop in the financial district) to poison rodent bait (as I'd learned from an embarrassing infestation in my own warehouse) to pinned insects (as I'd been warned by Scott Fortier at the Essig Museum). But the little bastards also feast on healthful vittles including dried fruits, beans, spices—and flour.

Dennis and Larry spent half a day in Mr. Constantanides' stockroom, inspecting and bagging up every dried good with a hint of beetles, cleaning the place with a high-powered vacuum, and providing supersized sealable containers to store new ingredients. With weekly spraying of crevices for the next couple of months, we prevented any hatchlings from starting a new plague.

Mr. Constantanides figured we'd saved his business and hailed me like a conquering hero whenever I stopped by. As usual, he began slicing succulent strips of lamb from the rotisserie the moment he saw me come through the door. The zealous Greek slathered the inside of a pita with tzatziki and stuffed it with meat, tomato, onion and French fries (which he insisted were traditional in his hometown of Athens).

While I ate, he basted the rotating meat and ranted about a Greek Cup match. I judiciously murmured my sympathy with his zealous critique of the officiating and nodded assent to his analysis that his Athens team was surely better than their low-class "eternal rival" from Piraeus. Agreement seemed prudent given that I hadn't the slightest idea about the sport of soccer and his diatribe was punctuated by waving a large, sharp knife.

I thanked Mr. Constantanides for lunch and headed to the shop, where I found Larry stocking shelves from a shipment of supplies piled by the garage door. He was deeply engaged in matching contents to packing lists—the sort of paperwork that never put him in a good mood—so I just nodded and he grunted as I headed to my office. I checked the phone book and found no listing for The Passion Place then went down the hall to find Carol.

Her radio was playing a song with a whispered one-word chorus, "passion," which seemed like some sort of warning. And the verses about dangerous nights, pitiless lovers, and twisted hearts were an ominous prelude to what I was going to broach with Carol.

"Hey babe, that song is almost musical," I said as a greeting.

"Don't patronize me, Riley. You appreciate Rod Stewart about as much as I enjoy Beethoven. I'm guessing that you're being nice because you want something." The woman was wickedly incisive.

"Okay, I was going to be delicate but I'll just come out with it. My investigation of the Linfords has led to a business that might be called The Passion Place, possibly located in the Tenderloin and run by a guy who could be named Mitch." She looked at me and rubbed her temples. A bad sign.

"And you figure lesbians know about sex shops because we're into kinky stuff?"

"No, that's not it," I lied. I imagined that atypical sex involved unconventional techniques, not that I thought about it all that much. "It's just that you and Anna live in the Castro where there are a few of these businesses, and you know everyone in the neighborhood. So I thought maybe you'd have some inside information."

"I'll let that lame explanation pass because of what's at stake for all of us." I smiled weakly. "But for the record, plenty of adventurous straight couples are into experimentation, based on what I've been told by several proprietors in the neighborhood."

"Okay, might any of the owners also have shops in the Tenderloin?"

"Doubtful. The influx of Asian immigrants hasn't been great for business in that part of the city. I'm sure that Vietnamese and Koreans are as kinky as the rest of humanity, but the new arrivals are too busy making ends meet, so to speak, to spend their entertainment dollars on dildos. But I can do you one better than speculating about the Tenderloin."

"How so?"

"A couple blocks from our apartment is a shop called Pleasure Palace, run by a woman named Michelle. And I know that she used to operate in the Tenderloin. Sounds suspiciously similar to what you're looking for." She was right. Lane's story was surely an extemporaneous permutation of the facts, and the near match was too close to be coincidence—even in a city famous for its entrepreneurial lustiness.

"Alright, we're onto something. Do you think Pleasure Palace might provide animals for deviants?" I asked. Carol sighed.

"I'm not sure what constitutes a deviant in your hopelessly heterosexual mind, but I know that Michelle has an impressive up-front inventory of sex aids."

"Up front?"

"Lotions, vibrators, ticklers, cuffs, strap-ons. The usual stuff." Apparently 'usual' had another meaning in this context. "But I've also heard that she provides special arrangements for S&M events, safe space for submission fantasies, and regular parties for furries."

"Furries? Do tell." I was beginning to feel like an adolescent coming across his first *Playboy*.

"You were asking about animals. Furries find it hot to dress up in animal costumes." I supposed that 'hot' didn't mean sweating inside a Yogi Bear outfit, which made me wonder why he and Boo-Boo wore ties while otherwise naked.

"Gotta say that I never busted a perp wearing a teddy bear costume. I did haul in a few hookers who were wearing nothing but teddies under their overcoats, but that's another thing altogether."

Larry strolled into the front office, evidently having picked up on our conversation. "Hey, whatever turns your crank," he said. "If nobody's getting hurt, then what the hell." He had a point, I guess.

"I'm not a fan of anyone telling consenting adults what they can do, but there have to be some limits. Right?" I was becoming increasingly, uncomfortably uncertain about what was normal.

"I guess so, but I wouldn't want the Moral Majority writing the rules," he said. "In any case, I might be able to help with your investigation, boss. My network of vets is tapped into happenings of all sorts if you get my drift."

"They'd know who might be providing animals to sex shops?"

"I wouldn't come out and ask 'em. Some of the guys in my Wednesday group are into kinky stuff. Mostly bondage from what I can tell. But if there's anything warped going down in 415, they might know about it. I'll see what's up with them tonight."

"Sounds promising," I said, appreciating the hip allusion to San Francisco's area code. "In the meantime, I'll stop by the Pleasure Palace and see what I can learn."

"Probably more than you can imagine," Carol purred and gave me a lewd smile.

The Castro's leading sex shop featured fake stonework, gilded chandeliers and red velvet to suggest the interior of a palace. As an ex-cop with a short but memorable stint on the vice squad, I know people get off in various ways. However, scanning the inventory while listening to Ravel's "Bolero" playing softly in the background and catching whiffs of lavender and musk raised some questions: why would the color of a condom matter, just what is the G-spot, and should good sex require batteries?

In contemplating the array of devices, I was reminded of a dinner at the home of a family from Delhi whose high-end flower shop had been infested with, ironically, Indian meal moths. The caterpillars were having a heyday in the dried arrangements despite the Kumars' enthusiastic spraying of insecticides. I could've advised an expensive fumigation, but instead I had them turn down the temperature in their walk-in cooler and freeze all of the dried plants for a week. This meant some logistical inconvenience as there was nowhere to keep fresh flowers but they saved a bundle compared to fumigation.

To express their gratitude, I was included in a dinner party of their business associates. We had all served ourselves from an array of dishes, including a heaping platter of chicken parts slathered in curry sauce. I'd picked up a fork and knife to cut the meat from the bone, in accord with fine dining etiquette. Mr. Kumar gestured discretely for me to wait and announced to the gathering: "My friends, eating is like sex." There were embarrassed smiles as he continued. "One should never allow an implement to come between you and the one you love." With that, he picked up a chicken leg, took a hearty bite, and licked his fingers. We all followed suit and joined the culinary orgy.

My marveling at the "triple-action diving dolphin" while contemplating whether Mr. Kumar's advice applied to whatever the hell this thing did for couples was broken by a provocative question. "How may I help you?"

The sultry voice came from a woman who had a good six inches and twenty-five pounds on me. She had piercing blue eyes, tight golden curls, and assertively unfettered breasts under a peasant blouse, carelessly untied at the throat. This had to be Michelle—like a blending of the most sensual elements of the Norse and the gypsies into a sexually intimidating presence.

"I was thinking that perhaps we might help each other." She cocked an eyebrow. "Our business interests might be complementary," I explained to move the conversation from flirtatious to financial.

"How so?"

"Let's just say that I can provide you with unusual inventory for discerning customers." She flicked her head toward the back of the store where a heavy black curtain covered the doorway to a small office with a steel desk, mismatched filing cabinets, a buzzing fluorescent light fixture and absolutely nothing to suggest the nature of her business. Michelle gestured for me to take a battered, wooden chair. She settled into an office chair with well-worn upholstery and lit a cigarette.

"You're neither slick nor bumbling enough to be a vice cop, so who are you and what do you have?" she asked.

"I go by Riley. I understand from one of your customers that you are a discrete retailer of animals for people with particular desires." She gave a subtle nod and took a drag on her cigarette, so I continued. "In my line of work as an exterminator, I come across creatures that might interest your customers."

"I have suppliers," she said. "Most requests from zoophiles involve warm creatures that can't be readily obtained from pet stores or at least not repeatedly without raising questions. Why would I need you?"

"Because I understand the world of six- and eight-legged animals. And you understand the world of unconventional appetites."

"What I understand," she said, taking a long pull on the cigarette and crushing it into an ashtray from the Stardust Hotel in Las Vegas according to the futuristic, gold lettering, "is that you are not here to wholesale cockroaches and flies. What are you after?" Those icy blue eyes had me nailed. Being on the other side of an interrogation was unpleasant so I opted for honesty, more or less.

"It's convoluted, but the bottom line is that my company is being drawn into a situation that, if the word gets out, could be disastrous for business. We didn't do anything wrong, but you know how the press loves a salacious story."

"Don't I ever. Hint at anything other than vanilla sex between a husband and wife and reporters get a hard-on faster than with any lotion I stock." She gave a throaty laugh. "So where does my shop come in—and how can I make sure it stays out of your 'situation,' as you call it?"

"I think you recently provided an individual with some lice which he used for purposes that may well garner the attention of the police."

"Thank you for leaving out names. My business requires anonymity. But I do recall this unusual request."

"A frequent buyer?"

She hesitated. I hadn't asked for a name, but had probed into a sensitive area when it came to the privacy of her clientele. "I'd rather not say." An awkward deflection can reveal as much as an agile answer. Lane Linford hadn't been sent by 'a friend'; he was a regular.

"I can tell you that my supplier of cold-blooded accessories is more accustomed to orders for tarantulas and earthworms than lice." I wasn't sure of the fate of these other creatures, but I was sure I didn't want to know.

"But he came through?"

"Yes, we filled the order. Tell me how the cops are involved."

"The lice ended up at the scene of two deaths. They were supposed to be the kind you'd find on humans, but your supplier evidently found it easier to acquire them from poultry than people. However, the customer didn't specify his purposes so the mistake was understandable."

"And traceable?"

"I managed to find you, although I'm smarter than most cops."

"That's not saying much. But what do you want from me? An apology for providing the wrong beasties?"

"I was hoping to get a clearer sense of what happened leading up to the deaths. And I have, but I'd also appreciate talking with your supplier, to fill in another piece of the puzzle."

"As I said before, discretion is everything. I provide customers with anything they desire, other than names." I thanked her and gave her a business card. She looked it over.

"Goat Hill, eh? I have a wealthy customer who occasionally seeks a goat. Maybe I'll get in touch sometime," she leered.

I left, found a pay phone on the corner and called Papadopoulos to let him know that I was following some twisted leads without providing him with details. He expressed his appreciation with being updated and said he could give me some time to pursue the case as long as I flew below radar and kept him informed. In his words, he had more pressing investigations than, "a couple of rich, old perverts who offed themselves."

I hung up and wiped my hands on the front of my faded jeans, wondering whose hands had last held the receiver—and what they'd touched just before that.

CHAPTER TWELVE

After inspecting a couple of apartment buildings that the guys had treated last week, I was ready to call it a day. I parked behind the shop and headed to our hump-day watering hole. The slate-gray clouds hid the upper floors of downtown office buildings and a fine rain blurred the waning, afternoon light. Like a soggy blanket, the moisture drew the smells of the bay up into Potrero Hill. The salty, sulfurous funk of ocean currents laced with rotting kelp plus the diesel vapors of cargo ships blending with the effluvium of fishing boats created eau d'San Francisco.

As I came into O'Donnell's Pub, the smells became yeasty and the cold drizzle was replaced by a feeling like the warm comfort of old slippers. I exchanged greetings with Brian, the pub's owner, weeknight bartender, and Tommy's godfather. Then I caught the eye of his wife in the kitchen behind the brass-railed bar. Cynthia came out, pushed an errant lock of strawberry-blonde hair behind her ear, and gave me a big kiss on the cheek.

"It's a wetting rain out there," she said, pulling the towel from her apron to wipe my face.

"I'd say rotten on its way to pissing," offered Brian. The Irish know their rain.

"How about a serving of your shepherd's pie to warm my gullet?" I asked.

"Is that all I mean to you, Riley?" Cynthia teased, giving me a playful shove. She headed back into the kitchen and Brian handed me a pitcher of Anchor Porter with a luscious head. It was nearly as good as the black stuff—Guinness—although I could get a knuckle supper if I shared this view with my countrymen.

"Your crew is two pitchers ahead of you," he said, gesturing to our traditional table where Dennis, Larry, Carol, and her girlfriend, Anna, were sitting along with Nina. I liked it when girlfriends joined our midweek gathering. "They can sure put it away when the boss is paying."

"That's the Wednesday deal," I said and he nodded approvingly.

Atop the battered oak table were a couple plates of potato skins—a culinary innovation that convinced people to pay for vegetable peels. But I had to admit that with sour cream and chives, the damn things were addictive.

Dennis was arguing that the Golden State Warriors had made a disastrous mistake trading Robert Parish for Joe Berry Carroll. And based on the game playing on the television at the end of the bar, Dennis had a point. Getting beaten by the Cleveland Cavaliers was about as bad as it could get.

"Sorry to interrupt a good tirade," I said, setting the pitcher in the middle of the table.

"You d'boss," Dennis said.

"And d'sugar daddy of suds," Larry added as Carol blew me a kiss.

"Enough of that," Nina said, "you're going to puff up his ego." She leaned over and gave me a sympathetic kiss which afforded a surreptitious glimpse of her cleavage. Or maybe not so stealthy, as she gave me one of those "behave yourself" looks and I shrugged without remorse. Her brown-and-tan plaid flannel shirt with the first two buttons undone combined with the Guinness-colored corduroys to just about beg me to stretch out on her couch and fall asleep on her lap. At least that's the message I was getting. As it turned out, it wasn't the message being sent.

"Now with the adulation out of the way," I said, "does anyone have anything that would help with the Linford mess?"

"That's why Carol brought me along. Well, that and free beer," Anna said. She was a big, healthy Swede, the kind of woman who would have made six months of darkness in northern Europe tolerable for a man—if only she'd been straight.

"What's the poop?" I asked. Larry rolled his eyes and Dennis shook his head at my lack of 80s jargon.

"Carol sort of filled me in. So, I asked around Haight Ashbury, where everyone knows something about herbalism." Anna worked at a New Age store that sold crystals, incense, Tarot cards and anything else that hip nitwits wanted in order to deceive themselves and dupe their friends. But she had something valuable—connections to folks who retailed plant extracts, tinctures, and my favorite, homeopathic elixirs which were little bottles of water that had one part per gazillion of some chemical. I'd thought about going into homeopathic insecticides. Hell, a drop of malathion would produce a tank car of marketable product, nobody could ever claim they'd been accidentally poisoned, and when the stuff didn't work I'd just blame the customer—or maybe the vermin—for lacking faith in magical treatments.

"And what did you discover?" I asked.

"HerbalVitae is the Bay area's largest wholesaler. They have competitors, but the Linfords are, or were, adapting rapidly. Last fall, the company came out with the hottest new herbal aphrodisiac."

"The best Afro-disiac plant is planting these Afro lips on a woman," Dennis said, puckering for the table just as Cynthia arrived with my shepherd's pie. She looked inquisitively at me.

"Don't ask," I said and gestured for Anna to continue as Cynthia walked back to the bar shaking her head.

"The rumor is that it's a blend of ginseng, ginkgo, some West Africa tree bark, and horny goat weed."

"You're shitting us," said Larry. "Horny goat weed? As in a weed that makes goats wanna screw?"

"It's named for the shape of the flowers, not its effect on livestock," Anna said dismissively, although I was right there with Larry.

"Just askin'," he said.

"The point is that HerbalVitae was doing fine," I said in an effort to get the conversation back on track. That meant Lane Linford's claim of fostering his grandparents' delusions as a way to allow him to save the family business was bogus. I couldn't guess his true motive, although I remembered Dr. Chen's warning that people hide their disorders—so maybe Lane was as screwed up as his elders.

I was pondering all of this while the conversation about aphrodisiacs slid into an argument about the role of technology in baby making. Larry and Dennis maintained that test-tube babies, the first one in America having been born a month ago, took the fun out of reproduction. Carol and Anna countered that having babies took the fun out of sex, a point the guys couldn't rebut.

"As interesting as all of this might be," I interrupted, "what Anna's information means is that I need to pay Lane Linford another visit. Something's not adding up."

"What do you figure, boss?" asked Larry.

"The kid told me this morning that he manipulated his grandparents so he could get them declared incompetent and modernize the business. I need to know the real story if we're going to protect our company's reputation, if and when the time comes."

"I'd like to go along," Dennis said. "I still got a dog in the fight, seeing as how I provided them with the insecticide."

"We've gone over that," I said.

"It's not your fault," Carol added, reaching to put a reassuring hand on his arm.

"There's more to tell," he said staring down at the tabletop. "What them old folks did with the flea collars I gave 'em is just like I did with my little brothers." We all sat quietly while Dennis took some deep breaths. "Mamma had gone to visit her sister who had cancer and my daddy wasn't around. So I was s'pose to take care of Reggie and Tyrone. Their friends had head lice and got tol' that they couldn't come to school."

"And so, you thought flea collars would help?" Carol said, squeezing his arm.

"If Reggie and Ty got lice, I couldn't look after 'em, go to my own school, and work every afternoon. I knew how cockroaches spread in the projects and figured lice would do like that. So, I boosted a package of flea collars from Walgreens, put 'em on my brothers and made 'em wear sweaters to hide the things so's not to get teased."

"Did it work?" Nina asked.

"Not sure. Ty got real sick a few days later, ralphing all night. Drove Reggie and me to sleep in Mamma's room. Mos' prob'ly my home cooking, but maybe the collar. I got scared and took 'em off. Reggie got lice after Mamma got back. For a week, she rubbed baby oil into his hair and made him wear a shower cap to bed, then shampooed his head to within inch of his life every morning."

"Mammas know best," Carol said.

"They do at that," Dennis said, looking up from the table. "But what I did is why this thing with the Linfords drags on me. Can you relate?"

"Big time, homey," Larry said.

I told Dennis he could join me tomorrow morning for a visit to Lane Linford. This prompted a discussion of "lame names," which then switched to cool names including Golden State's Lloyd B. Free who legally changed his name last December to World B. Free, which led to a debate as to whether "World" was a self-aggrandizing reference or a political statement.

Nina had been unusually quiet during the evening, just picking at the pub food and sipping her ginger ale. As the gathering started to break up, I took her aside and asked her if something was wrong. She said Petey hadn't come to the daycare again and she was getting worried about the kid. I offered to take her home, hoping that the flannel-and-corduroy signal would get me out of the workout at Marty's that I had originally planned. But she gave me a peck on the cheek and said she needed a long walk now that the rain had stopped.

Larry knew I wasn't keen on her neighborhood. He caught my eye, winked and asked Nina if she could tolerate a companion on her walk, as he wanted to buy tickets for the U2 concert at the Civic Auditorium which was on the way. She knew he was probably lying but didn't have the heart to refuse the big, protective lug.

I headed to Marty's Gym to sweat off the porter and pie. Marty came out of his hopelessly cluttered, dimly lit office to push aside the wrap I was using and tape my hands. Mostly he wanted to share his thoughts about the declining work ethic of young fighters who "pranced around the ring as if boxing was a goddamn ballet performance instead of a blood sport." As he chomped his unlit cigar butt, he tore into President Carter as a "world-class wuss" for having boycotted the 1980 Olympics noting, "maybe one in a hundred Americans could even find Afghanistan on a fuckin' map." Marty finished by declaring the US team "had better get its shit together for '84 or the commies are going to do in LA what they did in Moscow." Out of tape and having exhausted his irritation with the modern world, he grunted and headed back to his office.

While I was working the speed bag, Petros Hagopian was hitting the heavy bag. Petros was known for two things. He was a phenomenally demanding and effective coach for young fighters, having made the Olympic team for Armenia as a middleweight in 1964. He was also the hairiest guy that anyone had ever seen in the gym. From what I could tell, other than the palms of his hands, forehead and nose (excluding nostrils), the guy was covered in a mat of curly, black hair. I wondered if Petros would have enticed "furries," as Carol referred to those with a peculiar sexual inclination. Some mental images are not welcome, and today had generated more than its fair share.

On the walk up to my house, a cold mist was hanging in the air which felt good after my workout. It was especially soothing to my itchy hands. I was none too happy about the rash that had reappeared when I took a steam before my shower. That set me to thinking about the Linfords, lice and lust.

I'm not interested in telling people what they can't do in their bedrooms. When I was on the force, I was never big on busting prostitutes. If they weren't juveniles or pressured by some pimp and they just decided to make money with sex, it was their business—not mine. But what about selling animals for sex at the Pleasure Palace? There's gotta be a line.

So is it perverted to dress up like an animal? Seems so, but I liked it when Nina wore that black satin camisole. And she enjoyed outdoor sex. Would we be deviants if we weren't discrete while enjoying a romp among the sun-warmed dunes at Baker Beach or a rendezvous in a dappled forest glen at Mount Sutro? Maybe, but if exhibitionists and voyeurs want to team up for their mutual satisfaction, I'm not sure why it matters to me.

The whole thing about normalcy was becoming as irritating as the rash by the time I pulled off my sweatshirt and contemplated pinning a series of fritillaries from last summer. My itchy hands weren't up to the fine operations needed to spread the butterflies and my heart wasn't in it as I thought of Nina living in the Tenderloin. I was deeply appreciative of Larry's gracious offer to escort her without making it sound like he was going as her bodyguard.

I decided to combine Beethoven's 5th Symphony (Carlos Kleiber conducting the Vienna Philharmonic) with a generous pour of Bushmill's Black Bush (a dependable blend) to end the day. I settled into my battered recliner, imbibing a familiar symphony and a dependable whiskey. The unexceptional can be exceptionally comforting.

Chapter Thirteen

I grabbed a coffee and a couple paczkis from Gustaw's Bakery and tried to keep my breakfast dry while eating and walking down to the shop through the morning mist. Carol looked up from her desk as I came in shaking droplets from my coat and tossing a soggy bag in the direction of her trash can. I missed.

"Damn it Riley, you're getting water everywhere and throwing your garbage on the floor."

"And good morning to you, sunshine." She looked great in a Scotch plaid skirt and a butterscotch, ribbed turtleneck that was pleasingly snug.

"Pick up your trash and stop ogling your office manager. You have a girlfriend, you degenerate." I might've been wondering about what was normal last night, but this morning I was sure that a man admiring a nicely put together woman fell into the realm of normalcy. I picked up the wadded bag, banked it off the wall into the can, and bent over to give Carol a kiss on the cheek.

"What's wrong, babe?" I asked.

"Don't call me 'babe' and I won't refer to you as a degenerate." She sighed and ran her fingers through her hair.

"Deal. Now what's the matter?"

"Jobs are backing up and I'm trying to keep customers from getting grouchy, like me. I know you're juggling work around here with the investigation. And I know how important it is to figure out what happened with the Linfords to protect our reputation. But even with the lighter workload in the winter, things are jammed and now you're taking Dennis with you for the morning." Nobody took the business more seriously than Carol.

"We're busting butt to keep up," I pleaded. "Nobody's better than you with customers who want their roaches toasted yesterday. Anything I can do to take off the pressure, just say so."

"Well, there is something." I'd taken the bait and felt the trap slamming shut. Men can be such patsies. "My job would be much easier if I had one of those new Apple computers for the office, so I could keep track of our contacts, schedules and accounting." I understand computers even less than I understand women.

"I promise to consider it. Seriously. Give me a price quote and I'll make a decision." We both knew what I'd decide but it seemed important to maintain the illusion of my being the boss. I started down the hall to find Dennis and Larry.

"Oh Riley, one last thing," she called out. I stopped, turned back to her and waited, figuring that I was in for a final reprimand. Wrong again. "That big brotherly peck on the cheek didn't add to your degenerate quotient."

In the back, the garage door was open and Larry had pulled a van into the warehouse to load up for the day while staying dry for a few more minutes. Dennis was looking guilty for hanging with me rather than going out on jobs, so he was happy to take over the loading while I talked to Larry.

"No problem on your walk?" I asked.

"Not on the walk. You have one fine woman who can carry a conversation even with the likes of me. I'll be her escort anytime."

"By 'not on the walk' you mean there was trouble at her apartment?"

"Not really trouble, but there was a hoser hanging around who eyeballed Nina. So I laid low after she went into her apartment."

"A stocky guy with short hair, needing a shave and wearing an Army jacket?"

"That's him. I got sympathy for my fellow vets, if that's the guy's story. But this dude just leaned on the railing across the courtyard and stared at Nina's window. Like he was mental. Her curtains were half open, but I don't think he could see anything."

"How long did he stand there?"

"Until I went up the stairs and let him know it wasn't cool."

"What'd you say?"

"Didn't say anything. But he got the message."

"Does Nina know?"

"Nah, didn't want to worry her. I walked around to her door on my way out and quietly checked the handle. It was locked.

"Good. She's smart and tough, but that guy evidently didn't get my message the last time I was there."

"I'd be glad to send a message he couldn't miss, boss."

"Thanks, but I'll handle this. You did good with Nina. Did you find out anything from your pals last night about kinks around town?"

"Some, but I should jet if I'm going to get out to Pacific Heights and stay on schedule. Can I fill you in later this morning?"

We settled on meeting at my favorite diner on Ventura between his morning jobs. Larry took over the loading from Dennis.

On the way to the Linford place, I turned on KDFC. The announcer informed listeners of his *Morning with Mozart* program and introduced *Requiem Mass in D Minor*. After the Lacrimosa movement, Dennis declared, "that Mozart dude wrote some spooky shit."

"Probably not the way music critics would put it, but you're right. That's what you get when a composer dies in the middle of writing a piece commissioned by a Count to commemorate his wife's death."

"That's some bad juju. It's got me uptight along with our little visit."

"Nothing to worry about. Once we get there, I'm going to talk to Lane and make a point out of your needing to inspect for fleas since their eggs can last months before hatching."

"He'll buy it?"

"He'll be focused on me and won't figure a courteous black man is any danger."

"We be dangerous only if we be rude or be walking down the street or be moving into Ritz Cracker neighborhoods." I knew what he meant but didn't respond. There was work to do.

"What I need you to do is make it look like you're headed upstairs but loop back to Lane's wing. There's a series of rooms down the hall to the left of the entryway. I'll keep him busy while you see what you can find."

"Like what?"

"Like anything that might give us a clue as to what the kid is hiding. He's not telling the truth, so we need to find out why he was so dedicated to screwing with his grandparents' heads."

"Don't know what rich honkeys are s'pose to keep around, but I can see if anything looks warped by the standards of a po-lite colored boy."

Lane Linford was unhappy about our unannounced visit. When I told him I'd found serious gaps in his story and I needed some clarifications before we could finally part company, he grudgingly directed me to the cavernous living room. I told Dennis to inspect the upstairs for fleas and Lane didn't take much notice.

Lane flipped a switch and the enormous fireplace erupted in flame. He was wearing silk pajama pants and a smoking jacket which struck me as a pathetic effort to appear suave by a sallow, underweight kid with greasy hair. He slumped onto the divan or settee or whatever the hell the thing was called, which would've been a couch in my house but surely rated some classier term in this opulent setting. I opted for one of the wingback chairs upholstered in a fabric with vines and berries and birds.

"I thought we were done with this matter," he said, slowly rotating his too-large head around his pencil neck to produce a series of audible crunches.

"We would've been, had you told me the truth." He stopped lolling his head. "I tracked down Michelle at the Pleasure Palace in the Castro. You really need to practice your lying."

He shrugged. "What's the difference? Someone provided me with the lice." He rubbed the back of his neck.

"One difference is that no imaginary friend told you about the place. Why did you try to hide your connection to the Pleasure Palace?"

"Frequenting sex shops is not an approved pastime in my social circle." He started cracking his knuckles, one at time.

"Okay, let's talk about the bigger lie." I paused as he tortured his fingers. "Contrary to your story, HerbalVitae is doing fine. There are no financial reasons for you to take over the company. What you did to your grandparents wasn't motivated by a desire to save the family business." He gazed into the distance, as if spellbound by the fire. I waited. The rain had picked up and was pattering against the French doors leading to the back patio. There was no sound from the gas fireplace. Fake logs don't crackle and pop. If interrogations taught me anything, it was that no lie is as convincing at the truth. I leaned forward, trying to convey sympathy—my own lie.

"You wouldn't understand. Nobody would," he groaned.

"Try me."

He took a deep breath. "Michelle had video tapes that would've destroyed me if they ever got out."

"Blackmail, eh? Hardly original for a woman who specializes in unusual sexual diversions. But I guess you can't be innovative in all aspects of business."

Lane gave a slight snort and shook his head. "The bitch had me by the balls, figuratively speaking."

"What did she have, literally speaking?"

"You don't need to know. I'll go to prison before I'm humiliated to that extent. There's a witch hunt in this city for anyone that Grant Roberts and his Moral Majority tribunal deems perverted." It seemed the assistant district attorney's campaign was making life difficult for both sexually warped citizens and straight-laced cops, such as Lieutenant Papadopolous.

"I used to be on the force. I've seen a lot of stuff." Actually, I'd seen mostly unimaginative stuff, compared to what I'd learned in the last day, but it was worth a try.

"I have a condition, a habit actually. I can't break it, but I learned about my grandparents' condition while researching my own." Whatever he was doing was going to remain between him, Michelle and a VHS tape.

"Why not get help? You got enough dough to hire a therapist who would keep your secret." He shook his head.

"I have my own account, enough to pay a therapist if I thought one could help. But I didn't have enough to pay Michelle."

"So you needed control of HerbalVitae for long enough to access the company funds and make a blackmail payment. And having your grandparents declared incompetent was the answer."

"A hundred grand is a lot of money," he said.

"Must've been some video." There was a long minute of silence.

"Are we done?" He appeared oddly both agonized and relieved. Unlike our last visit, he wasn't sniveling, but drained.

"I thought we were yesterday, but then I also thought you were telling me the truth. I'm guessing we're getting closer now. At least you're being honest in what you won't reveal."

Lane looked at me for the first time since our conversation began and gave a wan smile. He rose and started toward the entryway, which I took to be my signal that we were done chatting. I called out for Dennis and hoped he had been keeping an eye on us. It wouldn't help my tenuous relationship with the presumptive inheritor of HerbalVitae if Dennis appeared in the hallway leading to Lane's wing of the house. But maybe it didn't matter.

The last day had made it clear that Lane couldn't be trusted. With his grandparents dead, rather than just merely pushed aside, he would presumably pay Michelle out of the company coffers and I still wouldn't know what dark secret of his led to the poisoning the Linfords. I was essentially back to square one. And if the newspapers latched onto the sordid story, there was no doubt Lane would throw Goat Hill Extermination under the bus. He'd say anything to protect his reputation—and he was getting in some good practice when it came to lying.

Dennis appeared at the top of the stairs, carrying a clipboard and looking every bit the professional. He joined us, flipped through a few pages, and declared that the upstairs was free of vermin. Even if he was overacting, I was impressed with his timely and convincing arrival on the stage.

When we were in the truck, I clicked on the radio and we caught Mozart's Symphony No. 25 in G minor, which I suggested was a much less "spooky" example of the great composer's work. We listened for a few minutes.

"It's not bad, I guess. Might be nice background music in an expensive restaurant or classy store."

I bit my tongue. "Setting aside your music review, what did you find in Lane's wing?"

"Most of the rooms had the fancy furniture and artsy doodads that I seen in rich houses before. But the dude had an insect zoo in his bedroom."

"I've seen his upscale ant farms. Even the insect neighborhoods in this city are becoming gentrified."

"Nice one, Riley. Did you check out his mealworm and cockroach condos?" That explained the smell coming from the covered terrariums. "Those was some badass roaches. But the real deal was in this office connected to his bedroom. There was shelves of scientific magazines." He paused to look through the notes on his clipboard. Dennis had taken his job seriously, as usual. "Our boy subscribes to the *Journal of Abnormal Psychology* and the *Journal of Sex Research*. These be *Penthouse* for college graduates, I s'pose. And then there was video tapes."

Now he had my full attention. "What did the labels say?" He flipped to another page.

"There was a mess of nature programs, like 'Secrets of the Ant' and 'The Swarming Hordes.' Then there was a few hand-labeled videos hidden behind the standard stuff. I couldn't make out some of the writing, but one had 'Formicophilia'—which I'm prob'ly not sayin' right—then it said 'LL October 1981.' Another said 'Crush: stiletto and crickets' and one said, 'Penis sting close-ups.'"

I was going to need another visit with Dr. Chen—and maybe some counseling afterward.

CHAPTER FOURTEEN

As I pulled in behind the shop, KDFC was finishing the Mozart program with *Eine kleine Nachtmusik* which Dennis judged as being pretty enough to play in the elevator of a nice hotel. I cringed, unable to decide whether my morning tutorial had been a failure or a success. At least he'd listened, which was something.

We went inside where Dennis checked the work schedule and started diligently loading the other van. He wasn't going to let down Larry by having played private eye with me rather than spraying for vermin. I headed to my office, ignored the "While You Were Out" notes festooning my door and called Dr. Chen, my reluctant, consulting psychologist.

As expected, I got the receptionist whose job it was to make sure that her boss never talked to anyone without an appointment and a checkbook. But this time I was ready for her.

"Hello, this is Dr. Müller." I drew out the long "u" as Mr. Müller, my 7th grade history teacher at St. Teresa's, had done. I figured that Freud was Austrian so a German name would sound important. In the haughtiest voice I could muster, I pushed on: "I am the head of the psychology department at San Francisco State."

"Ah, yes," she murmured with false assurance, which was good as I hadn't figured she'd know the faculty. But one could never be certain about the ignorance of others.

"Please connect me to Doctor Chen."

"May I tell her what this concerns?"

I sighed audibly. After all she was only a secretary and no self-respecting professor would deign to inform the office staff of professional matters. "I wish to invite the doctor to speak at the Cedric Riley Lecture series." Nothing like naming a prestigious event after oneself. There's no cause for humility when you're the imaginary head of an academic department.

There was a pause on her end as she processed this fabrication. Sensing her uncertainty, I bet that pomposity would trump doubt. In for a penny, in for a pound as my father used to say, despite the expression being British and his contempt for all things monarchical.

"Surely you've heard of the lectures. Anyone even vaguely familiar with the psychological profession knows that our series is nationally prominent. In fact, internationally. We had Dr. Gustav Marx here last fall." Okay that was weak, but Marx was the only Germanic name I could remember at the moment. It worked.

"Of course," she said as if it all made sense. "I'll put you through to Dr. Chen."

There was a few moments of silence followed by some clicking and then, "This is Dr. Chen. I understand you'd like me to give a lecture at your university?"

"Absolutely. A lunchtime lecture to an audience of one, but he's a very attentive fellow for being an exterminator."

There was silence as she tried to decide whether or not to simply hang up. "You are bordering on a diagnosis of being a pathological liar, Mr. Riley."

"Hey now, your receptionist is a wee bit protective. I had to come up with something to get through to you. Deception requires mental agility and deep understanding of other minds, don't you think?"

"I'm very busy. I've told you what you need to know about delusory parasitosis in your line of work."

"Yes, and you were a great teacher. But I have come across something even crazier."

"By which you mean mentally ill, I presume."

I'd failed to learn that lesson in professional terminology. "Right, sorry. What do you know about something called formicophilia?"

This time there was a long pause. "Where did you come across that term? It's a very unusual condition."

"I have reason to believe that a person involved in my little train wreck of mental illness and murder is mixed up in this practice or whatever it is. So, what is it?" I'd managed to work in the accepted terminology. Call me a teacher's pet, but it kept her talking.

"The condition was covered briefly in a graduate seminar on paraphilia, during a lecture on zoophilia in particular. I'd have to pull out my notes and I have a patient coming in a few minutes. But I'm intrigued if, in fact, you've encountered someone with this disorder. Skeptical, but fascinated, as a professional."

Michelle had referred to "zoophiles" which I'd inferred meant people who loved animals—and not in a platonic way. I wasn't sure about "paraphilia," but using my high school Latin, I surmised that it involved something about a person being in the vicinity of love. I didn't want to get us off track by asking for definitions. So, having set the hook, it was time to reel her in.

"How about lunch at Yee's Restaurant? You have to eat sometime and I doubt you'll find a more charming companion in the next two hours."

Dr. Chen sighed but evidently found my discovery of Lane Linford's condition to be irresistible and agreed to meet me at noon. If I'd only known the powers of obscure mental conditions to attract women, I might've been far more successful in my younger days.

I hung up and read through the pink messages Carol had taped to my door. The top one informed me that she was out getting quotes from ComputerLand and the Byte Shop. My technological fate was sealed. The other messages were from prospective clients, including a couple of potentially big contracts. Given my success in luring Dr. Chen, I figured I was on a roll and would try beguiling prospective customers with my enchanting repartee. But first, I had to find out what Larry had learned from his screwy pals.

The diner had been my hangout when I was on the force. I suppose the place had a name but there only was one of those pink and green neon signs with an arrow (as if people couldn't figure out where to go) and the word "Diner," so we just called it "The Diner." It was a couple blocks down Valencia from the Mission Station, and in the old days cops got free coffee which, given its quality, wasn't a great deal. Sometimes you get what you pay for.

To make sure police don't actually get to know citizens or cultivate relationships with local businesses, the Police Advisory Board in conjunction with the city's Ethics Commission issued a "professional standards policy" banning freebies shortly after I turned in my badge. I bet the appointed and anointed ones didn't pay for the coffee during their deliberations.

From what I could tell, the rules were the only things that had changed at the diner in the last thirteen years. The yellowed linoleum tiles, cracked vinyl seats, stainless steel counter and truly bad coffee took me back. From appearances, the waitress looked like she'd been working since the San Francisco earthquake.

The loss of complimentary java hadn't entirely dissuaded the cops from coming by. A couple of blues were at the table nearest the door, so I took a booth in the back to assure privacy. As Larry came through the door, my coffee arrived with half of it splashed into the saucer and the rest in a chipped cup. He slid into the opposite bench, winked at the fossilized waitress, and ordered a cinnamon bun to go with his coffee.

"Damn, that was a freaky job," he said, pulling up the sleeves of his moth-eaten rag wool sweater and resting his elbows on the table.

"From the schedule, I thought you were doing a simple roach raid at some swanky condo in Pacific Heights." I took a sip from my cup. The coffee was as bitter and acidic as ever, but you couldn't beat the atmosphere and service.

"Looked that way before I got there."

"Not so swanky, after all?"

"That's not it. The place was posh. Marble entryway, floor to ceiling windows, white leather upholstery, teak bar in the living room, cut glass decanters, you name it."

"So, you didn't find any cockroaches and sipped Bloody Marys all morning while trading interior design tips with a rich, sensuous and lonely housewife whose husband was making deals in London."

"The mister was at work but otherwise, wrong again—sadly. The roaches were rockin'. Turns out that the owners didn't want to be seen having an exterminator show up at their place. Our presence undercuts a couple's social standing. To avoid the shame, they put out those lame-ass roach hotels which probably just gave the roaches a grungy place to rent by the hour and crank out little roaches."

The waitress came with Larry's coffee and bun. He took a bite, washed it down with a swallow of coffee and continued. "Once the problem got bad enough, the husband, a lawyer, worried that their little house guests would invade the neighbors who would sue for damages."

"I gather that's how people get to know one another in those condo castles," I said, wondering if the sweetness of the bun would make the coffee any better. I decided to add a packet of sugar to mine. It didn't help.

"So, they called us. I did the usual, like convincing her that a bowl of dried cat food was like a soup kitchen for their growing family of greasy beasties. For a bimbette, she seemed sharp enough to see the connection. But when I brought up the sprayer, the missus wigged out like I was going to rain liquid death on their classy digs. She decided to go shopping to avoid the danger."

"Probably best for all concerned. But it doesn't sound all that freaky."

"Hold on, homey. In the course of the treatment, I checked all of the rooms for signs of infestation. There was a bodacious nightie hanging in the bathroom and in the bedroom there was this freaky device."

"A water bed? You know Larry, even decent folks have them these days," I teased as my coffee cooled and became even less drinkable.

"Try a swing hanging from a metal frame with ropes and straps and stirrups. The damned thing look like it was designed for a mountain climbing cowboy. I couldn't quite figure out what went where and it didn't help that I got dizzy looking at myself in the mirrored ceiling.

"With that freaky playground and funhouse, they were embarrassed with the neighbors seeing an exterminator in their condo," I said, adding more sugar. "But that reminds me of why we're here. What did you find out from your buddies last night?" The waitress came over and refilled our cups. At least the coffee was hot.

"It wasn't like conducting a police interrogation. More like nudging a conversation."

"I bet they have good reasons to be wary."

"The way vets get treated, trust is hard to come by and it doesn't help that it's such a fluid group. There's a VA counselor who runs the meeting, but he pretty much just asks us what we think about what someone says. It's horseshit but better than watching *Real People* which is real lame or *WKRP*, although Loni Anderson has a helluva rack. Don't tell Carol I said that. Anyway, we go out for coffee after. Better than this, which isn't saying much."

"I know. Go on."

"One of the guys knew about the Pleasure Palace. He's done some low-budget porn with the owner, Stefan, who directs quick-and-dirty films."

"I thought Michelle was the owner."

"She runs the place. Kinda like you and Carol, except they're married."

"Thanks for the comparison."

"Call 'em like I see 'em boss." He added sugar and creamer, took a sip and winced. "Turns out that Stefan is mostly into the money, but Michelle is into some really heinous action. Dangerous shit from what I could tell, but I didn't want to push too hard so I don't have any details."

"What you managed to find out is a big help. I didn't know about Stefan." I pondered for a moment. "Stefan and Michelle. S and M, eh?"

"Life's funny that way," he said, taking one more sip before giving up. "I'd better book in a few. Gotta save a lonely housewife in Noe Valley from a horrible death before lunch."

"Let me guess. We're at the leading edge of skunk mating season and the little bastards are spraying with greater enthusiasm than the nozzle heads at Orkin."

"More traumatizing. The note on Carol's work order said that there was a hairy, baby snake sprinting across the lady's kitchen floor."

"House centipede. About the scariest harmless creature around."

"Don't be so blasé. I'm about to rescue a fair maiden from a freakin' monster."

"Seriously, I appreciate your busting ass to hold things together while I'm playing gumshoe."

"No biggie. By lunchtime, I can tell the lady that the demon dasher isn't deadly and lay down some boric acid powder. Then I'll fuel up for the afternoon on a Cuban at Pequeño Habana."

"That new sandwich shop near St. Luke's Hospital?"

"It's only a sandwich shop like Placido Domingo is just a singer." I was impressed that he knew the name of the great tenor. "The owners are from Tampa, where they add salami to their Cubans which is righteous."

"But no lettuce or tomato, I assume."

"Would Domingo sing 'Muskrat Love'?" I had a hazy memory of lyrics concerning rodent romance, but I refrained from answering. "C'mon Riley, can you imagine him belting out 'You Light Up My Life'?" I hadn't a clue but supposed this was meant to be absurd.

"No?" I ventured.

"Man, you gotta start paying attention to Carol's radio or this century is gonna pass you by." He shook his head and got up.

I left a fiver on the table which covered the coffee, bun and a generous tip.

CHAPTER FIFTEEN

I spent the rest of the morning meeting with two prospects. Near Golden Gate Park, I caught up with a part-time super at 345 Aguello. He had a cramped office in a non-descript hulk of concrete constituting one of the nastiest excuses for public housing in the city. Tucked into the posh district of Inner Richmond, the project had more rats and roaches than the surrounding neighborhood had poodles and gardeners. We checked out the hallways and a few of the units where tenants were home. A fair number were in their apartments because they were old and disabled— and there was only one working elevator on the property. I scratched out a lowball estimate figuring that extermination wasn't at the top of the housing authority's budget list and the quality of life for the residents would be vastly improved with less vermin, fewer leaking pipes, and another elevator. But I could only do something about one of these.

My next stop was in the Tenderloin, where the minister of GLIDE Memorial United Methodist Church had assembled a coalition of soup kitchen directors from around the city. The Methodists had the oldest and busiest facility, but there were nearly a dozen other church representatives at the meeting. Their plan was to pool their resources and negotiate a good rate for exorcising six-legged demons. Once again, I penciled out a breakeven estimate and hoped to be rewarded in the afterlife. The sinful markup on home treatments in Nob Hill, Pacific Heights and other tony locales subsidized the housing projects and soup kitchens. I figured that if there was a God, he would be pleased.

As I was leaving, the Reverend thanked me for coming and shook my hand which disappeared into his baseball mitt-sized paw. Cecil Williams was very big, black, and brotherly—a fixture in the Tenderloin for two decades. Figuring that he knew everyone and everything, I asked him if he'd heard of a business called the Pleasure Palace that had once operated in his neighborhood. He not only remembered the place near Ellis and Polk, but added that the former owners still lived above the converted storefront—the street level having become a Korean grocery while the upstairs apartment was reputedly a sumptuous den of iniquity.

I had to park a couple blocks from Yee's Restaurant and make my way past laundries, jewelers, and groceries filled with dried everything from fruits, noodles, and mushrooms to sea creatures. Aquamarine lampposts were topped with oriental fixtures and provided street names in English and Chinese characters.

I paused to admire the crispy-skinned poultry hanging in the steamy front window of our lunch spot. Leaving the heads on the roasted birds was off-putting to some diners but I found it more appealing than pressing chickens into nuggets. Before I could open the door, a severe-looking woman with short gray hair and a shorter temper stepped up and asked my name through clenched teeth. I admitted my identity and she handed me a large manila envelope, saying the doctor was running late but wanted me to read the contents while waiting. Turned out she was the good doctor's receptionist, who didn't appreciate my earlier cleverness on the phone. Then she turned on her heel and left.

I went in and reminded myself that Yee's was known for its food, rather than its ambiance which was by-the-numbers Chinese shlock: woodcuts of tigers, washed out paintings of mountains, paper lanterns with red tassels, and gilded dragons. Having snagged a spot in the back corner, I ordered some green tea which a recent article in the *Chronicle* promised would cure cancer, burn fat, strengthen hearts, and shrink prostates. I just wanted something to stave off the damp chill.

Inside the envelope was a scientific article copied from the *Journal of Sex Therapy*. The case study described a man whose mother died when he was a child. When the kid was ten, his father caught him masturbating and beat him severely. Shortly afterwards, the socially awkward lad started keeping "a little zoo" of ants that he allowed to crawl over his inner thighs much to his pleasure (nothing was noted about how the ants felt). As an adolescent, he began masturbating while cockroaches and snails crawled over his scrotum. In his early twenties, he tried having sex with a woman but found it unsatisfying, two legs evidently not appealing to him. So he returned to his menagerie. He found his frequent insect encounters both irresistible and revolting.

At the age of twenty-eight, he sought treatment at a psychiatric clinic for what he called his "disgusting habit." Counseling improved his interactions with women, but after a year he was still sometimes drawn to his six-legged petting zoo. According to the therapist, this was a definitive case of formicophilia: "an uncommon form of zoophilia in which erotic arousal and orgasm are dependent on the sensations produced by small creatures creeping or nibbling on the body, especially the genitalia, perianal area, or nipples." The authors named the condition by combining the Latin words for ants (formica) and love (philia) while managing to heroically avoid any allusions to "ants in the pants."

Dr. Chen's reading assignment accounted for one of the videos Dennis found at the Linford's—and probably explained Lane's insect pals. I was hoping for a continued tutorial as the good doctor came into the restaurant looking somewhat harried. She composed herself on the way to the table, and greeted me cordially if not warmly. Before getting into the world of weird sex, we ordered lunch. I was intrigued by the "assorted pork guts porridge" but went with the less bold choice of roast goose lai fun. She opted for the onion and ginger noodle soup, which seemed a shame given the meaty temptations.

"Did you have a chance to read what Mrs. Miller delivered?" she asked, pouring a tiny cup of smoky green tea.

"I sure did. And it shed a great deal of light on the young man who's wrapped up in the dark mess I described when we last met."

"Darkness, indeed. He's living in the shadows of our society."

"Bestiality is a crime in California, although I'd bet nobody's ever been arrested for making it with the littlest animals."

"We prefer the term 'zoophilia' as it carries less baggage and refers to the attraction with or without consummation. In any case, you can understand how formicophiles would be quite reluctant to seek treatment, given the stigma."

"Now that I know there are guys who get off with insects, there were a couple of other videos you might be able to explain." Her eyebrows arched as she set down the tea cup. "Can you tell me anything about what might be shown on a tape labeled 'Crush: stiletto and crickets'?"

"You appear to have tapped into a most unusual subculture. To wit, there are men who are sexually aroused by watching women crush living organisms. The video probably shows crickets being macerated under a stiletto heel, although there are certainly variations on this theme."

"Variations? Such as grasshoppers and tennis shoes?"

"Not as far as I know. A few fetishists settle for fruits, but the more common objects are snails, worms, spiders, ants, cockroaches, and, of course, crickets. Sometimes newborn mice are used, as well. Tennis shoes aren't noted in the literature, but bare feet, socks, and sandals have been documented, with high heels being perhaps most common."

"Before our food arrives or my appetite departs, what can you tell me about a video labeled 'Penis sting: close-ups'?"

"My, you are a wellspring of unusual sex practices," she said while refilling her teacup.

"I'm not a cultural anthropologist, but there is reportedly an Amazonian people who use bee stings to enlarge the penis." I couldn't help but wince, which Dr. Chen found amusing if I interpreted her smirk correctly. "And in the Kama Sutra, there is mention of using wasps for the same purpose. I suspect the video documents penile swelling." I was left wondering whether her knowledge was purely academic or a tad lascivious.

"I have to ask another question," I said leaning forward. One eyebrow lifted and she nodded inscrutably. "How the hell do you know so much about the sickos who have become entangled, along with my business, in a death scene?" She started to answer but our food arrived and she wisely waited until the waitress was out of earshot. The crispy skin and succulent flesh of my goose trumped our unappetizing topic—and I was famished. Dr. Chen delicately slurped a few spoonfuls of her soup before adopting a scolding, professorial tone.

"Again, Mr. Riley, let us avoid imposing moral judgments on these individuals. Setting that aside for the moment, my knowledge of paraphilia— by which I mean individuals being sexually aroused by atypical objects, actions or situations—comes from my dissertation. Although my clinical internships were quite prosaic, my doctoral research on the etiology and treatment of sexual deviances included a cross-cultural literature review of fetishes."

"Like women's shoes?"

"Well, yes, in part. A fetish involves nonliving objects or non-genital body parts. And clothing, such as shoes or underwear, is the most common stimulus."

"Followed by?" I couldn't contain my curiosity.

"Materials such as rubber, leather, and soft fabrics. Fetishized body parts typically include feet, hair, and bodily fluids. But there are also rare stimuli such as stethoscopes, hats, and diapers."

"Diapers? You're shitting me." I thought my response was clever. She flashed a scowl and then resumed her implacable expression. Properly chastised, I tried another angle. "So, you treat deviants as part of your practice?"

"A few, yes. But there's actually little research on these individuals and even less information regarding treatments. For the most part, fetishists are happy with their lives and don't seek intervention unless the paraphilia is disrupting their marriage or other relationship."

"Like if a guy's wife figures that his having an affair with her shoes isn't quite normal," I offered, which produced the slow head shake of a despondent teacher with a near hopeless student.

"You must understand that what constitutes normal behavior is a cultural construct. In New Guinea, there is a tribe where it is typical for children to engage in sex by the age of ten. Mature women in a South Pacific society have sex with adolescent boys to teach them how to please future partners. Bachelors in a Columbian village copulate with donkeys to avoid the Catholic proscription against premarital sex. The list goes on."

"Your point being that who—or what—constitutes a socially acceptable sexual partner is a matter of tradition?" My goose was getting cold as I'd slowed my eating to a crawl while trying to take in Dr. Chen's tutorial.

"Yes, including here. Until 1973, homosexuality was considered a mental disorder by the American Psychiatric Association. And that change happened only in response to a massive, public protest at our national convention." She sighed and rather daintily slurped a spoonful of soup. "I'm afraid that the leaders in my field had to be forced into confronting their regrettably outdated biases."

"I suppose that every society dictates who gets to have sex with who," I said.

"Whom," she said, correcting my grammar with less reproach than the nuns of my youth. "But don't leave out when and where. Sex during daylight hours is prohibited by the Cuna people of Panama, while the Bambara of Mali believe that outdoor sex will cause their crops to fail." These rules would've put a real crimp in some of Nina's favorite trysts.

"So sex is like food, just a matter of taste." Again with the eyebrows, as she gestured for me to continue. "Most people find blood sausage from my homeland repugnant, and haggis from our Scottish neighbors doesn't appear on many menus in San Francisco." Sheep organs boiled in a sheep's stomach were on par with Yee's "assorted pork guts porridge" which was presumably not a big seller with the tourists. Nor were the famed thousand-year-old eggs, once a person caught a whiff of sulfurous ammonia emanating from the greenish-black lumps.

"I see your point. The last time I was at the Donghuamen Night Market in Beijing, shoppers could purchase chicken testicles and sheep penis. Or to tap into your line of business, one could also snack on fried scorpions, centipedes, spiders, cicadas, and crickets."

"And so we complete the circle, eh? Crushing crickets under high heels or between molars is just another source of pleasure." I rubbed my neck and tried to put together my thoughts, as the good doctor waited patiently. "Look, I can accept that whatever people want to eat is their business, but

I can't buy that 'anything goes' with sex. Gays and lesbians? More power to them. Nobody's getting hurt and somebody's getting satisfied." I was thinking of how happy Carol and Anna were together and how much Nina liked to include nature in our sex life. "But there has to be a line."

"If a person is being mentally harmed or physically exploited, then something's wrong. But that is a difficult standard to apply." She scooped the last of the broth from her bowl and blotted her lips.

"Meaning?"

"Meaning that consent between bondage partners can be complicated. That erotic humiliation is not a simple matter. That a dominatrix walks a fine line. That pornography is rife with ambiguity. And, I should add, that psychological damage can come from the shame of violating a religious edict." As the waitress cleared our dishes, I decided to take one last detour into the dark recesses of the human mind.

"Speaking of damage, a reliable source told me that 'dangerous shit'—in his words—was happening within the circle that might include my insect lover."

"Danger can be an aphrodisiac. Fear and sexual arousal are physiologically similar. Five percent of Americans engage in sadomasochism—and fear play is not uncommon. Sex and violence can be deeply interwoven." I remembered a high school girlfriend who was insatiable after watching me box in the San Francisco Golden Gloves tournament. And according to badge bunnies hanging around the bars, some of my fellow cops were into being handcuffed.

I paid the bill and thanked Dr. Chen for her time. She chided me for deceiving Mrs. Miller and said, "Such behavior will no longer be rewarded." I felt like the child of a psychologist-mother and decided there would be few worse fates for a kid. I also decided that I needed to pay Stefan and Michelle a visit to figure out Lane Linford's place in the depraved network. Maybe his perversion was a 'social construct' but it was my goddamn society and I wasn't going to look the other way if girls were squashing mice or guys were humping donkeys. Actually, I might've looked the other way if I hadn't been dragged into San Francisco's version of a vice cop's wet dream.

CHAPTER SIXTEEN

The buxom redhead at the Pleasure Palace told me that Michelle usually spent Tuesday and Thursday afternoons at home, "field testing" new products with Stefan. So I headed to the Tenderloin, looking for the address that Reverend Williams had given me. At the corner, I found the Korean grocery, along with an ambulance, a patrol car, and two cops doing their best to keep a growing crowd from getting out of hand. I parked a block away and moseyed down to the action which consisted of a ragtag mob of elderly Asians shouting in multiple languages while inadvertently preventing Pak Foods from selling any dried seaweed, fish sauce, or bean paste.

A wrinkled woman was declaring in broken English that the neighborhood would be improved without whoever was being removed by the ambulance, while a man whose weight and age were about the same shook his finger at one of the cops and said that this—whatever "this" was—would have been prevented if the police had done their job stopping the *pyuntay* (or something like that). Others grumbled about the *yang nom*—presumably the same people as the "filthy deviants" who those with a greater grasp of English were disparaging. I took this all to mean that Michelle and Stefan's recreational activities were well known and had led to a need for medical assistance.

With San Francisco's finest occupied by an impending riot of octogenarians, I made my way around the side of the building to the stairway leading to a second floor landing which I presumed the medicos had used to access the apartment. There, I found boxwood and holly in brightly colored pots on either side of an elegantly crafted door with stained glass inserts. The door was ajar and a yappy Yorkshire fervently and futilely guarded the opening.

The tiled entryway was a black and white checkerboard affair leading to a living room evidently decorated by Walt Disney on an acid trip. The furniture consisted of mismatched geometric shapes featuring primary colors. The rugs scattered around the polished, cherry wood floor featured abstract patterns of navy blue, fuchsia, pastel pink and sea green. Artwork, or whatever was hanging on the walls, was evidently the result of Escher and Picasso trying to outdo one another. I heard agitated voices coming from above, so I headed to a spiral staircase with no two stairs of the same color or material.

As I climbed upward, someone was frantically warning others to be careful and not get too close. Around the circular landing at the top were a number of doors, one of which was opened into the source of the excitement. I took it to be the master bedroom, although it might also have been a compromise between a playroom and a gym. In the middle of the room was a king-sized bed surrounded by thick, pastel ropes making it look like a Sesame Street boxing ring. And in the center of the bed, as if knocked out in a fight, lay Michelle. However, she wasn't wearing boxing gloves or, for that matter, anything else. And she wasn't unconscious—she was quite dead, as was apparent from the bluish tint of her creamy skin.

I could smell vomit and the white satin sheets and bearskin bedspread were stained with what looked to be frothy, pink saliva that was also smeared across her face. A distraught man wearing a short, silk robe with a gold-and-maroon paisley pattern and a white fur collar was standing between the paramedics and the body. I took him to be Stefan, and he was torn between wanting help and allowing anyone near the bed, as if whatever had caused Michelle's death was still lurking. One of the paramedics spotted me at the doorway and sidled over as his partner tried to calm Stefan.

"Sir, you'll need to leave," he said to me, keeping an eye on the drama. I expected my presence wasn't going to be welcomed, so I had a story ready to go.

"I'm with the medical examiner's office. The police figured the scene was worth our checking."

"The officers didn't come up, so how would they know?"

"I guess the crowd out there shouting good riddance to their decadent neighbor was enough to create suspicion."

"Okay, but I haven't seen you before," he said, not yet convinced of my legitimacy.

"Transferred from Sacramento. Too much heat, too little seafood." I patted my pockets and grumbled about leaving my identification in the car while explaining, "Dr. Machalek sent me, not that we're looking for work. I don't see anything to make this a crime scene, not that anyone's getting close to the body right now." The mention of the grizzled old cutter did the trick.

"It's a weird one, pal. The guy calls dispatch to say his wife is dying. We get here and he won't let us near the body. He keeps telling us to stay back like something in the sheets is going to get us. But he won't tell us what, if anything."

"Let me try." The guy shrugged and I stepped into the doorway. "Stefan," I said sharply to get his attention. He stopped in mid rant and looked at me quizzically. "These fellows are here to help. Come out here while they do their job." He paused. "Now," I ordered.

Stefan's head swiveled between me and his wife. "Okay," he said, still agitated but emotionally spent and vulnerable to a commanding voice. "But please be quick about it," he told the paramedics. I gestured for Stefan to step out of the room. He had slicked-back hair, a narrow face, and a neatly trimmed goatee. Stefan was as slight of build as Michelle had been sturdy. I told him to wait for a moment and went into the bedroom.

The paramedics had conducted their check of non-existent vital signs and were preparing the body for transport. While they did their job, I made a quick survey of the room and went over to the far side of the bed where I found an empty glass jar next to a large pile of gray fur, as if someone had skinned a giant rabbit. When I picked it up, the result was a cat costume—the sort of thing you might rent for a Halloween party, with one alteration. There was an opening in the crotch. One of the paramedics glanced over.

"Looks like the dude was getting a little pussy," he noted with a sardonic chuckle.

"The guy said that they'd been having sex when she collapsed," his partner said. "From the blood, I'd say heart failure and pulmonary edema. Must've been a wild ride."

"I've heard cats going at it in the alley behind my apartment. Scale that up to this lady's size, and I guess a body can only take so much," the first guy replied while setting up the gurney.

"Her husband didn't look like he could deliver a lethal banging," his partner observed, "but it's easy to underestimate little guys."

I left them to their medical repartee and went out to the landing, where Stefan was pacing.

"Stefan, we need to talk," I said.

"Are you a cop?" His eyes darted from me to the bedroom. "There's nothing to concern the police. We were just having sex when she became ill and . . ." he choked back a sob . . ." she died, right there in our bed."

"I'm not a cop, Stefan."

"Then how do you know my name?" I took his elbow and moved him to the far side of the landing, out of earshot from the bedroom.

"For the moment, let's just say that I'm an interested party who's aware of your business ventures. Now, for your own good, tell me what happened." I increased my pressure on his arm, he struggled and I clamped down.

"Like I said, we were having sex and—"

"Slow down, Stefan. Your version of sex involved more than a quiet afternoon featuring the conventional positions. I found the costume." He sighed and I relaxed my grip.

"Yes, okay then. We enjoyed livening up our sex life. Sometimes Michelle liked to experiment with animal costumes. There's nothing wrong with that."

"So, there you were humping your cat woman when she collapsed?" He looked back at the bedroom. When I released his arm, he started fidgeting with the belt of his bathrobe.

"That's right, we were just having sex." His speech slowed and he blinked rapidly. He repeated, "We were just having sex," but he might as well have said, "I'm just lying to you."

"And so, you removed her costume and called 911?"

"Yes, she was sweating and said her heart was racing, so I undressed her. When I got back from calling for help, she was dead. There was blood coming from her mouth. It was awful."

"I can imagine." I feigned sympathy to keep him talking. "So what's the problem with the paramedics getting close to the bed?" Stefan continued to twist the ends of his bathrobe tie.

"I was just scared."

"Scared of what?" He swallowed and took a deep breath. The guy was a terrible liar. Even Lane Linford was better.

"That they'd find the costume and try to humiliate me." Here was a porn film director supposedly worried that screwing his wife in a furry costume would be his undoing. I wasn't buying it.

Our conversation was interrupted by the paramedics wheeling the gurney out of the bedroom and struggling to work the body down the spiral staircase. When they got the whole assemblage out the door, Stefan collected himself and realized that I hadn't explained my presence.

"I want to know who you are and why you're here," he insisted. There seemed little reason for deception, so I opted for the truth.

"My name's Riley. And here's the short version of why I'm here. The Pleasure Palace had a customer, Lane Linford, who availed himself of your services in acquiring a six-legged alibi."

"Alibi? For what?"

"Murder, or at least two suspicious deaths which will put my business at risk if the whole sordid story comes to light. And that story involves a further financial transaction with your wife, who blackmailed Mr. Linford. I believe she was in possession of a videotape showing him engaged in a compromising activity."

"What is your business and how is it involved?"

"I am the owner of Goat Hill Extermination. Mr. Linford's efforts to acquire the money needed to pay your wife involved a poisoning, probably accidental. But my company could be implicated in having provided the chemicals. And, I might suggest that your business could also be dragged into the spotlight. So, to protect my interests, I need to find out just what the hell happened with Linford and your wife." Halfway through my answer, Stefan stopped listening and began to stare into space.

"My God, what incredibly good fortune. You're an exterminator?" Nobody had ever expressed such relief upon discovering my profession, let alone a man whose bloody, naked wife had just been hauled to the morgue.

"Yes. Flies, roaches, rats, pigeons, whatever you have that you don't want."

Stefan was suddenly giddy. "Do you have something to kill a spider?"

"Sure. Spiders are easy. Some insects have developed resistance to various chemicals and many species hide in hard-to-reach places. But spiders are susceptible to most insecticides and they tend to either hang out in easily found webs or wander around. Do you have spiders? Or maybe one particularly problematical spider? In that case, a well-placed shoe is more sensible that spraying a whole room."

"The bedroom. I want to have the bedroom sprayed. And I need it done today, right away. I'll pay anything, whatever you ask." Ah, those magical words from a prosperous pervert (Dr. Chen's admonition about terminology notwithstanding). I figured the standard price for a whole house treatment, added an affluence surcharge, tagged on my contemptible customer tax, and then doubled the result to reflect the emergency timeline. Stefan didn't blink when I gave him the number. I kicked myself for not aiming higher.

I didn't have a sprayer in my truck, so the fastest way to arrange a treatment was to call Carol and have her send one of the guys with the chemicals and equipment. Stefan directed me downstairs to the phone in the kitchen. The lemon yellow walls clashed spectacularly with the hot pink refrigerator. Where the hell does a person find appliances in neon colors? Carol said that Larry had just come back from a job and he'd head to the Tenderloin as soon as he loaded up. I told her to have him meet me at PhanTastic Coffee which was a block down from the spider caper.

After telling Stefan I'd be back shortly with the big guns, I headed to Phan's to put together a plan for dealing with a mysterious spider and a bathrobed dandy while savoring a cup of Vietnamese coffee. The French might've left behind a political mess in Southeast Asia, but their culinary legacy included amazing pastries and exceptional coffee.

Chapter Seventeen

Larry came into Phan's, nodded to me and went to the counter. He ordered ca phe sua nong in what was evidently passable Vietnamese. I'll never understand why he finds such pleasure in the cuisine of a place that holds such horrible memories for him. On the other hand, slowly dripping bitter coffee through a filter into sweetened, condensed milk makes a remarkable drink, perhaps because the damned thing takes so long to make. But Larry didn't appear to be in any great hurry, despite Carol having presumably expressed a sense of urgency in sending him to meet me.

He came over to the table, one of those white, wrought iron numbers that you'd expect in a Parisian café. Larry had his coffee and a plate of spherical, sesame seed-coated fritters.

"Glad you could find time for an afternoon snack," I said. He ignored my jab which wasn't fair given how hard he'd been working to fill in for my absence—and we both knew it.

"They're *banh cam*—orange cake. Try one." He slid the plate across the glass-topped table. I took a bite.

"Orange? Tastes like gooey rice with coconut and vanilla. Good flavor, bad name."

"*Mi chang* are so easily confused," he muttered. "The name refers to the appearance, not the flavor."

"Yeah, right. So, now that I've had my lesson and you've had your goodies, maybe we can get down to work."

"Absolutely, boss." He popped an entire orange cake into his mouth and chewed contentedly. After washing down the pastry with a slug of coffee, he pushed aside the empty plate. "What's the deal? Carol said it was an emergency job involving spiders, so I loaded up a tank of permethrin."

"Probably overkill. I suspect we're dealing with one spider."

"One? You had me motor across town to spray a spider? Maybe you could've stepped on it, although with your dancing talents that might've been a challenge." At the company Christmas party, we rearranged the bedraggled furniture in the warehouse to make space for a dance floor upon Dennis's insistence. I had a bit too much of the spiked eggnog and made the mistake of being coaxed into a pitiable attempt to move in synchrony to the throbbing beat produced by one of Carol's pop musicians. After the gang was done laughing, Dennis observed that the song, "Let's Work," was aptly named given how much labor I'd expended. My performance was fast becoming a Goat Hill Extermination legend.

"I'm glad everyone's getting such mileage out of that unfortunate holiday incident. As for today's job, stepping on the spider was not an option. The guy is frantic and wants the room sprayed. We're clearing a hefty profit from this one."

"I thought we didn't use insecticides unless they were needed. Isn't that sort of how we got into the Linford mess?"

"Good point, but I didn't see any chance of changing Stefan's mind."

"So he's mental, eh? And rich."

"That would about cover it. But I need you to take your time and poke around to see if you can find the spider."

"Won't this Stefan guy freak?"

"Probably, but I want him rattled, somewhere between anxious and panicked, to erode his defenses. He's connected to the Linford case. His wife was blackmailing Lane and I want to figure out what the hell was going on."

"You could ask him," said Larry, throwing back the last of his coffee.

"Tried that. He's hiding something."

"Yeah, a frickin' spider."

We headed up the street, with Larry carrying a two-gallon sprayer. At the apartment, he took in the surroundings and asked me if Pee-wee Herman was the interior decorator. Stefan was upstairs standing guard outside the bedroom.

Larry started systematically looking under and behind the furniture, working his way around the perimeter of the room. I focused on the bathroom as the creature's potential lair, although a spider would need pretty weird taste to choose a floor featuring pink marble and a haphazard mosaic of multicolored tiles. I made sure that the spider hadn't fallen into the square sink or the sunken tub.

Meanwhile, Larry was doing a great job of cranking up Stefan's dread by leaving the bed until last—the most likely place for the spider to be hiding. After rummaging through the sheets and tossing them aside, he dropped down on all fours to look under the bed.

"Holy shit," he said, reaching inside his coveralls for a penlight.

"Whatcha got?" I asked as Stefan retreated toward the door.

"There's a big-ass spider under here, at least four inches across including its legs. Black, shiny and definitely pissed." I knelt down beside him and had a look. The spider was rearing up and gaping its fangs like something out of a horror movie.

"You had a right to be unhinged," I said to Stefan over my shoulder. While crawling under buildings I'd encountered angry rats backed into corners, along with a memorable showdown involving an ill-tempered raccoon in an attic. But insects and spiders had the good sense to retreat from exterminators—with the notable exception of this bruiser looking for a fight.

"That is one mean mother. I take back anything I said about your not stomping on that fucker." Larry wasn't prone to using profanity in front of customers, except in extreme situations. This one qualified. "What should we do?"

"I don't want to mash it or we won't figure out what it is."

"Believe it or not, Riley, I think I know what it is. But I'll take a closer look once we have it subdued."

"We could try catching it in the jar Stefan left next to the bed," I suggested. "But that beast is damned serious about causing some hurt, and I'd rather not see either of us on the receiving end." It was still poised on its rear legs, with the front four legs waving in the air and its fangs held wide.

"I heartily advocate a dose of permethrin to even the odds," Larry said, reaching for the spray tank. I didn't have a better idea. In the background, Stefan was almost in tears, murmuring, "Just kill it, please just kill it," over and over. Larry hit it with a shot of insecticide and within a few seconds the spider was thrashing violently in its death throes.

Neither of us was excited about reaching under the bed and grabbing the presumably, but not certainly, dead creature. Larry took one of the paintings off the wall, slid it under the spider and pulled it out from under the bed like a pizza from the oven. The enormous, shiny black body on the glass contrasted with the sky blue background, hot pink squiggly lines and electric green saw-toothed shapes. The spider definitely enhanced the art.

"Okay Stefan, the drama is over. Now explain what the hell this was doing under your bed," I said. He answered from the doorway.

"Michelle was frightened of spiders, and we'd use them to get her excited. Usually, she'd get aroused just by having a tarantula in a jar on the bed. Sometimes I'd make her lie still and have the spider walk on her naked body. She'd become so hot that I could hardly get the thing back into the jar before she was all over me."

"Let me guess. This afternoon you took the spider for a walk across your wife but something went wrong."

"Exactly. I knew tarantulas didn't bite, but when this spider tumbled out of the jar onto her belly, it reared up and really terrified her. I tried to brush it off with a pillow, but it bit her several times like it was crazed before I could knock it to the floor. I trapped it under the jar."

"And then?"

"Well, she was definitely aroused but the bites really hurt. I asked her to put nipple clamps on me so we could share in the pain. We had really intense sex for about fifteen minutes and then it was her turn to decide what came next." Larry stood there, shaking his head.

"And she opted for the cat costume?" I was becoming unfazed, although I made a mental note that it was to their credit that one of them dressed up as a big cat rather than involving their little dog.

"Yes. She had it on when she became sick to her stomach. I thought it was a lingering effect of the fear and pain. But then she started sweating and trembling. I helped her out of the costume and went to get her some water.

By the time I got back, she said her mouth was tingling and her heart was racing. I tried to calm her down. When she started having muscle spasms and passed out, I went to call for help. That's when I knocked over the jar and the spider dashed under the bed. You pretty much know what happened after that."

Stefan looked sickly, so we took him into an adjacent room furnished as bizarrely as the living room. He laid down on the couch and I took a chair. Larry went over to examine a projection television with one of those gigantic, four-foot-wide screens. As the color slowly returned to Stefan's face, which had been almost as white as the ermine collar of his bathrobe, I marveled at what compelled anyone to engage in dangerous, even deadly, sex. Dr. Chen had explained the similarity of fear and arousal, but a woman needing foreplay with a spider doesn't say much for the guy's abilities. However, what with how easily AIDS is being passed around these days—and I guessed that Stefan's interests were not limited to women, let alone his wife—the possibility of lethal sex is becoming normal, whatever that means.

"Alright Larry," I said, as Stefan starting looking less nauseous, "you heard the plot for this afternoon's soap opera, but it would make more sense if I knew the characters. What did you mean when you said you knew what spider we had cornered?"

"When I was on my way to Nam, I was stationed for six weeks in Australia at Base Richmond, about thirty miles from Sydney. The Brits ran the operation, and they were gonzo about poisonous spiders and snakes. I guess there aren't any in England, so the RAAF training included having some guy from the Sydney Zoo come to the base, show us live specimens, and lecture about ways to avoid dying Down Under before giving the VC a chance to end our misery." He flashed the lopsided smile that tended to punctuate his less gruesome war stories.

"And one of the creatures resembled our little eight-legged voyeur?"

"To a T. I'm willing to bet a pitcher of Guinness at O'Donnell's that we hosed a Sydney funnel-web spider. Whoever provided that bad boy to our customer here was either really stupid—or meant to kill somebody."

"Any ideas, Stefan? Did Michelle's supplier have a reason to want her dead?" I asked.

"I don't know. Maybe. She had questionable dealings with some unsavory sorts." I couldn't keep my face from registering confused amazement. "I know, you think that I'm unsavory. Let me tell you, what I do with lovers is consensual."

"No need to explain yourself. Just tell me about these shady associates," I said.

"I told her we were making plenty of money without having to do business with psychopaths. But she was a fiercely independent woman. I can imagine she might have become involved in some sort of double-cross or extortion or whatever you call these situations."

"Okay, but why would anyone take a chance by using a spider? If someone wanted your wife dead, why not just stage a robbery or mugging that went bad."

"The police investigate shootings and Michelle's death appeared natural," he said. I might've questioned the naturalness of the setting, but I understood his point. The paramedics would report heart failure, the cops would concur, and there'd be no autopsy. Suspicious circumstances trigger a postmortem, but this was a just a case of weirdness—and San Francisco was up to her hairy armpits in weird.

"I'm not about to call the cops and have them digging into my sex life," Stefan declared. "That bastard in the district attorney's office, Grant Roberts, is waging a holy war on anyone who seeks satisfaction outside of biblical guidelines. Whoever gave her that spider knew that my reporting how she died would give Roberts what he needed to destroy the Pleasure Palace. They've already raided Big Richard's and The Pussy Cat on trumped up warrants."

"Or," said Larry, "maybe the spider provider was a nutcase with a twisted sense of drama." Dr. Chen probably would've objected to Larry's terminology. I found it appropriate to the moment. We sat in silence, each processing a very bizarre afternoon by anyone's standards. Finally, Stefan pulled himself together and spoke up.

"I have a business proposition, Riley. The way you handled those paramedics earlier suggests to me that you have more than passing familiarity with law enforcement. Am I correct?"

"That's quite perceptive for a man who was somewhere between distraught and hysterical. You're right, I was a detective with the San Francisco police before an unfortunate event led to my leaving the force and taking over the family extermination business."

"I don't think we need to know more about one another's past than is necessary. Wouldn't you agree?" I nodded and he continued, "We have a shared interest in protecting our businesses, and I have a particular interest in settling a score." How this little piss ant was going to get even with anyone wasn't my problem. Getting to the bottom of the Lane and Michelle show was. I glanced over at Larry who shrugged and gave me his you're-the-boss look.

"Go on," I said.

"I want to you to find Michelle's killer. Your investigative skills led you to her and I am asking you to keep going. I can pay very well and I am very discrete. Are you willing?"

I'd come this far. How much slimier could this get? At least that was how I saw things at the time. In retrospect, I'd consistently underestimated the potential of my fellow man to find pleasure in revolting behaviors. This didn't occur to me before I answered Stefan.

"I am willing, but our association must be covert. I have a license to kill pests, not one to investigate human vermin. Payment will be in cash at a daily rate the same as today's emergency treatment." I would've put the financial screws to him, but he might've enjoyed the monetary pain—and I felt inexplicably sorry for the guy. Sort of like the time I saw a greasy wharf rat satisfying its hunger with a used tampon.

"Most certainly," he said.

"Then we have a deal, under one condition."

Chapter Eighteen

"I need the truth," I said. "Your dark little secret about what was under the bed could've gotten someone killed. I have no intention of dying in the process of finding your wife's killer and keeping my business out of whatever the hell she had going with Lane Linford."

"I was scared," Stefan said.

"Let me put it this way. If you give me half-truths, I'll make sure that you are the one crawling under the bed. Not me or my people."

Larry grunted and headed to the bedroom to gather up his equipment and the lethal fetish which would make an impressive addition to the collection of creatures that he and Dennis had arranged in their warehouse living room. The spider would fit nicely between the mummified, foot-long tail that Larry had lopped off the biggest rat he'd ever whacked and the beach ball-sized paper wasp nest that Dennis had collected from under the eaves of the clubhouse at the Presidio golf course.

"If we're going to get anywhere," I said, "I need to start with your telling me who provided Michelle with her animals."

"You have to understand that confidentiality is critical to the Pleasure Palace."

"And you have to understand that without a lead, there's no investigation. We're done." I headed toward the door.

"Wait. Give me a minute to check our records," he said, brushing past me and disappearing into a room at the far end of the hall. Larry came out of the bedroom, gave me a wry smile, offered me good luck, and headed downstairs into the slate gray afternoon. I poked my head into the office where Stefan was rifling through a file drawer. While the rest of the apartment looked like a demented kindergarten, this room looked like a high-end lawyer's office.

"Find anything?"

"Michelle used a network of suppliers, depending on what was needed. Most customers didn't want to risk buying from pet stores, so she'd provide standard animals like gerbils and mice as well as more exotic creatures." I didn't want to think too much about how rodents were incorporated into the sexual practices of their clientele.

"And you didn't get involved in that end of the business—other than playing spider man when she needed some leggy arousal?" He looked hurt. I didn't much care about his feelings, but I needed him to stay focused— and the guy was starting to flag. He pulled out a stack of folders as if they weighed twenty pounds and plopped them on the desk.

"I handled the bookkeeping. Michelle worked with the customers. She was the people-person, cultivating the trust of those who society judged to be reprehensible. Her compassion and discretion were key to the success of our special orders, which were both exciting and lucrative. You can only sell so many dildos and vibrators before getting bored, you know." I didn't, but I could imagine titillation eventually becoming numbness, so to speak.

"And, I gather, you did some film directing on the side?"

"That was more of a hobby than a business. Michelle was also into videos, making shorts for a wide range of tastes. We sold a few out of the back room of the store, while keeping the standard stock out front." He continued to flip through the manila folders. "Here we go. This one has our payments to her supplier of insects and spiders. There's not tremendous demand, so I couldn't remember his name without finding the invoice." Stefan pulled out a piece of paper and hesitated. Providing their source was a violation of trust, and he was a principled pervert.

He handed me the sheet, which listed Bug Broker Ltd., a company at the Mission Rock Terminal, owned by Sam Scudder. The invoice described the company as "The West Coast's Leading Supplier of Live Insects and Spiders," and in smaller type proclaimed: "Providing film studios, zoological parks, pet stores, and private collectors since 1962." There was no mention of sex shops. The file contained invoices for Madagascar hissing cockroaches, death's head roaches, field crickets, lubber grasshoppers, Chilean rose tarantulas, Mexican red-kneed tarantulas, nightcrawlers, and banana slugs. The wholesale prices were impressive, five bucks for a meaty cockroach and twenty bucks for a leggy tarantula. The Pleasure Palace's customers presumably paid retail, but a fifty dollar spider is a better deal than a hooker if you take into account that the spider won't steal your wallet or give you the clap.

As I perused the paperwork, Stefan moved to an upholstered leather chair. He propped his elbow on the armrest and cradled his head in his hand, eyelids sagging. In one afternoon, the fellow had managed to have wild sex, lose his wife, survive a deadly spider, and betray a business confidence.

"Stefan," I said and his eyes snapped open, "you're wrung out and there's no sense pushing further today."

"Sorry Riley, I just nodded off for a sec."

"Get some sleep and then think long and hard about the last couple of weeks with Michelle and anything that could've made someone angry enough to want her dead. I'll stop by Sunday morning and hope that you've remembered something useful."

Stefan got up slowly and shook my hand with an effeminate grip. He was repugnant, but impossible to fully loathe. My memory flashed back to that disgusting wharf rat, doing what rodents do—using its natural tendencies to satisfy a biological hunger using whatever a screwed up world provided.

On my way home, I swung by Nina's place. The afternoon with Stefan had left me with an uneasy feeling about her stalker. I double-parked in front of the apartment complex and stepped out of my truck. Between the twilight and a misty rain, I couldn't see clearly across the courtyard. But furtive movement near a corner staircase caught my eye, and I headed over to see who was trying not to be seen. A bulky figure in a fatigue jacket scurried from the stairs toward the alley. I started to give chase, but he had a head start and panic on his side.

The guy disappeared before I rounded the corner. Although I didn't see his face, I had no doubt it was Tim—and wariness was all he had learned from my recent tutorial. On my next visit, I'd take his education to another level, leaving even the slowest student of 'boundaries'—as Nina put it—with an unforgettable lesson. I almost found pleasure in contemplating what he had coming, as if kicking a wharf rat made the waterfront any cleaner.

I headed to Finlay's in South Beach, the best fish and chips place in the city. The thick fries have a crunchy exterior with a fluffy inside and the fish is California flounder with a golden crust. You get a wedge of lemon, a container of malt vinegar and a sneer if you ask for tartar sauce. They wrap the whole works in newspaper and send you away with a side of mushy peas. I spread the feast onto my kitchen table and cracked open a Harp Lager I'd picked up on the way home as the perfect way to wash down the meal. The mail contained the normal assortment of advertisements and bills, but perusing the newly arrived BioQuip catalogue—with its selection of insect pins, black light traps, and collecting nets—made for satisfyingly mindless reading while eating.

After dinner, I treated myself to a glass of Tullamore Dew and put on the 1965 recording of *Salome* featuring Birgit Nilsson in the title role. Some aficionados prefer the studio recording from a few years earlier, but there's something less authentic when the performers are not on stage. Moreover, Fritz Uhl made a better King Herod than did Gerhard Stolze, whose energy faded in the later scenes, which is to be expected when there's no live audience to engage. And so my evening combined one of Ireland's finest whiskeys with one of Germany's strangest operas.

As I pinned and labeled a series of bees that Tommy and I had collected last summer from patches of gumweed and star thistle, I wondered what people would make of a fellow deriving pleasure from impaling dead insects while sipping a toxin (as I learned during my hard drinking days on the force). My source of entomological satisfaction wouldn't fall into what society deemed normal, but there's surely a difference between the gratification that comes from a cabinet of insects in my living room and a jar with a spider in another man's bedroom.

I remembered the time my father was first showing me how to make an insect collection and I didn't leave a California root borer in the killing jar long enough before pinning the creature. I was excited by having caught such an enormous beetle at our porch light—a female stretching nearly four inches including her antennae. Being a kid, I wanted to get the insect into my collection before bedtime. When I went to look at my trophy in the morning, the beetle was slowly flailing its legs while suspended on the pin. I was so horrified that I nearly gave up collecting, but my father dispatched the insect in the freezer and assured me that I'd made a beginner's error. He explained that what I'd done was not a moral failing unless I either intended unnecessary pain to the creature or failed to learn from my mistake. I learned that killing has to be done well. It matters how one takes life—or makes love.

Having pinned the well and truly dead bees, I refilled my glass and settled into the recliner with the readings Scott Fortier had given me a couple days ago after my louse lesson at Berkeley. The one that caught my eye was a copy of a chapter from Vladimir Nabokov's autobiography. Nabokov was the entomologist, or more precisely the lepidopterist, who wrote *Lolita*, the story of a middle-aged man who becomes sexually obsessed with his twelve-year-old stepdaughter.

Scott had paper-clipped to the chapter a copy of a review of the play based on the novel and performed at the Testiclovary Theater. The venue was named for the statistical peculiarity that the "average" person has one testicle and one ovary (as the theater notes on their marquee) by dividing the number of each gonad by the number of humans. This mathematical tidbit is supposed to undermine conventional notions of what is normal and natural. But it mostly undermines comprehension.

Lolita had been staged on Broadway last year and was panned by the New York critics using phrases that were about as brutal as pinning a live insect. Of course any theatrical production promising to meld perversion and art is worth reviving in San Francisco. However, the local review was about as lukewarm as Michelle's body when the paramedics strapped her to the gurney.

Also attached to the chapter was an article copied from Harvard's alumni magazine about the university's Museum of Comparative Zoology, including a sidebar that Scott had highlighted. Although lacking advanced training in entomology, Nabokov had been the museum's de facto curator of Lepidoptera. The museum houses Nabokov's "genitalia cabinet"—a remarkable collection of male genitals belonging to the 'blues,' a large subfamily of butterflies that Nabokov discovered could be distinguished by their sex organs. He spent so many hours studying the insects' privates under a microscope that he permanently damaged his eyesight. This struck me as an ironic demonstration that, "if you don't stop, you'll go blind." However, the magazine didn't make this connection—the Ivy League not being known for its sense of humor.

Scott's real purpose in giving me the chapter from Nabokov's autobiography was penned at the top: "Riley, check your collection for any of these." In the chapter, Nabokov described finding a rare, gynandromorph butterfly—a specimen with a genetic anomaly in which one half of the insect was male and the other half was female. The condition is relatively easy to discern in species where the sexes have distinctively different coloration. I figured that Scott was hoping I might have such a specimen unnoticed in my collection that I'd donate to the Essig Museum. But after an hour of careful searching, I came up with zilch. Seems I was better at finding bizarre forms of human sex than discovering weird forms of butterfly sexes.

I assuaged my disappointment with another glass of Tullamore, thereby affirming my lack of judgment and moderation. But the velvety warmth lusciously offset the cold, wet night. The sound of the wind and pattering rain complemented the grimness of the opera. I'd not paid attention to the music while searching for deformed butterflies, so I placed the stylus onto the outer third of the record, and drifted into the scene where Salome is being offered anything by Herod—her lecherous stepfather—if she will perform the dance of the seven veils, which some productions turn into a full-blown, high-brow strip tease. I read somewhere that Flaubert's version of the story described Salome as dancing like a gigantic beetle, a detail he extracted from a carving on a French cathedral showing the temptress dancing on her hands. Maybe Lane and his fellow formicophiles were onto something.

After her dance, Salome demands that the king, who was almost as turned on by her naked feet as the rest of her body, lop off the head of a holy man who earlier refused her advances—and deliver this payment to her on a silver platter. Herod is fine with incest but appalled by beheading. However, he makes good on his promise and watches his stepdaughter kiss the bloody head of the chaste prophet. While hell hath no fury like a woman scorned, Judea hath no rage like a king disgusted. So Herod orders his soldiers to kill Salome and they rush forward to crush her like a revolting insect beneath their shields.

I tossed back the last swallow of whiskey, turned off the stereo and the lights, headed upstairs and fell into bed. In the darkness, I reviewed the day, concluding that humans have been screwed up for at least a couple thousand years—and that having genitals and imagination but lacking morality is a very dangerous mix.

Chapter Nineteen

I woke up with a cottony mouth and queasy gut reminding me that moderation is increasingly advisable, perhaps virtuous, with age. Even a fine whiskey can punish a guy in his forties—not unlike how cheap beer can make a thirteen-year-old kid regret stealing a six-pack from Hill Top Grocery with his kid brother and getting caught by their father who teaches them a lesson about shoplifting and boozing by insisting that the big brother drink four cans while the younger is assigned two. Maybe virtue is its own reward, but wickedness delivers its own punishment.

I decided to start my morning at Gustaw's Bakery with a mug of his caffeinated sludge. Another instance of poor judgment, as it turned out. Ludwika noticed my condition, having had decades of practice with her husband. I soon decided that my father's lesson was a cakewalk compared to how a Polish babushka deals with a wayward man. I'd previously experienced her kefir—a thick, grainy version of sour milk designed to settle stomachs, or so she claimed. However, Ludwika was out of kefir, so she resorted to the alternative remedy for hangovers which she probably used to remind Gustaw that his vodka indulgences had unfortunate consequences. The old Pole shook his head sympathetically as his wife brought me a glass of pickle juice, whisked away my coffee, and commanded, "Drink. First sour, then fat. I make food to complete the cure,"

As she bustled back into the kitchen, I noticed a newly framed cover from *Time* magazine on the wall behind the cash register, proclaiming Lech

Walesa as man of the year. All it took was letting my gaze settle on the picture and Gustaw took his cue to regale me with a political tirade about the Soviet occupation of his homeland and the courageous countrymen who defied their oppressors. Like Walesa, Gustaw had worked at the Gdansk shipyard so he felt a bond to the leader of the nation's Solidarity movement. Gustaw insisted that more than a quarter of Poland had joined the trade union which seemed a tad exaggerated, but I wasn't about to challenge an impassioned former shipbuilder whose biceps, even with age and disuse, were damned near the size of my thighs.

"One month, Riley," he said pounding my table while ignoring the couple who'd come into the shop and looked to be calculating whether the goodies were worth engaging a colossal, agitated Pole, "that is how long Poland has been under martial law. If I could reach across the ocean I'd beat General Jurazelski with a hammer and slice him open with a sickle."

"He's the fellow who declared martial law, I gather." My efforts to calm Gustaw were working about as well was the pickle juice was working to settle my innards.

"A traitor. He's no Pole. The bastard is a *katsap*," he growled using what I took to be an insult but didn't figure that asking would help defuse the situation. Gustaw stepped back and folded his muscular arms across his massive chest. "At least President Reagan stops trade with the Soviet bastards after police shot mine workers in Katowice. Police are criminal dogs." I nodded supportively but was losing track of the diatribe as his English deteriorated. Ludwika came out of the kitchen, drawn by the tinkling of bells from the door and the absence of anything sounding like a greeting to the customers.

"Gustaw, shame on you," she said. "We are running a bakery, not a union hall. Behave yourself and help these people." The couple seemed relieved to have someone attend to them, even if it was a still grumbling bear of a man. Ludwika brought me ruchanki—apple fritters—and a glass filled with an orange concoction.

"Kogel mogel," she declared. "Drink."

"What is it?"

"Drink. I beat raw egg yolks and sugar, add whipped cream and then orange juice. Drink." It sounded better than kefir, which wasn't saying much.

As the couple paid for their poppy seed rolls, I washed down my deep-fat fried medicine with the thick tonic, left a fiver on the table and snuck out before Ludwika could impose further Polish treatments.

When I got to the shop, I was feeling better although still in need of caffeine. I poured a cup from Carol's coffeemaker. The scalding liquid was less painful than the insipid pop music. A pair of marginally competent crooners declared their endless love for one another. The lyrics and plaintive orchestration were more syrupy than Gustaw's sweetest pastry. I turned down the volume.

"Hey Riley, show some respect for Diana Ross and Lionel Richie," she said.

"I will, when they respect the taste and intelligence of the public."

"Well aren't you in a grumpy mood for a Friday."

"Not at all, babe. I have such good news that you'll be happy to have that vapid duo silenced."

"I'm waiting."

"Yesterday afternoon I landed a sizable payment for that spider extermination. And my pursuit of the twisted tale of Lane Linford has led to a lucrative contract for my off-the-books services as an investigator."

"The cash flow is welcomed, given the state of our accounts. But I'm not sure that it justifies your monkeying with my radio."

"Ah, my love, there's more." I'd made up my mind while munching on Ludwika's apple fritters, although recognizing that omens were not the best way to make business decisions. "I think this recent windfall provides what we need for you to buy your Apple computer." She jumped up from her chair, squeezed the sides of my face into a pucker, and gave me a big kiss followed by a breasty hug. If she'd been straight, Nina might've had something to worry about. As it was, I simply enjoyed the womanly, if platonic, warmth. We both knew her effusive gratitude was a performance for our mutual benefit, sustaining the appearance that the decision was mine to make and that it was possible for me to have said no.

"So, what are Larry and Dennis up to this fine, drizzly morning?" I asked once she turned me loose.

"I had them stocking a shipment of chemicals that arrived late yesterday. But while they were doing that, the public housing director called and accepted your bid for the job on Aguello. So now the boys are loading up for the big treatment."

"Okay, anything else I should know?"

"Yes. Lieutenant Papadopoulos called and said you should meet him at ten o'clock at some place called Sappho's Sweets in the Tenderloin. If you aren't there, then you become a 'person of interest' in the deaths of the Linfords—and he said he'd sure hate for that development to get out to the press, what with our business needing to maintain a good public image."

"Very subtle of him. I guess he's anxious for an update." I turned her radio back up to fill the air with the gravelly strains of some guy pleading for a woman to return to him. He evidently couldn't remember her name and just sung "Lady" to woo his true love. I suspect he was more successful attracting record producers than women.

"And Riley," she called out as I headed down the hall, "see if you can get through the calls on your desk before rendezvousing with your Greek pal."

Carol had crammed more "While you were out" notes into my inbox than dollar bills in a stripper's G-string. For the rest of the morning, I made calls and charmed customers with better lines than a pop singer in heat. Winter wasn't usually a busy season, but I guess even the vermin weren't keen on being outside in the cold rain. The little bastards were gathering in furnace rooms, kitchen cabinets, and bathroom sinks without having the good sense to stay hidden.

One distraught and unladylike woman with a talent for graphic description was beside herself having seen, "a cockroach with some huge thing out its hind end, either an erection or a turd and in either case I want the revolting creature out of my house." I explained that it was most likely a female extruding an egg case, but this didn't reduce her disgust with the exhibitionist insect. I put her down for a treatment early next week and she seemed pacified, although not pleased with having to live with six-legged flashers through the weekend.

After making a dozen calls, I headed to Sappho's Sweets on the corner of Turk and Eddy. The place wasn't a strip club, as the name might suggest, but a Greek bakery. I found Lieutenant Papadopoulos looking dapper, with an ankle resting on the opposite knee to draw attention to his two hundred dollar loafers. He was sipping coffee and munching on what looked like a biscotti, but I gathered from the menu board was a paximathakia.

"What's good in this joint?" I asked, feeling my appetite returning. Papadopoulos uncrossed his leg and dunked the cookie into his coffee.

"This 'joint,' as you call it, is one of the venerable, legit businesses left in the Tenderloin. We are just a block from the location of my father's shoe repair shop, which was a viable business back when people valued workmanship. He sold the store after the old neighborhood was drained of its vitality by the soulless bastards who built the Bay Bridge through the heart of Greek town. I'm glad he didn't live to see what's become of this neighborhood."

"Yeah, right. So, what is delectable at this fine establishment?"

"I'd recommend the koulouria, not too sweet, and the hint of lemon and vanilla is perfect with Greek coffee. And the kourambiethis will melt in your mouth like the finest shortbread." I grabbed one of each and returned to the table with a cup of coffee that rivaled Gustaw's for potency and a glass of ice water that the lady behind the counter insisted went with the coffee.

"So Lieutenant, what's on your mind?" He didn't look amused.

"I need an update on the Linford case."

"It's only been a few days. I'm trying to run a business while digging into the dark corners of the city's two-legged vermin."

"I get it, but Grant Roberts is chomping at the bit for some arrests that will please the righteous and wealthy who have what it takes to propel him from assistant DA to the top banana in the next election."

"So the sleazebag needs to bag some sleaze?" He gave a slight nod. "And I suppose that having your name wrapped up in a big case wouldn't hurt the chances of making captain." The shortbread was every bit as good as he'd promised.

"I'm just trying to solve murders," he snarled, setting his stout coffee cup onto the saucer with a clink to punctuate his annoyance. "And if I can do that and keep decent people from being endangered by freaks, so much the better."

"I'm making progress, if wading into a deepening cesspool of deviance counts as progress. But I don't want to bring the police into the sewage at this point because you'll just spook the bottom dwellers. Besides, you wouldn't want to get those fine shoes filthy." He plucked a handkerchief from the breast pocket of his coat and buffed the toe of a shoe.

"Okay, I'll give you until the end of next week."

"That's generous of you. In the meantime, I hope you can find one of those twofer deals—murder and vice all wrapped up and ready to deliver to the DA." The koulouria was arguably better than its buttery, sweet competitor. If I wasn't such a loyal guy and Sappho's was closer to my house, I'd be tempted to cheat on Gustaw.

"I might have caught just the case which is why I'm giving you a few days. Last night, the Tenderloin reverted to its namesake with a major orgy."

"C'mon Lieutenant, a bunch of folks sweating and humping is hardly the launching pad to captain. Besides, there's nothing illegal about group sex, is there?"

"Nothing, unless you charge admission, include sixteen-year-olds, and end the evening with a dead kid who was either the stupid result of erotic asphyxiation—or the homicidal result of an overzealous partner."

"Murder?"

"Depraved indifference, at least. In fact, that will probably play even better in the papers. Roberts will love working 'depraved' into the charges. There's not much doubt that someone, or perhaps several someones, at the pecker party knew the dumb shit was trying for the magic moment when a guy reaches orgasm and unconsciousness at the same time. It's supposed to be as good as a coke high."

"Wasn't there something in the *Chronicle* awhile back about a nutcase artist offing himself while trying to get off?"

"Yeah. It was before I moved to homicide, but vice was involved in the investigation. Some transvestite who went by the name of Von Boday or something like that. He or she or whatever thought comic books were art

134

and hanging yourself was foreplay. Never did nail anyone, although his kid was supposedly in the next room at the time. What do you tell a twelve-year-old boy?"

"Your old man dying has to mess with a kid's head, even without knowing about the masturbation and strangulation combo."

"Exactly, but this time we have the names of adults who were at the orgy and someone's going to hang—without getting any satisfaction in the process."

"Lieutenant, you keep chasing the hangers-on at the orgy, and I'll stay on my twisted tour."

Papadopoulos gave a little snort. "Oh for the good old days, when perverts had only a half dozen tricks and the Greek families had their neighborhood." He threw back the last swallow of coffee and headed into the grayness.

I bought a wedge of baklava and ate as I drove to Bug Broker Ltd., in the hope that Sam Scudder could give me the lowdown on the spider market. The flaky filo made a mess in the cab of my truck, but the day was about to get even messier.

CHAPTER TWENTY

Bug Broker Ltd. was squeezed between a rusting Quonset hut landscaped with a tangle of decomposing engine parts, oil drums, and steel cables, and Yat Sun's Imports which had a sign advertising: "Chinese Herbes and Spices are Speciality" (proofreading evidently not being their specialty). I pushed open a heavy metal door leading into Scudder's business. The office was a linoleum-floored, wood-paneled affair featuring movie posters of *Them!*, *Deadly Mantis*, *The Fly*, and other insect horror flicks. I assumed the rest of the building housed a menagerie of multi-legged film extras. Scudder was sitting at the battered metal desk, talking on the phone. He waved me toward a chair and continued his conversation.

"Yeah, I told you it would be twenty bucks a pop for the tarantulas, but my Mexican supplier jacked up his price because the rains have drowned so many of the spiders. Their burrows are underwater which means my business is underwater if I can't get fifty bucks a head." There was a pause and he ran a hand through his thick, curly hair which matched the black curls spilling from the top of his shirt and cradling an Egyptian scarab beetle pendant that dangled from a gold chain.

"Alright, I'll go thirty," he said leaning into the conversation, "but you gotta pay me the same as you're paying the stuntman. What with the rains, the only tarantulas available are Chilean rose which are much harder to predict than the red-kneed. If you want to keep your cast safe, then I'm going to have to absorb some risks handling the spiders. My initial estimate didn't include working with an aggressive species."

Scudder leaned back in his chair and put his feet on the desk, evidently satisfied with his negotiating tactics. The poor props manager on the other end of the conversation probably suspected he was being conned. I gave Scudder a conspiratorial smile and he winked. After a long interlude involving his alternately grunting assent and rolling his eyes, he said, "Alright, we have a deal. I'll amend the contract and fax it to you."

Scudder took his feet off the desk, hung up the phone, opened a drawer, and pulled out two glasses and a bottle of Old Crow. "If you're here to buy my services, I'll pour you one, "he said, filling his own glass to the brim, "but if you're here to sell me something, leave." It wasn't noon yet but I thought better of declining his hospitality.

"Pour me one. I'm in need of what you can provide." That was mostly true.

"And you are?"

"An admirer of your negotiating skills. We both know that Chilean rose tarantulas are no more dangerous than the Mexican red-kneed. And neither is going to bite anyone unless they're badly mishandled."

He flashed a crooked grin. "And how do you know that, Mr. . . . ?"

"Just call me Riley."

"That your first or last name?"

"Last, but using my first just caused trouble when I was a kid." I didn't explain that being named Cedric Vladimir Riley was the recipe for attracting taunts and getting into fights going back to elementary school.

Scudder shrugged and asked, "Okay Riley, so what brings you to Bug Broker?"

"I'm the owner of Goat Hill Extermination. So we're sort of in the same business. You bring 'em in and I take 'em out." He chuckled and topped off my glass. From there, we sipped horrible bourbon and exchanged stories about how we got into our respective lines of work.

Scudder had been in the navy, traveled the world, saw some amazing creatures, and made connections. When he was discharged, he was looking for an angle to work and the light went on when he saw the scene in *Dr. No* in which a docile, pink-toed tarantula co-starred with Sean Connery. Scudder figured there could be decent money in providing film studios with insects and spiders from around the globe—and he had the contacts. The movie business was lucrative but erratic. However, with some inquiries, he learned Chinese immigrants were thrilled to score singing crickets and Japanese businessmen were anxious to gain status by having the biggest rhinoceros or Hercules beetle on the block. With pet stores selling hissing cockroaches, museums setting up insect exhibits, and zoos stocking butterfly houses, he'd found buyers with less money than Hollywood moguls but who provided steady demand between major deals.

Scudder had become the go-to guy when anybody needed a creature with more than four legs that couldn't be plopped into a pot of boiling water along Fisherman's Wharf, dipped in garlic butter and fed to the tourists. From the looks of his office, he wasn't getting rich but neither was I.

I told him about my father converting his experience with killing mosquitoes in the Pacific during World War II into a thriving extermination business which I took over after leaving the police force. Before he could ask for details, I regaled him with an account of the fornicating cockroaches from this morning.

"Cock-a-roaches? She thought her house was infested with roaches dragging their giant cocks through her cupboards," he roared. "Shit, you gotta love it. You're okay Riley, but I still don't know what I can do for you."

"You can keep me from losing my business."

"Ya need me to import some badass termites and disgusting roaches to keep your customers on edge?"

"Nothing so dramatic. Without going into specifics, my company has been wrongly implicated in a recent homicide case. And yesterday, there was another killing which could draw your business into a sick story that would attract the press like flies to shit."

"Hold on, pal. I don't do anything illegal. Sometimes I stretch import regulations, but don't accuse me of being involved in murder." Scudder rose to his feet and his bulk was that of a former college lineman now in his forties—flab overlying a muscular core with a predilection for inflicting pain.

"Settle down," I said, raising my hands in a gesture of submission. He lowered himself into the office chair which emitted a metallic squeak. "I'm not accusing you of killing anyone, just telling you how things could go down if I don't get ahead of the story."

"What story?" He took a sip of his drink.

"Among your customers is—or was—the owner of the Pleasure Palace and she paid well for exotic spiders." He took another sip and leaned back with the tumbler resting on his gut. The chair emitted another high-pitched protest. "And one of your eight-legged products delivered a lethal bite."

"I would never provide an amateur with a deadly spider."

"But she was a regular customer, right?" I worked on my bourbon which was pretty bad. Actually, really bad, but I avoided wincing and insulting my host.

"Nothing large scale, but yeah. She ordered some standard insects like crickets and cockroaches for her shop. Can't figure what her customers wanted with them and I probably don't wanna know. She got real excited over spiders. The bigger the better. I figured she was into something kinky, herself."

"How'd you figure that?"

"The woman damn near had an orgasm when I showed her a huntsman from Indonesia. The thing was bigger than my hand. It was like she was a speed freak or something. You know how those guys need more and more to get tweaked."

"That's what I've heard." I took another swig and swallowed hard.

"But she never hinted that a deadly spider would get her off. And like I said, even if that's what she wanted, I only provide professionals with anything dangerous."

"So you do import deadly spiders?"

"Sure, if a customer has the background to deal with 'em. Zookeepers know the deal with a Brazilian wandering spider or katipo spider from New Zealand."

"Or a Sydney funnel-web?"

"Now, there's a piece of work. In fact, a couple weeks ago I sent one of those nasty numbers along with an Australian redback to the California Academy of Sciences for their special exhibit on deadly animals. Landed me five hundred bucks for those bad boys."

"Any other deliveries?"

"Not from me. I think they borrowed some poisonous snakes from the San Diego Zoo and a stonefish and lionfish from the Monterey Aquarium."

"Okay, so you provided a funnel-web to the Cal Academy. Is there any way it could've been sent to the Pleasure Palace?"

"Holy shit, that's what killed the lady? Look, I sent her a black house spider that I got from a contact in Christchurch. She was a good size and could give someone a painful nip but that's all. Made a fast C-note on that order." He threw back the last of his Old Crow.

"No chance of a mix up?"

"None, nada, zippo. I don't make mistakes like that. I transport dangerous and high-end products myself. I used a local delivery service for a couple years and lost nearly a grand worth of Amazonian butterflies when the fucking moron stopped for a couple of beers and left the engine running to keep the truck warm. When he was done with the suds, the leaky exhaust system had gassed my inventory." I finished my drink in a single gulp to minimize contact with the cheap bourbon.

"Scudder, I appreciate the conversation—and the drink. Anything I can do for you?" The old adage about honey catching more flies than vinegar describes a wide expanse of human relations.

He rose from his chair and leaned forward with his fists on the desktop. "Yeah Riley, you make damn sure that the cops and reporters don't drag me and my business into the mess you're uncovering." His posture reminded me of angry funnel-web spider. So much for the efficacy of honey.

I nodded assent and offered my hand, which he took with a crushing grip so as to leave no doubt as to how he'd deal with me should the police come knocking. I figured I could probably take him with skill and speed, but I didn't relish the possibility of finding out.

To keep following the sewage pipe that had led me to Scudder meant a trip out to Golden Gate Park for a visit to the Cal Academy's exhibit. If something got screwed up with spider identification and delivery, one of the curators should know or suspect something. The only other explanation was that a scary, sexy spider and a truly lethal species were switched after Scudder delivered the creatures. That seemed far-fetched, but I couldn't have imagined the depth of this whole moral cesspool a few days ago. What a tangled web we weave.

Tomorrow was my Saturday with Tommy, and we'd planned to go to "our secret site" in Redwood Regional Park east of Oakland. Our father had found a rock outcropping where tens of thousands of lady beetles aggregated for the winter, and we had made an annual trek to the site for at least twenty years. I'd set aside this weekend for our traditional outing, but now I needed to let my brother know the plan had changed. He wasn't good with disappointment, but spending the day in the Cal Academy's museum might be an easy sell given the weather was about as miserable as January gets in the Bay area.

I drove over to Saint Teresa's and found Nina in the daycare center, helping the variously challenged adults to assemble a gigantic scrapbook using gobs of rubber cement. Tommy and Karsa seemed to be enjoying peeling the adhesive from their fingers more than applying it to the poster-sized pages of the book that was going to be a birthday gift for Father Griesmaier. Nina was her perpetually patient self, gently directing her charges to remember the purpose of their task. I slipped into the doorway and caught her attention.

"What a lovely surprise," she said, looking over her shoulder before pulling me into the hallway for a very irreverent kiss.

"I've come to save you from a lunch of sloppy joes and Jell-O Pudding Pops," I said, "and to let Tommy know that tomorrow's plan has changed."

Nina scowled. "He's really excited about the ladybug expedition. I told him I'd tag along and bring hot chocolate. Why the change in plans?"

"I need to follow up on a lead with the Linford case while the trail is still warm. Don't worry, we're going to the Cal Academy which will be even better than the soggy woods. But right now, you and I are going to lunch."

"We have a dinner date tonight, right?"

"Sure, but something other than ground beef in tomato sauce on white bread will make for a lovely break from the glue vapors, eh?"

"Let me make sure that Gwen can handle lunch. She's a dream, but I don't like to ask too much of our volunteers. While I do that, you can break the news to Tommy."

I told my brother about Saturday's plan and he was okay with the deal as long as the weather was going to be cold and rainy, and Nina could still come along, and I promised that we'd see the lady beetles (not ladybugs, of course, as he insisted on using the correct, common name) next weekend. Gwen agreed to supervise sloppy joes, and I let Nina pick our lunch spot. She opted for a new place called Yum Yum Fish, which I hoped had invested more in their food than their marketing.

We headed across town to this newish hole-in-the-wall that Nina's friends had insisted was the best sushi restaurant around. As far as I'm concerned, slicing up raw fish isn't cooking and a place that doesn't cook isn't a restaurant. But sushi is all the rage—along with a toy called a Rubik's cube and a nighttime soap opera called "Dallas"—which says a great deal about how much a fellow should trust the judgment of society these days.

After my morning of sweets, I wasn't very hungry. Besides, nobody stuffs themselves eating raw fish and vegetables rolled with rice that's wrapped in seaweed. Perched on a stool at the counter and listening to Nina rave about a lecture she attended by N. Scott Momaday, the American Indian writer and Pulitzer Prize winner who's become her hero, made for a pleasant lunch— and, to be honest, the tuna roll was delicious. Maybe I was duped by the chef's ecstatic recommendation for the chu-toro cut which ran me nearly ten bucks, but sometimes you get what you pay for.

I had Nina back to the church by one o'clock. Sitting in the truck, she gave me a lingering kiss followed by a deep, humming sigh that meant she was looking forward to our romantic dinner—as well as dessert.

CHAPTER TWENTY-ONE

I finished the week where it started, back at the shop with normal people. It had been a wild ride since Larry had pulled me from Gustaw's Bakery on Monday and Carol had told me the police had some questions about a bizarre pair of corpses and their deeply disturbed grandson. I was ready for the weekend, following an afternoon with Carol devoted to deciding how long we could keep the utility vans before replacing them (almost eighty thousand miles of city driving was pushing our luck), where we should buy advertisements (billboards, bus stops and yellow pages being possibilities), who we might hire to audit our books (being a CPA would have been one of the circles of hell had Dante known about this profession), and how delinquent customers could be cajoled into paying without our resorting to a collection agency (I hate sending in the goons, but I can't afford to run a charity). Carol was an angel throughout these deliberations, but I could see her running out of steam. So, we called it quits at four, just as I heard the garage door open in the warehouse and the guys pull in to unload the vans.

By the time I shut down the front office and headed to the back, Larry and Dennis had settled into their makeshift living room. I could smell the Cubans wafting down the hallway, and the earthy smoke was far more appealing than the electric twang coming from the stereo.

"Hey chief, got any weekend plans?" Larry asked, resting his feet on the decrepit coffee table.

"Chasing down some leads and listening to some decent music," I said.

"Don't be dissing Merle Haggard." I could've admitted that the chorus, in which Merle begged for someone to stop the madly spinning world so he could get off, hit home after this week, but I didn't want to encourage Larry's musical taste.

"Yo Riley, if you got the time, we got the beer," Dennis said, pulling out a Miller from the softly wheezing fridge.

"Just one and then I need to hit the gym before dinner with Nina."

"Go easy on the grindage, boss. Last Saturday of the month is tomorrow," Larry said.

"Yeah, gotta save room for the dyno Goat Hill family dinner. I be askin' yo' mamma to adopt me if I could get that Irish soul food on a regular basis."

My mother made a feast for the extended family that comprised my business. She knew their hard work allowed me to support her and Tommy— and an Old World mother needed a houseful of family on occasion.

I settled into a faux leather recliner that was disgorging wads of foam rubber from the seams and tilting to the side like a capsizing boat. We talked about whether lite beer was actually beer (no), whether Jim Plunkett was better than Ken Stabler (no resolution, except that neither trumped Joe Montana), whether Reagan's military buildup made sense ("hell no" according to Larry), and whether Smokey Robinson was past his prime (Dennis defended the singer, while I tried to remember anything he'd sung). I finished my beer while listening to Mr. Haggard plead to be released from the depravity of the big city. Having spent the week mucking around in the bowels of humanity, I empathized with the plaintive lyrics but doubted that people were any less twisted in small towns.

At Marty's, I started with jumping rope, followed by a bout of shadow boxing, a workout on the heavy bag, a few minutes on the speed bag to catch my breath, and then some pushups, jump squats and a couple hundred sit ups. The last twenty-five hurt. A lot. Those were penance for the fattening sins of bakery indulgences. Drenched and panting, I draped a towel over my shoulders and walked over to where Marty was leaning on the apron of the sparring ring.

"The Mexican kid's outmatched," I said, watching the fighters.

"He's got heart," Marty said, chewing on the stump of his cold cigar.

"And the black kid has speed and power," I said as the Mexican absorbed a combination. The head gear would protect his brains, but his body was taking a pounding.

"Yeah, Clyde needs to step in since the corners won't." Marty lifted a hand to catch the referee's eye, then shook his head to signal an end to the fight. Clyde was the half-time maintenance man, sometimes trainer, and occasional sparring ref. He wasn't particularly good at any of these, but Marty had a soft spot for the former boxer who'd taken a brutal beating in the fight that ended his shot at an actual payday in the ring. Clyde stepped between the boxers and waved off the black fighter. The gutsy, outclassed Mexican briefly spread his arms in futile protest to salvage his dignity.

"So Marty, who's responsible?"

"For what?"

"For calling off the black kid. For a boxer ending up like Clyde?"

"You get into the ring and it's your deal," he said, spitting a few strands of tobacco between his feet. "Nobody makes you become a fighter."

"But most fighters won't stop a bout on their own. I've been there. Your pride won't let you."

"Sure, the ref can stop the action and your corner can throw in the towel," Marty shifted the cigar to the other corner of his mouth, "but when a man decides to be a fighter, he knows the deal. Sometimes he loses bad, sometimes he wins big. Better than being a cop, Riley. I never seen a cop take a beating for a million bucks."

"You mean the 'Drama in Bahama' last month?"

"More like the 'Trauma in Bahama' you ask me. Berbick pounded Ali in the last three rounds. It would've been a serious whoopin' if Ali had faced a world-class fighter."

"So the beating is on Ali?"

"Damn right. Getting into the ring at thirty-nine, what did he expect?" Marty shuffled off in the direction of his office where the phone had started ringing.

I headed to the locker room, knowing I was older than Ali and wondering if private investigation was a young man's game. This case with flea collars, insect foreplay, and spider seduction had me feeling like an old man, out of touch and yearning for the days when vice was simple and perverts stuck to trench coats and peep holes.

On my way up the hill to my house, I mulled over how Ali couldn't get a boxing license from any state commission based on reports he had brain damage, which is why his final fight was offshore. And I couldn't get an investigator's license based on having pled guilty to involuntary manslaughter after beating the location of a sick child out of kidnapper, which is why my pursuit of two-legged vermin was off the books. After the Champ lost to Larry Holmes in 1980, Ali said, "I shall return"—and he did, with Trevor Burbick who embarrassed him. In the ring, experience only goes so far against youth, strength, and speed. Whoever was behind blackmail and murder was probably younger and faster than I was. But, outside the ring, sometimes age and seasoning prevail. Sometimes.

I showered and checked for residual rash from Lane's botanical treachery. Pleased that the hot water had not revived the hives, I changed into clothes appropriate for a nice dinner, donned a woolen overcoat, and picked up Nina. We'd decided on the Tadich Grill a couple blocks from the Maritime Plaza. It was a Friday night and they've never taken reservations, so we knew what we were getting into—a long wait at the oldest restaurant in the state, for some of the best seafood in the city. We got lucky and nabbed a couple stools at the bar. I treated myself to a Connemara, Ireland's smooth, single peated malt whiskey, which someone described as smelling like a toffee shop had burned down. Nina had a virgin hot toddy, to stave off the chill. We didn't mind the wait, as the dark wood paneling softly lit with Art Deco brass and milk-glass fixtures provided a romantic ambiance. Like always, the place was noisy, but the voices mingle and meld in the high ceiling to create a background din assuring that each conversation is just between lovers.

Nina told me about her worry that Petey—the street kid who Tommy and Karsa had befriended—had not appeared all week. She didn't think he had the savvy to make it in the dark corners of the city without someone providing protection. Nina had contacted some of the vagrants in her

Indian community, a sort of extended family of social rejects. She trusted these people to keep tabs on a naïve white kid who was important to her, at least when they weren't drunk. But these half-sober half breeds hadn't seen anyone with a heart-shaped birthmark—except one possible sighting by Chief. I'd met him a few times while doing jobs in the back alleys downtown. A Chowok in his sixties, Chief was some distant relation to Nina's mother, which was probably the case for everyone in the tribe. He was tapped into the homeless network and had heard about a young man, new to the streets, who was hanging out with a refined white man dressed elegantly in black. When our table was ready, Nina shifted the conversation to a less grim topic involving her people.

"Riley, you absolutely have to read N. Scott Momaday," she enthused while scanning the menu. I was too busy contemplating dinner to focus on literature. "You'll understand both Chief and me if you read *House Made of Dawn*."

She had my attention. "I'll get my lover and her down-and-out third cousin twice removed? I'd say that your life is about as far from his as imaginable." The waiter appeared tableside and asked if we were ready to order. I could tell that Nina's mind wasn't on the dinner options, so I proposed that we split a bowl of cioppino and a Dungeness crab Louie salad. She quickly agreed. I added a glass of Chianti to my order and Nina asked for mineral water. Alcoholism had destroyed so many of her people, such as Chief, that she couldn't bear the thought of booze, but she never judged the drinking culture of the Irish.

"We come from the same people, but I found a path into respectability," she said.

"Being a bigwig in federal law enforcement and then deciding to care for handicapped adults is pretty honorable," I said with genuine admiration.

"Society sees me. I'm viewed as doing good work. But Momaday writes about coyotes and their gift of seldom being seen. Chief is like most Indians in the city, keeping to the edges and owning the night."

"I'm pretty sure the hookers and dealers own the night," I said.

"In a way, yes. But the street people recognize Chief for his wisdom, his rejection of wealth and power. By calling him 'Chief' they are saying that he, not the police chief or a chief justice, is the authority in their world."

"I see what you mean," I said, taking a sip of the wine that had materialized at my place, the waiter being something of a coyote himself. "I know there is a whole segment of society living in the shadows of the city. Sometimes they look after the vulnerable, but they'll just as readily slit a throat."

"They are—we are—often driven far into the darkness. But what about the Linfords and people of that class? It seems that they can be every bit as brutal."

"And twisted, I'm afraid." She raised an inquisitive eyebrow as our dinner arrived.

After a few bites, she pushed gently: "Did you want to tell me more about the case?"

"I don't want to ruin an exquisite meal with distasteful details. Let me just say that having money only buys you a better mask. The veneer of normalcy is as thin and fragile in the mansions of Nob Hill as it is in the gutters of the Tenderloin."

"I have to wonder," she said dipping a hunk of bread into the cioppino broth, "whether the veneer of wealth and power will crumble one day. Momaday wrote that the native people have assumed the appearance of their enemies but there is a quiet resistance, what he calls 'a long outwaiting.'"

"Are my people the enemy?" I asked, munching on a forkful of crab and asparagus.

"The Irish?" she laughed. "Hardly. Well, maybe that president that your people produced, but the white working class is not the enemy of the brown. Instead, it's the millionaires ravaging this city and country—and the big corporations who binge on labor and resources so they can puke up dividends and stock options."

"Maybe there's a kind of justice," I said. "What alcohol did to your people, cocaine seems to be doing to the upper class."

Our dinner conversation was hardly romantic, despite the sumptuous setting. But it hadn't been a week that lent itself to pleasant topics. We continued to exchange thoughts about what it meant to be hiding at the margins of social acceptability—in the literal basements and figurative sewers. The cockroaches, perverts, Indians, and retarded had something in common that polite company would not admit. At least we finished the meal on a high note, as Nina shared with me Tommy's afternoon of frenzied excitement about going to the Cal Academy tomorrow.

The clouds were delivering what the Irish call a hooring rain, meaning that we were drenched by the time we got to my truck and the windshield wipers couldn't keep up with the downpour. Back at my house, we shed our cold, wet clothes and shared a steamy shower. From there, we crawled under the covers. There's something enchanting about intimacy during a storm. She luxuriated in the sounds of nature, and I relished the murmurs of both the rain and my lover. How would society judge our lovemaking? If we'd been caught in the Middle Ages entwined in one of our favored positions that violated the 'natural order' of male-female roles or that resembled animalistic coupling, we would've been judged to be deviants and sentenced to years of penance. And even the modern Church wouldn't have approved of our purpose, which was most definitely pleasure and not procreation. But that stricture seems like deeming cioppino a sin because food is meant to fill the belly, not to be savored.

CHAPTER TWENTY-TWO

I rolled out of bed and winced. Our lovemaking had been lively but not the stuff of morning soreness. Rather, my muscle ache was the result of those last two dozen sit-ups at Marty's. I headed to the bathroom hoping that a hot shower would soothe my tender abdomen and allow me to stand fully upright. Nina came in as I stepped out of the bathtub and her help toweling me dry got me thinking that maybe there was enough time for an encore romp before we started the day. But she gave me a maidenly kiss and gently shoved me out into the hall which was undoubtedly the wiser course for the morning. Tommy had a difficult enough time waiting for a weekend outing without our being late.

He came lurching down the stairs of my mother's Victorian house as I parked at the curb. Tommy was bundled in a wool sweater that hung below a yellow rain slicker. He was shouting over his shoulder to my mother, who had come out to make sure that her boys were going to behave themselves. Having Nina along to keep us in line alleviated much of my mother's concern. Even so, she wanted to know my plans for breakfast before our visit to the museum. She insisted that a hot meal was essential to staving off pneumonia, which Mrs. Nagy had contracted—almost surely from becoming chilled while walking home from church in dress shoes, in my mother's medical opinion. Tommy was wearing galoshes.

I answered like any halfway intelligent son would do when confronted by a stern, maternal figure. I lied. Assuring her that we'd stop for omelets and sausages—acceptable if not quite up to the Irish standard of rashers and eggs, along with tomato, mushrooms, black pudding, and Irish beans—I herded Tommy and Nina toward the truck to forestall further questioning. My mother would have the day to shop and cook for the extended family dinner, which gave her incalculable joy.

I headed toward Nob Hill, which was not exactly on the way to the museum. Once we'd passed by City Hall on Van Ness and failed to turn toward Golden Gate Park, Tommy knew what was up.

"We're going to Bob's, aren't we?" he shouted.

"So it appears," said Nina. "Riley seems to have been less than honest with your mother." I could hear the disapproval in her voice, mixed with an undertone of conspiracy.

"This will be our secret," I said. "It's sort of like tricking people without being mean."

"I can't tell mom or else we'll be in trouble, right?"

My kid brother could cut through philosophical hair splitting and get down to the core of the issue.

"That's right," said Nina. "But remember it was Riley's decision, not yours. You won't be in trouble if she finds out."

"Thanks, sweetie," I said. Tommy was not the best keeper of secrets and now he'd been assured of immunity from prosecution. Bob's Donuts is one of the San Francisco's culinary gems—a Formica and linoleum temple to the gods of fried dough and sugar. Nina and I split a sticky bun and I got Tommy an apple fritter with the nutritional logic that the fruit was healthy— an apple fritter a day and all that.

At the California Academy of Sciences, which is really an enormous natural history museum with a fancy name, we walked past the banners featuring king cobras, poison dart frogs and box jellyfish advertising the "Deadly Animals" exhibit. I stepped into the administrative office at the entryway and asked the officious woman at the desk to call Dr. Rider, the entomology collection manager. I'd come to know Dave several years ago while I accompanied Tommy on "insect safaris" that Scott Fortier organized at the Essig Museum. Dave had been one of Scott's graduate students, and Tommy had bonded to him as being a fellow student—at least in Tommy's estimation—of the master entomologist.

I couldn't be certain that Dave would be in his office on a Saturday, but given the workaholic passion for multi-legged creatures that he acquired from his mentor, it was a good bet. And it paid off. The receptionist curtly directed me to the staff elevator and handed me a visitor's badge which I assumed would cover Tommy and Nina since asking anything more of the museum's gatekeeper seemed ill advised.

On the third floor, we made our way to Room 3467B. I chuckled at the notion of there being enough offices and labs to warrant such an elaborate code until we'd walked through a brightly lit maze for ten minutes, failing to detect any system to the numbering. At last, through no fault of our own, we found Dave's office. An athletic cup—the kind guys wear to protect their balls—had been spray painted gold and hung from the doorknob along with a sign saying, "Rider Cup." Pretty funny for scientists, the misspelling of the famous golf trophy notwithstanding.

Dave Rider shared two things with his mentor: a love of insects and an exuberant personality. Otherwise, he was as short and stocky as Scott was tall and skinny—and his office was as neat as Scott's was jumbled.

"Riley, great to see you," he said and then noticed Tommy behind me. "Tommy! My man, how nice to drag your brother along for a visit." Tommy grinned and shook hands with the jovial entomologist. "And, who is this?" Dave continued, as Nina stepped into the hyper-organized office, "A woman far more beautiful than Riley could hope to attract, so I assume you're his much younger, adopted sister." Nina's olive complexion and raven hair reflected her Spanish-Indian parentage and the complete impossibility of Irish ancestry.

"This is my girlfriend, Nina," I said. "And this is Doctor Dave Rider, a gifted scientist and renowned comic."

Nina smiled and shook his hand. I told Dave that I had a few questions regarding a sensitive matter. His eyebrows arched with interest. Although social acumen is not to be found in many scientists, he grasped how to proceed. When he opened the door leading from his office to the bowels of the insect collection, a twiggy brunette and a lanky redhead looked up from their microscopes. Dave introduced them as Brenda and Jason. She smiled; he grunted. Dave asked Brenda to give Nina and Tommy a tour of the insect collection. As she began to lead them through the narrow passageways created by stacks of steel cabinets, Jason returned to mounting almost invisibly small flies on triangular bits of paper with tiny dabs of glue.

"What's up?" Dave asked, assuring our privacy in his office by gently closing the door to the lab while I shut the one to the hallway.

"I understand you received some poisonous spiders for the museum's exhibit of deadly animals. And they came from a guy named Scudder, who operates Bug Broker Ltd." Dave settled into his chair and gestured for me to take a seat on the other side of the desk. He picked up a well-chewed pen and gnawed gently while deciding how to respond. I waited.

"Yeah, we've done business with him. Not the most savory sort, but he knows how to get specimens into the country and get the paperwork through the system." The chewing accelerated. "He supplied the spiders. And, for a finder's fee, he put us in touch with a reliable source of giant Japanese hornets and assassin caterpillars which we made arrangements to have shipped every couple of weeks during the exhibit since they're so hard to keep alive."

"He sold you an Australian redback and a Sydney funnel-web, right?"

"Along with a *Parotostigmus* centipede. A real beaut. So, what's the problem?" He put the pen down and shifted uncomfortably in his chair.

"I'm not sure, to be honest. Just tracking down a lead involving a woman who died from a spider bite a couple days ago," I said, not wanting to go into detail.

"Not from what we have here." He seemed oddly relieved, as if he expected me to be an undercover agent for the US Department of Agriculture ready to bust him for violating quarantine regulations. "Everything is locked up tight as Bo Derek's swimsuit."

"No chance of a Sydney funnel-web having disappeared?"

"We had one. But the old girl died a couple weeks ago, so she's not wandering the streets and killing anybody. Don't tell the visitors but, other than her, the other spiders aren't likely to be deadly. If I'd managed to get a Brazilian wandering spider like I'd hoped, then we'd be talking lethal."

Having reached a dead end, so to speak, we chatted for a while about our shared challenges of educating the public. He tried to get people to appreciate insects as sources of wonder and beauty, and I struggled to convince customers that finding cockroaches or their kin didn't always require dousing a place with insecticides. We were close to concluding that the ivory tower wasn't so different than the infested basement when there was a tap on the door.

"Brenda showed us everything! And you wouldn't believe how many insects they have," Tommy announced as Dave opened the door.

Brenda smiled at Tommy's unbridled excitement. Although probably a decade older than her, his childlike enthusiasm was endearing. Maybe brain damage isn't the worst thing that can happen to a person.

"How many, pal?" I asked.

"More than ten million," he said with grave authority. "Someday maybe we'll have a trillion insects in our collection, don't you think?"

"You and Riley will need to keep at it," Nina said.

"Can we go see the exhibits?" Tommy asked. "I read the brochure while we were waiting and they have a Sydney funnel-web spider. Dave, I've been collecting milkypleads or, um . . ." When Tommy was excited, his words tended to jumble.

"Millipedes and centipedes?" Dave asked.

"That's right," Tommy said, looking aggravated with himself and then quickly regaining his zeal. "And I've been learning lots about spiders, too."

"Well, I'm afraid that the funnel-web died," Dave said. Tommy looked crestfallen. "But we have her stored in alcohol. Brenda, can you go grab that specimen to show Tommy?" She headed into the labyrinth of cabinets, and I saw Jason watching us out of the corner of his eye. Brenda soon returned with a liquid-filled jar in which a large spider was floating.

"Here we go," she said handing the specimen to Dave, who passed it along for Tommy's inspection.

He grinned like having been handed a Christmas present, but as he slowly turned the jar his brow furrowed and the smile faded. "This isn't a Sydney funnel-web," he said hesitantly.

"Well, Tommy," Dave said, "you know how fast the colors change when you put a spider in alcohol."

"That's not it," Tommy said, "the back of the Sydney funnel-web is bald and this one is hairy."

"Let me see," said Dave, gently taking the specimen from Tommy and holding it up to the light. "I'll be damned, you're right. The cephalothorax is covered in dense hairs. And now that I look more carefully, the distinctive spinnerets of the Sydney funnel-web are missing. There should be two fingerlike projections at the tip of the abdomen. What do you think, Brenda?" he asked, passing her the jar.

"I'm not a spider expert, but this sure looks like a tarantula. Maybe a western desert tarantula. I saw plenty of those on my collecting trip to Organ Pipe National Monument last summer. Jason's better with spiders, but he must've left for lunch." A lab coat hung over the back of the chair where he'd been working.

Dave scowled and took back the specimen, turning the jar to read from the rectangle of paper floating in the alcohol. "There's been some mistake. Funnel-webs and tarantulas are both mygalomorphs, but this is definitely not *Atrax robustus*, as the label indicates." His doughy features squeezed into a scowl. Curators aren't bothered by failing to recall the names of people, but they loathe misnaming specimens.

"Can you explain what's happened, Brenda?" he grumbled. "Dammit, that funnel-web was a primo specimen that we could've used for display and education."

Tommy was looking anxious, as he was very sensitive to conflict. Dave was agitated with disorderliness and Brenda looked perplexed.

"No, Doctor Rider, I can't imagine how the mix-up occurred. But I'll see what I can find out and talk to Jason when he gets back."

"Do that," he said, turning back to us. "I'm sorry for the confusion. We are usually far more organized that this. Is there anything else I can do for you?"

"One last matter, perhaps—"

"Riley, can I go see the exhibits?" Tommy said, hoping to avoid any more tense conversations.

"Sure, pal," I said, "Nina can go with you and I'll catch up in a few minutes."

"Aw, can't I go by myself? Please," he begged. Tommy adored Nina, but he also liked being given some independence. It's tough being a thirty-seven-year-old man with a child's brain.

"Tell you what," Nina said, "If you'll thank Brenda and Doctor Rider for showing us the collection, then you and I can work out a deal for letting you have some time to see things on your own."

Tommy thanked the scientists with a blend of enthusiasm and haste, as he was both genuinely grateful and eager to explore the rest of the museum. After my companions took off, I talked with Dave about how a tarantula could've been switched with a funnel-web and where the latter spider might be. He reviewed the museum's meticulous protocol and recordkeeping, but we didn't come up with anything plausible. He was getting exasperated, so I took my leave and went to find Nina and Tommy—which turned out to be nearly as challenging as finding the missing funnel-web.

CHAPTER TWENTY-THREE

I found Nina at the geology exhibit on the third floor. I was never much into rocks but some of the crystals in the display cases were marvelously geometric and freakishly large. Based on my limited knowledge, I figured they probably came from caves, spaces that I've not particularly enjoyed after having the tide come in while I was exploring Secret Cave at Point Reyes with some high school buddies. Drowning in the dark seemed like a bad way to go. I'm not claustrophobic, having spent countless hours crawling under buildings and squeezing into attics to pursue pests, but there's something unnerving about being under tons of stone as the water is rising.

Nina had told Tommy that he could be by himself if he promised to stay on the second floor. We headed down to check on him, figuring he was likely to be glued to the glass of one of the aquaria outside of the theater, which was showing a documentary about the Great Barrier Reef. There was a series of bubbling tanks featuring poisonous marine life from Australia— a blue-ringed octopus, box jellyfish, cone shells, lion fish and stone fish. Some of these beasts could kill in minutes, while others could inflict enough pain to make you wish you were dead. Having a display of lethal creatures was a great way to rivet the public's attention after a movie about the reef. Based on what I knew about Australian spiders, snakes, and marine life, my desire to visit the country was about the same as my hopes for an evening stroll through Watts.

157

Tommy was nowhere to be seen. There wasn't much public space on the second floor other than the theater and a wide hallway where people assembled while waiting for the film to start. We thought maybe he'd slipped into the theater. Nina convinced the docent to let her peek into the darkness to see if she could catch a glimpse of him. I went down the hall, looking for where he might've disappeared. Seeing a sign for the restrooms, I headed that way and Nina caught up with me, having had no luck in the theater. From an alcove with a drinking fountain, the men's room was down a passageway to the right, the women's to the left. We could hear a tense conversation beyond our view, apparently outside the men's room.

"Hey, retard, let's see you walk a straight line," a voice said.

"Yeah, I wanna see a hunchback find his way to the workshop of a mad scientist," another added with a mocking laugh.

Tommy's neurological condition had worsened in recent months and his lurching caused a twisting of his back. The poor guy was increasingly bent to the side so that he couldn't stand fully upright without losing his balance. Physical therapy had helped, but when he grew tired the deformity was pronounced. I started to head toward the voices when Nina grabbed my arm and put a finger to her lips. My protective instincts were quelled. For the moment.

"I'm special," Tommy said, "and I'm smarter than you about things."

"Like being a gimpy retard," one of his antagonists said.

"No. Like do you know there's no antidote for blue octopus poison?"

"What the hell you talkin' about, loser?" demanded the other antagonist. He had a whiny voice, like he was trying to echo and please the first guy.

"And I bet you don't know that in Australia this is stinger season and jellyfish can kill you," Tommy said.

Evidently, my brother had been reading the text of the displays. He was good at memorizing facts, even if he didn't fully understand their meanings. Tommy was holding his own against the two tormentors who were becoming confused by the man-child.

"I don't care about some shitty jellyfish, 'cuz I'm not going into the ocean, you ignoramus," the first one said in an effort to regain the upper hand. I wouldn't have guessed the guy knew a four-syllable word.

"Yeah, and you walk like you been bitten by a poison jellyfish," the other added with his sniveling tone.

"Jellyfish don't bite, they sting," Tommy said, "And I know about poison spiders. They have a fumble web here but it died and it was really a tarantula and I could tell the difference." He was getting flustered while they were getting confused—and aggravated. But a museum is a bad location for beating up a retarded man who won't let himself be bullied.

Nina and I pulled back when we heard the two jerks mumbling insults as they headed toward us. The bigger guy was wearing a sweatshirt with Greek letters and his little buddy had on a letter jacket. Sweatshirt came around the corner of the alcove with frat boy attitude. I threw a shoulder into him. He stumbled backwards into Letterman, who crashed against the drinking fountain. Sweatshirt ended up on his ass, having lost both his balance and his pride. It was pretty comical, so I laughed. Nina scowled.

"Watch it, old man," Sweatshirt said, getting back to his feet and balling his fists.

"You couldn't outsmart my brother, and I guarantee you won't outpunch me," I said, grinding a fist into my palm. "But let's take it outside if you want to try."

Letterman took his place a step behind his buddy, a strategic position allowing him to look tough but let Sweatshirt do the swinging and bleeding if anything developed. Maybe he wasn't as dumb as I first thought. I waited and stared until Sweatshirt snorted and grabbed Letterman by the sleeve, shoving him past me and into the hallway while muttering about my not being worth his time. They left as Tommy came lurching toward us.

"Nina, those guys were mean—and Riley showed them. I'm glad you didn't hurt them Riley," he said turning to me, "but you would have if they didn't leave me alone."

"You had them on the ropes with what you learned about deadly sea life," I said, tousling his sandy blonde hair that looked no messier for my efforts.

"Yeah, I showed them who was stupid," he said. "I don't walk normal, but they didn't know about jellyfish or spiders or anything."

"I'm proud how you stood up for yourself," Nina said, giving him a hug, "but let's not call people stupid, even if they don't know things that we do.

And here's what I know, a visit to the gift shop would be a fine stop before we get some lunch."

At the gift shop, Tommy was struggling mightily to choose among wooden pieced-together models of insects. The cricket, mantis and dragonfly were studiously compared, selected, and re-shelved in a process that was both agonizing and joyful for him. I was looking at a rack of posters featuring images of Albert Einstein with various quotes meant to drive home the man's genius.

The museum had an exhibit devoted to the fiftieth anniversary of Werner Heisenberg's Nobel Prize, but nobody would lay out ten bucks for a poster of a physicist who discovered uncertainty. Hell, the older I get, the less certain I become and Swedish royalty aren't handing me a check and hanging a medal around my neck. But from what I could gather as we passed the exhibit on our way to the gift shop, Heisenberg did something complicated involving electrons—and whatever it was, Einstein disagreed and turned out to be wrong. I took pleasure in Einstein having been mistaken about something.

Tommy came over to where I was scanning the posters. "Who's that?" he asked. "He looks funny but nice. I like how he's sticking out his tongue."

"That's a famous scientist, Albert Einstein," I said.

"What did he do?"

"It's hard to explain because I don't really understand. But it had to do with some equation that explains lots of stuff about the universe." As I flipped through the posters, Tommy suddenly told me to stop and called over to Nina, who was looking at a coffee table book of birds.

"What did you find, Tommy?" she asked.

With a triumphant flourish, he lifted one of the posters from the rack and held it up for her to read. There was Einstein, standing at a chalkboard covered in mathematical gobbledygook with a quote: "The difference between stupidity and genius is that genius has its limits."

"See," Tommy declared, "a famous scientist said people are stupid. I bet he would have called those two guys who bothered me stupid."

Nina smiled and shook her head, being smart enough to know when she was defeated. Tommy settled on the model of the dragonfly with a one-foot wingspan because he said that in the days of dinosaurs, dragonflies got that big or even bigger. Another fact that had surely eluded Sweatshirt and Letterman.

Settling down at the Academy Café with our trays of food—hot dog and fries for Tommy, hearty bowls of chili for Nina and me—I hoped that the earlier excitement would fade from my brother's memory. The last thing I needed was his revealing to our mother that he'd had donuts for breakfast and an altercation at the museum. My hopes were futile.

"Riley, what's an inner anus?" he asked, dipping a fry into a paper cup of ketchup.

"A what?"

"An inner anus. That's what the mean guys called me. And I know that 'anus' is a bad word for your butt, so is the inner anus where the poop comes from?" I was baffled. Nina was doing her best to suppress laughter behind a napkin she was pretending to use.

"Oh dear, Tommy," she said, regaining her composure, "I think you mean 'ignoramus' which is just a fancy word for an ignorant person."

"So, it's like being stupid?" he asked.

"Sort of, but being ignorant just means that you don't know something," I said.

"Let me tell you a story," Nina offered. As Tommy chowed down on his lunch, Nina recounted the life of Will Rogers, explaining that he was one of the most beloved actors and humorists in the olden days before television. I had no idea where this was going. Nina explained that she had learned all about Will Rogers because he had something in common with her. They both had Indian heritage. He was part Cherokee, having been born in Indian Territory which became Oklahoma. She was half Chowok, her mother having come to the city from the reservation when the government forced her people to relocate.

"That's a good story," Tommy said, "but Will Rogers wasn't stupid, was he?"

"Not at all. In fact, lots of people thought he was very wise. And he said something important about being ignorant."

"Tell me," Tommy said, wiping up the last of the ketchup with the end of his hot dog bun.

"He said, 'Everybody is ignorant, only on different subjects.' So, I'm ignorant about football, and Riley's ignorant about knitting."

"And I'm ignorant about checkers," Tommy said, "But Karsa knows everything about checkers, like I know about insects. He knows how to move the pieces and sometimes he can beat Father Griesmaier."

After lunch, we hit the African wildlife hall and the earthquake exhibit. By the time Tommy got to the hands-on gallery with the antlers, bones and furs, he was running out of gas. On the way home, he fell asleep on Nina's shoulder. I dropped them off at my mother's house, so Tommy could nap before dinner and Nina could lend a hand chopping, stirring, and shredding.

I headed down Van Ness to The Groove Cellar—the best record store in the city. Cassette tapes may be outselling LPs, like sales of Michelob Light are outpacing Anchor Steam at O'Donnell's Pub, but Americans have never sought quality in music or beer. Or politicians, food, or clothes. Or films, cars, or tools. Or . . . you get the idea.

I was after a hard-to-find Grant Still album as a surprise for Dennis at dinner. If anywhere had this recording, it would be The Groove Cellar, and if anyone could unearth it from the overflowing, cobwebbed shelves, illuminated with a single sixty-watt bulb in the back storeroom, it would be the owner, who I'd befriended years ago through our shared taste for classical music.

I waited in the front, aimlessly flipping through albums and concluding that although the worst classical music is probably more listenable than the best popular music, the rock groups have the upper hand when it comes to album covers. If only they were as adept at composing musical scores and lyrics. My ruminations were interrupted by the owner proudly producing the 1974 recording by the London Symphony, which included one of the most aesthetically interesting album covers I've seen on a classical LP—a feature I hoped would please Dennis, along with the music.

Back at my house, I did some chores while listening again to the Metropolitan Opera's recording of *Rigoletto*. For some reason, that story drew me back. The opera opens with an orgy hosted by the Duke of Matua, disdaining fidelity and laughing at the jealous husbands of the women he beds. He mocks his hunchbacked jester, Rigoletto, who has no hope of partaking in his "kingdom of pleasure." Verdi's tale of depravity, set in the sixteenth century, was darkly reminiscent of my last week.

While mopping the kitchen, it occurred to me that the Riley brothers had much in common with Rigoletto. He was a social outcast because of his deformity—and Tommy constantly battled being different. But unlike Rigoletto, my brother had the goodness to resist becoming bitter.

As for me, Rigoletto wanted to shield Gilda, his vulnerable daughter, from the corruption of the world, the same as I wanted to protect Tommy. But despite—or maybe because of—his passionate concern, Gilda's innocence drew her to a horrible end. Maybe Nina was right about allowing Tommy to stand up for himself.

The opera was as pungent as the mixture of turpentine and linseed oil I used on my insect cabinets and oak worktable. Rigoletto's perverse fate leads him to make happen the very thing he most fears. I was left buffing the wood and wondering if my efforts would end up assuring the death of innocents.

Chapter Twenty-Four

A soft, amber light leaked through the gauzy curtains. From the cars parked in front of my mother's house, I could tell I was the last to arrive. I didn't bother knocking as the clamor of voices and music would've masked any effort to announce my arrival. The women were packed into the kitchen having a lively conversation about whatever was simmering on the stove, baking in the oven, and cooling on the counter. As much as Carol objected to stereotypical sex roles, she and Anna were having a grand time in their roles as sous chefs. Sometimes activism gets in the way of having fun.

My appearance at the kitchen door produced a fleeting acknowledgment in the form of a quick peck on either cheek from my mother and Nina, who then gently shoved me toward the living room where the guys had gathered. I brushed the floured handprints off my tweed jacket which was too warm for the house, given the steaming kitchen and the long-suffering radiator that could never put out enough heat to satisfy my perpetually cold mother.

Larry and Dennis were in the midst of Tommy's new, favorite card game. He derived as much pleasure from telling his opponents to "Go Fish!" as actually winning. Prokofiev's *Peter and the Wolf* narrated by Peter Ustinov with the London Philharmonic Orchestra played in the background. That poor, scratched record had probably been played a thousand times and Tommy knew every word and note but never tired of listening. It calmed him during chaotic times such as our monthly dinners, which is almost certainly why my mother had it playing.

Once the guys had counted their points with Larry coming out on top, I handed Dennis his gift. He let Tommy unwrap it while Ustinov described hearing the duck quack inside the wolf which meant the symphonic fairytale was reaching its end. While putting the new record on the turntable, I explained that Dennis's appreciation—however painfully phrased for a classical music lover—of Mozart a couple days ago gave me hope that he might enjoy Grant Still's *Afro-American Symphony*.

The opening strains feature the plaintive notes of a muted trumpet giving the piece a bluesy feel on top of the classical music, before sliding into a more symphonic movement and later picking up on a jazz theme.

"Reminds me of Gershwin," Larry said. I must've looked stunned because Larry adopted a smug look and stroked his jawline with affected snobbery.

"How do you know about Gershwin?" I asked, knowing that Larry's tastes centered on the lamentable collision of country western and rock music, a blend consistent with chicken-fried Oreos which appeal to Nashville stoners.

"Who dat?" Dennis asked.

"My good man," Larry said, continuing his self-satisfied performance, "Gershwin was a famous composer of . . ." the stroking slowed, ". . . of stuff that sounds like what we're hearing."

"You're bluff is showing," I said.

"Okay, I know Gershwin from the musical," he said. "*An American in Paris* is etched into my memory because it was the only flippin' movie my unit had to show during lulls in the action. I must've seen that thing twenty times. It was more entertaining than building rattraps from empty C-ration cans, by baiting them with cheese and blasting caps, then counting little explosions all night."

After the music reached its big finish, I told Dennis about Grant Still being the first African American composer to have a symphony played by a world-class orchestra and the first to have an opera performed by a major company. He was impressed, particularly by the revelation that Still had died just a few years ago, since Dennis figured all classical music had been written by white guys in powdered wigs.

Our discussion was abandoned as the women brought dinner to the table, festooned with candles and eight settings of Belleek china. Along with an enormous potato casserole loaded with bacon and sour cream, a tray of garlic-roasted cabbages, a heaping platter of boxty, and an overflowing basket of Irish brown bread, my mother took great delight in having worked with Nina to prepare cocido—a wintertime stew from Spain composed of every edible part of a pig, along with turnips, potatoes, and cabbage.

My mother was thrilled by the similarity to skirts-and-kidneys, a dish from my childhood involving pig parts and potatoes, which was increasingly difficult to make given the paucity of pork ears, feet, and innards in today's grocery stores. Nina explained that cocido is usually served in three courses: soup, vegetables, and meat. But she'd learned the difficulty of moving about in a dining room filled with Goat Hill Extermination's extended family.

Nina had also brought special wines from her parents' restaurant. The Monastrell and Bobal were intense, red wines that complemented the rich flavors of our melded meal. If my very Catholic mother could accept Carol and Anna being a couple, then intermingling Irish and Spanish cuisines was not so radical. What mattered was that her loved ones were happy—maybe not sinless, but that was God's business.

For a while, everyone dug in and murmured approval. The talk was all about the food, which was fantastic. Simple and honest. I'd flipped over the album to play some works by Samuel Coleridge-Taylor, a mixed-race composer called the "African Mahler." It was enough to prompt my brother to use his new vocabulary.

"Mom, Dennis was ignorant of the music Riley gave him," Tommy declared, once the dishes has been passed a second time and our plates refilled.

"Goodness, Tommy," my mother said, "that's not a nice thing to say. Wherever did you hear that word?"

"Nina told me what it meant. It just means that you don't know something," he said.

"Sounds about right to me," Larry affirmed while sopping up cocido broth with a slab of brown bread.

"I don't like it when people are ignorant of what it's like to be retarded,"

Tommy said, sticking with his topic and heading in a problematical direction, "Like those mean guys at the museum—"

"You're right, pal. Most people don't know what it's like to be you," I interrupted, hoping to avoid a recounting of the museum altercation. My mother knew that Tommy was often teased, so there was no reason to upset her with the morning's events. "But then, we're all different in some way, right?"

"Mos' people don' know what it's like to be Black," said Dennis, "havin' folks watchin' you all the time and wondrin' if you gonna grab a purse."

"Or to have fought in a war," said Larry, "to do what your government says is right and get called a baby killer."

"Or to love another woman," said Anna, looking at Carol who flashed a smile.

"But that's not like me," insisted Tommy. "You're all regular grownups. I want to be like you."

"What do you mean, dear?" asked my mother, slipping another boxty onto my plate, knowing how much I loved the potato pancakes.

"I want to be normal," he said and then paused. "I wish I was smart like all of you, then nobody would make fun of me."

"What matters," Nina said, "is not what's in your head, but what's in your heart. I think you're more honest and kind than anyone at this table. And these are some of the best people I know."

"It's normal for adults to lie and be mean," said Carol, setting a forkful of potato casserole on her plate to focus on Tommy. "So being normal isn't always a good thing."

"You know what you are?" Larry asked. Tommy looked at him with pure admiration. Larry had a special place in the kid's world. "You're one hundred percent natural."

"No jivin' homefry, you be legit." Tommy didn't follow the slang, but he loved it when Dennis laid it on thick because it made him feel included.

"Heck, it took me years before I admitted to Riley that sometimes I came late to work because nightmares kept me from sleeping," Larry said, pouring the rest of Tommy's bottled Coke into his glass. "I lied and told him I had a broken alarm clock or my car wouldn't start. Anything but the truth because

I thought I wasn't normal. But you're the real deal, Tommy. I wish I was honest like you."

"And I wish we could dig into those desserts," Anna said, folding her napkin and starting to clear the plates. Everyone pitched in and within minutes the table was graced with three Porter cakes—named for the essential ingredient: Irish stout. Nobody seems to know the difference between a porter and a stout (at the pub, Brian simply asserts, "Six o' one, half a dozen of the other"), but it's called Porter cake and my mother decided to conduct a culinary experiment making one with Murphy's stout, one with Beamish stout, and one with Guinness. We all had a modest piece of each and voted—the winner was Murphy's, which Tommy declared as being, "better than donuts for breakfast, like Riley and Nina and I had this morning!"

"I guess honesty has its downsides, eh?" I offered weakly.

"Riley, don't take me for a stook," my mother scolded. "I know you're out acting the maggot with your brother on Saturdays." Translation: she was no fool, but I was.

"The cakes are delicious," Carol said, in a valiant attempt to redirect the conversation away from my shortcomings.

"Thank you, dear. The secret is freshly grated nutmeg. And I use currants and dates, rather than raisins, to keep the cake from being too moist."

"Raisins are what's normal in cake," Tommy said and then chattered along in the excited way that invariably ends up in some unexpected place. "But sometimes normal isn't so good, right Carol? Riley, insects are normal aren't they? I read a library book about how some of them make babies in ways that are really strange. But that's natural, so it's okay, right?"

"Well pal, I'm not sure that's great dinnertime conversation," I said.

"But Riley, remember that time we saw the girl mantis eating the head of the boy mantis while they were mating? That's what you told me they were doing, and you said the boy mantis was feeding the girl so she'd have more eggs. Isn't that right?"

"That's right. And there's an assassin bug that glues dead ants to its body for camouflage and a kind of spider where the babies eat the mother. Nature does some strange things," I said, trying to direct the conversation away from sex. No luck.

"Remember those bugs with their butts stuck together? You said they were so-scary bugs and they could mate for more than a week. That's a really long time, isn't it Riley?"

Nina was covering a smile with her napkin, while Larry and Dennis were nodding appreciatively. Carol and Anna were just shaking their heads. "Those were soapberry bugs, pal."

I figured that Tommy was next going to tell everyone, as he'd excitedly shared with me a couple weeks ago, how he'd learned from an entomology book that a drone bee, in his words, "gets his penis stuck in a girl bee and it rips out his guts" which is technically correct but not ideal dinner conversation. But fortunately, Carol stepped in.

"Yes, a week is a long time. And speaking of time, we've been here quite a while and maybe it's best for us to let your mom have a rest, seeing that she's been on her feet shopping and cooking the whole day."

While my mother packed up leftovers for everyone, people gathered up coats, exchanged hugs, and headed into a rain somewhere between rotten and pissing, in the Irish catalogue of weather. My mother put Tommy to bed while Nina and I did the dishes. I found handwashing dishes soothing, even pleasurable, especially with a sensuous woman gently bumping my hip and brushing my shoulder as she reached across the sink in the course of rinsing and drying.

We had the mess cleaned up by the time my mother came back downstairs. She asked us into the living room, a space filled with enough lacey doilies, gilded frames, flocked wallpaper, and floral upholstery to be the envy of a Victorian aristocrat. She poured each of us a glass of sherry, an unusual indulgence, as she wasn't one for drinking more than half a glass of wine at dinner.

There was an agenda to go along with the nightcap. After some awkward starts and oblique references to disrobed women, she came out with it— almost.

"I was cleaning Tommy's room and I found a magazine under his bed."

"A *Playboy*, I'd venture to guess," I said.

"Well, yes. A nudie magazine. I don't know what to do."

"He's a grown man. He's curious. I'm surprised that you didn't find anything like that until now," I said.

"But Riley, he doesn't know about such matters. He's like a child."

"If I may," Nina said, "he has the understanding of a child but the body of an adult. It must be very difficult for him. He sometimes holds hands with a girl, actually a woman in her thirties, at the daycare. I don't think there's anything more to it than that. But surely it's natural for him to wonder about women and, well, sex."

"Yes, you're right," my mother sighed. "And that's probably his fascination with insect mating and all that." She took a modest sip of sherry.

We chatted for a while longer, convincing my mother that Tommy's hiding Miss January under the bed didn't mean he was a deviant. Nina agreed to talk with him about his new hobby which, I was quite certain, was only newly discovered by my mother.

At the end of the evening, I drove Nina back to her apartment and did a quick reconnaissance to assure myself that Tim wasn't lurking. I headed home and climbed into my own bed, digesting a gutful of food and anticipating an unholy Sunday featuring a visit with Stefan. I slept poorly, dreaming about running naked through the city while being chased by giant spiders with pendulous breasts.

CHAPTER TWENTY-FIVE

I once overheard Father Griesmaier telling an offended parishioner after Mass that the church welcomes sinners as well as saints. The congregant had been put off by a visitor who did his best to look like a woman. The butt-hugging silver lamé dress was out of place, but the glittery pumps were a fashionable addition. Given the priest's attitude, I figured that spending Sunday morning with Stefan would be approved by God—if there is one, which I highly doubted, particularly given recent events.

Stefan had pulled himself together since Thursday, having made a pot of coffee and set out a tray of pastries. No reason a pervert can't be a good host, I suppose. The man's decorating taste was appalling, with a kitchen featuring neon appliances and a zebra-striped tabletop, but he could make a tasty drink.

"This is outstanding coffee," I said after the first sip.

"It's light roast from one of the Vietnamese grocers, and I make it with a French press," he said. I wasn't familiar with this device, but it struck me as vaguely erotic, which made sense given Stefan. "Would you like cream or sugar?"

"No, I take it black. You don't pour sauce on a good steak."

"Understood, although embellishment can take sensuality to another level," he said, slipping a chunk of pastry to the Yorkshire terrier sitting at his feet. The dog expressed its gratitude by trying to hump Stefan's leg, affirming that debauchery was a household practice.

"I'm sure it can, which brings us to the point of my visit. Have you come up with any reason somebody would have embellished your bedroom with a deadly spider?"

"I've been reflecting on the days leading up to that horrible moment." Stefan sighed and slowly stirred his coffee. I waited. "She was anxious about something. At the time, I dismissed it as an issue with the business, perhaps a difficult customer. But it was more than that."

"How do you figure?" I said, taking a bite of apricot pastry.

"Michelle couldn't let it go. She wasn't eating well, even when I made her favorite foods. And a couple of nights I woke up and heard her crying. Something was going on, but I couldn't get her to share it with me. So I just tried to be supportive." Stefan began twisting the fringe of the pink-and-green plaid lambswool scarf he'd loosely wrapped around his neck. No lamb should've been shorn to produce that thing.

"Not much to go on."

"No, it's not. That's why I spent yesterday going through her notebooks, business letters, photo albums . . . and videotapes."

"And?"

He fidgeted with the end of his scarf, like he'd done with the tie of his bathrobe on Thursday—a sure tell that he was holding back. The man wouldn't last an hour in a poker game.

"Come upstairs with me, please. I need to show you something."

We went up the multihued spiral staircase to the room with the projection television. I settled onto a lime-green couch with asymmetrical lavender cushions while Stefan put a videotape into the player. He sat on the edge of a chair that looked to have been upholstered in Dalmatian skin, but given his affection for the Yorkie, I figured the dog fur was fake.

"You told me when we first met that Michelle was blackmailing Mr. Linford with a video showing him in some embarrassing situation. I was dubious, to be honest. Michelle did make specialized films, but she scrupulously protected the identity of anyone in scenes that could harm their reputations."

"So faceless pornography?"

"Not always. Professional models want their fans to recognize them. But Michelle wasn't into standard bump and grind stuff. The major studios have that covered. She was interested in distinctive material for niche markets."

"And Lane Linford filled a niche?"

"Indeed, he did. Let me show you."

A man was lying on a plush, forest-green carpet. The camera showed him from the waist down. He was naked. Pale, skinny legs. A close-up of his flaccid penis and black pubic hair trimmed very short. On the four-foot wide screen, the image was life sized. The camera pulled back and the man's hand came into the picture holding a small, Tupperware container.

He peeled off the lid and sprinkled a dozen ants onto his genitals. A close-up ensued as they crawled about. The sound of his breathing became audible. Next, he added some half-inch-long black beetles, which I guessed were mealworm adults. For a couple of minutes he nudged them around, becoming aroused.

Then into the picture came a tropical cockroach, slowly exploring its new surroundings. The camera panned up the man's body. He was so focused on his pleasure that he didn't seem to notice his face being filmed. Lane Linford's eyes were half-closed, his mouth gasping.

"That's enough. I get the picture." Stefan hit the pause button and Lane's face was frozen in twisted ecstasy.

"I found her record of cinematic projects," he said. "She documented every date and location, along with abbreviations of the performers," Stefan handed me a spiral-bound notebook opened to an entry: "January 4 / 9212 Jackson Street / LL: Begin supine. Add ants, beetles, cockroach. Arousal to orgasm required. Anonymity guaranteed. Payment in-kind for product delivery."

"What's that last bit about payment mean?" I asked.

"There's an earlier entry indicating that Michelle restocked his colonies after they were killed off by an exterminator who was treating the house for fleas," Stefan said. "I guess he allowed her to film in exchange for a new supply of insects. Plenty of people with kinks enjoy performing, as long as the videos are anonymous."

"There seems to have been an agreement to that effect. But she broke the rules and filmed his face. Michelle must have been using the video to blackmail him," I surmised. "He wouldn't tell me what she had, but now it's obvious. The upper crust of San Francisco can look the other way when it comes to one of their own screwing the help, snorting coke with celebrities, or crashing the Bentley after a bender. But getting off with insects would be more than the well-bred could ignore."

"Yes, zoophilia is an unforgivable sin in our world. Animals can be food but not lovers. Given the choice of being skewered or screwed, I think most creatures would prefer the latter, don't you?" he asked.

"I suppose, but Lane wasn't doing either," I said.

"No, but Michelle and society provided a motive for murder. Perhaps we've found her killer."

The couch, which had been designed for style rather than functionality, was getting uncomfortable and Lane's orgasmic expression was still frozen on the screen. Plus, I needed time to consider this newest twist before answering Stefan. So I suggested continuing our conversation over another cup of coffee, which would keep him occupied while I did some thinking.

On the way to the stairs, I paused at the master bedroom door which was cracked open. I could still catch a whiff of vomit and see the remnants of the paramedics' work scattered alongside the rumpled, satin sheets. Stefan mumbled about having a cleaning service coming tomorrow but doubting that he'd ever go back into that room. I didn't like such a revolting man being able to evoke my sympathy.

As Stefan heated water and ground beans, I mulled over what I knew. Lane Linford had manipulated his grandparents into a lethal delusion and taken over the family business. He needed access to a large amount of money to pay off Michelle, who had devastating videos of him with insects perking his pecker. The blackmailer had met an unpleasant end, courtesy of a poisonous spider that she'd mistaken for a safer version of foreplay. A good, clean American story of capitalism at its finest.

From here, things became messier. The spider's inclusion in the ménage à trois was evidently not a simple matter of mistaken identity, given the knowledge needed to acquire and handle a Sidney funnel-web. So who had sent the eight-legged assassin, how had they acquired the creature, and why did they want Michelle dead?

"Riley, you look like you're in another world," Stefan said, setting the coffee pot between us and pulling up a chair to the kitchen table.

"Just thinking about what I know and what you suspect. I can't make Lane Linford fit into the puzzle of Michelle's death. At least not as her killer."

"Why not? He had a reason to want her dead," he said, pushing the plunger into the glass pot.

"I'll grant you the motive, but what I can't figure is how he would've acquired the Sidney funnel-web." I knew that Scudder had provided one to the Cal Academy and there was confusion as to its whereabouts. But I didn't see any connection of Lane to the science museum, nor did I see him having the skills to handle an aggressive spider. There was, however, no reason to share this information with Stefan. His role was to provide me with answers and payments, not to collaborate in the investigation.

"Maybe from that wholesaler, Sam what's-his-name," he said, pouring the coffee into our cups.

"Not likely. But there's a bigger problem. Linford had already gone through extreme measures to acquire the money before the spider did its work. And you don't pay dead blackmailers."

"So, what's next? If Lane Linford didn't do it, who else is a suspect?" he asked, pursing his lips and blowing across his mug. Somehow he made the simplest acts look dirty.

"There's still a promising loose end. Why was Michelle blackmailing Linford? You two seem to have plenty of money," I said, taking a sip. Too bad Stefan ended up with a sex shop rather than a coffee shop. But I suppose there's more money in grinding and heating human beings than coffee beans.

"Good question," he said, setting down his mug. "I've been so focused on her killer that I'd not thought about why she betrayed the confidence of a customer. There must have been some extreme circumstances. And that's what had her so upset of late."

"Right. The implications for your business would be enormous if your clientele knew of her double-crossing Linford. So, what would be the explanation? We're looking for a hundred thousand reasons, Stefan."

Stefan got up from the table and paced the kitchen. His leather slippers made a rhythmic shuffling. I poured the rest of the coffee from the pot into my mug and marveled at the simplicity of how the plunger formed a seal with the glass to keep the grounds from getting into the coffee. There was something far more elegant about a mechanical, two-piece device than my Mr. Coffee with its rocker switches, paper filters, and power cord. The metronomic pacing stopped.

"I'm sorry, but I can't think of what she needed money for. A hundred thousand dollars is beyond anything we ever talked about in terms of expanding the business. We'd discussed finding a new place to live closer to the shop. Maybe a nice loft or even a house. But there was no urgency or desperation. If there was any sort of medical issue, she would've told me. And our health insurance premiums are always paid up, so that couldn't be it."

Stefan was a totally inept liar, and nothing in his voice or movements suggested he was being less than honest. He wasn't even fiddling with his scarf. The guy really had no clue.

"Alright, but she needed the money for some reason. And once I know why, I'll know a whole lot more about who planted the spider. Give me something. Anything."

He paused for a long minute before saying, "Well, there's Luis at the Pleasure Palace. He'll be at work tomorrow."

"What about this Luis? Could Michelle have owed him money?"

"No, no. He's our longest serving employee, as good and honest as they come. But he might know something you could use."

"How so?"

"He specializes in BDSM. Luis knew all of the wholesalers and trends. He always had us stock the most updated supplies and equipment. He was also very knowledgeable about zoophilia, especially where it overlapped with sadomasochistic practices. So he and Michelle would talk about marketing opportunities and sales strategies."

"You figure he might shed some light on whatever had Michelle uptight and why she needed a hundred thousand dollars?"

"Maybe, but you'll need to be subtle, Riley. And to be honest, it's not your forte." He was right. I wasn't going to be assigned to any diplomatic posts, unless some tinhorn dictator in South America needed an ass kicking. I shrugged and he continued, "Remember, Luis and other folks in his community are used to being ridiculed and vilified. These days, the police and prosecutors are just looking for ways to make their lives miserable."

It occurred to me that sadomasochists enjoyed misery, so maybe the cops were doing them a favor, but I thought better of sharing this insight with Stefan.

"Don't worry. I can fake being adorable and charming, when necessary. Anything else?" I asked swallowing the last of my coffee and heading to the front door.

"Yes. I've been thinking about our deal. I asked you to find Michelle's killer, and I still want you to do so. I'm paying you well for that information."

"But?"

"But I reserve the right to decide if you go to the police with the information I've paid for—or whether I'll handle things on my own."

"Let's see how this unfolds, Stefan. I have an arrangement with a police lieutenant who's involved in this whole mess. I might not be able to withhold information altogether, but it's possible you could have some time between when I know the killer's identity and when I go to the cops."

Stefan gave a thin smile and a slight nod. I had to begrudgingly admire a fellow with the guts to settle a score himself, even if I couldn't imagine this girlish pervert being able to inflict harm on anyone who wasn't tied to a bed.

Chapter Twenty-Six

I spent the early afternoon doing laundry. Having bought my own washer and dryer, I missed the warm rumble of Laundry Land but didn't miss shoving quarters into the machines. Then I rewarded this domestic diligence by working on my insect collection to the strains of beautiful music. Earlier in the week, I'd put some sulfur butterflies in a cigar humidor to soften the specimens so they wouldn't break during pinning. Tommy and I had spent a pleasant afternoon last fall collecting these intensely yellow insects in fields outside of the city and they'd been tucked away in my freezer until now. For some reason, Ravel's *Daphnis and Chloe* seemed like the right musical accompaniment to take me away from the twisted world of human perversions. And there's no better recording than the enchanting 1959 performance by the Parisian symphony conducted by Manuel Rosenthal, who was the last of Ravel's students.

I settled into my chair at the work table and began gently removing the butterflies from the hydrating chamber and slowly extending their wings beneath strips of acetate. As I lined up the specimens on the spreading board, their subtle color variations became apparent. Most were rather typical Orange Sulfurs, but a couple had characteristics similar to those of its kissing cousin, the Clouded Sulphur. Conversely, among the few specimens of Clouded Sulfurs was one with an unusual amount of orange coloration—a feature normally found in the other species. The identification guides fit specimens into square and round holes, but what I had were a few oblong pegs that didn't fit neatly into either hole.

I'd attended a public lecture at the Cal Academy a couple years ago by an entomologist who studied insect hybrids. He explained that populations of sulfur butterflies were sometimes composed of individuals with features of both the Orange and Clouded species. This was something like lions and tigers producing ligers, except the cats require the matchmaking intervention of lecherous zookeepers. Setting aside the butterflies that didn't fit nicely into either of the well-established species, I decided to show them to Scott Fortier the next time I was at Berkeley.

Thinking about how insects courted and mated with the "wrong" species—evidently being fornicating, not just kissing, cousins—got me wondering about Lane Linford. Sure, a human deriving sexual gratification from a cockroach is a larger leap than what happens between two butterflies. But then, Stefan's little dog tried to satisfy canine urges using his owner's leg, an encounter which wasn't going to produce any more offspring than Lane and his mini-menagerie. Crossing the species line in the pursuit of sex seems to be natural, whatever the hell that means.

After the butterflies were pinned, I tossed the clothes into the dryer and returned to my insects. For the most part, my specimens were organized into conventional, taxonomic families. But I've also assembled groups of insects representing crimes—or what would be crimes if humans engaged in similar behaviors. Along with murder, theft, and fraud, I had a box devoted to vice. There were species that forced themselves on unwilling mates, copulated in public with reckless abandon, and exchanged payment—usually a bit of food—for sexual services. My conversation with Lieutenant Papadopoulos convinced me that although orgies are not technically illegal, their inclusion of underage participants and admission fees warranted a new tray in my collection.

The music was drawing to a close, having passed through an achingly beautiful softness. Playing loud is easy. True artistry comes with *pianississimo* of the sort found in Ravel and Debussy—the moments sumptuously contrasting with and leading up to the throbbing, shattering climax of instruments and voices. Making music is like pinning insects. A hulking beetle under glass impresses the casual viewer, but the fineness of a collection comes with the most delicate flies, double mounted by piercing the thorax with an exquisitely thin, minuten pin which is then set into a piece of cork which is itself mounted with a standard insect pin.

My pinning tray of orgiastic insects included various midges and gnats that formed mating swarms—such as those annoying clouds of tiny flies around a person's head, although few people would guess they are the site of a six-legged sex party. I also included some March flies, aka lovebugs, which gather in enormous swarms of horny individuals, similar to the mass emergences of mayflies in their rush to copulate within the few hours of adult life they enjoy.

In the midst of the gloriously shattering musical climax, the phone started ringing. Nina had left her beloved Aran sweater at my mother's house and, if I was not too busy, would it be possible to pick it up and bring it over? She didn't want my mother to think she didn't value the Christmas present. And she wanted it for Monday because there was a meeting with the finance council of the diocese where the sweater would make a good impression. And it was so wonderfully warm to wear around her apartment. And her Datsun 210 was notoriously unreliable on wet days despite my having replaced the cracked distributor cap and the spark plug wires. And so I didn't have much choice.

I was getting stiff from sitting indoors on a damp day, so I figured that a long walk would do me good. My well-worn trench coat and a woolen paddy cap were appropriate for heading into the drizzle. It was only a couple blocks to my mother's house, but two miles up Van Ness to Nina's neighborhood. The wind would've been miserable if I hadn't stuffed her sweater under my coat. I looked like I needed to lose twenty pounds, but comfort trumps appearance in my book. The late afternoon light was a silvery gray by the time I got to Nina's.

"Riley, thanks so much for fetching my sweater," she said, giving me a hug. A long, clinging hug.

"Sure. What's wrong?" I asked.

She paused and then said, "Wrong? Nothing. Nothing's wrong," she said, tucking a few strands of loose hair behind her ear.

For being an ex-cop with lots of interrogation experience, she wasn't terribly adept at deception. I peeled off my coat, tossed my hat onto the coffee table, settled onto her couch and said, "It's chilly out there. How about we have some tea?"

She headed to the kitchen.

"I'll take mine strong," I said, "with a splash of milk—and truth."

Nina returned with two steaming mugs, set our drinks on the table and took the overstuffed chair across from me. She was wearing stirrup pants beneath an oversized turtleneck sweater that reached past her bottom. A pleasant look on a miserable day. I sipped my tea and waited.

"Tim pushed the boundaries too far, but I don't want you doing anything. I can handle it," she finally admitted.

"And 'it' would be?"

"I went downstairs to take the garbage to the dumpster. On my way back, he met me in the alley."

"And?" The muscles in my neck and shoulders tensed.

"And, well, he exposed himself. Then he ran down the alley. I think he was ashamed."

"Probably was. The sicko didn't pick a very good day to feature his goods. The cold probably shrank him to unimpressive dimensions."

"Riley! Please, he's not well. I was scared and I'm still a bit rattled, but I don't think he's dangerous. Just starved for attention. I wasn't even going to tell you because I was afraid that you'd do something."

"A reasonable guess," I said.

"Tim needs help, not punishment. I'll talk to him."

"Nina, this has gone on long enough. He's had his chances. Stay away from him. He knows the deal and more talking won't help," I said, taking a sip of my tea.

Nina kept Lyons tea for me and brewed it until nearly as black as coffee— as it should be. She preferred herbal teas, gentle and soothing.

"I don't want him hurt," she said.

There it was—comeuppance versus compassion, and I wasn't going to lie about my intentions. Someone was going to get hurt, and I'd be damned if it would be Nina.

"I'm not looking forward to hurting him."

"But you will."

"Probably."

"Because that's who you are. That's how you see the world. I can accept you or not, but I won't try to change you. I couldn't anyway," she said.

I finished my tea and we kissed goodnight. She said that she loved me, even when she didn't like me. There were tears in her eyes. Sometimes, even when you're with someone, you're still alone.

On my walk home, I mulled over how to handle Tim. Of course, my confrontation would just shift him to another, easier target. That's how NIMBY works. You keep the mess out of your backyard which means it ends up in someone else's. This was just like advising citizens to put deadbolts on their doors and bars on their windows. These don't stop thieves, they just move the burglars to your more vulnerable neighbors.

And what about Tim? Maybe the guy needed help, but not as much as Nina needed protection. In a sense, he was no different than the libidinous gnats and lustful March flies, seeking to do whatever their biological urges demanded. People are animals too, but that's not all we are. Part of our nature is self-restraint, moral boundaries, and human dignity. And screwing with abandon, seeking arousal from other species, or finding satisfaction in exposing our genitals isn't right. It just isn't.

Back at the house, I warmed up the leftovers from the family feast. The potato casserole went into the oven and the cocido into a sauce pan on the stove. While those were heating, I pulled out some lady beetles from the freezer. Tommy and I had decided to challenge ourselves by collecting one of every kind found in the state, which was going to be a very long-term project, as Scott Fortier informed us there was something like two hundred Californian species. We'd made a small dent in our objective last summer, and I had pill bottles stuffed with beetles neatly arranged in my ice trays.

My dinner was hot at about the same time as the insects were thawed, so I took a plate to my worktable, along with a glass of Guinness—a perfect complement to the stew which had become even tastier with reheating. I was particularly pleased with a nice series of the Ashy Gray Lady Beetles which included a black form. The common names of these insects are often a riddle, such as the California population of the Ninespotted Lady Beetle which has no spots. The best name, however, was surely the Two-stabbed Lady Beetle, so-called because its obsidian-black body has two, blood-red spots as if the creature had been attacked by a miniature Jack the Ripper. And in the last few years, the department of agriculture has been busy releasing the Asian Multicolored Lady Beetle in eastern states, so there's speculation that it will make its way across the country and potentially outcompete our native species. I figured Tommy and I had better get cracking before California loses any of its local beauties.

Savoring food from Ireland and Spain while puzzling over insect names, pondering Lilliputian knife attacks and contemplating lady beetles from Asia, coalesced around my evening's choice of music. Add a week of people acting out their strange desires and the only choice was Puccini's last opera, *Turandot*. I put on the 1977 recording, not because it had the best soprano in the title role (Montserrat Caballé was solid but Birgit Nilsson was much better two decades earlier), but because Pavarotti was brilliant in the role of Calaf, the suitor of Turandot and this was a live recording from the San Francisco Opera, so I felt a twinge of loyalty.

I pinned a couple dozen beetles during the first act, while the beautiful, cold-hearted princess Turandot, whose ancestor had been ravished and murdered by an invading foreign prince, took out her bitterness toward men. Yet another suitor failed to answer her three wickedly difficult riddles. Had the poor bloke gotten them right, he would've gained a wife. Instead he lost his head to the delight of the assembled masses. Nonetheless, Calaf is smitten and decides to court the Chinese princess.

During the second act, I put away the pinning supplies and settled into my recliner with a glass of Connemara, Ireland's whiskey challenge to Scotland. To be honest, I think the Scots do a better job incorporating peaty flavor into their Scotch, but the smoky aroma of Connemara is perfect on a cold, damp night. While I sipped, Calaf answered the three riddles—my favorite being the final: What ice can make fire? The answer is Turandot. But she gets mad at losing the game and refuses to marry him, so he offers her a deal. If she can learn his name by dawn, he'll go to the chopping block. If not, she goes to the marriage bed.

In the final act, we learn there is a person who knows his name—his father's servant who has an unrequited crush on Calaf. But rather than revealing his identity to Turandot, she kills herself. However, in a gallant gesture, Calaf tells the princess his name, rather than forcing himself on a woman who does not desire him. At dawn, Turandot proclaims to the gathered crowd—hoping for another gory execution—*Il suo nome è . . . Amor!* ("His name is . . . Love!")—and the couple is soon wed.

As I finished my whiskey, I couldn't decide whether I liked or hated the happy ending, a feature that so many operas manage to avoid. My recent days made clear that life provides an abundance of perverse passion, depraved violence, and complex riddles, but in my experience there are rarely blissful conclusions. *Turandot* should end with Calaf's beheading in my estimation. That's what happens to romantic suckers who think screwed up people will return their warmth. Maybe Lane and Stefan had the right idea. At least they weren't figuring on insects sharing a candlelight dinner or spiders going for a long walk on the beach. My challenge would come when I found whoever was at the end of this dark drama because I was damn sure that his name was not Love.

CHAPTER TWENTY-SEVEN

Opulent whiskey and operatic weirdness, following a long walk in the cold rain while contemplating a good way to handle a bad man, all conspired to create a restless night. In the morning, I rushed through a shower and headed to Gustaw's for a quick bite. From there, I looked forward to a morning of degenerate dialogue at the Pleasure Palace—the perfect start to a week.

"Riley, you look a little rough this morning," Ludwika said as I came into the bakery.

"Nothing that a cup of Gustaw's coffee can't fix," I said.

"He put together a special treat for you, knowing you never miss a Monday morning with us."

"Gustaw is a good man," I said.

"Good inside, yes. But not so much the outside. He is growing a moustache like his idol, Lech Walesa. Gustaw looks more like cave man than revolutionary hero."

The Polish Neanderthal came out from the kitchen, approached Ludwika from behind, wrapped his burly arms around his plump wife, and nuzzled his bristly upper lip into her neck.

"You cannot resist such a virile man," he said as she squirmed unconvincingly to escape his grasp. Ludwika managed to turn and playfully push him away, declaring that if he didn't shave soon, he'd look like the bigfoot creatures that villagers reported in the Tatra mountains along the border with Slovakia. She was a big fan of yeti and had even dragged Gustaw up to Humbolt County a couple summers ago after a flurry of reports about furry sightings. They didn't find the creature.

While I took a seat and tried to decide if the coffee was stronger than usual, Gustaw went back into the kitchen and returned with a plate of pierogi and a big grin.

"To celebrate the people of Poland and Ireland, I make special breakfast for you, my friend," he said.

I poked curiously at the stuffed dumplings which were not filled with anything as prosaic as fruit, which one might expect for breakfast. The dockworker-turned-baker had an affinity for hearty food to begin the day.

"Both our people love cabbage and potato to make us strong."

Gustaw lifted his chin and pounded his chest. I could see what Ludwika meant about the reference to ape men.

"In your honor," he continued, "I add corned beef to pierogi!"

I tasted the concoction, a melding of Polish dumplings with corned beef hash. The result was genuinely pleasing—and far more down-to-earth than the unaccountable passion for quiche that has swept the country, with half-baked cooks dumping every imaginable frou-frou ingredient into curdled eggs and a soggy crust.

"This is a perfect start to a damp day," I said.

"Not so cold as Chicago, where cousin Jerzy lives. He tells it was twenty-seven below zero. I say San Francisco is more like Gdansk. You get chilled but not turned into ice cube."

"Maybe your next recipe should be something to stave off the chill at the end of a day. Perhaps a blend the finest Polish vodka with the best Irish whiskey, although I'm not sure the result will be satisfying for either nation."

Gustaw stroked his whiskers and looked into space, contemplating the possibilities.

"Do not tempt him, Riley," Ludwika scolded. "He does not need to be encouraged. He drinks too much vodka without an excuse from you."

Other customers seeking more conventional morning fare began to come in, so I figured it was good time to leave my payment along with an extra fin in appreciation of the custom breakfast—a tip that the Polish couple would never accept if handed to them. But I knew that running a two-person bakery was less lucrative than running a four-person extermination business, and I wasn't exactly rolling in dough.

I stopped by the shop and nabbed a couple of work orders in the hope of doing something less revolting than my primary task for the morning. Given that it's only two miles from Potrero Hill to the Castro and that morning traffic was at a crawl, I could've walked faster than driving to the Pleasure Palace. But the rain had increased from spitting to rotten, the weather equivalent of a sulky teenager. The heavier the precipitation, the slower the commute—which didn't reduce speeds enough to prevent a vegetable truck from overturning at 18th and Guerrero. The resulting salad bar became an impromptu bonanza for a half dozen homeless men who were gleaning the windfall, while the uninjured but outraged driver tried to shoo away the scavengers. Meanwhile, the cops did their best to create gridlock, as if a tipped-over delivery truck was an armored car heist.

For my part, the traffic jam provided a chance to listen to the entirety of Camille Saint-Saëns' *Carnival of the Animals* on KDFC. Tommy had recently come to relish this musical suite nearly as much as Prokofiev's *Peter and the Wolf*. He figured out how each movement captured the qualities of an animal: rooster, tortoise, elephant or—his favorite—the kangaroo, which Saint-Saëns portrayed by hopping fifths and grace notes. The composer covered the spectrum of vertebrates—fish, reptiles, birds, and mammals—but omitted the spineless creatures. Presumably then, as now, most people considered insects, clams, and lobsters to be something other than animals.

The tangle of cars made its way through the chaotic intersection during the twelfth movement: Fossils. Even the inanimate impressions of extinct creatures counted as animals. Insects just don't get any respect. Saint-Saëns echoed his own *Danse macabre* in which he summoned humans from the grave and used the xylophone to evoke the sound of bones clattering in a darkly humorous allusion to death. Tommy loved listening for the riff on *Twinkle Twinkle Little Star* in this movement as it made him feel like a musical connoisseur. According to the radio host, the inside joke of this movement is Saint-Saëns' allusions to musical pieces that the composer considered to be fossils in his time. Today, there might be snippets from the big band era—one of the last times that popular music was both fashionable and melodious.

Although the musical carnival was light and playful, the piece had a disturbing quality in light of my morning's venture. The menagerie of animals providing entertainment was ominously reminiscent of the zoophilia that was insinuated in Stefan and Michelle's "dance macabre." And now I was headed to their store in search of Luis—her confidant in all things sadomasochistic and animalistic. But to be fair, Saint-Saëns married a nineteen-year-old girl when he was nearly forty, became estranged from her, and probably preferred men over women when all was said and done, although nothing was publicly said or unquestionably done. Such was the nature of sex a century ago. Maybe in another hundred years, foreplay with spiders will be considered normal and people with be trolling the Castro in search of an eight-legged threesome. I'm glad I won't be alive to see it.

I bypassed a prime parking spot in front of the Pleasure Palace and found a metered place around the corner. It was ridiculous, but I didn't want to be seen—by whom, I couldn't say—parked in front of the sex shop. I couldn't tell if I was being prudish or discrete, but there was a kind of guilt-by-association. I'd rather be caught crawling through an attic filled with bat shit or a cellar infested with cockroaches than perusing a store filled with whips, furry costumes and triple-action diving dolphins.

The voluptuous redheaded salesgirl would've been more enticing, but Luis was a fine specimen in his own right—a Latin American with intense brown eyes, coffee skin, and a torso that was a testament to sit ups. He wore black-framed glasses that conveyed a scholarly demeanor despite a body builder's physique under a white tee-shirt tucked into black jeans. I'm as straight as they come but this guy was a tribute to the human form. I feigned interest in a rack of sex guides including: *The Joy of Kink, Cindi Love's Sexercises,* and *The Tao of Orgasm.*

"Can I help you?" Luis asked, having quietly moved from behind the counter. I'd already decided that dishonesty would be the best policy.

"Maybe. These books are not as creative as a guy might hope," I said.

"Meaning?" His eyebrows arched. I gathered that in his world, one had to be cautious about unfamiliar sorts. Grant Roberts was gunning for vice arrests and undercover pervert patrols were a fine way for the cops to score points with the assistant district attorney.

"Meaning that Stefan told me you specialized in less humdrum practices."

"You know Stefan?"

"I do. And I know about Michelle. That's a terrible loss to those of us seeking pleasure beyond the dull boundaries of social norms."

Luis glanced around the shop. I was the only customer. Even so, he lowered his voice, "What do you know about Michelle?"

"There was an accident involving a spider. Nobody's fault. And hey, lots of people die of heart attacks during boring sex. I'd rather go while doing something imaginative."

"And what do you imagine?"

"Maybe something at the intersection of animals and your expertise," I said, trying to be a bit coy as I wasn't really sure where the hell this was going.

"My expertise?"

"Yes. Stefan says that you're a connoisseur of BDSM. That's really quite a buffet of possibilities, eh?"

"Well put. I can offer you anything on that menu, although my tastes run to domination and masochism," he said. Given his build, I would've thought Luis was more into giving than receiving. But then, I was way out of my league in making guesses in this underworld.

"A kindred spirit," I lied.

"I might have something for you," Luis said. "Michelle and I collaborated on some projects, and I'm sensing that you could find one of our products to be exciting."

He led me to the back of the store, where he gestured for me to wait as he disappeared through the black curtains draped over the doorway to Michelle's office. I perused a pegboard holding riding crops, fuzzy handcuffs and feather dusters, like a supply store for offbeat equestrians, cops and maids, although I undoubtedly misunderstood the precise function of the merchandise. Luis reappeared holding a videotape.

"Here you go," he said. The cassette had a handwritten label: Stiletto Squash. "There's another one with a barefoot dominatrix, but I think the dialogue is better in this production. More natural and intense," he said.

I took the video case and followed him to the cash register. This was all fine and good—actually sick and bad—but I needed access to whatever was happening behind the scenes. Michelle needed money and Luis was my best hope for figuring out why. But watching a videotape of high-heeled women talking dirty and crushing cockroaches wasn't going to get me any closer to an answer.

"That'll be fifty dollars," Luis said.

I grimaced and said, "A bit pricey, no?"

"We produce these in limited quantities and high quality. If you want standard porn, we have an extensive inventory," he said, flicking his head toward a wall covered in films of Bambi and Debbie losing their virginity in locker rooms and hospital beds for the hundredth time.

"I understand. Of course, if there was a way to get closer to the action I'd be willing to pay a premium," I said, handing him my credit card and hoping that the Pleasure Palace used discretion in recording transactions. Not that anyone would see the billing statement, but having "Stiletto Squash" on my purchase history was like having the nuns tell me that my juvenile indiscretions would go on my "permanent record," which at the time I took to mean a document that God would scrutinize when I stood at the pearly gates.

Luis looked at me, apparently deciding whether I could be trusted beyond purchasing dubious videos. "Tell you what," he said, "meet me for lunch at the Anchor Oyster Bar and we can discuss the possibilities."

I thanked him and left, figuring I was in for an interview to determine if I would be allowed access to something more sinister and vile—and hopefully more connected to Michelle's murder. I wasn't sure this line of investigation was leading anywhere, but I had nowhere else to go. Thankfully, my normal business could occupy me at least until lunchtime.

It was a short drive over to Eureka Valley, a quiet residential neighborhood that used to be filled with working-class Irish families. A few were still there, but nowadays there were lots of homosexuals which accounts for the district having elected the first openly gay politician to the San Francisco

Board of Supervisors. The Irish Catholics and homosexual atheists made their community work rather harmoniously, Harvey Milk's murder notwithstanding. The devoted and gay public servant was assassinated by an asshole whose lawyer got him a slap on the wrist with the infamous Twinkie defense—blaming junk food for the murder. Now there's a perversion of justice.

According to the work order that sent me into the hybrid neighborhood, Mrs. Moynihan was, in her words, "being driven mad as a box of frogs" by a chirping insect in her house. It took me about ten minutes to determine that the nice old lady was suffering from a combination of an underperforming hearing aid and a weakening smoke detector. The former wasn't telling her where to look and the latter was telling her it needed repair.

My treatment involved walking down to the corner market and picking up batteries for both devices, thereby exterminating the chirps and allowing Mrs. Moynihan to hear *Days of our Lives* and *General Hospital* without the volume turned high enough to vibrate the windows. The kindly widow served me Earl Grey tea while watching her shows. I figured that my day was shaping up more like *The Edge of Night* and *Another World*.

Chapter Twenty-Eight

Luis had nabbed one of the few tables at Anchor Oyster Bar, which consisted of a long, narrow room with gleaming walls and a floor of white, honeycomb tiles set off with black grout. Between a counter running the length of the dining area and four tiny tables, there was seating for a couple dozen customers. The ambiance was pure hokum with a nautical motif, but the food was the real deal. I ordered a platter of oysters on the half-shell and a glass of Riesling. Luis went with a bowl of steamed, black mussels from California (sweeter and richer than the greenlips from New Zealand, if you ask me) and a Bartles & Jaymes Tickle Pink wine cooler—not a drink to match the guy's physique, but to each his own. After we'd made a dent in our lunches, Luis cut to the chase.

"So Riley, what's your angle?"

"My angle?"

"Yeah, you're not into kink," he said.

I slurped an oyster and waited in silence.

"You did your best to play the role at the store, but I could see through your act. I called Stefan and he was pretty cagey. He said I should trust you but didn't explain what you're up to. I know it's not domination and animals. So, who are you?"

"I'm an ex-cop operating an extermination business."

"Ex?"

"Yeah. I'm done with law enforcement or vice versa." The wine was perfect with the oysters, which tasted like the sea itself.

"So, what's the deal with Stefan?"

"Long story. But the short version is that my business is at risk through a series of events linked to Michelle's death. Something went wrong with the spider Stefan used to arouse her, and whoever messed up their foreplay is likely connected to a couple other deaths."

"You can't suspect me," he said, no longer interested in plucking the orange meat from the blue-black shells. "Michelle meant a great deal in my life."

I cocked my head and arched my eyebrows. It was enough to keep him going.

"Okay, we were lovers. She didn't hide it from Stefan, and he didn't hide his interest in going both ways. Not with me, but I know other guys who he enjoyed."

The slippery tissue of the oysters had become uncomfortably sensual. I put some lemon on the last couple to make them taste fresher, cleaner.

"Michelle and you were into sex but maybe looking for something more?"

"Like what?"

"Like money."

"I suppose so. We were putting together some funding for a series of films on topics of our shared interests."

"How much were you talking about?"

"Five, maybe ten, grand."

"Chump change. I want to know why she needed a hundred thousand bucks."

Luis looked pained. I could tell that he had answers but they weren't going to come as easily as his admission of banging his boss. I needed to deal Luis one more card to force his hand.

I leaned forward and looked him in the eye. "Luis, the trail leading to Michelle's death ends with her breaking confidentiality and blackmailing a guy who was supposed to be anonymous in one of her films. Stefan said this was totally out of character." I found the notion of any of these people having "character" to be ludicrous. They had urges and cravings. Luis would show me otherwise.

"We need to find a more private place," Luis said.

The lunchtime noise seemed more than sufficient to drown out our voices, and nobody had shown the least interest in our conversation. But whatever he had to share was apparently even darker than what we'd discussed so far.

Luis and I walked down 19th Street in the cold grayness. We ended up at Kite Hill, a small park with a captivating panorama of the city on a clear day. The low, skittering clouds eliminated any hope of a view. The winter rains were beginning to transform the parched grass into a verdant green. Nina and I had picnicked on the hill last spring, when she'd shown me a lily unique to California. Her people crushed the bulb of the "soap plant" into a foamy lather for cleaning and, when food was scarce, they cooked it like a potato. There can't be many plants that are good for both shampooing and eating. But then, Luis and his sort figured out how to use animals for unexpected purposes. If nothing else, humans are inventive.

"Let's sit here," Luis said, gesturing to a picnic table. The benches were soaked but a wet ass was the least of my discomforts. We sat across from one another. He gave a deep sigh and began. "I'm a member of the crush community. Do you know what that is?"

I nodded, sensing I wasn't going to like what was coming.

"We get together and stage crushes. Michelle was our crush mistress— the one who performs. She totally understood what we wanted and always said the most erotic things." He lapsed into a falsetto imitation of her voice, "You're just a wriggling bug, trying to escape. Here, let me pin you to the floor. Squirm you little maggot. I'm going to squish you between my toes. You're just a disgusting, greasy spot." He sighed and shrugged somewhat apologetically.

"Okay, where are you going with this?" I asked.

"Well, she'd bring the crickets, cockroaches, or worms . . ." He paused. I waited. " . . . or whatever."

"Whatever?"

"Insects and stuff like that." Another pause. This was getting tiresome, but I could tell he had something on his mind, and I hoped it would be useful to my investigation. "At least until the last couple of months."

"Go on."

"The group was drawn into some really wicked shit by this guy, Eunectes."

"That's some name. Is the guy Greek or what?"

"Maybe. He kinda looks the part, but it's not his real name. Everyone uses an alias for confidentiality." That meant tracking his actual identity would be nearly impossible, if such information turned out to be important, which seemed increasingly likely.

"So what's this Eunectes up to?

"We were all into soft crush, but he wanted to take it up a notch."

"Meaning?" There was a long silence. "Look Luis, you dragged me up here because you're in some sort of bind—and it's evidently not the kind involving fuzzy handcuffs. You can either bet on me or roll the dice yourself." Luis was maybe twenty years younger than me, so I took a chance with using my best paternal voice to trigger both trust and trepidation—a potent combination when it worked.

"Okay, okay. We started getting into hard crush. At first pinkie mice, the little newborns. Then adult mice. And in the last month, he brought kittens. Just strays from the alleys. They'd end up dead anyway, he said."

"And Michelle went along with this?" The icy water soaked into my pants, but the discomfort seemed like a kind of penance for what was unfolding.

"It was weird. He was, like, charismatic. Even mesmerizing. Nobody argued about his suggestions or opposed him. Michelle seemed to be enchanted by his smooth talk. I know they were lovers and he probably pushed all of her buttons, even ones that I wasn't into. I suspect she told him everything. He was irresistible."

"Okay, so we have this guy who entices everyone to follow his lead, progressing—if that's what it should be called—from squirmy creatures to cuddly animals. And Michelle is pulled along as the 'crush mistress.' I'm not quite seeing where the money comes in, but I suppose anything this messed up generates the potential for extortion or blackmail."

"Maybe so . . ." Another long pause while my ass went from chilled to numb.

"Goddammit, Luis, we've come this far. How much worse can it get?"

"It gets really bad," Luis said, as if stomping on kittens wasn't so awful. "Things have gotten out of control." He took a deep, stuttering breath. "Eunectes is talking about crushing a person."

It was my turn to sit silently. We'd gone from weird, to sick, to evil. "What do you want from me?"

"I need your help."

"You don't know me."

"Stefan vouched for you. Things are sliding downhill, fast. I've got nowhere to go, so I'll take my chances with an ex-cop who can stand up to Eunectes."

"You're pretty ripped, Luis. Why can't you challenge this weirdo?" He dropped his head in shame.

"I'm strong, but I'm not courageous, Riley. I have the body of a lover, not a fighter. Stefan said you could 'solve problems' and I'm desperate."

"Maybe Eunectes is all bluff or fantasy," I said. A soft rain started to fall. "I can't see how anyone is going to lie down and let some woman trample him." I was trying to grasp what Luis was saying and struggling to imagine anything so twisted.

"Like I said, Eunectes is alluring. He'll find a woman to replace Michelle. As for the guy, I don't know what he's planning. Maybe the dude will be drugged or something."

"You make it sound like Eunectes has some poor sap lined up. I need the whole story if I'm going to help you and maybe figure out how this connects to Michelle's death," I said, pulling the collar of my jacket around my neck to keep the water from running down my back. Luis didn't seem to notice the rain.

"Shit, I've taken you this far. So here's what I know." Luis slumped as if weighed down by what he was about to say. "One of the guys in our group is sort of like Eunectes's disciple. He told me that Eunectes has some retarded kid living with him. And—"

"Slow down, Luis. Let's start with the disciple. What's his name?"

"He goes by Redbug."

"Any reason?"

"Yeah, he has red hair and works at some insect laboratory. He's occasionally supplied beetles and roaches for crush nights."

"What about the retarded kid?"

"Not much to say. I've seen him around Eunectes's car a couple of times after our events. He doesn't join us, but crush isn't everyone's thing."

"That's a safe bet," I said. Luis flashed a crooked smile. "Describe the kid."

"My sense is that he's your basic gutter whore, although Eunectes probably fixed him up. At least his clothes are clean. He looks to be late teens, sandy blond hair and sunken eyes. He has a reddish purple blemish on his face, like maybe from being burned."

"Or a birthmark?" There were hundreds of homeless youth wandering the alleys of San Francisco, but Eunectes's adolescent companion, or captive, was a disturbingly close match to Petey—the kid who Nina was worried about.

"Could be. Hard to say, given he stays in the shadows, like he's hiding but not scared enough to ditch Eunectes."

"I might know who he is. Or to be more precise, I know somebody who might care a great deal about him. And if I'm right, then whether or not my wading into this filthy swamp does any good for Stefan or you, I need to make sure that this kid isn't hurt—or killed. But I'm wondering whether we're getting in over our heads. Maybe it's time to go to the cops."

"No!" Luis sat bolt upright, as if jolted by an electric shock. "They'll sweep up everyone, and most of the guys aren't doing anything illegal. The prosecutor will humiliate all of us to please that Moral Majority asshole in the DA's office."

Apparently Grant Roberts had put the fear of God into anyone not using the missionary position, although crushing creatures for kicks didn't strike me as the sort of behavior that warranted social approval. But neither did it require arrest in a city with plenty of homicides, burglaries, and rapes to keep a police force productively occupied. When we get to the point where a bunch of guys getting off on a woman mashing insects is the biggest problem in San Francisco, we'll be close to utopia.

"Alright, we can keep this unofficial. For now. But if I'm going to make any progress, you need to get me access to your little crush carnivals," I said.

"There's a performance tomorrow night. I might be able to get you in, but there could be a test of sorts. The guys are pretty anxious about newcomers and you don't come across as a genuine crush freak."

I took that as a compliment. But I didn't know what he meant by "a test"—and I didn't want to ask. Sometimes a swamp is best entered without knowing what's beneath the fetid water. We walked back into the Castro, and Luis said he'd give me a call. Then I drove up to Hayes Valley to solve a problem I could understand.

In the early part of the century, the district was ethnically mixed like Potrero Hill, but after World War II, Hayes Valley became an African American neighborhood. The streets were reasonably safe during the day, but no place to be at night. I stopped at a sagging Victorian townhouse on Grove. According to Carol's work order, the owner had found, "smelly worms with lots of legs" in the laundry room.

I knocked on the door and a big, black woman answered. She led me to the kitchen and showed me the invaders she'd trapped in a margarine tub. Just as I expected, she had a cozy little collection of millipedes. I explained that they wouldn't do any harm and she explained that, "I don' care if they be hurtin' any folks. I want 'em gone." Fair enough.

I checked the yard and found a rock garden built up against the house, along with a pile of scrap wood and a bed of roses with a thick covering of mulch. The woman loaned me a rake, and I spent a half hour removing millipede habitat from around the foundation. The house was just south of where the 1906 fires stopped, making it historically valuable and structurally questionable.

Back in the day, builders mixed beach sand into the concrete. When the salt leaches out of the sand, the result is a crumbling foundation—and job security for exterminators. All sorts of creatures move through the cracks and holes in search of a better, indoor life. Given our cold, wet winter, the millipedes were undoubtedly tickled to find a warm, dry home. I spent an hour hunting millipedes in the basement and devoted four tubes of caulk to sealing the foundation. Between the outdoor mud and the indoor dust lurking behind appliances and storage boxes, I was effectively tarred and feathered.

Finally, I went upstairs and explained what had happened, how the problem was fixed, and why there was no need to spray insecticide. She seemed somewhere between pleased and dubious, telling me, "You be the expert Mister Riley, but if'n they's back in da' house, I be callin' you." Fair enough.

I drove back to the shop, feeling filthy—inside and out.

CHAPTER TWENTY-NINE

Back at the shop, there was a stack of phone messages. Carol had checked the "Urgent" box on one from Lieutenant Papadopoulos and added a parenthetical note: "Not a nice man." I began by returning calls from several potential clients and a couple of disgruntled customers. Of the latter, one was convinced our work had insufficiently scorched the earth. I assured him that having every single living creature, other than the family dog, "tits up"—Larry's term, which I didn't use with the homeowner—within a day of treatment wasn't our goal and shouldn't be expected as this would mean the house was a toxic waste dump. The other customer complained that our scheduled inspection was unnecessary because he hadn't seen a cockroach or earwig around the apartment complex in weeks. I explained that not having vermin was like not having blood in your urine or oil on your driveway—a sign that your doctor and mechanic were doing their job and everything was copacetic. But the absence of a symptom didn't mean it was no longer necessary to have an annual physical or a regular tune-up. Having assuaged these concerns, I called the dithering detective.

The station operator connected me to Papadopoulus. "Lieutenant," I said, "how can I make your Monday more pleasant?"

"Stow it, Riley. I need a status report on the Linford case."

"Hey, our deal was that I had until the end of the week."

"The new deal is that the DA's office has caught wind of something perverted in the works, and Roberts' God squad wants a bust to placate the holy rollers."

"I can assure you the pieces are starting to come together."

"I can assure *you* that obstruction of justice is a felony," he retorted.

"Look, you'll be the first to know when I have something worth reporting."

"I let you pursue this as a favor, but if things don't start happening I'm taking over—whatever it might mean for your little business."

"Things are happening, Lieutenant."

"And understand that if those things happen in ways that require code two assistance, I've never heard of you." Translation: if I needed emergency backup from law enforcement, I was on my own. He hung up.

I took care of ordering some chemicals and supplies, while thinking through my next moves. I called Dr. Chen and explained my need for some professional insight regarding a situation that could be headed toward another murder. That was enough for her to make time to meet with me tomorrow. The afternoon appointment was workable, given that the freaks weren't going to gather until evening.

These best laid plans, which might involve both mice (squished) and men (excited), gave me the opportunity to contemplate what to do about Nina's stalker. Now there was a problem I could handle on my own. I unlocked my filing cabinet and opened the bottom drawer. The snubnosed .38 Special was tucked into a gorgeous, custom holster with "Erin Go Bragh" tooled into the side—a gift from my father when I made detective. The smell of full-grain Italian leather melded with the vapors of Hoppe's No. 9 gun oil.

I could hear Carol shutting down the front office, so I went up the hall to ask her for a favor which was crucial to what I had worked out for the evening. I needed to pick her up around eight o'clock, have her wear a bulky coat and hat, and drop her off at Nina's place. There, she'd go into the apartment, turn on the lights, leave the front curtain open a crack, disappear from sight, and wait until I knocked four times as a signal to come out.

She was dubious, but I told her that Nina was in danger and her role in my evening's drama was critical to making the situation safe. Carol's response was typical of what she'd come to understand after years of working with me: "I doubt whatever you're planning is legal, but I have no doubt it's the right thing to do. Or at least you're making the best of some awful situation. I'll be ready at eight. Please don't tell me anything more."

I love that woman.

My next stop was Marty's Gym for a short, hard workout before dinner. Jump roping, interspersed with bouts on the heavy bag, had me gasping and sweating. I cooled down with some speed bag training, then wandered over to the sparring ring. A big, black fighter with a sculpted torso was getting schooled by a focused Mexican kid with solid footwork and impressive hand speed. I sidled up to the old codger, who was leaning on the apron and grinning mischievously.

"What's up, Marty?"

"Watching a man learn a lesson," he said, shifting the unlit cigar to the other side of his mouth.

"You figure it's okay for the pretty boy to take a pounding?"

"Absolutely."

"How so?"

"Two reasons. First, he got into the ring." Marty spit some errant strands of tobacco onto the floor.

"So he consented."

"Yup, he knew the deal. And second, he was over confident. Figured he was too pretty to lose and didn't respect his opponent."

"So he deserves what he's getting."

"Brainy sorts have yapped about this shit for centuries in highfalutin books. Nothing like a boxing ring to clarify what some people want to make complicated."

I took a quick steam, showered, and headed up 18th to Van Ness, where I met Nina at Whiz Burger—a romantic setting in my book. A run-down, neon-signed drive-in that's been in business for a quarter of a century evokes sweet nostalgia, like a ratty, leather motorcycle jacket from 1955. We grabbed a couple of stools at the counter.

I ordered a Whiz burger, along with fries and a malted. They still call it a "malted" which resonates with the ambiance. My father used to love double-rich chocolate malted milk from the Walgreens soda counter, a drink reminding him of the best moments during the worst times in the Great Depression. Nina opted for the Junior burger with a diet Coke. She was watching her weight, although I found her to be perfectly sumptuous. In fact, admiring the profile of the sweater she was wearing as she leaned over to take a bite of burger had me feeling lusty. I prefer sex to violence, but tonight was going to be focused on the latter—a reality I was keeping from her. However, there was another unpleasant reality I needed to explore.

"Nina, I might've found out something about Petey," I said without the nonchalance I'd hoped to evince. She sat bolt upright, turned toward me, and almost knocked over her drink,

"What? Is he okay? Riley, tell me what you know."

"Slow down. I don't know anything specific—"

"Goddammit Riley, don't play games. This matters to me. A lot," she said, latching onto my wrist as if preparing to apply a submission hold.

"I have a vague description of a street kid who might match his appearance and who might be in danger," I said.

"What kind of danger?" her grip tightened.

"Sexual. Whoever this is might be part of a violent fantasy."

"Jesus," she said, "What do you need from me? How can I help?"

"Give me whatever you can about him. Anything."

"I haven't seen him in a couple of weeks. When he dropped in at the daycare, he was needy—like a child making his way on the streets. He'd barely speak, except to Tommy and Karsa, but I could tell he was easy pickings for predators." Her grasp began to relax.

"Okay, good. You said he had a birthmark on his face. Give me a full description."

Nina lapsed into police mode. "Five-eight to five-ten, late teens maybe early twenties, thin and reedy, hundred-and-thirty or -forty pounds, curly blond hair over his ears. He usually wore ripped jeans, a raggedy sweatshirt, and red sneakers."

"Good."

"Meaning?"

"Meaning, not good. The kid I heard about could be Petey. I should know by tomorrow night. Until then, there's nothing to do but sit tight."

Nina let go of my wrist and leaned against me. "I'm scared, but I trust you'll protect him."

I gave her a long hug to convey a confidence I didn't possess. Then I managed to get her onto another subject while we finished our meal. She was heading to a knitting circle this evening. The women provided social support (hence their self-appointed nickname, "stitch and bitch") and shared a love of all things fibrous. Nina's people had a long history of weaving. As a girl, she'd learned to harvest willow, wild grape, and bear grass, prepare the materials, dye the fibers using berry juices, and form the baskets which were beautiful and functional. The Chowok passed down the knowledge from one generation to another but now that the tribe was scattered, having other women to teach her about knitting made her feel connected. I alluded to our knotting the sheets tomorrow night, and she rolled her eyes—but then gave me a lusty kiss.

While Nina headed off to a peaceful evening, I headed into a violent night. I picked up Carol, who was dressed so that from a distance she could pass as Nina. I went over the plan on our way to Nina's apartment, gave Carol the key, and dropped her off a block from the place so my truck wouldn't spook Tim. I retrieved my gun from the glove box, crossed to the other side of the street and watched her head to the apartments. I avoided the streetlights and loitered in the shadow cast by a New Zealand Christmas tree, like an armed Santa deciding if my quarry was being naughty or nice. It was soon apparent that Tim was awake and hadn't been watching out.

Carol left the drapes in the front window open a few inches and within minutes Tim had slithered out from under a concrete staircase, quickly glanced around and slowly started up to the second floor. He'd made it halfway to the top by the time I crossed the street into the courtyard. The guy was entirely focused on his goal, so I was just a couple stairs behind him when he sensed my presence. I reached up and grabbed the back of his fatigue jacket.

"Hey man, let go. I'm not doing anything," he said, struggling to escape.

"Tim, we need to have a talk. Come downstairs with me, or I'll bounce you down the steps."

When we got to the ground level, he made my decision easier by shooting off his mouth. "This is a free country. I ain't doin' nothing. Just out for an evening walk and you grab me. I should call the cops."

"Look, I gave you fair warning. You knew the deal," I said, taking a fistful of his jacket and pushing him into the shadows under the stairs.

"You better not hit me or I'll press charges," he said.

"I'm not going to hit you, Tim. That would mean messing up my hands, and maybe you really would be stupid enough to call the cops from the emergency room. Then, I'd need to explain my bloody knuckles and your broken face to the cops." Pulling the .38 from my holster and putting the muzzle under his chin, I continued, "I don't have time for that, Tim."

"What the fuck? You can't shoot me. They'll find you and gas your ass," he said with a tremor in his voice, trying to convince himself that I wasn't going to pull the trigger.

"Ya know Tim, you're right. I can't blow your brains out. Too messy. So I'll do the next best thing."

I moved the gun to an inch from his left ear, took a step back, angled the barrel toward the concrete overhang—and pulled the trigger. I was using the "Treasury load" that Winchester provided exclusively to police—or to those who had buddies inside law enforcement agencies. When I'd been a cop, we had round-nose lead bullets which didn't penetrate for a damn. To improve stopping power, you had to move up to a .38/44 or a .357 Magnum, which had their downsides. In the 1970s, a jacketed hollow-point became favored by the Secret Service—hence the "Treasury load." These babies exceeded the industry-standard pressure limits, so cops had to sign a waiver acknowledging the potential for firearm damage. But the upside was damage to the target, compared to the old ammunition.

Some of my pals on the force complained that the new load was dirty, especially in a short-barreled gun like mine. And firing them made a lot of flash for a .38, along with an earsplitting crack. This last feature was, for my purposes this evening, a virtue rather than a drawback.

When the gun went off, Tim grabbed the side of his head and crumpled to the ground. My skull was ringing but I knew he was in far worse condition. Tim writhed in a fetal position, screaming about being deaf. And he was, since the blast had burst his eardrum, or so I judged from the blood trickling out his ear and down his neck. After a minute, he stopped moaning, and I jerked him to a sitting position against the cinderblock wall.

"Here's the deal, Tim," I said into his right ear that was likely still ringing but not bleeding. He grunted so I figured he could hear me well enough. "You won't be hearing anything for a long time, maybe ever again, in your other ear. Take that as an ongoing reminder of what will happen if I see you anywhere near these apartments." His face was screwed up in pain, but his eyes shifted in my direction so I knew he was listening. I jammed the gun between his legs and he winced. "That's right Tim, next time you end up with vaporized balls rather than just a ruptured eardrum. Now get out of here before I decide not to wait with your .38 castration."

He stumbled to his feet, shuffled out the back of the breezeway to the alley and disappeared into the night. I retrieved Carol from Nina's apartment, locked up, and listened for sirens, but it seemed that nobody was sufficiently worried about a gunshot to call the police. Nice neighborhood.

CHAPTER THIRTY

Coming through the front door of Goat Hill Extermination the next morning, I was greeted by the sounds of Carol tapping away at her new computer while her radio featured a guy crooning the vacuous lyrics of a love song to his partner in bed. I shook the raindrops off my jacket and turned down the volume just as the lead singer and his twanging band slid into a chorus of "feels so right." I rolled my eyes.

"Riley, don't make fun of that song or you'll have more than me to deal with," she said.

"Let me guess . . . Larry."

"That's right. He has a stack of Alabama albums in the back. How'd you know?"

"I can't imagine Dennis being a fan of a group that sounds whiter than new-fallen snow. Speaking of which, if it gets any colder out there, we might see a repeat of '76. Remember that?"

She shook her head and smiled sheepishly. "I sure do. A friend of mine got her car stuck trying to drive up to Twin Peaks. Five inches of snow is more than enough to bog down a Ford Escort with bald tires," she laughed.

I hoped to be of some value in the never-ending pursuit of six-legged vermin and cash flow for the business this morning. Rather than pressuring Luis about the upcoming crush event, I wanted to give him time to work on getting me access and to give myself a few hours of normalcy.

"What's on the schedule?" I asked, pouring myself a cup of coffee.

"The guys have the work orders in the back," she said. I turned up the radio and started down the hall when Carol called out, "Riley, one more thing."

I came back to her desk and said, "Shoot, babe."

"Call me 'babe' again and I will shoot. Except talk about gunshots reminds me of last night. I need to know, did anything happen that, well . . ."

"Well?"

"That I need to cover for."

"Cover for?"

"C'mon Riley, just tell me, should I have a story ready if the police come asking about your whereabouts?"

"They won't. But if they do, keep it simple. You spent the night at home and have no idea where I might have been. I can assure you there are no bodies or trails of blood. Just a chunk of concrete missing from an overhang and no reason for anyone to suspect that you or I were there. Especially you. Relax, doll."

That last bit had the desired effect of breaking the tension. Carol threw a roll of tape, which missed me and plunked Mr. Coffee. I headed to the back where Larry and Dennis were laughing at a recording being played over their boom box.

"What are you guys listening to?" I asked.

"Shhhh," Dennis said, "Larry be educating me through his boy, George Carlin."

The comedian was riffing on homosexuality. He was sardonically observing that guy parts and girl parts match up and fit together, while homosexuals have to share the parts in ways that don't seem natural, whatever that means. As Carlin put it, people were more inventive than nature, adapting the sexual apparatus to our purposes.

"You gotta love this Riley," Larry chuckled, "Carol listened yesterday and told us it was righteous. The man tells it like it is." Dennis shushed him.

The comedian observed that rubbing against a naked person in a dark room feels really good. But when the light goes on, if your partner is the same sex, society dictates that you scream in horror. But, it felt *really* good. And to be honest, generating pleasure seems entirely normal—whether or not it's natural.

"That is one funny honkey, but he be no Richard Pryor," Dennis said as Larry turned off the recording.

"Good point, m'man. Carlin didn't set himself on fire," Larry said.

"That's harsh, homey. True, but harsh."

"The dude wigged out, for sure. Free basing is bad shit."

"So Riley, what you make of Larry's killer comedian?" Dennis asked.

"Nothing wrong about two people enjoying one another's bodies. But what if one of the bodies isn't okay with what's happening? What if one of the bodies is being damaged for the other's pleasure?"

"Sheeit, boss," Dennis said, "you being a major downer."

"Yeah, 'sup with that?" Larry added, looking annoyed.

"Sorry, guys. My investigation has run into some dark corners."

"Like with those messed up videos at the Linford's house?" asked Dennis.

"And that heinous spider shit between Stefan and his lady?" added Larry.

The guys had been talking and knew about what each other had seen, so I filled them in on the rest of the story—at least as much as I could understand. When I was through, they looked bewildered.

"This Luis dude, maybe he just be yankin' yo' chain, Riley," said Dennis.

"Maybe, but one of those videos you found in Lane's office had a title about crushing crickets, if I remember," I said.

"Watching a chick step on some insects is one thing, but crushing another person? Man, that's too twisted, even for this warped city," said Larry.

"Maybe, maybe not. I'm meeting with an expert on psychological disorders later today. I should know more after that," I said.

"And after your freak show tonight," said Larry.

"So, what do you need us to do?" asked Dennis.

"Two things. First, be ready to roll with whatever comes. Whatever happens could come quick—and I might need you guys to provide support."

"We be yo' homeboys," Dennis said. Larry nodded.

"And second, we need to get after the work orders that Carol put together. Dennis and I can take the job at the Summit Towers penthouse, as that could mean some serious cash flow and having two people will impress the client. Larry, you take the rodent job for Mrs. Orbison."

"You mean Mrs. Robinson," Dennis said with a leer.

"What are you talking about?" I asked.

"Tell him, you bodacious stud," said Dennis, giving Larry's bicep an affectionate squeeze and getting his hand slapped away.

"It's nothing, Riley. Mrs. Orbison is an attractive woman in her fifties. And Dennis figures that she's as seductive as Anne Bancroft in *The Graduate*, which means my co-worker's mind is in the gutter," Larry said.

"She not just into boy toys, she be into weird shit. That woman make me nervous," said Dennis.

"How so?" I asked.

"You know how some customers get juiced by nailing a mouse in a snap trap. Bang, and the little pest that's been nestin' in the dish towels is pancaked. But, Mrs. Robinson—"

"Orbison," Larry corrected.

"Yeah, whatever. She be quivering when I set them mole spears in her backyard, wanting to know how they worked. I thought she was goin' to start moanin' when I tol' her about the scissors trap. No way that this boy is headin' back to that house. She be all Larry's."

Moles could make a mess of a lawn, even during the winter. If the ground didn't freeze, the little varmints didn't hibernate. The traps either the impaled or sliced the unsuspecting rascals. Apparently, either fate was enough to get Mrs. Orbison's imagination cranking in disturbing ways. So, Larry took one van while Dennis and I took the other. It was unlikely that our prospective customer would see what pulled up, but even from the twentieth floor my truck might look pretty grungy.

Winding through downtown traffic on the way to Russian Hill, I tuned into KDFC. Apparently listeners who preferred dogs to cats had called in about last Tuesday's program celebrating the connections between felines and classical music. Dennis approved of my "choice jams," trying to figure out what movie the first piece we heard came from. I explained that "The Ride of the Valkyries" was written by Richard Wagner in the 1850s and came from the second opera of the famed Ring Cycle and therefore didn't originate with Francis Ford Coppola's *Apocalypse Now*.

Dennis wasn't impressed with my knowledge, being much more intrigued by the radio host drawing a connection between Wagner and canines. The great composer supposedly played his work to a cherished spaniel for approval, although just how the dog expressed its judgment wasn't mentioned. One of Wagner's dogs is buried at his master's feet in Bavaria, which Dennis found touching. It struck me as weird, but I was suspicious of unusual expressions of affection between humans and animals these days.

The radio program's next selection also met with Dennis's approval, which is saying something for classical music. The announcer noted that Carl Orff had a beloved dog, which seemed like a stretch of the morning's theme. But the first movement of *Carmina Burana* is undeniably powerful, and Dennis reported that it was the soundtrack for an epic battle scene in *Excalibur*—a movie I had boycotted on political grounds. The story of the legendary King Arthur establishing a British empire encompassing Ireland was too raw given the hunger strikes by Irish republican prisoners last May.

We were about halfway through Orff's masterpiece when we reached the luxury condos. After the doorman called up to Mr. Nye, we were given access to the elevator serving the penthouse. The place was as opulent as they come—glittering crystal chandeliers, shiny brass hardware, a thick red carpet with gold threads, and a thin black butler with white gloves. He showed us to the study, where Dennis couldn't resist asking about the woodwork: Macassar ebony flooring and East Indian rosewood cabinetry. Like a high-priced call girl, it sounded expensive and looked nice, but you had to wonder if the pleasure was worth the price.

Mr. Nye joined us in short order. He had the distinction of wealth—perfect grooming, elegant manners, and dapper styling. The man exuded class but not pretention. I don't usually like rich people, but he was the sort who didn't need to make others feel less significant so he could feel more important. He shook our hands warmly and said we'd come highly recommended by a dear friend, whose collection of mounted hunting trophies we'd saved from a beetle infestation. He explained that the housekeeper had found little piles of "fine sand" on his library shelves which he inspected and deemed suspicious—for good reason.

The room had its own climate control system to dehumidify the air and provide an optimal temperature for the rare books, including volumes from the sixteenth century. Our inspection left no doubt that Mr. Nye had a colony of drugstore beetles enjoying the comfortable, indoor weather. I found some adults in a pendant fixture—one of those giant glass bowls which are perfect for trapping insects attracted to light. Using a magnifier, I showed him that the drugstore beetle had clubbed antennae and pitted wing covers, in contrast to its bothersome relative, the cigarette beetle, which had saw-toothed antennae and smooth wing covers. Mr. Nye took the time to look carefully at the insects and gushed at my entomological knowledge, which wasn't as impressive as he seemed to believe. But he blanched at what this all meant for his beloved books.

Instead of trying to find every book with any sign of beetle larvae, I told him that the surest tactic would be for us to put his entire collection into individual plastic bags, take them to a commercial freezer facility, stack them carefully to assure complete and even cooling over the course of at least three days, thaw them slowly, and leave them bagged to watch for activity by any survivors. Given the cost of his books, some of which undoubtedly exceeded my annual income, he said he'd hire a professional conservator and an armed guard to work with Dennis and Larry to assure proper handling and security of the books during transport and freezing. I offered to inspect and treat, if necessary, other areas of the suite where beetles might be hiding and he didn't bat an eye. I could've named almost any price for the whole operation but gave him a fair estimate. Respect is a mutual deal.

After a quick lunch with Dennis at my favorite hot dog cart in the Financial District—while we hunkered in something between a fog and a mist that the Irish would label, "a grand soft day"—we headed back to the shop. The guys had planned for a few hours of calibrating sprayers, cleaning equipment, and changing oil in the vans—while arguing about whose music played on the boom box. An ideal afternoon in their estimation, given the chance to work in warm, dry conditions.

The rest of my day was shaping up to be less optimal. Carol told me that "some guy named Luis called but wouldn't give his last name or a phone number, only saying to meet him at the store." I took this to mean he'd found a way to get me into the crush show, but he understandably didn't want to pass along the details in a phone message. Carol looked suspicious, and I told her the Linford investigation was coming to a head, to which she offered sage advice.

"Goddammit Riley, be careful and remember you're not as quick or brawny as you used to be."

"And you're not as gentle with my ego as you used to be," I said.

"A little brutal honesty," she said, "might keep you in one handsome piece for Nina to enjoy."

Having Nina enjoy me sounded like a great idea for this evening. But instead, I was planning a dive into deviancy with the coaching of Dr. Chen who, I desperately hoped, would give me some useful insight as to what I'd gotten myself into—and how the hell to get out, along with Petey.

Chapter Thirty-One

When I got to the Pleasure Palace, Luis was consulting with a customer who was trying to decide among various bondage devices. It was not a shopping challenge I'd ever face. I slipped down the adjacent aisle and pretended to be interested in assorted instruments of pleasure and pain which reminded me of giant fishing flies, as if designed to lure a horny human into latching onto one of them only to find himself punctured, pierced and played to exhaustion. I supposed if the quarry was lucky, the game ended with catch-and-release.

The customer was explaining that she'd used bondage tape and a spreader bar with her lover to their mutual delight. I could almost guess what these involved. When Luis suggested a ball gag, she demurred and coyly murmured that they'd like to expand on the sensations provided by the Wartenberg wheel he used on her. I was stumped, Luis was not.

He took her to my aisle, so I moved over to the shelves of vibrating gadgets and edible lubricants which I suppose a lusty couple might combine for an erotic version of the electric toothbrush. The consummate salesman proposed that she try a flogger or spanking paddle and then launched into the nuances of leather, rubber, nylon and rope floggers, along with the pros and cons of paddle designs. I was transfixed by the combination of technology and deviancy. A soft, naked body under flannel sheets on a chilly night sure did the trick for me.

The woman settled on Emmanuelle's beginner flogger and a Singapore stinger paddle for $18.57 which seemed pricey given the ready availability of pain in this world. As she was leaving, Luis glanced around the shop, checked the concave mirrors in the corners of the store to assure that the aisles were empty, and flicked his head to the back.

We retreated to the office, where the stale odor of Michelle's cigarettes still hung in the air and the light fixture buzzed overhead. Luis was too agitated to sit, so he leaned on the desk. I settled into a hard, wooden chair that was uncomfortable enough to be put on the S&M aisle, but I wanted to ratchet down Luis's anxiety by conveying nonchalance. The guy was wound tight as a top or a length of bondage tape if my imagination was correct.

"Okay Riley, I got permission from Eunectes, actually Redbug, but it's just as good. You can come to the performance tonight, but let's arrive separately." His leg was jackhammering and he kept crossing and uncrossing his arms.

"Jesus Luis, would you relax? You're about as smooth as a speed freak looking for a fix. Eunectes is going to know that something's up if you don't dial it back."

"Sorry, but if this goes wrong I don't know what'll happen," he said.

"Let's just stick with the basics. When and where?"

"Eleven o'clock. There's a row of warehouses on Natoma and 6th."

That put the place in the South of Market neighborhood—the epicenter of the gay leather community, which had converted warehouses into sex clubs and bars. I'd heard that joints like the Caldron were nonstop orgies featuring thematic evenings. Initially, I'd figured this was an exaggeration, but based on my recent descent into decadence I was ready to believe most anything about my fellow man.

"Which place is your venue?"

"It's the one farthest from the street. There's a painting of an Orange Crush can on the door."

"Crush, eh? Cute. So I just go in and find a seat?"

"No, there'll be somebody at the door. I've paid your membership fee and dues for the month—"

"What did that cost you?"

"Plenty, but it's worth every penny to have your help."

"So, do I flash a membership card?"

"No, just give the password. Tonight it's 'grape.' We rotate among the flavors."

"Clever. No reason why brutalizing animals has to be humorless."

"Nobody was into hard crush until Eunectes took over. People step on insects all the time without being judged or labeled," he said.

"Relax pal. We're in this together, possibly to keep a kid from being killed. I grant you it's a long way from mashing crickets to crushing people."

"I was grilled by Redbug, so I had to give him some information about you. I figured it would be best to keep things close to the truth." Luis's leg had stopped shaking and he appeared to focus on our plan. Maybe there was hope after all. "I told him you were an exterminator who I met at the shop and you get off on watching insects being crushed, but you're open to anything. I also said you were the quiet sort. So you don't need to say much, which should keep you from blowing your cover."

"Good thinking for a guy who looked ready to melt down a minute ago."

He gave a cockeyed grin. "I do okay when I'm in the moment. It's thinking about what's coming that gets me nervous. Speaking of which, you should prepare for the possibility of a test. They've started doing this recently to make sure that we're not being infiltrated by Grant Roberts's morality goons."

"Meaning I'm supposed to know some inside secret about crushing?"

"Nothing so easy. You might be challenged to prove you're legit by assisting the crush mistress on stage."

"On stage? What the hell, is this a theater?"

"We'll be in a room at the end of a hallway. When you go in, there will be floor lamps so you can find a chair or a place on a couch. Then, the room is darkened and a spotlight shines on a low stage. If asked, you'll need to go up there and do what the crush mistress tells you. She'll whisper commands to you, while she talks dirty to the animal, like it was a man."

As I contemplated this bizarre scenario, there was an electronic beep indicating the arrival of a customer. Luis told me to slip out the back door "just in case," and he headed to the front to provide advice on latex, leather, and lace.

Nob Hill and the Castro might as well be on different planets. And in keeping with this cosmic separation, Dr. Chen's office had absolutely nothing in common with the Pleasure Palace—other than a shared interest in abnormal psychology. The receptionist was curt and suspicious, probably because: I wasn't a patient, she didn't like my having deceived her earlier, and she was protective of her employer. All good reasons.

I read a *Time* cover story about video games which furthered my belief that the end of western civilization was on the horizon, just in case the perverts didn't manage a takeover. I was, however, impressed that the magazine was less than a month old—a remarkable accomplishment for a doctor's office. When I was told that Dr. Chen would see me, I headed into an elegant, minimalist office exuding calm confidence.

"Nice digs," I said. Dr. Chen rose from her chair behind an uncluttered, glass-topped desk to shake my hand. I settled into a surprisingly comfortable, sleek chair. She was wearing a floral print dress that didn't quite reach her knees and I admired a pair of taut calves beneath the see-through desk.

"My office reflects the principles of feng shui, a thirty-five-hundred-year-old discipline. The selection and arrangement of objects facilitates the flow of 'chee' or what might be called energy."

"I could use some of this vibe in my shop. I don't suppose that steel filing cabinets and Army surplus desks are part of the formula, eh?"

She smiled patiently and said, "Chinese scholars recognized earth, fire, water, wood—and metal. So perhaps your furnishings are not beyond redemption." A little fountain burbled beneath a window with half-opened lacquered shades. "But you're not here for interior design guidance. You said that your investigation indicated the possibility of an imminent murder. That's a very serious matter and perhaps you should be speaking to the police rather than a psychologist."

"The case involves one of the deviancies we discussed at lunch."

"If so, you may be in over your head, assuming your information is reliable."

"That's why I wanted to talk with you."

"Go ahead." She leaned back and crossed her legs. Nice thighs, as well.

"I have good reason to believe that there's a group of men who meet in secret to watch women step on various creatures. My source doesn't look like a pervert, and he sounds on the up and up."

"So, he doesn't wear a raincoat and offer candy to school children? Riley, perfectly normal-looking people engage in what society deems to be abnormal behaviors. The crush fetish is unusual, but it's not dangerous."

"Unless you're a cricket or a kitten—or maybe a kid," I said. She cocked her head and leaned forward, resting her elbows on the desktop.

"What are you suggesting?"

"Let me back up to get a handle on whether what I'm about to tell you is believable. Just what is this fetish? Why do men get turned on watching animals being crushed?"

She sighed deeply and ran her fingers through her lustrous black hair. The woman reflected the calm confidence of her surroundings. She leaned back and went into professorial mode.

"Our best theory is that the men, and it's always men as far as we know, desire domination. When they are watching a performance, they imagine that they're the ones being crushed—and the woman adds to the fantasy by talking as if it is a man under her foot."

"And that gets them off?"

"For them, being powerless to the point of death is erotic. The proximity of sex and death in the human psyche is profound. Perhaps you're familiar with *la petite mort*—the little death?"

"No." But I was learning that my sexual education had been sadly neglected. The football coach at St. Teresa's had warned us about the clap and pregnancy, not little deaths.

"It refers to the likening of orgasm to death or to the post-orgasmic state of unconsciousness that some people experience."

I decided my bedroom technique needed work. Or maybe not. "Okay, so the guys want to be totally dominated and substitute animals for themselves. Is it like a drug? Do they need more and more to get aroused?

"More?"

"More realistic performances. You know, first a few grapes, then a handful of crickets, next a couple of mice, and then?" She fell silent, seeing where this was heading.

"Perhaps. From what we know, the vast majority of fetishists are satisfied with soft crush—the use of invertebrates. From there, a small proportion go on to hard crush, using higher animals. But this practice is kept far underground, so researchers know little beyond anecdotal accounts."

"Do the two groups mix?"

"Generally speaking, the soft crush community is critical of hard crush practitioners."

"Why? Seems odd for cricket crunchers to be judgmental of mouse mashers." She didn't appreciate my analysis and gave me the Sister Mary Leon look that I used to get when being a smartass in junior high. "Isn't soft crush a gateway to the hard stuff?" I asked, trying to regain professional decorum.

"As I said, not usually. I know this is hard for you to understand, and even professionals such as myself struggle with the notion of abnormality. But think of it this way, as a soft crush fetishist who visited my graduate seminar explained. Killing insects for sexual gratification is a choice, a way of finding pleasure at the cost of a living creature. But, he asked, what about those who choose to eat beef or pork? Sentient animals are raised in factory farms and brutally killed so that meat eaters can derive sensual fulfillment. Nobody needs to see worms crushed or to consume cattle flesh. We do it because it's enjoyable. But who has the moral high ground—the fetishist or the carnivore?"

I thought about my juicy Whiz burger from last night, but there was no way I could see how my meal was the same as asking Nina to skip sex and crush a roach. Not wanting a philosophical argument, I returned to the topic we'd been avoiding.

"Here's what I meant when I talked about kittens and kids. Is it possible that for someone on the hard crush track, the ultimate high would be to watch a woman smash a human being?" There was a long silence as Dr. Chen closed her eyes and rubbed her temples.

"I've never imagined that the fetish could lead to murder," she said. "But yes, it's conceivable." She stopped rubbing and leaned forward. "So what's your next move?"

"I'll go to a crush performance tonight and try to determine if the whole story is just the anxious imaginings of a scared guy . . . or whether there's actually a plan to kill someone."

"Riley," she said, fixing me with her deep, brown eyes, "what you've described is beyond anything I've studied—probably beyond anything in the literature. This is . . ."

"Evil?" I suggested.

"If there is such a thing, then perhaps yes. Or madness, which also isn't a term I would use professionally."

"Call it whatever you want. If it's real, then I need to stop it."

"Not the police? You might be dealing with a very dangerous, psychopathic individual."

"I'm in touch with a detective, but I can't share the details with him. I made a promise to my source. And besides, the cops are likely to blunder in and flush the suspect, who'll scuttle like a rat into some other filthy alley where he'll start over with a new batch of twisted followers. This is on me." I stood up and Dr. Chen escorted me to the door. Before she opened it, she turned and took my hand.

"Be careful. I know we haven't hit it off, but I sense you're a decent, even a good, man. Maybe violent, but caring . . . a strange combination." She gave my hand a gentle squeeze and said, "And that pair of qualities could be dangerous . . . for you."

"My plan is to make it dangerous for the bad guy," I said returning the squeeze. I released her hand and reached for the door knob and then turned back to her. "It's true what George Orwell said. People sleep peacefully at night because rough men stand ready to do violence on their behalf."

She laughed softly and said, "I suppose in a way, cops and exterminators are society's sleeping pills."

I opened the office door and smiled at the good doctor to convey my gratitude and express my confidence. The former was genuine, the latter was not.

CHAPTER THIRTY-TWO

The upper floors of the skyscrapers in the financial district were shrouded in clouds like a gauzy lampshade. The city lights reflected back onto the streets and bled into the South of Market district to provide an artificial, unending dusk. I parked around the corner from the warehouses, turned my collar against the cold and damp, and waited for Luis. After a few minutes, he came walking down the other side of the street, threw a glance in my direction and kept going. I fell back a half block and followed him.

Luis turned down an alleyway, passed a couple of warehouses, and then stopped. He looked around, as if to assure he wasn't being followed when, in fact, he wanted to be sure I hadn't lost him. He pulled open a metal door with a crudely painted image of a soda can. This was the place.

I waited a minute, then walked to the entrance and went inside. There was a guy standing in the dimly lit entryway. His chest and gut were so big he couldn't quite cross his arms over his metal studded leather jacket. I gave the password. Nothing. So I handed him twenty bucks. He flicked his bowling ball head toward a hallway illuminated by a series of fluorescent fixtures with half the bulbs dark and the other half flickering like stroboscopes. At the end of the passage, a Grape Crush can was duct taped to a door.

Inside, a few torchiere floor lamps cast their light upward into blackness. The walls were also black, making it difficult to get a sense of the size of the room, which was furnished with flea market rejects. My heart skipped a beat when I saw, on the far side of the room, Jason—the lanky redhead who'd been working in Dave Rider's laboratory at the Cal Academy. Luis had told me about Redbug's connections to "some insect laboratory" but I was too focused on the unfolding tale of perversion to make the connection.

Jason being Redbug could go a long way to explain the missing funnel web spider and the mislabeled tarantula. I couldn't be sure exactly how this piece fit into the twisted puzzle, but my first priority was to avoid being identified. Redbug's knowing I'd been at the Cal Academy could've been problematical, but it seemed unlikely he'd recognize me in the dim light after our brief encounter in Dave's laboratory. However, I wanted to have the upper hand with respect to identities.

Luis was sitting in a rocking chair on the near side of the room, keeping to himself while some of the dozen or so men chatted in clusters reminiscent of an audience awaiting a concert or a play. I sidled over to Luis and plucked the knit cap from his head. He looked up at me with startled curiosity, and I raised a finger and shook my head to preempt any question. I pulled the cap over my ears and selected a floral print armchair next to him. My disguise wasn't brilliant, but oftentimes even a small change in appearance is sufficient.

Settling into the chair while trying not to think about who had been sitting there previously and what they'd been doing, I took in the ambiance: the grassy sweet smell of pot smoke and the background music of hard rock. The volume didn't preclude conversation, although if it had that might've made it easier for me. Most of the lyrics were impossible to understand, although I did catch "let's get it up" which struck me as apropos if lacking in subtlety. A few minutes later I picked out the lead singer—using the term loosely— screaming about evil walking and talking and sleeping and arousing you, as if anticipating the evening's events. Amid the pounding jumble of electric guitars, I actually caught some of the lyrics admonishing fans to break the rules, and I started wondering if a contact high accounted for my newfound capability to understand rock musicians. My reverie was interrupted by a tall man dressed entirely in black, who managed to approach with such graceful movement that I failed to notice him. Or maybe what seemed like a catlike arrival was also attributable to the secondhand smoke.

"Is our newest member an AC/DC fan?" he asked, directing his question into the space between Luis and myself. I assumed that the reference was to the rock band, not electrical systems, although I knew nothing of the former and fair amount about the latter.

"Eunectes," Luis said, rising from his rocker, "this is the guy Redbug approved."

I stood up and remembered Luis telling me the crush freaks didn't use their real names. On the spot, I decided to use a shortened version of my middle name.

"Vlad," I said, extending my hand. Eunectes's grip was strong and lingering, which matched his appearance. The man had the physique of a dancer, with elongated musculature and not an ounce of fat. I figured him for six-three, maybe six-four. His lush, black hair was perfectly trimmed, and a hint of stubble along his strong, unblemished jawline provided an aura of sophistication. Thick, arching eyebrows perched above intense, green eyes evoked a sense of cold calculation.

"A perfect name, chosen, I assume, from the fifteenth century Romanian prince." I must have looked perplexed because he continued graciously. "A darkly sensuous tale, as you surely know, although for Maso's sake, will you allow me a brief explanation?" 'Maso' wasn't the most original alias for an S&M fan, but Luis didn't seem prone to linguistic creativity.

"By all means," I said, feeling as if I was at a swanky cocktail party rather than awaiting a revolting, sexual performance.

"You see, Vlad was orphaned, betrayed, and exiled, before he regained control of his former kingdom. To assure that his enemies would think twice before attempting to invade, he tortured and executed captives by impaling them along the road to his castle. As the story goes, when an advancing army encountered a forest of twenty thousand skewered and decaying corpses, they quite reasonably decided to return home. Vlad the Impaler was also called Vlad Dracula and became the inspiration for Bram Stoker's classic horror story."

"He impaled his enemies on sharpened poles? Alive?" Luis asked.

"Exactly. Just like mounting insects on pins, although I gather that most collectors kill their captives before impaling them. But penetration can be so erotic, however it occurs. Don't you agree, Vlad?"

"Absolutely," I said, trying not to think of my collection as a Lilliputian forest of impaled six-legged corpses.

Eunectes glanced at his watch. "I think it's time to start," he said and started to walk away but then turned back to Luis. "Vlad knows what we have planned for our ultimate event, right?" Luis nodded and Eunectes headed to the front of the room. On his signal, the floor lamps dimmed and a spotlight illuminated a wooden stage about a foot above the cement floor. Toward the back of the platform was a card table with several boxes. At center stage were sheets of blank newsprint. The music faded away and murmured conversations fell silent, as Eunectes glided into the circle of light.

"Good evening, my friends," he said with a smile and a sweep of his arms, ending with his hands clasped in front of his chest. "We have a new member joining us this evening, but we'll see more of him in a bit." I assumed that this was reference to the upcoming test of my legitimacy, as Luis had warned.

Eunectes continued. "Before we begin the show, let me provide an update on our progress toward the triumphant culmination of our journey." He made it sound like everyone was on board, a nice move when a leader senses his followers are uncertain.

"Ours is a grand voyage," Eunectes said with the dramatic intonation of Christopher Columbus or Francis Drake preparing his crew. "On the horizon is the greatest possible sexual ecstasy. Together, we will share in the climactic experience, a distant shore that every one of us has imagined." His voice rose to a fever pitch. "We will realize our most glorious, erotic fantasy!"

There was a long pause before he began again in a soft, diabolical tone. "Tonight is the last time we allow a new member to join our adventure. And this is also the last opportunity to turn back. Now is your chance to leave. But understand that anyone who speaks of our voyage outside of the group will wish that he was the one being featured in our grand finale. Does anybody wish to disembark?"

There was the sound of a prolonged exhalation from behind me in the darkness, but no movement. And then silence.

"Good. Very good," Eunectes said with sinister satisfaction. "I will provide details of time and location as the plan comes together. But the elements are falling into place more quickly than anticipated. So expect to hear from me as soon as tomorrow." Then his tone shifted to that of a late night talk show host, providing a warm welcome to a performing artist. "Let me introduce our new crush mistress, Courtney."

There was scattered applause as Eunectes disappeared into the darkness and a too-thin, too-blonde woman wearing a too-tight, too-short dress stepped onto the stage. She looked to be in her early twenties, although her breasts and hips seemed adolescent. Courtney began her patter almost shyly, but became more forceful as the men grunted their approval. She looked over the audience and said, "You're shit to me. Nothing but weak, putrid scum." There's not many venues where a performer would succeed with this line, but Courtney's Crush Theater was aberrant in so many ways.

Courtney continued her insults while she reached into a box and pulled out a handful of cherry tomatoes which she proceeded to seductively mash under her bare feet, squirting their contents onto the newsprint. I'd never thought of tomatoes as lewd but now I'd never look at a salad in quite the same way. The men moaned their submissive encouragement as music began to fill the room with the voices of angry women and the pounding beat of heavy metal. Courtney rubbed her body in synchrony with the music. She teased and danced until the audience became restless for more of what they'd really come to see.

With rock lyrics declaring something about being a victim, the crush mistress dropped a wriggling mass of earthworms onto a sheet. She ground them into the paper while declaring, "You're not going anywhere. I say when you can leave—and when you can spurt."

Next came the crickets. Courtney plucked the hind legs from the insects, flicking them into the audience and continuing to degrade the men over the sound of the music. Calling them worthless vermin, she dropped each cricket onto a clean sheet of paper, watched it struggle, mocked its efforts to escape and pressed her heel onto the insect. For my part, I was not so much disgusted with Courtney as disheartened with humanity. But my part quickly changed.

With Eunectes's encouragement from the wings, Courtney invited me onto the stage. As the music throbbed, she whispered to me, "Pick one of them, pin it to the floor, and guide my foot. I'm not sure I can do this alone. I'm sorry." She directed me to the table while she slipped on her high heels and Eunectes slipped behind a video camera on a tripod. I assumed my role was being documented to assure I was completely enmeshed in the perversion should I attempt to betray the group or its leader. This was about the only thing I fully understood of what was happening. Blackmail is rational.

In the largest box on the table were four mangy kittens with matted fur. I selected the runt, a reject unlikely to survive in any case. Or so I reasoned. It didn't help. I could feel its toothpick ribs under the tissue paper skin. It flailed weakly, squinting under the bright light, mewing without its littermates.

When I was in high school, Deacon Roland taught a class on Catholic morality which seemed like a really good idea given the temptations of cars, beer, and girls—although not necessarily in that order. He told us that ethics was not about choosing between good and evil. If we were unsure of what to do when confronted with such a stark choice, then we were simply psychopaths and he couldn't help us. Rather, moral dilemmas were about choosing lesser evils, accepting venial sins to avoid mortal sins, doing a small wrong to prevent "a horrible malignity" (I looked up this word, thinking it might entail some juicy taboo, but I was disappointed).

I brought the tiny, doomed creature, shivering with fear, to center stage. Over the music's throbbing drums and bruising guitars, the lead singer howled in despair and wailed a warning to "watch your step," with the last words ominously repeated. The warning evoked a memory of when I beat a thug in an alley to extract the location of a kidnapped girl. She needed medicine—and the guy knew where she was being held. Between his ruptured spleen and some bleeding heart do-gooders, we found the kid and I lost my job as a cop. I'd told the commissioner that I could live with trading the life of a street punk for that of an innocent child—and my career. He understood.

I knelt down and shifted my lower leg to momentarily block the view of the audience. My only excuse was a version of George Orwell's assertion, allowing the creature to die peacefully at night because a rough man knelt ready to do violence on its behalf. Pretending to position the pathetic thing for Courtney, I delivered a sudden twist, breaking its neck.

As the tiny creature's spasms quickly subsided, I swung my leg out of the audience's sightline and glanced up at Courtney. She turned her back to the audience to provide a clear view of her stiletto heel hovering above the kitten, looked down at me, and silently mouthed a thank-you. Then she launched a debasing monologue for those whose existence society wants desperately to deny, along with the vermin in their crawlspaces and basements.

CHAPTER THIRTY-THREE

After the performance, there was no applause, just murmurs of approval. A musty odor had replaced the grassy sweetness and the music was reduced in volume and quality—not that heavy metal has notable artistic virtue, but it is more genuine than the insipid blend of flutes and chimes that followed. The spotlight was dimmed and the floor lamps were turned up enough so nobody stumbled over the scattered furniture on their way out. The audience exited wordlessly, evidently satisfied with the evening and on board with what Eunectes had coming next.

Outside, Luis and the others headed toward the street. I went the opposite direction, seeking solitude in the labyrinth of warehouses. Coming around a corner, I saw in the shadows a woman doubled over, holding her gut. Not one to abandon a damsel in distress, I drew closer and the stench of vomit hit me like a warm, wet pillow. Courtney retched and then stood up, swaying like a punch-drunk fighter.

"You alright?" I asked. She looked at me dizzily.

"Sure, bud. Classy ladies always spew on their shoes in upscale neighborhoods." She wiped her mouth on the back of her sleeve. "We do it to attract refined gentlemen, asshole."

"Hey, just asking. I'll let you get back to your charming endeavor." I started to head down the alleyway.

"Hold on," she commanded. "You're the guy who assisted me on stage, right?" She stepped into the glare of an industrial, vapor lamp. Her face softened.

"That's me, the kitten killer. We made a helluva team tonight."

"I should be thanking you, not mouthing off. Christ, I knew what was coming, but I hadn't done it before." Her eyes filled with tears. "That was fucking messed up," she whimpered.

I never know what to say at these moments, so I tried the comforting platitude, "What's done is done," followed by the even less helpful cliché, "It's all over now," which evoked a trembling in Courtney reminiscent of the pitiful kitten.

She gave a rasping inhalation. "I gotta figure a way out."

I stepped toward her and she collapsed against me, sobbing. Long, rattling breaths finally giving way to deep sighs as if she'd fallen asleep. Courtney looked into my face with the desperation of a hostage, then dropped her eyes and wiped futilely at the mess she'd left on the front of my coat.

"I'm sorry. I don't even know your name and here I am blubbering away as if you should care or help. God, I must look disgusting," she said.

"Not at all. I'm Riley and I find women covered in puke and snot to be irresistible." She looked at me with a mixture of uncertainty and revulsion. "I'm kidding, doll. My desires don't go much further than silk sheets and soft music—and the only kink in my sex life can be found in my lower back the morning after a night of lovemaking that pales in comparison to whatever the hell happened on stage tonight."

"So, why were you there? You're not a cop or something are you?"

"Not a cop. Maybe an 'or something.'"

"Can you help me get out?" She had the desperate tone of a panicked child.

"Slow down. I'm not sure what you're in. Let's go somewhere and talk."

Courtney clung to my arm with daughterly dependence and wobbled along beside me. After a few blocks we found a bar where a middle-aged man escorting a young woman wouldn't draw attention. The place had crumbling brick walls, exposed ductwork, and rough wooden flooring which was either a stylistic effort to evoke an industrial ambiance or a financial move to avoid improving the decor. In any case, it was poorly lit, blessedly quiet, and sold beer, which was all we needed. Courtney went to clean up while I ordered a couple Budweisers—the least offensive of what they had on tap and took them to a table in the back corner.

"I should be less disgusting, now," she said, taking a seat across from me.

"You look fine. Lovely, even. Which makes me wonder—"

"What's a nice girl like me doing in a place like that?"

"Yeah, something along those lines," I said, sampling my beer. It was cold, which is about as much as you can say for the standard American brews.

"I'll give you the short version," she said, taking a sip and leaning forward. There was nobody near us, but she was clearly anxious about being overheard. "I came to San Francisco with my younger sister. She's sixteen. I'm twenty," she said taking a long, defiant drink. Great, I was buying booze for an underage girl who evidently perceived me as a father figure. But given our earlier collaboration, beer seemed morally harmless.

"We used to live in Sacramento with our mother, a junkie, and our stepfather, a fuckbag who regularly beat the shit out of us. Hooking was a way to get enough money to escape. My stepfather's pals were into S&M, so I learned some things that paid well. Very well. So when we got here, we connected with Eunectes and he got me some lucrative gigs as a dominatrix."

"And your sister?"

"Followed my mother's example and went into the family business. She whores to make enough money to get her next fix. I love her and hate who she's become. Not that I'm any role model. But that's how this shitty world works."

"Speaking of which, why don't the two of you start over somewhere else? You can't do much worse than tonight, no matter what it paid," I said, draining my beer and signaling the barkeep for another round.

"I want to. It's not that causing men humiliation and pain bothers me. I just imagine they're my stepfather. They consent to it. But animals? Mice and hamsters and kittens . . . ?"

The beer arrived. I tipped the guy ten bucks and asked if we could have some privacy. He grunted and turned the chairs upside down on the table next to us. It wasn't going to cost him any business on a Tuesday night.

"So what's keeping you here?"

"A nightmare named Eunectes."

I took a drink and waited for her to explain.

"Last week, he set me up with a customer. Told me it was a special arrangement that was going to pay a premium, like triple the normal charge.

The deal was a choke scenario and the guy wanted it filmed. I knew what I was doing, how to bring a guy along, how to avoid damaging the windpipe. You know." I didn't, but I nodded. "And I also knew to wear a mask if there was going to be a videotape." She took a long pull on her beer. "So I get into my costume and go into the room. The guy is lying on the bed and looking pretty fucked up, but what the hell, it was his party. After some preliminaries, I straddled him and started pressing on his carotids and releasing. He didn't signal me to stop, so I kept going.

"Eunectes was behind the camera and kept nodding to encourage me to apply pressure longer and longer. The trick wasn't looking so good, but the payday was. On about the fifth or sixth round, he passed out. And then stopped breathing. Eunectes freaked out, yelled that I'd killed him, and told me to start mouth-to-mouth resuscitation. I took off my mask and tried to save him, but it all turned out to be a scam."

"So, the guy wasn't really dead?" I'd forgotten my beer at this point, but Courtney reminded me of our refreshments by draining half her glass. I followed suit.

"Oh, he was dead alright. But I hadn't killed him. After Eunectes shut off the camera, he started laughing. He says, 'Sweetie, I got you good. I have you on film killing a guy with kinky sex.' I looked at him and started crying. And then he says, 'But what's not on the video is my giving him an overdose before you came in. You were just yanking his cock and pinching his arteries until the junk stopped his heart.'"

"Nice guy, that Eunectes," I said.

"Yeah, he's stroking my hair like he's my friend or something. And in this soft voice he says, 'Now here's the deal. I'll send this tape to the cops and I'll give your baby sister a needle contaminated with AIDS for her next fix if you don't do me one, big favor.' Then he grabs my hair, pulls me backward, and pins me to the bed next to the dead guy."

"Let me guess, he invited you to be the crush mistress for his ultimate fantasy. You're chained to the oars of his ship and rowing to the distant shore of sexual ecstasy, to borrow from your vile captain's imagery." Courtney dropped her head and stared at the tabletop. When she looked up, her eyes were filled with tears which she wiped away angrily.

"If it was just me, I'd run. I've hidden away enough money to get to New York or Florida or somewhere the cops wouldn't find me. I'd have to go underground for a while, but I don't figure that the dead guy was anyone important. Eunectes just needed a corpse on film. The police will lose interest once enough bodies of whores and junkies and runaways pile up. But . . ."

"But what? Take your sister and get out."

"She won't come. She thinks Eunectes is her savior. He supplies her with Johns and smack. She's set up in this studio apartment a few blocks from here, not far from where Eunectes lives, although I don't think anyone knows exactly where that is. Her place is a shithole but it's the safest place she's ever lived. If I bolt, she's facing a death sentence, a sure, slow, miserable death from AIDS. I know that bastard will infect her to get back at me."

"So, by your figuring, there's no way out."

"Not unless *you* come up with something. I shouldn't be dumping this crap on you, but I'm so fucking scared, and I don't know who can help. I could see in your eyes when you broke that kitten's neck that you're not one of them. I don't know why you were there, but you're my only hope."

"I'm gonna be honest. I'll help you if I can, but my concern is for the kid Eunectes has lined up for his finale. I'm *his* only hope."

"That's for real because I can't help him," she said, finishing her beer. "If I don't follow through with the final crush, Eunectes will find some other chick. Unless you can do something, the dude's going to die sooner or later."

"Are you sure that Eunectes is serious, that he really has some guy lined up?" I asked, putting away the rest of my beer.

"He's a lying, manipulative son-of-a-bitch. So it's possible he's just screwing with the crush freaks, seeing how far they're willing to go. He's all about power. He wants to be dominated, to imagine himself utterly debased by a woman. But at the same time, he wants to have complete control over others. Redbug told me that he's serious, but that sicko's just creaming his pants in anticipation."

"So, you figure it's going to happen?"

"Probably. But we won't know until it actually comes together," she said, pushing back from the table. I caught the bartender's eye in thanks and he nodded an appreciative reply. Back on the street, I told Courtney what I needed from her was as much advance notice as possible about the place and time of Eunectes's crowning—or crushing—glory. I gave her my number and she paused for a moment, seemingly unsure what to do. Then she stood on tiptoe, whispered a thank-you into my ear and delivered a quick peck on my cheek. Looking a bit embarrassed, a presumably unpracticed emotion in her life, she headed up the sidewalk, the glare from the streetlights in the fog casting an angelic, or maybe hellish, glow around her.

By the time I got home, I was brooding and angry. A frozen pizza and a glass of low-end Jameson were about all I wanted—along with the third act of *Rigoletto*. Sometimes when you're in a funk, going deeper feels good. Or at least it feels right, as if wallowing in rottenness is more genuine that pretending the world is filled with goodness. The pizza crust was burnt around the edges and soggy in the middle, just the way the damned things are designed to cook. Along with the cheap whiskey, it became a kind of penance. Maybe not ashes and sackcloth, but something that resonated with my long-rejected Catholic roots.

Piero Cappuccilli accompanied my dinner with his heartrending baritone. I stopped eating to savor the part when the Duke's voice, singing a reprise of "La donna è mobile," can be heard echoing in the streets of Mantua. In this ominous moment, Rigoletto realizes that the shrouded body he's preparing to dump in the river—the payoff from his hired assassin—is not the corpse of the Duke who defiled his daughter. The anguish as he opens the sack to discover his own dying daughter is beyond words, which is exactly why the music of opera is necessary.

I could feel his disbelief in the horrific outcome of his plan—a combination of the love of a father for his child and the rage of a deeply flawed man against a cruel world. Having been degraded by the elite, the humpbacked jester had lashed out bitterly in the Duke's court, evoked a curse from an elderly Count he'd viciously mocked, and thereby sowed the seeds of tragedy. Are we supposed to feel sympathy for Rigoletto or disdain? Tonight, I felt a disturbing kinship. When my plan reached its end, who would be in the sack? Would the body reflect honorable motives or moralistic rage? Crappy food and drink bring out my melodramatic side.

I contemplated driving over to Nina's to fulfill my promise of knotted sheets in the hope that late night lovemaking would break the gloom. But I knew if there was going to be a time when my libido failed, tonight would be a good bet. So I called her and offered a feeble, rambling explanation with assurance that both body and soul would be hers tomorrow night. She gave a soft, throaty laugh and assured me that celibate solitude could be its own seduction. I hung up and ruminated on her having once told me that while she could keep me from being alone, nobody could keep me from being lonely. "That's who you are," she told me, "and I love you anyway."

I considered thawing some scarab beetles from the freezer, but pinning insects conjured images of Vlad the Impaler's forest of corpses. So I threw back another shot of Jameson, stumbled up the stairs and crawled into bed. Alone.

Chapter Thirty-Four

In the morning I felt like Courtney's shoes—the ones behind the warehouse, splattered with puke. The weather was an unrelenting drizzle, although the radio promised that a high pressure system was on its way. But we've also been assured that computers will make life easier, nuclear energy will make electricity cheaper, video games will make children smarter, and the Army will make young men all they can be. So, I wasn't counting on sunshine later in the week.

Fungus gnats know that the best way to get out of a dark place is to find a ray of light, which accounts for their swarming around windows after emerging from the soggy soil of houseplants. Given the rot I wallowed in last night, fungus gnats seemed like fine models. So after a shower and a late breakfast of coffee and cold pizza—the stuff is actually improved by refrigeration—I headed over to St. Teresa's for a bit of light in the form of moral decency. And I was hoping Nina could use her skills to gently extract some more information from Tommy and Karsa.

The daycare was fully engaged in a craft project. Over the years, blobs of tempera paint and Elmer's glue had created a reasonable facsimile of a Jackson Pollock canvas on the cement floor of the undercroft, despite the best efforts of the custodian. I explained to Nina that events were unfolding quickly, and anything I could learn about Petey or his whereabouts might be valuable in determining if he was actually in danger.

"Tommy's pretty excited this morning," Nina said, sneaking a kiss while her charges were occupied with their art. "The theme is Saint Brigid of Ireland since this is her feast day. Your mother is bringing scones for mid-morning treats, and Tommy's Irish pride has him going full tilt on the craft project. So I'm not sure that I can redirect his attention, but it's worth a try."

Tommy was sitting on a bench beside his pal, Karsa, and they were shaping clay into figures and arranging them on the table. Nina sat across from the two friends and I stood behind them, trying to listen without intruding. Tommy glanced over his shoulder, greeted me and went right back to his sculpting.

"We're making cows and babies," he said, rolling a ball of clay between his palms that was going to be head of another infant judging from what he had lined up on the table. "Today is for Saint Bridges and she's a patron saint of Ireland, where mom and dad came from."

"And she's the patron saint of cows and babies, too," Karsa added which explained the clay figures.

"And dairymaids and midwives," Nina added. "Remember what you learned from our reading this morning?"

"Yes," said Tommy, "but those are boring. They just milk cows and help women have babies."

"Wouldn't it be fun if Petey was here to make cows and babies along with you?" asked Nina. The two men paused in their work. "If we sent Riley out to find him, where should he go? Can you remember anything about where Petey said he lived?"

"Petey liked watching bridges go up and down. He told us it was like living in a castle," Tommy said, and the two fellows went back to their clay.

I figured these had to be the Fourth Street Bridge and the Lefty O'Doul Bridge. O'Doul, a good Irish name for a European mutt, played for San Francisco's minor league team in 1917. He was drafted by the Yankees and then traded to the Red Sox, where he set a record that still stands. He allowed thirteen runs in a single inning as a relief pitcher. I guess the bridge honors his efforts to introduce baseball to Japan rather than his getting clobbered on the mound.

Karsa broke my reverie with another detail about Petey. "He slept in a park sometimes. It would be fun to sleep on the grass. Except he said there were lots of bad men selling drugs. But they didn't bother him, so it was like camping out, I guess. Father Griesmaier said he'd take us on a campout this summer when it's warm."

At that point, Tommy and Karsa decided that their sculpted babies and cows were having a campout, which delighted them and had Nina laughing as they arranged the figures. From what Karsa described, Petey had been sleeping at South Park, a few blocks from the drawbridges. That put him in South of Market, where I'd been last night. Where Eunectes lived. Shit.

I called Carol from the church to pull together the crew. Her plan was to connect with the guys and snag us lunch from Goat Hill Pizza—two extra-large, special combo pies with sourdough crusts. The pizzas had nothing in common with last night's dinner other than the coincidence of a name.

The food was more than sufficient to draw Larry and Dennis back from their work on a termite control project which, by the pathetically muddy looks of them, had advanced to the final stage of treating around the foundation. They washed up, which led Carol to warn if she found mud in the bathroom sink their asses were going to be chewed like pizza crust, which sent them back down the hall—a very wise decision. They returned and Larry pulled a six-pack of Miller from the fridge, setting it on the dilapidated coffee table. I generally had a rule against drinking before the end of the day, but I could tell that they sensed this was not a normal lunchtime gathering. They were right.

We settled into the scruffy furniture of the warehouse living room, which wouldn't suffer in the least from pepperoni grease stains. Most of the pizza had disappeared by the time I'd brought everyone up to speed on the case.

Dennis leaned back into the over-stuffed, under-hygienic couch cushions and started the summary. "Sheeit boss, lemme get this right. You be tellin' us that you've moved from two dead, rich old folks, to their twisted son—"

"—who was being blackmailed for jacking off with his six-legged playmates on a video made by a sex shop owner," Larry continued and then paused to wash down a mouthful of crust.

"Who," Carol picked up the thread, "was killed by a spider—"

"A very righteous spider," Dennis interjected, reaching for the last slice of pizza.

"You bet your jive black ass," Larry affirmed and continued the synopsis. "And now her kinky hubby is paying Riley to find who swapped out their foreplay spider for an endplay spider, which might be some redhead guy from the Cal Academy."

"Which then led Riley to meet up with a Hispanic hunk working at the sex shop, who's into watching women crush crickets," Carol added, moving the sordid tale towards last night.

"But who doesn't have the balls to stop a twisted sonofabitch from planning to mash some sweet, misguided dude as the ultimate fantasy," Larry went on, tossing a wadded napkin toward the trash and missing. "So he wants Riley to put his ass on the line, which he'll do because some equally sweet and misguided chick has been sucked into doing the dirty work when the time comes."

"And because Riley, being a most triumphant investigator, figures that there be a connection between the evil asshole and the spider lady," said Dennis.

"And, let's not forget," said Carol, "at the end of this sick trail is Goat Hill Extermination's reputation, which our hero will save from being besmirched by the newspapers."

"'Besmirched'? White folks sure do have some goofy shit ways of saying simple things," Dennis said, shoving the last bite of pizza into his mouth and washing it down with a gulp of beer.

"Okay gang, you got the outline right and the details don't matter in terms of our next move," I said.

"And that would be?" asked Larry, finishing his beer and opening another. Carol scowled at him, and he looked contrite, pouring half the drink into a mug on the table and shoving it to Dennis. The taste of Miller beer couldn't be harmed by coffee dregs.

"Eventually, I need to figure out how Eunectes and Redbug fit into Michelle's death—"

"That'd be the king of crush, his lieutenant and the spider lady, right?" Larry asked.

"Yeah, well done. Sorry if I'm moving quickly. But my real concern at the moment isn't those three. It's Petey—the retarded kid who Tommy befriended—who, from what I can tell, is slated for crushing. And if saving him means also saving our reputation by tracing this moral mayhem back to the Linfords, then all the better."

"Got it, boss, humans first, business second," said Larry.

"Seems right by me," said Dennis.

"You guys are aces," said Carol.

"Alright, enough of the love fest. It's time for some action so we can get back to business as usual." I considered one of the beers and thought better of it, given its quality and my need to stay sharp.

"So what do you need us to do?" asked Carol.

"Just be ready," I said. "I don't know when or where the Big Crush is going to happen. But from what I gleaned, it's likely to be soon."

"And not where you hung with yo' homies last night?" asked Dennis.

"Apparently not. It would help if I knew how Eunectes plans to make it happen," I said.

"Shit," said Larry, "could be driving a car onto a guy or lowering a weight from an overhead crane. This is messed up, but it probably involves some big space indoors to generate the force and maintain secrecy."

"Maybe, but it could be simpler," said Carol. "I read about how in the Salem witch trials they put a guy under boards and piled on rocks to press him to death.

"A dude?" Dennis said.

"Yeah, mostly they hung women—"

"Okay, I hate to break up our history lesson, but we're just guessing about the how, which doesn't tell us much about the where. Courtney will call me with the location as soon as she knows. I'm hoping that will give us enough time to formulate a workable plan. So Larry and Dennis, for the next few days I need you to be near a phone or to call into the office every hour while you're working. I know it's inconvenient, but we might need to act fast."

"No problem, boss," said Larry.

"I still feel like I got us into this scene and—"

"No Dennis, we've been through that. It's nobody's fault and we're fixing it together," said Carol. "Speaking of which, what's my role?"

"I need you to coordinate communication among the three of us—and be there for whatever the hell comes up that I can't predict, which is most everything. As for the takedown, you'd stick out like a sore thumb."

"Or a crushed one," Larry mused.

"Other than the crush mistress, it'll be a men's only event," I said.

"Yet another upside to being lesbian," Carol mused.

"As soon as I get word from Courtney, we'll need to do a recon of the place and decide how to stop the action and grab Eunectes. He's key to fitting together the last pieces of this perverse puzzle."

"And there's a price for him to pay?" asked Larry as he moved to the weight bench.

"And you be the collection agency," said Dennis.

"We'll see," I said.

"You'll let the other crush creeps go?" Carol asked.

"Redbug might have some useful information, but the others are worthless. They're into some freaky shit, but people do lots of weird things for pleasure," I said. "Swallowing raw oysters, jogging in circles, breeding goldfish—

"Listening to opera," Dennis said.

"Touché," Larry said, working the barbell.

"My point is that the crush freaks are just following Eunectes, lacking the guts to resist a charismatic leader. In the end, they're like most people."

"Damn straight," grunted Larry, finishing a set of curls.

The guys headed into the rows of shelves, stocking the van for an afternoon job. I told them to wait for me while I made a phone call, and Carol expressed mock amazement that I was going to do some actual work that generated income for the business. That stung a bit, but she was right. I hate it when she's right.

I went down the hall to my office and pondered whether or not to make the call. On the one hand, Stefan was generously compensating me for finding his wife's killer. And he had made it clear that he wanted to decide the fate of whoever I fingered. I hadn't exactly agreed to his terms, telling him that I also had an obligation to the cops without mentioning Lieutenant Papadopoulos by name.

On the other hand, I wasn't certain how the spider swap occurred. I figured Redbug and Eunectes were somehow entangled in this homicidal web, but understanding what they did and why they did it wouldn't be evident until I squeezed it out of them at the culminating crush. I didn't exactly admire Stefan, but a deal's a deal. I picked up the phone.

"Stefan speaking."

"Riley here."

"You've found Michelle's killer!"

"Not so fast. First, I have a decent idea who was involved but no proof. Second, there's an event in the next few days that should provide definitive evidence. Third—"

"I want to be there. I insist on confronting whoever orchestrated that horrible—"

"Third, and don't interrupt me, you can be at or near the location, but only if you follow my directions to the letter. If you don't, you could screw up the whole thing."

"Okay, okay," he sighed.

"Stay by the phone at your apartment or the store for the next few days. I'll call you when I know when and where it's going down. I'll only call each number once. If you don't answer, I'll move on my own and let you know what happened after it's over."

"I understand," he said.

I hung up and went back to the warehouse. Spending an afternoon killing vermin with a couple of loyal guys while checking in every hour with a trusted Girl Friday seemed like just the thing to give me a glimmer of hope for humankind.

CHAPTER THIRTY-FIVE

"Well boss, I gotta say that an afternoon of splashing through puddles to outsmart seagulls beats the hell out of a morning of slopping around in mud to outflank termites," Larry said, pulling tight the hundred-pound monofilament and tying it off.

"That be right," Dennis said, fastening brackets at regular intervals and occasionally looking out to the Bay and into the swirl of drizzly fog.

We were putting down a grid of fishing line for a block of shops and restaurants on Fisherman's Wharf. The guys had already strung line above the parapets and now came the process of stretching a grid a few inches above the flat roofs. The idea was to discourage seagulls from gathering on the rooftops and turning the building facades into something resembling a giant cake—except the icing dripping down the storefronts was bird shit. Apparently the dribbles of what could have been sugary confection streaked with brown caramel weren't fooling the tourists, making it bad for business.

"So, the theory is that the gulls get wrapped up in the fishing line?" asked Larry.

"And the other ones swoop down and eat their tangled homies. That be how these nasty birds see the world," said Dennis.

"Not quite," I said. "According to the experts, gulls don't like places where they can't get a long run before taking off or landing. The lines don't snag the birds. They're more like obstacles on seagull runways."

"Bird hurdles, cool," said Larry.

I kept tying Palomar knots to secure the line at each bracket while wondering if this new method was going to work as well as the company who sold us the system had claimed. The business owners had agreed to give it a shot. They'd tried putting fake owls on the parapets and within days the seagulls had expressed their disdain and frosted the avian mannequins. For my customers' willingness to experiment, I'd given them a big discount, figuring that if the approach was successful, we'd have another arrow in the quiver of Goat Hill Extermination and I'd make up the shortfall with future contracts.

Larry looked up and stretched his back. "Now, we just need a way to keep Eunectes and his flock of sex freaks from roosting in the city."

"I be down with that," said Dennis.

"To be honest guys, what we're doing here is moving the pests to some other rooftops. It's not like they're going to head out to sea and find a desert island to take a crap," I said.

"I suppose gulls and perverts are just heeding nature's call. We provide full dumpsters and empty warehouses and then wonder why nasty creatures show up," said Larry.

"But people don' need to be acting like animals," Dennis said. "That be the whole point of getting ourselves civilized. Can't just graze garbage or—"

"Bang bimbettes—" Larry added.

"Or steal shit," Dennis finished, clearly pleased with their spontaneous poetry.

"Agreed," I said, "but we've been telling people since the Sixties that when it comes to sex, sin is for uptight suckers. So, the moral dumpster is overflowing and the deviants are having a feast." While I wasn't comfortable with society approving and prohibiting sexual positions and partners, there had to be a line. And at least on this soggy rooftop, the lines were regular and tight.

Once the rain shifted from spitting to wetting to pissing, having skipped over rotten, we decided to call it a day and head to O'Donnell's to get warm, dry, and merry—or maybe even gee-eyed, but not baloobas. The Irish have even more words for inebriation than for rain.

I stopped by the office to check on messages and found nothing from Courtney. Knowing that Nina was planning to join us at the pub where the Goat Hill crew was likely to bring up Eunectes and his band of twisted men, I gave her a call to fill her in on developments without going into grisly details. By the time I made it to the pub, the gang had nearly emptied a pitcher of Guinness to acknowledge my long-standing contention that, other than whiskey, this was the best way to warm a bone-chilling day.

Behind the bar, Brian greeted me with, "What's the craic?" and another pitcher of the Irish stout. As I got to the table, Larry, Dennis and Carol lifted their glasses with "*Sláinte!*"—the traditional Irish toast to health. And given my mother's conviction that hot food was the best way to stave off a cold, it was good to see them chowing down on a plate of blaa that Cynthia had turned into sandwiches. There's nothing better than one of her tender flour-dusted rolls folded around a sausage sizzling off the grill.

Buíochas le Dia (the Gaelic phrase for "thank God" and one of the few expressions from the Old Country that stuck with me from childhood), Brian and Cynthia had refused to serve those awful bread bowls that were all the rage. Spinach gunk in pumpernickel or clam chowder in sourdough are about as appetizing as Frito pie and Cheez Whiz.

Having emptied a second pitcher while arguing whether the craze over Rubik's cubes or CB radios was a surer harbinger of cultural collapse, we ordered another and started to debate who was the most important person to have died in the previous year. Such was the nature of hump days at O'Donnell's—passionate disputes about probably irresolvable and undoubtedly inane issues, much like every day at the United Nations.

Carol made a case for Edith Head, who she called the most famous and glamorous costume designer in the history of Hollywood. The lesbian diva held the record for the most Academy Awards by a woman and, according to Carol, when asked about the important men in her life, Head replied, "There were eight of them—they were all named Oscar." Carol found this awfully damned funny and I was reluctantly amused. Meanwhile, Dennis was advocating for Bob Marley and Larry was pushing for Bill Haley, so reggae was battling rock-and-roll for cultural importance neither of which seemed a great leap forward for music in my estimation.

I was trying to decide between Bobby Sands, the Irish nationalist who led a hunger strike from prison during which he was elected Member of Parliament, or Joe Louis. I was explaining that the "Brown Bomber" was maybe the best heavyweight boxer of all time when my brilliant analysis was interrupted by Nina's arrival.

Brian greeted her with a virgin Irish coffee, a concoction he'd developed for her during the wintry months. His secret was very strong coffee (never instant), brown sugar (never white), heavy cream (never whipped), and a teaspoon of brandy flavoring that he kept behind the bar just for her special drink. Nina came over to our table and shed her overcoat. She was rain-soaked and gorgeous, with water dripping from the tip of her nose. The cold had worked its way into her body, from what I could discern beneath a tastefully tight sweater.

She gave me a hug and whispered, "Keep your eyes above my chest, you dirty old man."

"My apologies," I murmured while nibbling her earlobe, "but it's been nearly a week since this aging fighter was in the ring."

She purred a wordless agreement, then wrapped her down vest around her body, while I figured that the next couple of days would extend my bout of celibacy. And if I couldn't get the weirdness of Lane, Michelle, and Eunectes out of my head, my libido might be doomed for even longer.

"So Riley, what's your reason for nominating Joe Louis as the most important dead bro' of last year?" asked Larry.

"Or *sister*," Carol corrected, taking a defiant slug of beer.

"He destroyed the Nazi claim to Aryan superiority by putting away Max Schmeling in the most important fight of the century," I said. "Two minutes into the first round, the German's corner threw in the towel."

"That be a serious whoopin' of a lame-ass honky by a brother," said Dennis.

"Gotta think the dude enjoyed giving the kraut a lesson in racial superiority," Larry noted between bites of the stuffed blaa, which can't be pronounced without sounding like a sheep. Very Irish.

"Seems a good bet," I said, "but boxing isn't only about inflicting pain. Really, that's not what a fighter is thinking. Sure, he wants to win and he does that by hurting his opponent—"

"He or *she* does so," Carol interjected, having amassed hours and earned a formidable, if unfeminine, reputation at Marty's Gym. The old codger had told me that she'd sparred with some of the upstarts who initially pulled their punches, until she'd land a couple jab-cross combinations and then tag them with a jab-jab-cross. Marty waxed poetic about how she'd transition into a stick-and-move style, slipping punches and frustrating the studs who'd eventually land a hard shot or two, rocking Carol and forgetting about chivalry.

Carol launched into a lecture on Cat Davis—who appeared on the cover of *Ring Magazine* a few years ago—and concluded by filling my glass and asking, "So Riley, you think a woman could put a hurt on you in the ring?"

"Like I was saying, it's not really about inflicting pain."

"Way to bob and weave, Riley," Larry said.

"What it be about if not messing up the other sucker?" asked Dennis.

I thought hard about his question, then took a long draw on my Guinness.

"Ah shit, Dennis. Now see what you've done," said Larry. "When Riley gets that look, you hafta know we're gonna get another of his stories. Time to cover up and take what's coming." He refilled everyone's glass, except Nina's. He gave her a wink and she smiled back.

"I'll keep it to a single round," I said. "Back when I was in the fight game, there was this bruiser, Swede Nilsson. He was damned good in the ring if all you considered was winning, but not how."

"He cheated?" asked Nina.

"Not really. Oh, he'd work in a kidney punch during a clinch, and he threw more than his fair share of low blows. But the sonofabitch was a master of the corkscrew punch."

"Marty's not taught me that one," said Carol.

"And he won't," I said. "It's an arching, overhand punch that twists on impact. The goal is to cut the other guy. Swede liked nothing better than working his opponent to the edge of a TKO and then drawing out the match—and drawing blood. Winning wasn't as important to him as hurting the other fighter."

"So he was a sadist?" asked Nina.

"I guess so, but maybe worse. When I saw his face after a fight where he'd really damaged the other guy, Swede looked more than just pleased. Almost, well, ecstatic or . . ."

"Say it, Riley. Orgasmic," said Carol.

"Yeah. It was disturbing. The ring is a place where a man—or woman," I nodded to Carol, "is defined. Where a person's character is revealed. At the end of a fight, most boxers feel a deep respect for their opponent, whatever the outcome. They hug because they've come through the pain and fear together. But for Swede, it was about domination."

"Crushing the other man," Larry said.

"You sayin' some boxers and the freaks we be stopping are the same?" asked Dennis.

"Maybe whether a guy gets off on giving or taking a beating doesn't matter much." Larry said.

"Except that the satisfaction in the ring doesn't come from humiliating your opponent. At least not if you're a decent human being," Carol said.

"It's what's in a person's heart that matters," said Nina quietly. "But only that person knows what's behind a punch—or a kiss."

"Really? A kiss?" challenged Larry.

"Jesus was betrayed with a kiss," she said, biting into one of Cynthia's sandwiches.

"Nina be a woman you don' wanna go toe-to-toe with, m'man," said Dennis, who then decided Nina would be the judge between Bob Marley and Bill Haley. The heavyweight conversation became a free-for-all that no courtroom would abide as the guys made their respective cases without decorum.

Our gathering broke up when Nina declared they were both wrong and William Holden was the most handsome, if not the most important person, lost to world last year. I defended her judgment, noting that he was everything a guy could hope for in *Golden Boy*, a film in which he played a promising violinist who wanted to be a boxer—and ended up with Barbara Stanwyck. My assessment generated a round of eye rolling from the guys and distinctly unladylike raspberries from the women.

Back at my house, I brewed a cup of Lyons tea and defrosted a container of treasured insects that Tommy and I had spent days hunting in the woodlands along the American River last summer, staying each night in a cheap motel outside of Sacramento. The valley elderberry longhorn beetle is a gorgeous creature with sweeping, inch-long antennae. The satiny black and vividly crimson body reminded me of a Flamenco dress.

But my real excitement was because this beetle is slated to be listed as "threatened" which will put an end to collecting—not that insect nets are doing any harm compared to the real estate developers who are leveling the insect's habitat to build houses. Even so, we kept only one female so our collection would have a matched pair. The rarity of the beetles meant the trade value of my extra, male specimens to fellow collectors would be fantastic.

With the beetles pinned and labeled in fine form, I poured a shot of Jameson and put on a recording of Debussy's solo piano works. Settling into my recliner, I turned on the television to a random channel without sound in a desperate effort to stop my mind from running circles around impaling organisms and labeling them with the name of who had delighted in their capture. Watching professional wrestling and listening to Debussy's *Nocturne* left me spellbound with humanity's potential for barbarism and beauty.

Chapter Thirty-Six

"Pin him, goddammit!" The face of Mr. Rossetti, my high school PE teacher, was twisted in rage. A suffocating pressure squeezed around my chest. I fought to breathe, to escape from the grasp of my opponent. Cheerleaders chanted in their taunting cadence: "Hey, alright. Pin your man tonight." I smelled the acrid stench and felt the hot moisture of a body pressing against me relentlessly.

In a desperate effort, I arched my back, turned my opponent and reversed positions, now on top and inflicting my own punishment. "Your turn— that's it, dominate him," the teacher yelled, his face inches from my own. I tried to identify the other wrestler but perspiration stung my eyes and kept me from focusing. I wiped my face on his torn sweatshirt and saw that I was grappling with a skinny, blonde kid. For some reason, he was wearing worn out jeans and red sneakers. He looked scared.

"You have control. Now humiliate the weak, putrid scum," a voice commanded as I watched Mr. Rossetti's face morph into Eunectes's. When I looked back down at my opponent, he'd become a pale cockroach, his six legs flailing desperately at my body.

I leapt up and he rose onto his hind legs, metamorphosing into a man. The antennae drooped and thickened over his face to become a white, biker moustache as my opponent transformed into Hulk Hogan. "I'm your master," he sneered, circling me inside the ropes of a professional wrestling ring. He rushed forward and wrapped his arms around my chest and drove me onto my back.

Eunectes had become the referee, wearing a striped shirt, and I was being crushed against the canvas. Somewhere in the darkness, a crowd was screaming. The referee looked at Hogan and smiled. "Humiliate the fucker, make him squirm like vermin," he hissed, raising his hand as if to signal an end to the match, but refusing to slap the mat.

I tried desperately to tap my submission, but Eunectes just smiled. I thrashed and writhed trying to escape, the pressure of my opponent's massive body slowly, mercilessly bearing down on me.

As I squirmed, my tormentor transmogrified into Birgit Nilsson, arguably the finest Wagnerian soprano in operatic history. As the hefty singer pressed on me, "The Ride of the Valkyries" drowned out the roar of the crowd and the insane, piercing battle cry of the female warriors punctuated my gasps for air.

Nilsson straddled my chest, her thighs squeezing my rib cage. The fat lady's voice rose toward a climax until she collapsed onto me. The diva engulfed me in a suffocating embrace as the crowd roared their approval, with thunderous applause and shouts of "Brava!"

I turned and inched desperately to the edge of the mat, wriggled from beneath her, rolled under the ropes and fell into the darkness. Falling and falling, until I landed with a jolt.

Suddenly awake, utterly disoriented, gasping for air, I looked around. What I first thought to be the wrestling ring rose above my prostrate body. In the silvery darkness, the corner post began to look a whole lot like the end of a headboard. With dawning relief, I realized that I was on the floor next to my bed, drenched in sweat with the sheets wrapped around me like a whole-body tourniquet.

Disentangling myself, I decided that pinning insects, watching professional wrestling on late night television, listening to impassioned classical music, mixing Guinness and Jameson, and pondering sexual deviancy was a very, very bad combination. The alarm clock read 4:30 which I inferred to be AM, a deduction about which I took absurdly great pride, but any flash of rationality seemed worthy of celebration.

The thought of returning to the jumbled, damp bed and lapsing back into a twisted dream was extremely unappealing. So I started a pot of coffee and then stood under a searing shower until the hot water ran out. I dressed and returned to the kitchen to find Mr. Coffee sputtering and coughing the last of his hot water into the grounds.

I fried up a rasher of bacon and used the fat to fry some eggs over easy. A thick slice of Irish brown bread to sop up the runny yolk and a steaming mug of coffee made the early morning dampness outside seem almost refreshing after my disturbing night.

While eating, I perused a recent copy of *Pest Control Today* and was drawn into an article about ecologists finding Burmese pythons in the Everglades and speculating that the snakes could become a serious problem for wildlife—and a major challenge for pest control operators if Fido and Fluffy started becoming snake snacks in Florida neighborhoods. I was pondering the legendary success of St. Patrick, the famed Irish exterminator of serpents, when my eye caught a photo of two enormous snakes with the caption: "The Burmese python (*Python bivittatus*) and the Green anaconda (*Eunectes murinus*)."

Eunectes. I'd figured the exotic alias was an allusion to some Greek island or Roman god. But knowing that the name referred to a genus of snakes that crushes their prey made me loathe my twisted nemesis all the more for dragging another animal into his creepy world.

Carol had me scheduled to spend the morning with her in the warehouse doing inventory. I found this task about as welcome as a bowl of soggy bran flakes for breakfast. But when Carol wheeled in a cart with her new computer and old radio, I could tell she was in heaven. This was a chance to play with her new toy while listening to pop music—and making me scurry among the rows of shelving to call out the names and amounts of products. Being stoically resigned to my fate as the alleged boss of Goat Hill Extermination while knowing Carol was the brains of the operation, I started enjoying the work. At least I managed to forget about Eunectes and the impending murder by focusing on the stockpile and the music.

Between calling out the number of various sticky traps, I caught a singer plaintively repeating "just the two of us" enough times to almost root for the poor sucker, if not the cocktail lounge backup group. The Romeo's appeals to raindrops, rainbows and castles didn't seem to be wooing his Juliet, so I thought he might have better luck by working some unicorns and fairies into the song.

"So, what do you think of Grover Washington's voice?" Carol asked.

"It's unremarkable, although the lyrics are remarkably sappy. However, the music had some decent moments when Grover was drowned out by the saxophone at the end," I said.

"Riley, you can be such an ass. Can't you appreciate anything other than classical music? Wait, don't answer. Here comes the Pointer Sisters . . ."

The seductive voice of a woman serenaded my counting of snap traps. Grover might have been well advised to curtail his lyrical lament and listen to what amounted to a foreplay instruction manual put to music by the Pointer Sisters. The sultry plea for a man with "a slow hand and an easy touch" struck me as fine advice in a world where speed is an unconditional virtue and going faster is the unchallenged goal.

"Okay Riley, now there's a song a straight guy should find alluring. C'mon, tell me you weren't thinking of being with Nina," Carol teased. She was right, but I wasn't going to confess.

"The music wasn't on par with Ravel's *Bolero*. Of course, the lyrics were doing most of the work. And what they lacked in subtlety they made up for in sensuality. That's better than the vapid drivel of most contemporary ballads."

"Nice dodge Riley, but we both know where your mind wandered during that song." I didn't reply, except to tell her that we needed to make sure Larry and Dennis didn't mix the mouse and rat snap traps in a single bin because it made inventorying a pain. Carol's station played a series of advertisements for car dealers, insurance agencies, and "friendly, neighborhood banks" while I worked my way down the shelves sorting mole and gopher traps.

During a song with some guy whining that his baby had "lost that lovin' feeling," I began to think that maybe Grover wasn't so bad after all.

"Don't say it," Carol shouted to me across the rows of shelves when the music was over. "I know you hated that song, but two summers ago Anna and I had a wonderful time at a Hall & Oates concert."

"Maybe 'Haulin' Garbage,' rather than oats, would be a better description of their talents," I said.

Carol told me I'd misunderstood the duo's name, but I wasn't following her explanation. She gave up on my capacity to appreciate pop music and decided to test my ability to admire computers. During another bout of advertisements, Carol regaled me with the comparative virtues of the Apple II versus the TRS-80 and IBM-PC. When she started to wax lyrical about memory and monitors, I began to miss Grover's singing. His hearing crystal raindrops fall made as much sense as my hearing about 64K RAM. I tried to be excited about her being excited, but I was faking it along with the Pointer Sister in bed with the man who didn't appreciate the value of a "slow hand" with a woman. I emerged from the shelves to find a cup of coffee. Carol brought a carafe from the front office and continued her tutorial. She advised me to look into a Commodore VIC-20 for keeping records of my insect collection at home.

"Carol, I really appreciate your educational efforts," I said, sipping from the Styrofoam cup. "But I'm reminded of my father's bit of Irish wisdom: 'Don't give cherries to pigs or advice to fools.' And I'm afraid you're dumping a bucket of juicy advice into the trough of this clueless swine."

She laughed and gave me a sisterly kiss on the forehead to let me know I was a hopeless but adorable boss. "Tell you what, you've been a good sport, so while you count up boxes of masks, gloves, and booties and I feed the data into VisiCalc, we can switch to your radio station."

I hadn't a clue what was VisiCalc was, but I knew KDFC was featuring popular pieces from opera. This seemed a great way to make my point about the wonders of classical music. The selections were tuneful standards, with the announcer providing just enough context to enhance the songs. The first was the Queen of the Night's aria from Mozart's *The Magic Flute*, followed by the drinking song from Verdi's *La traviata*, then Musetta's waltz from Puccini's *La bohème* and "Habanera" from Bizet's *Carmen*. My chest tightened with the announcer's description of the next piece. Carol looked at me with concern.

"Riley, are you alright? Geez, I'll admit the music is touching, but you look pained."

"I'm okay, it's just that 'The Ride of the Valkyries' hits a little close to home."

"How so? Did you lose a bunch of money on some horse named Valkyrie?" she teased.

I went over to the radio and turned down the volume so that Wagner's most famous number wouldn't evoke last night's bizarre dream—and I came up with a quick cover story to avoid having to explain why a grown man didn't want a song to remind him of a nightmare. As Carol tapped at her keyboard, I explained.

"With all the sick sexuality I've encountered lately, this opera pushes my buttons. The story is about a young woman who escapes from the man she was forced to marry. The fellow she runs away with turns out to be her long lost brother. The fellow's father is a Norse god, and his wife, who isn't the fellow's mother because the god sleeps around, is the goddess of marriage. The spurned husband is chasing down his wife and would-be lover, so the god was going to send his favorite Valkyrie to aid his bastard son."

"And a Valkyrie is?"

"A warrior woman produced by the god and the earth goddess."

"Another of the god's trysts, I see."

"So his wife is unhappy about both her husband's infidelities and the adulterous, incestuous liaison about to happen. She makes the god command the Valkyrie not to interfere, but the Valkyrie is so moved by the love between the brother and sister that she tries to stop the murderous husband. However, the god shows up and breaks the mighty sword he'd given his son, who's then killed."

"A big old sword, eh? How phallic."

I wasn't going to tell her about the god's massive spear, so I just continued, "The god is enraged at his defiant daughter. She escapes and takes along her now-pregnant half-sister. The god catches the Valkyrie and condemns her to being mortal. He puts her into a deep sleep and surrounds her by fire which can only be crossed by a heroic mortal."

"Let me guess, a hero arrives to kiss the sleeping beauty," Carol said.

"Not until the next opera in the series. And her rescuer, a handsome young man who she calls a 'valiant child,' becomes her lover—and he's none other than the son of her half-sister who died in childbirth."

"Holy crap, Riley, it's like Mrs. Robinson in *The Graduate*. Hell, there's no difference between soap opera and classy opera, except one is watched by bored old ladies who eat bonbons and like following messed up lives on television and the other is watched by rich old ladies who sip champagne and enjoy listening to people sing about screwed up relationships on a stage."

I was about to protest her comparison when the phone rang in my office. I hurried down the hall and grabbed the receiver.

"Riley here."

"This is Courtney," a voice whispered. "It's going to happen at nine o'clock tonight. Come to a place called Hoffman Fabrication, a couple blocks south of Folsom on Sixth."

"Got it. Are you okay?"

"Can't talk. Just be there. Please."

The line went dead.

CHAPTER THIRTY-SEVEN

I told Carol to get hold of Dennis and Larry and have them meet me across the street from the venue for the evening's depraved entertainment. Hoffman Fabrication was a windowless shop in the middle of a block featuring a bar, auto mechanic, furniture upholsterer, locksmith, used clothing store, and barbershop with the traditional pole twisting hypnotically. The skyline consisted of a highway overpass, which the city unwittingly provided as a shelter from the rain for those buying and selling dope. From what I could see, business was brisk.

I'd finished scoping out the neighborhood when the guys showed up, looking as grim as the surroundings. We walked around the corner and down an alley running behind the shops to assess escape routes from the designated venue. The back door had a narrow, grimy window providing a limited view of the interior. From what I could see, the place was dominated by a large room with a counter separating the work space from a small entryway at the front door. One light had been left on within a bank of fluorescent fixtures, providing enough illumination to make out metalworking machines and workbenches around the periphery of the space.

Having reconnoitered our objective, we headed back to the street and down to Joe's, the watering hole on the corner where we hoped to stay dry and inconspicuous. There were a couple of big, ugly hunks of marginal humanity perched on bar stools near the entry. Their bloodshot eyes lit up for a moment at the prospect of causing some trouble with visitors to their hovel. But the three of us—and particularly Larry's you-don't-want-a-piece-of-this demeanor—silently convinced them to return to their drinks. I paid for our beers with a ten-spot, pushed the change back to the barkeep, and asked if he'd mind turning up the radio. He took the money, gave a knowing half-wink, and filled the air with country western twanging. We settled into the darkness of the back corner, assured that our conversation would be private.

"Okay, so the perv party is at a metal shop," Larry said.

"Seems like a weird location to this black man, but you white folks be some kinda crazy," Dennis said, taking a long draw on his beer.

"Batshit crazy would cover tonight's gathering from what Riley's told us," Larry said, "but those are the cards we've been dealt. So, Riley, how do we play our hand?"

"Nothing fancy. I learned in the ring that being clever usually means getting hurt. We'll rendezvous around the corner from this joint, out of sight from Hoffman's. Be there at eight forty-five sharp. Bring your choice of weapon—but no guns—for what I have planned."

"Which is?" asked Larry, draining his glass.

"Simple. You guys wait until everyone's inside, probably by nine fifteen. Then Larry, post yourself by the front door and stay out of sight as much as possible. Dennis, go around back and set up in the alley."

"That be right. Put the black man by the servant's entrance," said Dennis.

"In this white man's neighborhood, having you stand out front will generate more attention than our honky thug," I said, nodding toward Larry. "And besides, you get to oversee your very own flunky."

"Who dat be?" Dennis's eyebrows converged into a skeptical frown.

"My client, Stefan."

"Sheeit, Riley, why's I get him? What Larry be doin' while I be babysittin'?"

"I don't want anyone extra out front drawing attention. And both of you will be doing the same thing. When the shit goes down inside, I need you to make sure that Eunectes and Redbug don't escape." I described the demented duo, knocked back my beer, and asked if they had any questions.

"So, we're the 007s in Riley's secret service, eh?" Larry asked with a soft belch.

"Not quite," I said. "I'm not issuing a license to kill—only a license to thump."

"We got it," Dennis said.

I was confident they understood the deal. They were good men, able to deliver as needed and to hold back when necessary.

When I got back to my shop, I called Stefan and told him when and where to meet us. He sounded worrisomely eager but acceptably obedient—perhaps not unlike his former approach to carnal encounters with Michelle. Just as I hung up, the phone rang. It was Redbug informing me of the evening's event. He seemed less assured, maybe even unnerved, by what was unfolding. Perhaps the fun was draining from the fantasy as it was becoming real.

I told Carol what was up and that she should be ready for helping with whatever fallout came her way. To keep busy, I reorganized supplies in the warehouse until I heard Carol getting ready to leave. I went up front, where she said nothing but gave me a kiss on the cheek and headed into the dying light.

I killed the next few hours by taking a nap to make up for last night and preparing a TV dinner. Carol kept some frozen food in the warehouse for late nights at work. The toaster oven did a middling job of heating a mediocre Salisbury steak, mashed potatoes, cubed carrots, and apple cobbler. Preparing my .38 was a more appealing project. I decided to stick with the Treasury Loads that Tim had experienced. I wouldn't be looking for flash and thunder tonight, but these hollow points had shallow penetration and reliable expansion. So, if I ended up taking a shot inside Hoffman's workshop, there'd be less chance of the bullet passing through somebody and doing unintended damage. At least my plan was more plausible than the claim of "Delicious Homestyle Gravy" on the packaged dinner.

I headed out at eight-thirty to meet up with the guys. Stefan arrived on time, wearing a trench coat like he was a cross between Humphrey Bogart in *Casablanca* and Marlene Dietrich in *A Foreign Affair*. Larry was carrying a thirty-four inch, thirty-two ounce, Louisville Slugger and Dennis had a police riot baton. When I expressed my curiosity, Dennis said he'd found the straightstick when he was twelve and scouring the debris after the Hunters Point Riot in 1966. If I'd been waiting outside, my weapon of choice would've been the shillelagh I'd found in the back of my father's closet. The stout, blackthorn stick had a noggin-busting knob that would've put down anyone trying to make an unauthorized exit from Hoffman's.

I gave my final instructions, telling Larry and Dennis to keep an ear out for trouble. Then I turned to Stefan and explained in the clearest possible terms that I had no intention of letting him mess up the operation. Translation: If he got more than an arm's length from his babysitter, Dennis had standing orders to clobber him. Dennis slapped the baton against his palm to leave no doubt that braining Stefan would make the evening a success whatever else happened.

While they waited for the attendees to arrive, I spotted Luis and followed him through the front door of the machine shop. This time, there was no lummox asking for passwords. The place had the pungent smell of machine oil and metal grindings. It smelled like hard work. I liked it—and hated how the space would be debased this evening.

In the glare provided by the bare fluorescent bulbs illuminating the entryway counter, I could see that along one wall stretched a battered workbench, with a pegboard holding a multitude of files, assorted hammers, every imaginable type of pliers, and an array of calipers, depth gauges, and dial test indicators. The edge of the bench held a series of vises ranging from petite to monstrous, and spaced along the surface was a selection of electronic pan scales and three-beam balances. On the opposite wall loomed a milling machine, lathes, a couple of drill presses, and a grinding machine. The far end of the room featured a hulking metal press and off to the side was a battered wooden door, leading to an office.

The center of the room was normally an open space, but tonight it was filled with folding chairs. As the men took their seats, they faced a pair of black-draped objects on the cement floor. They were harshly spotlighted by a couple of gooseneck lamps clamped to the workbench at the far end of the room.

Eunectes emerged from the office door. With his black beret and turtleneck sweater, he looked like a beatnik poet who drifted in from North

Beach. He turned and swept his arm toward the door by way of introducing Courtney. She came out in a masochistically tight sapphire-sequined cocktail dress that I figured Eunectes had provided for this occasion. She looked confident as he gave a lascivious smile and gestured for her to come forward. As she did, he stepped back into the shadow, pulsating music started playing from a boom box, and she began her demeaning patter. She wriggled between the rows of chairs, sneering at the men, calling them filthy names. One guy tentatively touched her hip and she slapped him across the face, hard—calling him a disgusting maggot.

Then she made her way to the first of the draped objects at the base of the metal press and whipped off the cloth to reveal a punch bowl with a couple dozen crickets scrambling to climb the smooth sides. She mocked the insects and slipped off her black satin pumps. Courtney lifted a bare foot over the bowl—and then stopped, resting her foot on the edge. She taunted the audience—or maybe the insects—telling them they were too insignificant for her to bother with.

Courtney then sat on the lap of a guy in the front row, violently grinding herself against him while strapping on her shoes. The others voiced their envy, and Courtney inflamed their crushing desire by slowly approaching the other object and bending over provocatively. She yanked the cover from a second punch bowl to reveal a scrawny kitten curled in the bottom. Expressing her disgust at its submissiveness, she lifted her foot—and hesitated, again. The cruel foreplay was driving the men into a state of frenzied anticipation.

At that moment, Eunectes reappeared from the office doorway, gently but firmly guiding another person whose head was covered in a black hood. As they stepped into the makeshift spotlight, Eunectes turned the fellow to face the audience. He paused dramatically and removed the hood with the same flourish Courtney had used for the bowls with the crickets and kitten, as if the person was the natural continuation of the series. There stood Petey—a heart-shaped birthmark on his cheek leaving no doubt.

"This evening, as promised, we will complete our journey of sensuality with this young man. He is nothing more than a pathetic, useless stray, like the mangy creature that Courtney was so tempted to crush." When Petey tottered unsteadily, Eunectes grabbed his elbow and continued. "In fact, should he be allowed to wander the streets, this smack rat will overdose within a few weeks."

There was no sign of comprehension on Petey's face as he was led to the metal press, where Courtney had directed the light of the gooseneck lamps. I could see the manufacturer's sign riveted to the front of the press: Atlas Machine, with a picture of the naked god bent beneath a globe, over which was lettered, "20 Ton Hydraulic Press."

Eunectes grabbed the back of Petey's neck and steadily pushed his head and shoulders down onto the flat, working surface of the machine. Petey steadied himself by holding onto the edges of the metal plate, while Eunectes moved a lever and the upper unit slowly descended. Petey rested compliantly, breathing slowly, almost as if asleep, except his eyes were open and twitching slightly as he looked unseeingly into the room.

From the back row where I sat, I heard Luis mutter, ""Fuckin' A." To my left a guy murmured, "This shit's for real," and I recognized Redbug's voice whispering, "Holy fuck," from near the front. Just as the press barely pinned Petey's head and shoulders against the base plate, Eunectes stopped the descent and smiled. Now held firmly in place, Petey relaxed his grip, utterly unaware of his fate. Eunectes bowed to Courtney and moved aside.

Courtney stepped forward and began her patter, with a slight quaver. She looked into the audience and caught my eye. There was a flash of desperation, to which I gave a slight nod. She seemed assured I was somehow in control, that what was happening wouldn't be allowed to reach its gruesome climax. Her voice became more confident: "You're such a typical man—weak and disgusting. I wipe gutter scum like you from the bottom of my shoe." She sneered and dragged her foot across the floor to drive home her insult.

As Courtney's belittlement became increasingly vile, the crush freaks were enthralled, their earlier disbelief was giving way to vivid fantasy. They no longer had to imagine themselves as insects or kittens but could project themselves into the pathetic man being held in the grip of the metal press.

When I looked over at Eunectes, he was rhythmically rubbing his crotch against the corner of the workbench. He'd clamped his left hand into a bench vise and his right hand was gradually turning the crank as he stared rapturously at Courtney. Slowly, she reached for the lever to lower the press. With her vulgar monologue flowing like the riff of a demented jazz musician, she looked into the audience and our eyes met. Her desperation had transformed into horror. Again, I nodded.

I needed to know what Eunectes and the others would allow to happen. I needed to know the depth of their evil and depravity. I needed to justify the smoldering rage in my gut and burning violence that was about to erupt.

CHAPTER THIRTY-EIGHT

Lengths of iron pipe were stacked against the workbench, providing me with a show stopper. I grabbed a two-foot section, slammed it against the entryway counter, shattering the Formica, and yelled "Stop!" The outburst froze everyone for a moment, except for Courtney who pushed the lever on the metal press to halt the imminent, grisly spectacle. From his vice-gripped position, Eunectes commanded her to continue, but she didn't move. He unclamped his hand and raged at the interruption of his grand fantasy.

"Think of your junkie sister and your cinematic debut in a snuff film," he snarled to Courtney. "There are much worse fates than being crushed while high on smack."

She looked horrified with her options but was unwilling to restart the press.

Eunectes shook his head in disgust and stepped into the semi-circle of crush freaks, his acolytes in homicidal perversion. "This is merely a minor interruption from a disloyal coward," he said coldly and then angrily addressed Redbug: "I told you we shouldn't take on a new member so late in our voyage."

Redbug looked around, hoping the others would come to his rescue. "It was Luis," he said, trying to shift the blame.

"No matter," Eunectes said with a malevolent smile. "We will simply restart the proceedings once we've dealt with this traitor. Take him—and we'll have a double feature this evening."

I slapped the pipe against the palm of my hand. Nobody moved.

"If you allow this gutless bastard to leave, he's sure to snitch to the police." Eunectes left a dramatic silence and then continued, "And he knows what each one of you looks like." I could sense the collective anxiety as heads turned from Eunectes to me. But still nobody rose.

"Redbug, this man will destroy your life when he sends the cops to the museum and you're arrested for lewd and lascivious acts and sexual abuse of animals. Imagine the humiliation, my friend, as you're judged by the hypocrites of this great state."

Evidently, Eunectes didn't figure that Luis was behind my *crush interruptus*. While Luis remained frozen, Redbug grabbed a length of pipe. The audience pushed aside their chairs to create space for him to stalk me. I saw some of the others eying tools and scraps of metal, as if screwing up the courage to join the fight. I considered calling out to Dennis and Larry for backup, but figured that three against fifteen was still bad odds. Even with experience in the projects of San Francisco and the jungles of Vietnam, they'd wind up a bloody mess—and I might end up a human pancake if the melee didn't go our way.

So, I opted for smart over tough. I dropped my pipe and pulled the .38 from the holster inside my waistband. Redbug paused when I took what my police academy instructor called a tactical stance and aimed the gun at him. This posture avoids the downsides of alternative positions which look more cop-like but provide less stability and impede movement.

"I will shoot you," I said, "and anyone else who brings a pipe to a gunfight." Redbug must have figured the odds were still in his favor or I wasn't serious or maybe he was just desperate. In any case, he continued to advance. I didn't feel like playing games, but neither did I feel like killing the dumb shit. At the academy we were told that if you draw your gun, you do so with the intent to shoot. And if you shoot, you do so to stop a threat—not with the intent to kill. This latter caveat always struck me as bullshit to appease the public. Cops aim for center mass to stop a threat, which means a good chance of hitting a vital organ and killing somebody. The best way to stop a threat is to stop his breathing.

Redbug moved slowly, closing the gap to eight feet. I figured a shot into his shoulder would shift the group psychology in a constructive direction regarding the outcome of the evening. I pulled the trigger.

The Treasury load provided an impressive explosion in the confines of the shop. The slug spun Redbug around, and he crumpled to the floor. His screams of surprise and pain broke through the ringing in everyone's ears and did a fine job of adjusting the attitude of those gathered. Now, rather than rushing me, they decided scrambling for the exits would be advisable.

Some pushed their way to the front door and onto the street, while others realized there was less of a throng trying to get through the back door and into the alley. From the crowd jostling at the front, Luis turned to me and mouthed "thank you." I was in a piss poor mood, disgusted that he and the others had allowed themselves to fall under Eunectes's spell and let the insanity develop to the point of passively watching a drugged, street kid get put under a twenty-ton metal press to gratify their sexual fantasies. I mouthed "fuck you" in reply. His face fell momentarily, but then he gave an apologetic nod. I almost felt bad.

At the same time, Eunectes had shoved his way through the front door and reached the sidewalk. Larry had no problem picking out the ringleader and based on a dull, meaty thump, followed by violent retching, I surmised that the perverted puppeteer had been subdued.

With the party over and the puppets scattered, Larry dragged Eunectes back inside and Dennis brought Stefan into the room, now filled with overturned chairs, abandoned coats, and powerful machines. I told Stefan to tie Eunectes's hands in front of him, and my weasely client applied his bondage skills to something worthwhile. As he worked the knots, I raised the metal press to release Petey, who curled into a fetal position on the concrete floor. I stuffed one of the leftover coats under his head.

Courtney was sobbing softly and Larry draped his coat around her shoulders in an uncharacteristically chivalrous move. He led her to a chair, where she crumpled and clung to him. Meanwhile, Redbug was bleeding and blubbering his innocence, insisting that he'd been duped by Eunectes. I told him to shut up or the next shot would put him out of my misery. I tossed him a discarded denim jacket and suggested that applying pressure would stanch the bleeding.

Eunectes looked at me with contempt. Whatever he thought meant nothing to me, but I wanted to know the rest of the story—as Paul Harvey would say. When I muscled Eunectes's bound hands onto the lower plate of the metal press, his arrogance became tinged with fear. I directed Stefan to lower the machine's upper plate and Eunectes clenched his fingers into fists—as if that would help.

"The truth, you sick bastard," I said as his hands became pinned and Stefan stopped the machine. "Tell me what happened with Michelle," I demanded, figuring his reply would fulfill my obligation to Stefan who'd paid very well for the answer. Eunectes sneered, so I lowered the press until his face twisted in pain.

"Stop, enough," he groaned. "Here's the deal. When Michelle started wavering, I gave that cunt a choice. She could either be the crush mistress for the kid or she could buy him from me."

"Let me guess, the asking price was a hundred grand," I said.

"Yes, an entirely reasonable sum, I'm sure you'll agree. And either way, I came out on top, so to speak." For a man whose hands were pinned between two slabs of steel, he was doing a remarkable job of recovering his pomposity.

"How so?"

"Either I ended up achieving the ultimate sexual fantasy. Or I ended up with enough money to allow me to pursue my passions without having to work some shitty job." His voice had become increasingly throaty with pain, as the pressure on his hands took its toll.

"But she failed to pay up, eh?"

"Yes, and I began to sense that she was becoming dangerous to my voyage of carnal delight. Morality can be such an impediment to achieving the peak of pleasure," he sighed. "I was worried she'd go the cops about what was in the works, even if it meant she'd be sacrificed on Grant Roberts' altar of righteousness."

"So?"

"So, with Redbug's assistance, I switched spiders for the little game that Michelle played with her sorry excuse for a husband. There are upsides to having bootlickers and weaklings when executing grand ventures."

Dennis had to restrain Stefan as he described Eunectes in the most colorfully profane terms I'd heard strung together in a very long time.

265

Meanwhile, Redbug dragged himself into a sitting position and leaned against the workbench. From there, he interrupted Stefan's harangue and insisted that he didn't know what Eunectes had planned for the deadly arachnid that he'd provided from the museum.

"It was, dare I say, a devilishly elegant murder," Eunectes said with evident pride and then exhaled with a ragged laugh to mask his discomfort. "Rather more complicated than necessary but poetic in its performance. I replaced Michelle with Courtney, who was readily convinced that her role as crush mistress was better than the alternatives."

"How'd you get access to this place?" I asked. The answer didn't really matter, but Eunectes's sliminess held a kind of dark fascination. The man wasn't stupid by any means. Evil, but not stupid. And I wasn't sure what I was going to do with him or the others, so I was stalling for time while trying to figure out my next move.

"Quite simple. The proprietor, Mr. Hoffman, enjoyed socially unacceptable amusements. A photograph of the corpulent fellow stripped naked while Courtney stood next to him bearing a whip and baring her lovely breasts was a problem for him. Add a swastika armband and jackboots to complete her minimal costume and trading the negatives for a key to the shop seemed entirely reasonable."

"And finally, what did you give to Petey to sedate him?"

Eunectes groaned softly and shifted his weight. "Heroin. And probably his first dose from what I can tell. The kid's naturally dimwitted, which I initially took to be evidence of his being an addict. So now he's just a drugged cretin. But no matter. An imbecile wandering the streets of the city has a life expectancy of a junkie or prostitute." He took a shuddering breath. "I gave him his best chance to bring something interesting into the world, something memorable. He wouldn't have felt a thing while my people would've had the sexual experience of a lifetime."

"You figured heroin would've made the whole process of having his head crushed like a grape under a woman's heel painless? Let's give you a dose of what you were going to make Courtney deliver." I felt a monstrous fury, a depraved desire to inflict pain. I've beaten and killed people who deserved it, but I never sought to create agony as an end in itself. I grasped the control lever and watched the steel plate descend another inch. Bones snapped and ligaments popped, like the meaty sound of breaking apart raw chicken. A gurgling scream lowered the red curtain on my rage, and I stopped the press.

Eunectes had passed out and now hung limply from the machine. The room was quiet except for a weeping dominatrix and a crush freak whispering, "Holy fuck," over and over in response to the condition of his former master. Larry and Dennis were silent, wondering what I'd do with this shambles of humanity—and inhumanity. I was wondering the same thing.

Who deserved what? I could reveal the whole demented story to Lieutenant Papadopoulos, who would turn the case over to Grant Roberts, who would call a press conference to reveal how he'd scrubbed moral slime from the filthy streets of San Francisco. Eunectes would throw Luis and other crush freaks under the bus—or the metal press, as the case may be. They'd be trotted out as exhibit number one of the prosecution's case against deviancy. The Moral Majority would declare a major victory over sin. But why does God's lawyer get to decide who is a sub-human degenerate and deserves to be punished? The only thing more revolting than a woman crushing innocent animals would be the government stomping on citizens, including harmless perverts—harmless, unless you happen to be a cricket or a kitten.

And if the front page headline was going to read LINFORD CASE REVEALS BLACKMAIL, PERVERSION, AND HOMICIDE, then a story on page two of the *Chronicle* would drag Goat Hill Extermination through the mud. We'd be implicated in the murder for having provided the poisons. The tabloids would have a journalistic orgy describing my company's role in the moral mayhem that concluded with naked, delusional geezers using our products to unwittingly off themselves with the encouragement of their sicko grandkid.

The whole mess had begun with Lane Linford, who abused his grandparents to get the money he needed to pay Michelle, who had blackmailed Lane with an insect porn video to get the hundred grand she needed to buy Petey from Eunectes. And then there was Stefan, a furry freak who killed his wife by accident, courtesy of Redbug's pathetically misguided devotion to Eunectes. Off to the side sat Courtney, who was trying to keep herself from being portrayed as a killer and her sister from being provided with a contaminated needle by Eunectes. Every sick path through weakness and perversion led back to this one man—and to my solution.

I told Dennis to haul Redbug to San Francisco General, drop him off at the emergency room entrance, and get the hell out of there. I told Larry to drive Courtney to Carol's house with instructions for her to take care of the feminine wreckage however seemed best. That left an agitated Stefan wanting justice and an unconscious Eunectes dangling by his mashed hands from the metal press.

I thought back to a job involving an infested basement a couple months ago. A guy can learn a lot about the world from vermin.

Chapter Thirty-Nine

I decided to let nature takes its course. That is, to the extent that whatever the hell Stefan and Eunectes did in their private—and not so private—lives bore any resemblance to nature.

My decision emerged from remembering how I'd solved a problem in the dank basement of a customer who was upset by her creepy boarders. There were a dozen wolf spiders and a passel of silverfish scampering around the baseboards. It struck me that a batch of hungry predators wandering among a bunch of tasty prey was a "problem" on its way to solving itself. Sort of like the comedian who riffed on seeing a wanted poster that described a notorious criminal as being both armed and suicidal—maybe the FBI could just wait for this case to resolve itself.

Likewise, I suggested to the lady of the house that rather than spraying poisons, she had the makings of a built-in solution if she just let things unfold in their own way. I assured her we'd check back in a couple of weeks to see if the spiders had taken care of the silverfish and, owing to a shortage of food, might've headed back outside for better hunting. Sure enough, when I returned, there was nary a silverfish and just a couple of spiders. I caulked some cracks in the foundation to keep out moisture and wildlife, helped her clean up the old books, cardboard boxes, and potting soil that had fed the silverfish, and wished the basement spiders well with whatever slim pickings were left as an errant earwig wriggled under the washing machine.

That's how I figured that Stefan would do a fine job of working out whatever resolution would be befitting a pervert seeking justice from a deviant.

"I'm outta here," I told Stefan.

"What should I do with him?" he asked, gesturing to his unconscious foe.

"Up to you," I said. "You're the one who wanted in on the action and now the ball's in your court. Press the flesh, call the cops, leave him here for Hoffman to find in the morning. Be creative."

"He's a serpent, a poisonous viper," Stefan said half to himself, trying to either figure out a course of action or justify whatever he had in mind. I couldn't tell which, although his allusion to the cold-blooded nature of his wife's killer reminded me of a Saint Patrick's Day toast.

"He calls himself 'Eunectes' which is the genus of the anaconda. Clever, eh? As an Irishman, I'll leave you with this little ditty: St. Patrick was a gentleman; who through strategy and stealth; drove all the snakes from Ireland; here's toasting to his health." I lifted an imaginary glass toward Stefan and said, "Looks like you're San Francisco's St. Patrick." He was no saint and no gentleman, but the snake was at his mercy.

Stefan stood staring at Eunectes's unconscious body draped beside the metal press. I knelt down and nudged Petey, who responded with a drowsy protest and mumbled a question about where he was. I dragged him to his sneakered feet. He was dopey but able to walk with my support. We made our way through the clutter of chairs, out the front door, and staggered down the sidewalk like a couple of drunks. Petey seemed to be coming around by the time we got to my truck and I stuffed him into the cab. As I slid behind the wheel, he flopped against the door with his head resting against his bony chest.

I drove aimlessly, the rain having created a sheen on the streets that complemented the drops accumulating on the windshield between beats of the wipers to turn the city into an expressionistic painting of neon lights. The rain ramped up to bucketing and reached hooring by the time I cruised through the Tenderloin. The thrum on the truck's roof provided a soothing cocoon of white noise, masking the traffic sounds and the wet shush of my tires. I didn't know where I was going, but I figured I should be ready to get

Petey medical attention if his trip took a bad turn. He started lifting his head every so often and his breathing seemed less shallow, so I was hopeful.

I turned on KDFC which was featuring Wagner's entire Ring Cycle in their evening *Opera Tunities* (classical music lovers not being renowned for their humor or marketing prowess). The announcer broke in to remind listeners that we were coming to the second scene of the first act of the second opera—*Siegfried*. This meant the program was not quite a third of the way through the seventeen hours of opera that the station was spreading across two weeks of nighttime broadcasts.

Petey gave a deep sigh and a shudder as I circled the Civic Center, paying just enough attention to the streets so I could get us to St. Francis Hospital, which would be the closest emergency room, if needed. At a stoplight I looked over and his eyelids fluttered. I figured he was on his way back to the world. Meanwhile, I turned my attention to Wolfgang Windgassen who was singing the role of Siegfried as gorgeously as any heroic tenor has ever done. Siegfried and Petey had one thing in common—they were orphans whose lives were screwed up by evil men, a dwarf in Siegfried's case and a snake in Petey's case.

Siegfried despises his foster father, but he's the only person who knows the young man's parentage. Under pressure, the dwarf explains that he took in the kid's mother who died in childbirth, leaving the homely gnome with a bawling ward and a broken sword. One thing leads to another, as happens in Wagner's epic operas, and Siegfried tells his ersatz father to use his blacksmithing skills to repair the sword his mother left behind. Dad lacks the ability to fix the blade but possesses the capacity to fix up a plan to use his adopted son to acquire a magical, gold ring—which is the accursed goal of the entire four opera marathon. Siegfried is a perfect chump, being strong and fearless. Really, the guy had never experienced fear.

The bombastic music and fantastical plot took me back to the moment when Eunectes stuffed Petey under the metal press and the kid showed no fear. Heroin explained his drug-induced, apparent courage. The glassy-eyed innocence in the minutes before his impending death was haunting. In that moment, it occurred to me that there was another orphan in the machine shop who showed no fear. I headed back to rescue the one left behind.

271

I parked in the alley behind the shop and hoped Stefan left the back door unlocked. He had and I went inside, fumbling to find a light switch. Failing in that part of my mission, I relied on the illumination provided by the headlights of my truck reflecting into the darkened space. I made my way along the wall and then down the workbench, banging my shin against an overturned chair. Reaching down, I pushed aside debris and shuffled to the end of the room where the gruesome performance was to have taken place.

Just as I was thinking about going back to the truck to look for a flashlight, my foot bumped into the rim of a bowl on the floor. I reached inside and felt the soft warmness of the kitten, curled in the bottom. Not sure that the creature would appreciate being snagged in the dark and not wanting to tangle with a frightened stray, I tried to lift the entire bowl which shouldn't have been much of a challenge. But the damned thing was stuck to the floor and I had to give a hard yank, which almost sent me tumbling backwards. I regained my balance and pushed back through the scattered chairs.

Once I reached the doorway, I saw what had adhered the bowl to the floor—blackened blood with red clots clung to the bottom. In the dim light, I could see the kitten was looking pitifully upward and didn't seem at all interested in defending itself. So I set down the bowl, stuffed the creature inside my coat to keep it dry, and dashed to the cab. Petey was reasonably alert and gave a weak smile as I handed him the kitten. On the way to my house, I explained what he'd missed without going into more detail than necessary. Neither he nor the kitten seemed up to handling the depths of human depravity.

When we were inside, Petey said he was hungry in so many—or so few— words. I went into the kitchen to whip up some sausages and colcannon. While the potatoes and cabbage were boiling, I put on a record of Samuel Barber's music and showed the kid my insect collection. He stared in rapt wonder at the specimens, which spoke highly of his capacity for curiosity despite his intellectual limitations. My kind of guy.

Petey asked if he could pin some insects, so I pulled a margarine tub of miscellaneous beetles from the freezer and showed him how and where to insert a pin through the body. While he was busy impaling beetles, I gave Nina a call and conveyed the good news and bad news. The former being that Petey was fine, the latter being that my plan for a tryst was nixed by having the kid safely ensconced at my house. I had the sense that she was more relieved than randy, which was understandable but not a boost to my Irish machismo.

When the food was ready, I called Petey into the kitchen and set out three plates—two heaping platters on the table for us and a saucer with diced up sausage on the floor for the kitten. It had been slinking along the baseboards in an effort not to be noticed, which was likely how it had lasted this long in the grunge of the city. The waif approached the grub with a mixture of caution and hunger until an empty stomach got the better of him and he pushed his face into the food.

Petey asked me to "play that pretty record" again, so I moved the needle back to the beginning of the LP. We listened to the sweet melancholy of *Adagio for Strings* and ate wordlessly. In fact, throughout the entire night, the kid had said a total of twenty words: Where am I? (from the shop floor); What happened? (in the truck cab); What's his name? (in reference to the kitten for which I had no answer); I'm hungry (twice); Can I try? (regarding insect pinning); Play that pretty record again (his longest sentence). Petey offered up three more words, "This is good," after taking a second helping of my makeshift dinner.

While I cleaned up, Petey returned to quietly pinning beetles with a poignancy that reflected the somber mood and Latin lyrics of Barber's "Agnus Dei": "The Lamb of God; Who took away the sins of the world; Have mercy upon us." A lamb, indeed. I went out to the living room as the record ended. I was tempted to put on Debussy but decided on Ravel. His Piano Concerto in G Major was a change from Barber, the music being upbeat, playful, and jazzy. And you can't beat André Cluytens conducting the Paris Symphonic Orchestra with Samson François at the keyboard.

Petey smiled but said nothing. That was okay with me. People generally talk too much. "Sharing" is overrated and is usually synonymous with whining. The police shrinks were always trying to get us to talk about our experiences after some bad shit went down and this never did any good. Living is hard, killing is necessary. We didn't write the rules. God did, according to the police chaplain. And he could never explain why the Big Guy was such an asshole in setting up the game.

Emboldened, the kitten joined us, scrambling onto the kid's lap and then tried to climb onto the worktable. My firm rap on its nose set him straight—a version of the technique the nuns at St. Teresa's used to maintain order among their miscreant charges. A ruler to the knuckles provided an effective reminder as to the limits in Sister Mary Leon's classroom. Soon, the kitten nodded off in my recliner and Petey was fading fast. I led him upstairs and directed him to my bedroom, where he could enjoy a safe night of decent sleep.

Back downstairs, I went into kitchen, boiled a pot of water, slowly added oatmeal, and turned off the heat. Having taken care of breakfast preparations, I poured a generous dose of eighteen-year-old Jameson, a whiskey older than the kid in my bed. I kept this bottle for special occasions and tonight seemed to qualify. There were loose ends that I'd need to deal with tomorrow, but tonight I could celebrate having kept the world from becoming uglier than it had been this morning. Not a glorious victory, but goodness is primarily a rearguard action.

I put on Verdi's *Otello*, slipped an afghan under the kitten and stretched out in my recliner. Sipping slowly, I listened for "Iago's Credo," arguably the darkest aria in all of opera—and Tito Gobi had the baritone to convey the depth of this musical malevolence. Iago was evil personified, manipulating people into committing horrendous acts of betrayal and brutality. But we never learn his fate. In the final act, Otello kills his beloved and faithful Desdemona, then realizes his error and stabs himself—as Iago, the evil puppeteer who is finally revealed for his duplicity, escapes.

Nodding off, I wondered about Eunectes's fate. I didn't so much care, as I was curious. They say that curiosity killed the cat, but at about two in the morning, it was clear that inquisitiveness wasn't lethal to the kitten, which surely wondered about the unfamiliar comfort to be found on the blanket draping my lap.

CHAPTER FORTY

In the morning, I deposited my feline lap warmer on the floor, massaged out the stiffness in my neck from a night in the recliner, and headed to the kitchen. While whipping up a batch of my special Irish oatmeal I heard the water running in the bathroom and wondered how long it had been since the Petey had enjoyed a steaming hot shower. I added some milk, Irish butter, and a pinch of salt then reheated the pot that had cooled overnight. The Irish know their oatmeal—and how to make it.

I like both Flahavan's Pinhead and Macroom's oatmeal, which are available through the Green Mafia (my mother and her network of Irish ladies on Potrero Hill). Not having had a recent delivery from the Old Country, this morning I went with McCann's steel-cut oatmeal which is perfectly acceptable and locally available if you know where to shop. I want nothing to do with the dietary fiber craze for bran flakes, which are the equivalent of dried leaves, nor Grape Nuts, which are twigs and pebbles. A few months ago, Nina convinced me to try these abominations for my health. My view is that culinary masochists don't live longer by eating lawn clippings for breakfast, it just seems that way.

The key to Irish oatmeal, in addition to using toasted grain and dipping each spoonful into a bowl of cream, is topping the porridge with soft brown sugar which includes the molasses that is often removed for reasons that elude me. I shared a wordless breakfast with Petey, then grabbed a shower while he had a heaping bowl of seconds and played with the kitten.

We—meaning Petey and I, the feline remaining at the house and enjoying a saucer of cream—headed to St. Teresa's. Nina was ecstatic to see the kid was hale and hearty, and Petey said more in the first two minutes with Tommy and Karsa than he'd spoken to me in the last twelve hours. He regaled my brother with having pinned beetles, and Tommy affirmed the immense good fortune at having been provided with such a special opportunity. Petey proceeded to tell Karsa all about the kitten which elicited a curiously raised eyebrow from Nina. I just shrugged, which seemed the best explanation. There was no talk of last night, drugs, metal presses, sensuous women, or gun shots.

"So, it's over?" Nina asked, stepping away from the chatter of the man-child trio.

"Not quite. I still have to figure out how I'm going to play this with Lieutenant Papadopoulos once I learn what Stefan decided to do with Eunectes."

"I'm not sure I know what you mean," she said, "nor am I sure that I want to. But maybe you can give me enough of a picture so I can help Petey in the coming days, while allowing me to plead ignorance should the police pay a visit."

I provided a general outline of what happened last night without self-incriminating detail. I skipped over as many sordid particulars as possible while keeping the account coherent and relevant to Nina's caretaking.

"Jesus, Mary, and Joseph," she said, borrowing my mother's most extreme expression of disbelief. "They were going to crush him in a machine press? And what about the kitten?"

"The little guy was a teaser during the warm-up act. So, I came home with two orphans. I was hoping you might look after both of them." Again Nina gave me the one eyebrow, which I knew meant trouble. "I'll try to keep Petey out of the story I tell the cops," I said. "If I play it well, Papadopoulos will close the case and move on to the next lurid investigation."

Petey's prognosis on the streets was grim, but better if he could avoid cops and perverts—and get support from St. Teresa's. He was a loose end that was likely to fray in the future, but at least for the moment he was chattering away with his buddies.

"And if not?" Nina asked.

"I get booked for attempted murder by San Francisco's finest, Goat Hill Extermination's reputation gets trashed, a crush mistress gets charged with god-knows-what to please a sanctimonious prosecutor, and . . . I could go on."

"Don't. All I need to know is that Petey is safe. All you need to know is that I am not going to adopt a kitten. And . . ."

"And?"

"I know you'll do the right thing. Or the best you can do," she gave my hand a soft squeeze. Nina understood that the world doesn't provide many opportunities for uncomplicated goodness. Usually, it's a matter of minimizing bad shit.

"And I know one more thing," she said, glancing over her shoulder to see if anyone was eavesdropping. I leaned closer. "I know that if I don't get you into the sack soon, I'm going to become a nun and join Saint Teresa in a life of mystical prayer and womanly frustration." She gave me a lingering, moist kiss.

I swung by a Walgreens to get cat litter, a litter box, and a few tins of chow. I wasn't sure what I was going to do with the kitten, but I didn't want it making a mess or starving in the meantime. Stopping by my house, I set out a food bowl and the litter box while musing that I could just dump the former into the latter and cut out the middle man, or creature in this case. The smell of tuna brought the houseguest mewing into the kitchen. Having taken care of my new charge, I headed to the shop.

My crew had already exchanged stories of last night, so I gathered everyone together and filled in the gaps. Dennis had dumped Redbug at the emergency room for patching and Larry had taken Courtney to Carol's house for safekeeping. Carol had given Courtney a soft bed, hot breakfast, and two hundred bucks—the latter courtesy of Goat Hill Extermination's petty cash lockbox which was now nearly empty. I was going to fuss, but thought better of second-guessing the woman who kept the books and hosted a traumatized vagrant overnight without complaint.

"I got here late," she explained, "because I picked up Courtney's sister and took the two of them to the bus station. They're on their way to Los Angeles where they have a distant relative and a shot at something better."

This loose end was about as likely to have a happy resolution as Petey. But at least LA is warmer in the winter than up here, and a relative couldn't be more abusive than Eunectes was. That second part wasn't true but I was going with it anyway. The little lies we tell ourselves make the world tolerable.

"So what's the story with Stefan and Eunectes?" Larry asked, leaning against Carol's desk. "The little dude was looking like he'd wig out."

"Mental," Dennis said, shaking his head. "That scrappy honky be juiced on revenge."

"I don't know, but I have a suspicion that it wasn't a pretty ending," I said.

"My guess is that Riley is going to find out soon enough," said Carol. "When I got in this morning there were already three messages on the machine from Lieutenant Papadopoulos. Each one became less polite or, I should say, more rude. The first two were requests, the last one was an order for Riley to meet him at Central District Station at ten thirty or he'd send a black-and-white to take you in for questioning."

"Good luck boss, we gotta' bounce," said Larry draining his Styrofoam cup and heading to the warehouse.

"We be battling bad guys by night and bad bugs by day. Regular super heroes, Larry and me," said Dennis with a grin. "Be sure to have a wicked good time with your homey in blue," he added, following Larry to the back. Then he stopped and turned, "Riley, you know I appreciate you doin' all this, bein' as I sorta got things started."

"Shut up and get to work," I said. Dennis flashed me a grin and headed down the hall with his trademark saunter. I headed to the Linford estate.

"I've seen the videotape," I began. Lane Linford's defiant gaze dropped to the Oriental rug. "Since last Wednesday, your trail of blackmail led to a woman dying in agony, a kid nearly crushed to death, a pervert being shot, and a pool of blood that will undoubtedly lead to a very unpleasant scene." I leaned forward from my overstuffed leather chair by the fireplace in the Linfords' opulent study.

The heat felt good given the chill wind of the morning which was supposedly ushering in sunny weather for the first time in weeks. I was dubious since weathermen lie with the same frequency as deviants and criminals. Lane had abandoned his affected clothing for a track suit and running shoes. I doubted he'd taken up exercise, but perhaps jogging relieved stress. I can't see any other plausible reason for this fad.

"And will the trail lead back to me?" he asked, rolling his head to produce that infernal crunching of neck vertebrae.

"It's up to you."

"What can I do?"

"I'll keep you out of this sordid tale under one condition." I wasn't absolutely sure that I could protect him, but what I was about to propose was for his own good, whatever Papadopoulos had ginned up for me later this morning.

"Get help. I have the name of a psychologist." I plucked one of Dr. Chen's embossed business cards from my shirt pocket and put it on the polished coffee table.

I continued as he fingered the card. "She's very good and doesn't judge. If you'll contact her, I'll do everything in my power to keep your name out of the police report." That much was true. The other truth was that I was in over my head in terms of crazy. Lane wasn't an axe murderer or a deranged rapist, either of which I would have been more than willing to turn over to the cops. He was a sicko who'd more-or-less accidentally offed his grandparents to avoid public humiliation. Let Dr. Chen decide whether to call in the police. That's why shrinks get the big bucks.

"It's no use, Riley."

"You're miserable. And you're a sitting duck for the next person who wants to convert your shame into cash." He took a deep breath and hung his head. I waited. The ticking of a grandfather clock and the crackling of the fire were the only sounds. At least this room didn't have one of those gas log gimmicks that were about as convincing as inflatable sex dolls.

Lane Linford started talking. I don't know why he decided to confide in me rather than waiting to spill his guts to Dr. Chen. Maybe because

I wasn't charging a Jackson an hour to murmur "uh huh" or perhaps he wanted to practice on a guy before telling his story to a woman. In any case, he described how he'd been shy in elementary school, never wanting to play "rough games" with the other boys. His father had been a tyrant and his mother had been tender but unable to stand up to her domineering husband. Lane had kept an ant farm and liked the feel of insects crawling on his thighs. When he was in fifth grade, the gardener's son, a boy about Lane's age, would take him into the tool shed and they'd rub against each other. One day, Lane's father caught them and beat the other boy bloody. Only the gardener's arrival with a pruning hook upon hearing the screams saved his kid. After that, Lane didn't have any close friends and in adolescence he struggled to relate to girls. So he expanded his collection of creatures and began masturbating while the insects wandered over his genitals. However, after every episode with his pals he felt disgusted but powerless to resist. He tried to learn about his condition by reading psychology journals—and that's where he got idea of how to use his grandparents' delusions to gain access to the money needed to pay off Michelle.

"Helluva story Lane," I said, having settled into the overstuffed chair, marveled at his twisted tale, and thought how much I could've used a whiskey even if was 10 am. "Seems that if your 'dirty habit'—as you call it— is filthy enough to motivate a deception that turned into negligent homicide, then it might be time to give therapy a try." I was dubious that Dr. Chen or any other head-peeper could fix this guy, but throwing a psychological haymaker seemed better than throwing in the towel.

"I'm so tired," he said, lifting his head. He seemed too drained to bother brushing the straggly hair out of his eyes.

I reached across the coffee table smacked him, hard. His shook his head and glared at me. "Good, you're mad. That's better than this despondent bullshit." I was confident that thumping patients wasn't among the techniques taught to therapists. Probably should be.

"Here's the deal pal, you call Dr. Chen by noon or I call Lieutenant Papadopoulos. I can deal with sexual weirdness. Shit, we all have our quirks—including at least a few kinks that fill our fantasies, if not our lives. But I won't put up with self-pity." I headed out of the room and paused at the doorway. "I'll call the shrink after lunch and if she's not heard from you, then expect your life to get way more screwed up than your little game of six-legged foreplay."

Back in my truck, I figured that Luis was happy with his fetish, as long as he stuck with soft crush. So there was no point in recommending my favorite shrinkiatrist to him. My real problem was going to be not getting mashed under the tassel-toed, Italian leather loafers awaiting me in the office of Lieutenant Papadopoulos.

CHAPTER FORTY-ONE

The furnishings in the lieutenant's office were as non-standard issue as his clothing, unless the SFPD had started providing cherry-veneer desks, along with faux-leather chairs and pseudo-Tiffany lamps. Papadopoulos featured a charcoal pinstripe, three-piece suit, his jacket on a hanger (not a hook) behind the desk. The room reeked of cologne, my host being slathered in Yves Saint Laurent's Kouros.

My odiferous knowledge was based on Nina having bought this scent for me on my birthday. She explained that Kouros referred to ancient sculptures of nude Greek youths that she lovingly, but unconvincingly, associated with my own physique. I was willing to bet that Papadopoulos was fully aware of this connection and saw himself as statuesque. The cologne was more like perfume in my book, so I returned to tried-and-true Aqua Velva—a smell that reminded me of my father. But I kept the bottle of Kouros on my dresser to use on special occasions for Nina.

Papadopoulos offered me a cup of coffee from the pot in the grimy squad room outside his ostentatious office. I yearned for Gustaw's wickedly strong brew, or even Carol's version, rather than this swill. A heaping spoonful of sugar and a generous shake of chalky creamer covered up the bitterness, sort of like how a bad steak can be made almost edible with some A1 sauce.

"So Lieu, what's on your mind?" I said, settling into a chair that was far less comfortable than his but figuring that whoever started asking questions was usually in the better position.

Papadopoulos leaned forward, resting his forearms on the desktop. His chair was a couple inches higher than mine. Nice move.

"There was a very strange death last night," he said. "It was outside our district, but the captain in the Southern Station knew of my interest in the Linford case and figured that maybe there was a connection."

"Another pair of naked, dead geezers wearing dog collars? Really, this needs to be stopped before the elite of the entire city is wiped out," I said.

He wasn't amused. "This morning, the owner of a machine shop near Folsom and Sixth reported finding a body crushed in the metal press. And I suspect you might be able to shed some light on what happened." That neatly, or messily, explained the blood adhering the kitten's punch bowl to the floor.

I sipped my coffee, contemplating what evidence I might've left behind in the chaos. "Do tell, Lieutenant. Was the corpse a fellow exterminator? To be honest, I find that killing vermin at a reasonable price is far more effective than killing my competitors."

"Cute, Riley. We don't know the victim's identity because his head and hands were pancaked into a quarter-inch slab of meat and bone. There won't be any usable fingerprints or dental records."

"Sounds like a terrible, industrial accident. A guy shouldn't mess with power tools unless he knows what he's doing," I said, trying to play dumb. It's one of my finer skills.

"We don't think the victim worked at the shop. Some guy showed the owner compromising photographs of himself and exchanged the negatives for the keys and a night's access to the joint. The place was set up for some sort of spectator event, with rows of folding chairs."

"Evidently not a safety seminar, eh? But I'm still wondering why you think I know anything about this." Papadopoulos shook his head and tented his fingers. A corner of his mouth twitched in his version of a smile as he was quite evidently pleased with what he was about to reveal.

"We found a couple of items you might be able explain."

"Gee Lieu, I'll do my darnedest," I said with the most innocent tone I could muster while trying to imagine what he had to link me to the scene.

"A gunshot victim was dumped at San Francisco General's ER last night. The docs patched up a gaping hole in his shoulder. The guy bolted when a black-and-white rolled up. The nature of the wound was consistent with a Treasury Load, the sort of ammo that an ex-cop with connections to the force might use."

"A well-connected ex-cop, along with a few thousand other people, including the Secret Service, Customs officers, highway patrol, active cops, retired cops, the wives and kids of cops, range rats, and brass-scrounging reloaders from every walk of life."

"Thou doth protest too much, but let me continue," he said. I wouldn't have given Papadopoulos credit for being able to paraphrase Shakespeare since the Bard wasn't Greek. Maybe the lieutenant was slightly deeper than his smarmy facade indicated. Probably not. "The victim in the metal press had a pair of vice grips locked onto his balls."

Stefan had both determination and a sense of poetic justice. The little guy must've wrestled Eunectes's unconscious body up onto the metal press, as I'm sure the bigger man wouldn't have been cooperative if awake. But then what? My bet was that he lowered the press just enough to pin Eunectes in place and waited for him to regain consciousness. The vice grips would have provided Stefan with satisfaction only if his wife's killer had been alert enough to experience a version of crushing that was surely less stimulating than his fantasy. I might've felt a twinge of sympathy for Eunectes except his fate was exactly what he planned for Petey, although without sedation. Of course, I didn't really know what happened and never would, which was fine with me.

"Let's see, vice grips are probably found in the garages of about ninety percent of San Franciscans. If that's all—" Papadopoulos raised his hand to stop me.

"I've saved the best for last. But you probably knew that, since I suspect you were there or nearby. There was a punch bowl of crickets on the floor and an empty one near the back door." He paused and reclined in his chair, clearly satisfied with himself. "Now then, let's see you do a little more math. How many citizens of our fair city are connected with odd deaths, sexual depravity, and insect weirdness? I can think of exactly one."

He didn't really have anything on me—a flattened corpse, vice grips, and a batch of crickets. This flimsy, however bizarre, circumstantial evidence wasn't sufficient to put me at the scene. But Papadopoulos had been decent enough to give me time to extricate my business from the Linford deaths and scandal-hungry reporters. This was my chance to shape the story—but I had to give him something that would work in the worlds of police and politics.

"Here's what I know. To begin, the Linfords' deaths were a tragic accident caused by their delusions of being infested." The lieutenant grunted his doubt, but I continued. "Although their grandson, Lane, can't be implicated, in the course of my investigation I discovered that he was tangled in another mess. Lane starred in videos showing him doing some very nasty things."

"Porn? That scrawny-assed punk?" Papadopoulos said.

"Takes all kinds to make this deviant world go 'round. I don't know who the filmmaker was—"

"Hold on. You don't know or you won't give me the porn producer's name?"

"Don't know," I lied, having also left out the blackmail element and skipped over the whole Marcia and Stefan angle, since the cops hadn't determined her death to be suspicious.

"You're full of shit, but please continue," he said, pulling a pad of paper from a desk drawer and a silver pen from his shirt pocket to take notes.

"The kid's information led me to a group of perverts who get off watching women crush insects underfoot."

"That's even sicker than you could invent, Riley. Continue."

"So this guy in the crush club was getting nervous about where things were heading—"

"I don't suppose you caught his name either."

"They used aliases to protect themselves against infiltrators, having gotten the message that the assistant DA has a hard-on to round up anyone not using Biblically approved methods of intercourse."

"Okay, but this story had better start getting useful," he said, clicking the button on his pen.

"We're nearly there. Turns out that a charismatic leader calling himself 'Eunectes' seduced the group into taking on a more realistic and extreme fantasy. You see, when insects get mashed, the men are imaging themselves underfoot because they crave domination by women." Papadopoulos resumed taking notes.

"Shit, I could've given them my ex-wife's address," he said while neatly printing on the legal pad.

"They might've taken you up on that because they needed a crush mistress who would go the extra mile."

"Meaning?"

"Meaning a woman to stomp on mice, at first."

"At first?"

"Right, and then building to the ultimate—crushing a man."

"How do you know this?"

"I worked myself into the group."

"Let's back up. I gather they found a crush mistress. And I'm going to guess you didn't catch her name or she also had an alias," he said. I shrugged.

"Sorry Lieu, I'm out of practice when it comes to police procedures. I'm just a lowly spray jockey following a grimy trail to make sure Goat Hill Extermination isn't dragged into the gutter when this story breaks."

"And so, you figure Eunectes and his gang of deviants were at the machine shop last night?" He rubbed his chiseled chin. "That explains the folding chairs, the bowl of crickets, and the body in the metal press. But this whole story is just a little too convenient, a little too neat."

"How so?"

"It explains everything and nothing. In particular, your inability to come up with any names that would allow me to check your account of last night makes me pretty damned sure you're withholding evidence. And we've been over what a charge of obstructing justice means. I believe this interview is over—at least until I convince the DA to charge you with a felony or . . ." Papadopoulos pushed back from his desk and then paused for a moment.

"Or?"

"Or maybe I should just detain you right now as a material witness." He reached to the small of his back and pulled out a pair of handcuffs with dramatic flourish. "I figure you were at the murder scene and can explain the vice grips along with providing names. Once my officers make some high profile arrests, you take the stand in a few weeks and then get back to chasing the vermin you're licensed to pursue."

Here was my moment of truth, or more accurately my culminating moment of deception. If I could sell this chapter of my story, I might wriggle free.

"I wasn't there, but my guess is something went wrong in their plan. Somebody got angry, maybe betrayed. Mad enough to pull a gun. We might never get that part figured out." Papadopoulos started to get up. "Hang on. The case comes together if I'm right about one element of the crime scene."

The lieutenant sat back down. "Go ahead, but this had better be good and fast."

"I'm betting that something else went very wrong for Eunectes." Papadopoulos put the cuffs on his desk blotter and lifted one eyebrow. He took the bait and I set the hook. "Was the body in the press around six foot three, a hundred and eighty pounds, and dressed in black?"

Papadopoulos opened a file folder on his desk and scanned the contents. "According to the preliminary report, the victim was wearing black. We'll have to wait for the ME to get a height and weight. Why?"

"Eunectes always wore black, and I'll bet the autopsy comes back with my numbers. It looks like one or more of his followers turned on their leader and he ended up as the main act of the evening."

"So what am I supposed to do with your story?" Papadopoulos asked, fingering the chrome-plated cuffs and staring menacingly at me.

"Simple Lieu. You close the case on the Linfords as the accidental poisoning of a nice old couple who were struggling with mental illness and tell the press their heartbroken grandson wants to mourn in private. And then you tell Assistant District Attorney Grant Roberts that you cracked the case of a sex operation which involved torturing animals for shocking purposes and culminated in the well-deserved death of the ringleader whose identity is being investigated but may not be ascertained due to the condition of the body. It's even better than the high-profile arrests you were hoping to make.

"At the press conference, you say that while the police are continuing to pursue the other participants in the secret society, we can be sure that the sicko leading this sexually depraved group has been stopped. Roberts then goes to the podium and announces that the good people of San Francisco can rest easy knowing this criminal activity has been thwarted and its immoral adherents are on the run. The headline reads: DISTRICT ATTORNEY ANNOUNCES MAJOR BUST OF PERVERT RING."

I leaned back and waited. Papadopoulos slowly shook his head. I waited. He gave a deep sigh. I waited some more. He looked pained and then resigned.

"You're full of shit, Riley. But this just might work. I get to quietly close one case and publicly close another." He paused to stroke his chin and put the other pieces into place. For my part, I was smart enough not to interrupt by noting that I got to keep Goat Hill Extermination out of the whole story.

"The perverts get back to exploiting one another and not endangering the public," he continued, "unless the citizenry includes bugs and rodents. And the political payoff is that Roberts gets a victory in his holy war and moves onto the next threat to the moral fabric of society."

"I'm guessing that he has you waging a crusade against cleavage?"

"Almost," he sighed, the tension in the room dissolving. "There's a 'serial exhibitionist' who's been exposing himself to tourists on Pier 39."

"You have to admire a flasher with the confidence to show his goods when it's fifty degrees and raining."

"Get the hell out of my office before I change my mind about running with your story," he said. I could swear that Papadopoulos flashed an actual smile.

On the way back to my house, the sun broke through and blue sky began to replace the blanket of gray. The forecast had been right—the temperature was rising noticeably. I called Dr. Chen while rummaging through the refrigerator in search of lunch fixings. She told me that, "a certain individual called and made an appointment based on your recommendation." So Lane was headed into the kooky carnival of psychotherapy. At least he had the money to pay for the fun house, carousel ride, and sideshow. I thanked the doctor and silently wished her patient well.

As I was contemplating the possibilities of rewarming leftover colcannon, Nina knocked on the front door. Her hair was pulled into a pony tail and she had on a Giants sweatshirt worn to a cottony softness and a pair of loose, khaki shorts. She took my hand and led me to her rusting Datsun hatchback, explaining that she'd convinced Gwen to take over at the daycare. In the backseat was a picnic basket atop a raggedly quilt that we used for beach excursions. Nina started the engine while I clicked on the radio and tuned it to KDFC.

The station was playing Mahler's *Resurrection Symphony*. The composer included detailed instructions but left much to the artistry of the conductor, particularly the pace. Bernstein liked it slow which felt right to me. The key to the whole thing is controlling the instrumental softness at the end of the fourth movement. The music must be exceptionally quiet before bursting into an explosion of two hundred singers, along with eleven French horns and two timpani drums. The *Resurrection Symphony* is among the most powerful, glorious and memorable finales in all of classical music.

CHAPTER FORTY-TWO

We drove across the Golden Gate Bridge and headed north for an hour, listening to music and chatting aimlessly about nothing. When we arrived at Point Reyes National Seashore, Nina wound her way down to Limantour Beach and parked on the sandy asphalt. There were a half dozen cars in the lot—including a black Pontiac Firebird with an eagle painted on the hood, a cherry-red Mustang putting the Firebird to shame, a beat-up and dented Pinto, an even sadder, burnt-orange Gremlin, a two-tone VW bus with bumper stickers declaring the end of war, poverty, and clothing, and a Thunderbird with a peeling vinyl roof—easily one of the least practical features in automotive styling. Nina's oxidizing, forest-green Datsun with cracking, butterscotch vinyl seats melded into the eclectic gathering.

There was a soft breeze coming from Drakes Bay and the sun had finally emerged in all its glory, doing its best to make up for more than two weeks of miserable rain. I grabbed the picnic basket. Nina took my hand and tucked the quilt under her other arm. She led us down from the parking lot into the gently rolling dunes. The sand was soft and warm as we made our way between sprawling patches of ice plant with succulent leaves and stiff clumps of beachgrass with erect stems whispering in the wind. The murmur of the surf breaking below us on the beach matched Nina's sighs of pleasure as we stopped to kiss like amorous teenagers and then continued to walk wordlessly in search of privacy.

After glissading down a steep, sandy slope, Nina spread the blanket in a sheltered valley between two dunes and shed her clothes. I followed her lead. Her desire to make love in the open air, with the sun and breeze washing over us felt completely natural, not the least bit deviant. Public nudity is illegal, but we weren't exhibitionists. We weren't trying to be seen. In fact, quite the opposite, although in the next minutes it didn't much matter as the world collapsed into the space of a threadbare picnic quilt. For all the waiting we'd endured, the sex was sumptuously slow. At least for a while, a long while.

What the Pointer Sisters sung about a woman wanting "a man with a slow hand" was so much more subtly and sensually evoked by Gustav Mahler's music. He fell in love with a woman that friends judged to be too beautiful for him, while his family considered her to be dangerously charming and flirtatious. Mahler was a difficult husband in many ways but he was passionate about his wife. Perhaps the Mahlers' lovemaking was the inspiration for his compositional technique in which extended, hushed— almost inhibited—musical foreplay teased the listener before erupting into an ecstatic climax.

After a languorous nap with Nina's head on my chest, we were both deeply satisfied and famished. She tugged on the Giants sweatshirt which mostly covered her, and I pulled on my pants. The sun on my shoulders melted away the tension of a morning spent with a pitiable pervert and a crabby cop. As Nina unpacked the picnic basket, I wondered whether my judgment of Lane Linford was fair. How many of us can claim to be normal? For that matter, why is normality such a good thing? After all, Nina was the only woman with whom I'd made love in the past year. So, I was abnormal given that the annual number of sexual partners for a man in San Francisco was undoubtedly more than one—especially if you included other men and species in the total. But somewhere in all of this, I couldn't get past fidelity being good, whether or not it was normal.

My ponderings were unsophisticated, but the lunch was exquisite. Nina had packed a crusty baguette (which her father insisted was a "barra" the

Spanish not wanting to cede bakery ground to the French), burstingly ripe tomatoes, plump, purplish olives, a firm and supple wedge of Manchego cheese, paper-thin slices of salty serrano ham, and a bottle of "young Tempranillo" which provided a juicy and tart coupling with the food. Nina propped herself on one elbow, the sweatshirt migrating upward to reveal a smooth, coppery, and very captivating, buttock.

"Damnit Riley," she said, tugging down the end of her minimal clothing, "you're incorrigible."

"Isn't it a good thing that I can't keep my eyes off you?"

"Well, yes. I suppose," she smiled with alluring reluctance. "But I was hoping to have a conversation, as well as being ogled."

"It'll be my pleasure. What's the topic?" I asked, not sure where this was heading but guessing it wasn't going to be as pleasant as the last hour of flesh and food.

"Nothing in particular, but I do have a question." I knew women well enough to understand that this meant: Something very specific about which she was about to demand an answer.

"Yes?"

"I haven't seen Tim around the apartment complex since the beginning of the week. He's usually somewhere nearby, offering to carry groceries, hold an umbrella, or whatever." I sat with my knees hugged to my chest and looked toward the ocean, squinting into the sun. There was a long pause. Nina took a deep breath.

"I won't ask if you did anything to him," she said. I nodded slowly to convey my appreciation of not being made to lie to my lover. "But I will ask whether you know if he's alive or badly hurt."

"The last time I saw Tim, he was most certainly alive. He was in some discomfort but nothing that would require medical assistance." That much was true. Maybe he decided to go to the ER, but a ruptured eardrum would've put him somewhere down the triage list along with bleeding noses and dislocated fingers. "I suspect he decided to move on to somewhere less dangerous." Again, true.

"You know, he wasn't a bad person," she said. "He was confused, or maybe 'disturbed' is a better word."

"I was a cop long enough to learn to appreciate that being bad is a relative term. Manslaughter is bad; first-degree murder is worse. The man who planned to kill Petey was plain evil. By that standard, Tim wasn't a terrible person."

"He just wasn't normal. And we don't know what to do with people like him." Her voice had become wistful, as soft as the breeze. I didn't want to break the spell of our afternoon, but I wanted her to understand me. Or maybe I wanted to understand myself.

"Being normal is a tough standard. Tommy isn't normal. I'm okay with abnormality. That wasn't the issue with Tim," I said.

"What was it, then?"

"He couldn't resist his urges. Whether or not he was capable of doing so isn't for me to say, but I know he was capable of doing harm to others. To you." I reached over and ran my fingers through Nina's silky black hair. "There's lots I don't know, Nina. But I know a funnel-web spider can kill a person. And I know if there was one on this quilt coming toward you, I'd crush it."

"And here's what I know. I love you Riley, but not always everything about you." She put her head in my lap and sighed. "I also know that I can't change you. Nor do I want to, even those parts I don't cherish." In the next minute, her breathing became tremulous, heavy-hearted.

"I make you sad, don't I?"

"Sometimes," she whispered.

"Like now?"

"Oh, it's not you, Riley. You are a good man. A hard man, but I know that's your world."

"If not me, then what—or who?"

"I was just thinking about Petey. All that he's been through. All that is yet to come in his life."

"He had some twisted and brutal days. I wonder what those will do to him," I said.

"I watched him carefully all morning. I could tell Tommy was worried about him because he invited Petey to join our outing tomorrow. And I know how special those expeditions are to your brother."

Nina and I were planning to hike the Stream Trail in Redwood Regional Park with Tommy to make up for having missed out on this expedition last weekend. We were going in search of the massive piles of beetles that form under branches and rocks. The well-named, convergent lady beetles exhibit this natural, but very strange, behavior. Supposedly the aggregations function to provide warmth and mates, which seem like fine goals in the winter sogginess of the Bay area. The "lady" part of the insect's name refers to the Virgin Mary—a beneficent figure. And the beetles are widely interpreted as signs of good luck. The Irish call them *bóin dé* or "God's little cow" much to Tommy's dismay. He knows that lady beetles are predators, munching on aphids rather than grass. Despite his pride in our family's Irish roots, this entomological error is unforgivable in his mind.

"So, maybe Petey will be alright, at least with the security of St. Teresa's to provide refuge from the streets during the day."

"If only," Nina said pensively. "When he wasn't goofing around with Tommy and Karsa, he just sat and stared. I asked him if something was wrong and he looked puzzled. I was reminded of how N. Scott Momaday, the Kiowa author I told you about, described one of his Indian characters, a crippled old man: 'He wondered what his sorrow was and could not remember.' Petey feels like an old soul in a boy's body."

"These last days have left me wondering, too."

"About?"

"About humanity, about sanity, about freedom to be whoever we want to be—even if that deviates from what others deem acceptable. I've made decisions and I'll make no excuses. I did what I believed was right."

We rested in silence. I continued to stroke her hair, lifting the strands for the breeze to catch.

"But?" Nina always seemed to know when there was more needing to be said. She could wield single word questions with penetrating wisdom.

"But I'm feeling more uncertain than I've been in a long time. Or maybe naïve, which surprises me." She rolled over onto her back and looked into my face.

"Or?" Again she probed the unsaid. Jesus, this was starting to feel like one of those fifty dollars sessions with a shrink.

"Or maybe stupid. I'd rather be stupid than naïve."

She chuckled softly. "Oh dear, Riley. You are a lovably strange man. But you know what Pope John Paul said about stupidity?"

"I thought Popes preached about the sinfulness of gluttony, sloth, envy and lust," I said, sliding my hand under her sweatshirt and gently massaging her breast to punctuate my list. She shook her head in mock dismay. I knew she appreciated my appreciation of her. "So now the pontiff is condemning nitwits?"

"He's not against foolishness. The pope says that stupidity is a gift from God, but we shouldn't misuse it."

"What the hell does that mean?"

"We all have failings. And we can use our limitations to live humbly."

"Being humble is fine. But in my experience, people too often use humility like a crutch, to avoid making hard decisions. It's a way of turning cowardice into a virtue. A cop or an exterminator has to make judgments and then take action, which sometimes means doing bad things for good reasons."

"The Pope didn't mean you can't act. He meant you have to allow the possibility that what you're doing is mistaken, uninformed—wrong." She paused and murmured, "Although what you're doing at this moment is very right."

We lapsed into silence for long minutes, until I reached over to tilt the picnic basket and asked, "Did you bring dessert?"

Nina gave a sly smile and slowly wriggled her hips against the quilt, the sweatshirt sliding upward. "Yes," she said, "but it's not in the basket."

I knew what she meant. I wasn't *that* stupid.

—THE END—

But wait, there's more . . .

Don't miss the first two
Riley the Exterminator Mysteries

POISONED JUSTICE: ORIGINS

What if an exterminator learns
that the worst pests have two legs?

When an activist ecology professor is found dead in his hotel room, the police chalk it up to natural causes, but his wealthy and fiery widow is convinced it's foul play. She needs someone who can operate behind the scenes—in the dark cracks and gritty crevices of San Francisco. Riley the exterminator fits the bill.

Riley's career as a police detective was cut short when do-gooders saw him beat information out of a child kidnapper. Now running his father's pest control business, Riley pursues two-legged vermin on the side. Turned out an ex-con can be licensed as an exterminator but not a private eye.

Winged ants and dead flies at the death scene suggest something's amiss to a man who knows insects. The dead professor's students, each harboring a secret, reveal that their environmentalist mentor had plans to take down the pesticide industry. But he needed cash for the operation—and that put him on a collision course with a most unusual drug lord.

When Riley's investigation unexpectedly reveals that the drugs that poisoned his own brother might be connected to the professor's death, extermination is in order. But he'll need to join forces with an intoxicating South African beauty—a reluctant ally, armed with lethal poison.

Can Riley rid San Francisco of its most deadly vermin?

**Get your print or ebook copy now at
www.Pen-L.com/PoisonedJustice.html**

MURDER ON THE FLY

San Francisco, 1981.
Danger is in the air and nothing is as it appears.
But then, neither is Riley.

The body of a gay cop who committed suicide, a radical commune in the hills above Berkeley, and a pest outbreak that will cost California $10 billion if not controlled would be sufficient problems by themselves. But the maggots don't match the policeman's time of death, the hippies aren't as peaceful as they claim, and the Medfly is spreading faster than it can move on its own.

Knowing that police detective-turned-exterminator Riley has what is needed—knowledge of both two- and six-legged vermin—an old flame draws him into a perilous search for the mastermind behind the most devastating insect outbreak in the nation's history. Riley must determine whether the Medfly infestation is the work of a government insider or a radical environmentalist.

As crops are reduced to worm-infested mush, Riley and his loyal crew at Goat Hill Extermination zero in on the perpetrators of gruesome murder, brutal kidnapping, and economic devastation.

But it's revenge, not money, that has bullets drawing blood and wasps delivering venom in a battle to determine who lives and who dies. Between romance reigniting and terrorism smoldering, Riley knows he's likely to get burned.

Get your print or ebook copy now at
www.Pen-L.com/MurderOnTheFly.html

ABOUT THE AUTHOR

Jeffrey Lockwood is a most unusual fellow. He grew up in New Mexico and spent youthful afternoons enchanted by feeding grasshoppers to black widows in his backyard. This might account for both his scientific and literary affinities.

He earned a doctorate in entomology from Louisiana State University and worked for fifteen years as an insect ecologist at the University of Wyoming. He became a world-renowned assassin, developing a method for efficiently killing billions of insects (mostly pests but there's always the innocent bystander during a hit). This contact with death drew him into questions of justice, violence, and evil.

His career metamorphosed into an appointment in the department of philosophy and the program in creative writing at UW. Unable to escape his childhood, he's written several award-winning books about the devastation of the West by locust swarms, the use of insects to wage biological warfare, and the terror humans experience when six-legged creatures invade their lives.

Pondering the dark side of humanity led him to the realm of the murder mystery. These days, he explores how the anti-hero of crime noir sheds existentialist light on the human condition: In the end, there are no excuses—we are ultimately responsible for our actions.

Find Jeffrey at:
Website: JeffreyLockwoodAuthor.com
Goodreads, Facebook
Email: Lockwood@uwyo.edu

Dear Reader,
If you enjoyed this book enough to review it for Goodreads, B&N, or Amazon.com, I'd appreciate it!
Thanks, Jeff

Find more great reads at
Pen-L.com

www.ingramcontent.com/pod-product-compliance
Lightning Source LLC
Chambersburg PA
CBHW051242260626
47162CB00002B/570